MORE THAN A KISS

"I should go," she murmured again, her aquamarine eyes still on his.

"Don't go yet."

He stepped closer to her, causing his heart to pound in his head. Every single nerve in his body tensed at the closeness of her. Maybe it was the wine he had with supper. Maybe it was her light, sweet violet fragrance that surrounded him, enveloped him. Maybe it was inevitable. But he had to kiss her just once, and then he would send her home.

Just one kiss.

In one quick movement, his arm reached out and encircled her, pulling her up against his chest, and his mouth came down over hers possessively. As he lost himself in the feel of her seductive lips, the soft silken touch of her mouth responding wildly to his, he held her even tighter, the length of his body pressed intimately against hers.

He had Colette Hamilton in his arms just feet away from his bedroom.

He knew then with a dreadful certainty that this would not end with just one kiss . . .

Books by Kaitlin O'Riley

SECRETS OF A DUCHESS

ONE SINFUL NIGHT

WHEN HIS KISS IS WICKED

Published by Kensington Publishing Corporation

WHEN HIS KISS IS WICKED

KAITLIN O'RILEY

ZEBRA BOOKS
Kensington Publishing Corp.
http://www.kensingtonbooks.com

ZEBRA BOOKS are published by

Kensington Publishing Corp.
850 Third Avenue
New York, NY 10022

All Kensington titles, imprints, and distributed lines are available
at special quantity discounts for bulk purchases for sales promo-
tion, premiums, fund-raising, educational, or institutional use.

Special book excerpts or customized printings can also be created to fit specific needs. For details, write or phone the office
of the Kensington Special Sales Manager: Attn. Special Sales
Department. Kensington Publishing Corp., 850 Third Avenue,
New York, NY 10022. Phone: 1-800-221-2647.

Zebra and the Z logo Reg. U.S. Pat. & TM Off.

ISBN-13: 978-1-4201-0446-2
ISBN-10: 1-4201-0446-2

First Printing: April 2009
10 9 8 7 6 5 4 3 2 1

Printed in the United States of America

For my sister, Jane.
I truly could not have done this one without you.
Thank you for everything, especially the champagne and bacon.

And for Dad.
Thanks for being my research department.

Acknowledgments

I give my most heartfelt gratitude for all their love, support, and wisdom, as well as for helping me in vast and various ways, to the following people:

My West Coast contingent:
Jennifer & Greg Malins, Maureen Milmore,
Billy Van Zandt, Adrienne Barbeau, Jaime Merz,
David Horvitz, Eric Anderson, and all
my wonderful friends at CH.

My East Coast contingent:
Jane Milmore, Richard Vaczy, Janet Wheeler,
Scott Wheeler, John Milmore, Yvonne Deane,
Kim McCafferty, Michele Weiner, Jeff Babey,
Lynn Kroll, Laurence Cogger (*merci beaucoup!*),
Jane Dystel, Miriam Goderich, and John Scognamiglio.

(And a special thank you goes out to the
inspiration for the character of Jeffrey Eddington.)

Note to Riley:
You make me proud every minute of every day.

Chapter One

You Can't Judge a
Book by Its Cover

London, England
May 1870

"Hello!" a deep masculine voice called. "Is anybody here?"

The words echoed through Hamilton's Book Shoppe, a small but quaint building on a side lane off Bond Street in Mayfair, London's most fashionable district. Lucien Sinclair, the Earl of Waverly, looked around the dark and cluttered interior searching for signs of the proprietor.

Growing impatient, Lucien ventured another call, this time a little louder. Honestly, one would think Mr. Hamilton had no desire to do any business if he were not present to greet potential customers when they arrived.

"Just a moment, please!" a dulcet voice exclaimed from the back of the shop. "I shall be right with you!"

Finally. A response of some sort. Well, that explained the delay, Lucien thought to himself. Apparently a woman was left to tend the shop. Perhaps Mr. Hamilton was out for the day, in which case his little venture would be for naught. He highly doubted the lady in the back room would be able to assist him.

He had met the owner of the shop over a year ago and had found him to be most agreeable. A kind and genial man who was very intent on helping Lucien choose the exact type of literature that would interest him, Mr. Hamilton wouldn't rest until Lucien was totally satisfied with his selection of authors. Lucien had only purchased the books out of boredom one day, hoping to ease the restlessness that plagued him from time to time, but once he returned home, he had lost interest in the little stack of books chosen by the eager bookseller, and he became immersed in his demanding social life once again.

However, a few weeks ago his father's sudden illness required him to spend more time at home to look after the weakened man and keep him company. Lucien began to read to his bedridden father, finally putting the forgotten books to good use, and surprise of surprises, he had actually enjoyed them. He realized how much he missed reading for pleasure, since he had not done much of it since his days at Oxford. Now he wanted to speak with Mr. Hamilton, not only to thank him, but also to ask his suggestion for new books he and his father might appreciate.

Glancing around, he noticed the little bookshop was not quite how he remembered it, but then again it had been over a year since he had visited there last. If he was not mistaken, the bookshop had been remarkably like any other that he had seen in his life; dark, disordered, and fairly dusty. Now it appeared to be undergoing some sort of transformation. Wooden crates, some of which were stacked and some open, and an assortment of hundreds of leather-bound books lay scattered in haphazard heaps on the floor, large buckets of paint and various sized brushes rested on a work table, and long sheets of canvas covered half the room.

"I'm so sorry to keep you waiting." That clear and gentle voice intoned once again and Lucien turned to see a woman walking toward him. "Welcome to Hamilton's. How may I help you, sir?"

Never one to miss a pretty face, Lucien instinctively noted the one belonging to the lady in front of him. From her small stature, he judged her to be very young, perhaps seventeen, seeing as there was a youthful air about her. Still, she approached him in a businesslike manner. She must be minding her papa's store for the first time. He frowned.

"I was hoping to speak to Mr. Hamilton," he responded in his most imperious tone.

As she stepped closer he revised his initial impression of her, for she was more than passably pretty. In spite of the dirt smudges on her fair skin, the dust motes sprinkled in her rich brunette hair, and the drab, shapeless gray smock that covered the navy dress she wore, her face was stunningly beautiful in its perfection. Her deep blue eyes, insightful and steady, regarded him with what seemed like skepticism. Even disdain. Her demeanor shocked him. Such an odd thing! Couldn't she tell he was a nobleman? What would prompt the beautiful girl to look at him in such a condescending way? As if she knew more than he did? As if she had dealt with his kind before?

"I am Miss Hamilton, his daughter. I can assist you."

The challenging, practically defiant, tilt to her head almost knocked him over. Once again he realized he was in error. She was older than he first thought, for she handled herself far too confidently. She must be closer to twenty. Again he frowned. He refused to deal with a haughty shopkeeper's daughter.

"I'm sure you are quite a charming young lady, but I was hoping your father could assist me. Perhaps I shall return at another time when he is available to offer his expertise. Would you please tell me when I could expect him?"

"My father passed away six months ago." She stated this matter-of-factly, revealing no emotion, her face calm and serene.

Feeling like a callous idiot, he said earnestly, "I am very sorry to hear that, Miss Hamilton. I only knew him briefly, but your father seemed to be a good man. Please accept my sincerest condolences on your loss."

She nodded her head in acknowledgment of his sympathy. "Thank you."

After an awkward pause, he asked out of polite curiosity, "Who is responsible for running the bookshop now?"

"I am."

That truly took him aback. A mere woman, this little slip of a girl, maintaining a business? It was preposterous. Ridiculous. Unheard of. She ought to be safely married with a home to manage, not working in a store.

"How old are you?" Lucien asked without thinking.

"Old enough. How old are you?" she countered quickly.

Her slightly sarcastic response irritated him. "Surely you have help? You could not handle such an enterprise on your own. A brother or an uncle or a male cousin must be overseeing you," he said.

Again that defiant look crossed the elegant features of her face, making her appear more assertive than he had first anticipated.

"You are aware that a woman is running our country, are you not?"

"Well, that's different," he sputtered in his defense.

"Queen Victoria was born and raised to rule and has advisors and counselors to guide her."

"I too was raised to oversee this shop. I have no male relatives to help me, yet I manage quite well without the assistance of men, thank you," she responded with unmasked condescension.

Lucien did not approve of women having to work, and for some reason her particular situation upset him. This girl was far too beautiful to be in charge of a business with no male to guide her decisions and ease her burdens. From his point of view, it was simply wrong. A woman should be taken care of, not left to fend for herself.

"You seem rather too delicate and too young to shoulder such weighty responsibilities, Miss Hamilton."

She sighed heavily, her manner revealing she had explained this many times before. "I've been assisting my father since I was a child. I assure you, I am quite capable of running the bookshop on my own, Mister . . . ?"

He gazed at her skeptically, but answered her unspoken question. "I apologize for not introducing myself sooner. I am Lucien Sinclair, the Earl of Waverly. It is a pleasure to make your acquaintance, Miss Hamilton."

"How can *I* assist you today, Lord Waverly?" she asked with a decidedly lofty tone.

He could not help but notice the unmistakable emphasis she placed on the "I" when she spoke. Irked by her obvious confidence, he glared back at her. She really should be more solicitous of him as a potential customer. And as a gentleman. Something about her made him want to rattle that self-assurance of hers a little.

"I came to speak to your father about selecting some books, but since you are here, let's see if you can help me. I need to purchase a gift. A present for"—he paused with deliberateness, raised one eyebrow, and grinned daringly at her—"a lady."

She gave him a withering look and he wondered if she treated all her customers with such disdain or just him in particular.

"Was there a specific type of book you had in mind for this *lady*?" she questioned with an air of superiority.

Noting her skeptical inflection of the word *lady*, Lucien felt slightly vindicated. "Are you knowledgeable about poetry?" he asked, for Lord knew he was not.

"Knowledgeable enough."

Something about the shape of her mouth intrigued him and he could not stop staring at her lips. They were full, sensual looking, and the color of summer-ripe berries. He found himself wondering what they would taste like and if they would be as sweet as they looked. How was a girl this beautiful not married yet? She must be an awful harridan. It was the only explanation that made sense.

"What about love poems?" he continued. "Do you know anything about love poems?"

"I think I know what you have in mind," she stated dryly.

He was trying to bait her and she refused to be reeled in. Miss Hamilton merely turned and made her way carefully to a stack of books in the corner. She picked up a small, red leather-bound book and handed it to him.

"This should do."

He glanced at the gold-lettered title, *A Collection of Romantic Love Poems*, and laughed. "Now, how did you know this was exactly what I had in mind?"

"Experience," she retorted without hesitation.

He shook his head in mock surprise. "My, my, Miss Hamilton, I wouldn't have expected it of you."

Ignoring his innuendo, she gazed at him wearily.

"Have you read this?" he asked out of perverse curiosity.

"Yes."

"Which poem do you recommend as being the most romantic?"

"Page seventy-four." She folded her arms across her chest and sighed. "Now, is there anything else I can do for you today, Lord Waverly?"

"Most definitely, Miss Hamilton, but I don't believe you would agree to it," he surprised even himself by saying. Something about the woman set him on edge. He wanted to read the poem on page seventy-four, but found himself staring at her instead.

On impulse he stepped toward her and she instinctively backed away from him. Now that was a reaction he expected. He moved forward and she predictably moved back until she was pressed against a table laden with stacks of books and could retreat no further, her hands braced on the edge of the table behind her. He closed in on her, standing mere inches from her petite body.

At this proximity he was able to breathe her scent. It was something floral and delicate and reminded him of a summer meadow. She smelled heavenly, even though she had obviously been immersed in cleaning before he arrived. Being that she barely reached the middle of his chest, she was required to tilt her head back to see his face. Wide eyes, the color of the sky on a cloudless June morning, stared up at him with mixed emotions. Surprise. Expectation. And again that determined look of defiance. But not fear.

Not this girl.

He had the oddest sensation that she could see right through him, leaving him feeling off balance. A feeling he was decidedly unaccustomed to having. Yet the beauty of her face mesmerized him. Such a dainty little nose! She had perfect skin, as smooth as fine china, with not a freckle or a blemish to be seen. Although the inclination to wipe the dirt smudges from her soft cheek overwhelmed him, he held himself in check, his hands at his sides, his fingers clenched tightly around the book of poems.

Instead, their intense stare continued for what seemed an endlessly long time as her intelligent eyes held his in an unwavering gaze. Something intangible sparked between them. An unexplained intimacy, a sense of knowing, an ethereal bond, a chemistry of sorts. Lucien had heard or read dozens descriptions of such sensations before but never had he felt something this intense himself. It was as if they were suddenly the only two people in the world, and a wild desire to kiss her, to taste for himself those luscious lips, charged through every vein in his body. Lucien realized he was holding his breath, and if he were not mistaken, Miss Hamilton held hers also. That intrigued him and made him want to kiss her even more, to set her world off-kilter, too.

What would she do if he leaned down and kissed her? Would she scream in outrage? Would she slap him in indignation, as she rightfully should? Or would this woman let him kiss her pretty, tempting mouth, pressing his lips ever so softly against hers, just to start? He had earned himself quite a reputation over the years, and many women had gossiped about his romantic talents.

Then again, he had never advanced on an innocent woman he had just met all of five minutes earlier.

What had come over him?

He wanted to kiss her, and he did not like how desperately he wanted to kiss her. He didn't even like the type of woman she was: independent, defiant, and self-assured. All attributes that he found objectionable in women. Still, unable to stop himself from touching her, he slowly reached out his hand to her. He saw her tremble, felt her expectation, but she did not resist. She did not so much as flinch from him, which made him grin. Her blue eyes rose upward as they followed the movement of his fingers to the top of her head.

Very carefully, and ever so gently, he removed a fluffy

dust mote from her silky, coffee-colored hair. Holding the bit of fuzz on the tip of his index finger, he blew on it with a puff of his breath. They both watched in mute fascination as it floated lazily to the ground at their feet.

Suddenly Miss Hamilton pushed by him, spinning back around to face him, her long navy skirt twirling around her legs. In an instant she became all business once again, the intensely intimate yet unexplored moment between them lost, leaving him battling a sense of sharp disappointment at the evaporation of all that moment had promised.

"Since this book of poetry is all you require today, shall I wrap it for you, Lord Waverly?" The frostiness of her tone of voice matched the cold look on her beautiful face. All traces of the warm and inviting woman who had wanted him to kiss her had vanished.

She behaved as if that astonishing feeling had not just passed between them. That a highly charged connection had not sparked so wildly in their eyes. That he, a complete stranger, had not almost kissed her there in broad daylight in the middle of her father's chaotic little bookshop.

She was not easily ruffled, that was for certain. Whereas he was more unsettled than he cared to admit to himself.

"That would be lovely, Miss Hamilton." He handed the book of poetry back to her with a gallant sweep of his arm and followed her to the counter. He leaned leisurely on the polished wood, resting his chin on his hand. "Does Miss Hamilton have a first name?"

She glared at him. "Of course I do."

He grinned at her, his most charming, most winning smile. The one that got him his way with every female he had ever encountered. It truly came in most handy at times.

"May I have the honor of knowing your name?"

"No."

"No?" He echoed in disbelief, raising an eyebrow, a bit stunned by her refusal.

"No." She did not meet his eyes.

"Then I shall have to guess your name," he persisted. "Let's see . . . Katherine? Mary? Victoria? Margaret?"

She shook her head at each suggestion as she methodically wrapped the little red leather book in brown paper. Her elegant fingers moved with efficient skill as she folded the paper with sharp, straight creases.

"Nothing traditional, then? Because your father owned a bookshop, perhaps your name has a more literary inclination. How about Lydia? Tess? No, not quite. Alice? Goldilocks?"

He noticed the glimmer of a smile playing at the corners of her sensuous lips and felt his stomach tighten in response to her. He continued his guessing game. "Ophelia? Juliette?"

"Juliette is my sister's name," she admitted with slight reluctance.

"Ah, I'm getting warmer. It seems your father had a passion for Shakespeare."

"No. Juliette is just a coincidence."

"So it's simply an affinity for French names, is that it?" She nodded her head.

"This should be interesting now. I didn't suspect you of having an exotic French name. Is it Desirée? Jacqueline? Angelique?"

She rolled her blue eyes heavenward in exasperation. "It's Colette."

"Colette? How very intriguing."

In an odd way the French/English name suited her perfectly. Colette Hamilton. She was a woman of contrasts. Beauty and business. Youth and maturity. Sensuality and innocence. He could not stop thinking about her.

She continued to ignore him as she artfully tied a pretty

green ribbon around the brown paper package. The bright bow added a distinctive flourish to the wrapping.

"Nice touch," he commented on her handiwork.

"Thank you." She held out the gift-wrapped book to him.

"No, it is I who must thank you for your most able assistance, Miss Hamilton." Once again he grinned devilishly at her. "I gather that no one calls you Coco?"

She eyed him evenly. "No one."

"You are a lady of few words, aren't you?"

"When prosaic conversation warrants it."

"Point taken." He laughed. He glanced at her lovely profile. "Colette and Juliette. Pretty names for pretty sisters. And it seems you have no brothers, correct?"

"Just three more sisters."

"There are five of you?" Could such a thing be possible? The thought of five women like her boggled his mind.

For the first time, she smiled; her entire face lit from within. The effect was stunning and he had to catch his breath.

"After me, there is Juliette, Lisette, Paulette, and Yvette is the baby."

"You are the eldest?"

She nodded in a way that was becoming familiar to him.

"And you all work in the bookshop?"

"Every day."

"I have even more sympathy for your father now." He reached inside his coat pocket and took out some money.

She accepted the payment and gave him his change. "Thank you and please come again," she said with unmistakable sarcasm.

"I wonder if your father would approve of your insolent attitude toward a paying customer," he could not help but respond, enjoying provoking her.

"My father is no longer here to approve or disapprove

of anything I do, Lord Waverly." She challenged him with her eyes, her chin tilted upward.

"Unfortunately, that is the truth. And that is a shame." He tipped his hat to her. "Good day, Miss *Colette* Hamilton."

Lucien turned and exited the quaint little shop, the bells above the door jingling a gentle good-bye. As he made his way through the bustling London streets, he wondered why he felt so flummoxed after meeting Miss Hamilton. She was quite irritating. Captivatingly beautiful, but irritating nonetheless. What did it really matter, though, in the end? He need never see the impossible woman again, for the logical decision would be to simply find another shop from which to buy books.

Which he had every intention of doing.

Chapter Two

The Root of All Evil

"I expect you both to be a credit to me and comport yourselves with the utmost decorum. Your aunt Cecilia and I have spent all the money we could spare on this little venture, and we count on a large return from the two of you," Uncle Randall warned for at least the hundredth time, as if Colette and Juliette were a pair of idiots and not aware of the urgency of the situation.

Colette fought the desire to stick her tongue out at him, as Juliette was currently doing behind his back. She knew better than to act that way. Besides, Uncle Randall was looking directly at her. Maintaining a neutral expression required what little self-control she had left, after her unusual encounter in the bookshop that afternoon with the handsome Lord Waverly.

"I hope you understand that if you both don't marry money quickly, then we are all out in the cold," he continued in his pompous manner, his bushy eyebrows furrowing ominously. "I cannot continue to provide for all six of you, as well as my own family. You need husbands to take care of you and help support your mother and sisters. It's more than past the time for you to have married already, Colette. Twenty years old and not yet a wife! Why your father let you remain unwed so long is something I will never understand, but then I never did understand Thomas."

Randall, her father's older half brother, inherited the title of Lord Hamilton and the Hamilton estate, but he had run out of funds to support his lavish lifestyle, which included his haughty wife and his wastrel of a son, Nigel. Since Nigel was too spoiled to foist upon an unsuspecting, wealthy heiress for a few more years yet, Uncle Randall had appointed himself guardian of his brother's five daughters.

Although he appeared the benevolent uncle, Colette was perceptive enough to see through to his true motives. In his role as their guardian, Uncle Randall would benefit from contracting the wealthy marriages of his nieces, which was the only reason he'd decided to launch Colette and Juliette during the coming Season. By selling their beauty to the highest bidder and reaping the financial benefits of two fat marriage settlements, he would also rid himself of the responsibility of his brother's family once she and Juliette married.

Uncle Randall continued with his repetitive speech, pacing between them, his coattails flapping. "With the Hamilton name and your stunning faces, most men will overlook your lack of dowries. You should both fetch a fine price. I have a few suitable gentlemen in mind for you already, and you will be charming and gracious to them when I introduce you."

As Uncle Randall turned, he almost caught Juliette making a face at him. In an instant, a look of angelic innocence replaced Juliette's scornful scowl as Uncle Randall ranted on, oblivious to what was happening. From across the room their mother shook her head in despair, silently pleading with Juliette not to anger their uncle.

"*Mais bien sûr.* They are my daughters. They will behave as expected, Randall," Genevieve Hamilton whispered in a faint voice, always somewhat fearful of her overbearing brother-in-law.

"They had better be." He gave Genevieve a hard look, which conveyed volumes and Colette understood quite clearly.

"We will be." Unlike her mother, Colette didn't fear her uncle, but neither did she respect him. However, she was wise enough to understand his reasoning.

As much as she hated to admit it, marrying well would ease the burden on her entire family. Unfortunately, she had absolutely no interest in marrying at the present. If only she had more time, she knew she could make the bookshop a great success. The changes she had in mind would transform the place. Changes her father had never allowed her to make. But now she had the freedom to do as she wished with Hamilton's. If only they weren't so pressed for money. If only her younger sisters weren't depending on her. If only her mother would stand up to Uncle Randall . . .

She glanced at her mother, who reclined wearily on a chaise. Visits from Uncle Randall or Aunt Cecilia drained her more than usual. Her long gray hair, which had once been a rich brown like her own, now hung loosely from a ribbon at the back of her neck, while her pale eyes lacked any life or spirit.

Years ago Genevieve La Brecque Hamilton had once been a raving beauty and the toast of London, or so Colette had been told a thousand times. How Genevieve ever managed to marry Thomas Hamilton, a quiet man with a love of books and the second son of an insignificant lord, always mystified Colette. Now Genevieve could never be thought of as anything but a shadow of her former self. After bearing five daughters and being constantly disappointed in her married life, Genevieve had retreated to her bed, acting as an invalid. By the time of little Yvette's third birthday, Genevieve had become a complete recluse who never left the house or entertained guests. Colette, not sure if her mother's constant illnesses and injuries were real or imaginary, had been the one to take care of her younger siblings in her mother's place, as well as the one to help her father with the shop.

"And when you marry well, it will no longer be necessary for you to have to work in that deplorable bookshop any longer," Uncle Randall stated with undisguised contempt, his dark eyes narrowing.

"I don't mind working in Father's shop," Colette said, holding her anger in check by biting her tongue. The bookshop had always been a contentious issue between them.

Oh, if he would only leave already! Uncle Randall had no idea how much effort Colette had put into the shop, nor did she want him to know just yet. He thought her incapable of making the store a success, simply because she was a woman. His beliefs infuriated her, as most men's did. Just as that odious Lord Waverly's had done earlier that afternoon. One day she would show all those superior, smug males just how wrong they were about her.

"You know how I feel about the Hamilton family being in trade," Uncle Randall persisted. "It's quite beneath us. It was embarrassing enough when my brother opened the shop, and now it's even more humiliating that my nieces are running it. But I shall not delve into a discussion about it with you at this moment, Colette. I haven't the patience for it tonight, and I'm late for a supper party with the Davenports as it is. Have all your gowns and fripperies been delivered?"

Colette nodded. "Yes, Uncle Randall. They arrived yesterday." She had to admit that she loved all the gorgeous new clothes that had been made for her and Juliette to wear during the Season.

"Good. Your aunt Cecilia and I will be here at seven o'clock on Friday to escort you both to the Hayvenhursts' ball." Uncle Randall stared at her with a pointed glare, his balding head tipped menacingly in her direction. "And I'm counting on you, Colette, to keep your sister here in line during the Season."

His reference to Juliette annoyed her, for she had no more control over Juliette's behavior than anyone else did, but Colette nodded in deference to him. She had learned long ago that if he thought she agreed with him, he left her alone. She pretended to agree with him now.

"Yes, Uncle Randall."

"Good, then. I shall be on my way for the evening, ladies. Genevieve." He nodded to her mother and took his leave after a disapproving look at Juliette.

"*Dieu merci, il est parti.* He has always treated me shabbily, just because I am French." Genevieve gave a petulant frown when the door to their living quarters above the bookshop closed and they were alone once more. "Now I have a dreadful headache." She touched her hand to her forehead dramatically and closed her eyes with a heavy sigh.

"He makes me so angry!" Juliette exclaimed, rising from her chair.

At nineteen, Juliette was stunning and would no doubt have many offers of marriage during this Season. All the Hamilton sisters were beautiful, or so everyone said. Their beauty was the only reason Uncle Randall was bothering to launch them at all. Colette loved her sister and they were very close, but Juliette could be unexplainably obstinate. If only Juliette would be more accommodating once in a while . . . She fought against everything so much, often to her own detriment, that at times Colette had given up trying to reason with her.

"Keep me in line, indeed!" Juliette declared adamantly, stamping her foot, her dark blue eyes flashing. "I don't even wish to have a Season!"

"Juliette, you should be grateful to your uncle," Genevieve admonished in a weary voice from her position on the chaise, not even bothering to open her eyes. "Your father left us little enough to survive on. Now you have an opportunity you wouldn't have had to make a grand marriage and live comfortably. Make the most of it. Don't make the same mistakes I made in life. *Ne sois pas insensée.*"

"I don't want to marry some stuffy lord who will order me about and tell me what to do all the time," Juliette complained, folding her arms across her chest and falling back into the armchair she had been sitting in for their uncle's lecture on proper deportment during the Season. "I'm not ready to get married."

"Is it safe to come out now?" Lisette asked from the doorway of the bedroom and glancing around the parlor. Their comfortable home life had been interrupted by their uncle's visit, and Lisette and the other girls had escaped to the bedroom to avoid him. "I no longer heard Uncle Randall's voice."

Colette nodded in relief. "Yes, he just left."

Lisette entered the room with their younger sisters in tow. She immediately went to their mother's side, helping her get comfortable and placing a small lavender-scented pillow behind her head to help ease her headache. Paulette and Yvette sat themselves beside Colette on the sofa. Yvette snuggled against her while Colette smoothed her pretty blond curls. She was almost fourteen already, but being small for her age she appeared younger than she was and they still referred to her as the baby of the family. And perhaps treated her as one far more often than they should.

"Well . . . What did Uncle Randall have to say this time?" Lisette asked as she began to rub their mother's shoulders, soothing her as only she could. Lisette had a calming quality about her, and Genevieve relied heavily on her middle daughter because of that very fact.

"Oh, the usual marching orders. How Colette and I have to marry well or the entire family will starve on the streets and it will be all our fault," Juliette snapped, her eyes flashing.

Yvette stared at them with wide eyes. "Are we all going to starve?"

"No one is going to starve," Colette said firmly, hoping they believed her. "Least of all us. We're not destitute."

Not yet, anyway. The thought nagged at her. They were not destitute yet, and with any luck they would not end up that way.

When he died six months ago, their father had left the shop in financial chaos and Colette was barely sorting through it all. Her mother and sisters, and even Uncle Randall, had no idea how close they were to actually losing the shop, and consequently their little home above it. But they would not be forced to move in with Uncle Randall and Aunt Cecilia or thrown out on the streets, because Colette would die before she let that happen. She was not unaware of the dislike Aunt Cecilia had for her nieces, and living with her aunt would be only a drastic last resort. She had to make the shop a success and knew without a doubt she would get no help from her uncle in that regard. She had to do it all on her own.

As much as it pained her to admit it, marrying well at this point seemed the only option open to them. She should be grateful to her uncle for providing the

opportunity of a Season, not only to her but to Juliette
as well, in order to double their chances. Marrying
wealthy husbands would alleviate all their troubles.

If only she had a little more time to make the shop
over . . .

"Everything will be fine. You'll see," she reiterated to
her sisters, as well as to herself.

"At least you get to wear all those pretty gowns and
dance with handsome gentleman at fine parties!" Yvette
exclaimed with a dreamy look on her face. "I wish I
could go with you!"

"I have no doubt that you will someday." Lightly Colette kissed the top of Yvette's head. Yvette had been enchanted with the arrival of Colette and Juliette's new
wardrobe and had been playing with their lace fans and
walking around in their high-heeled slippers all day. "But
for now, it is time for you to help set the table, sweetie.
Paulette, you come help Julie and me downstairs for a
little while before supper."

"Can I paint the signs now?" fifteen-year-old Paulette
asked, her sweet, earnest face brimming with excitement.

"Yes, you can start, though I doubt you'll finish them all
tonight." Colette stood, eager to get back to work in the
bookshop. There was so much that still needed to be done.
Once she began the Season, her time in the shop would be
limited to business hours. She wanted to get as much accomplished as she could before then. She left Lisette and
Yvette to prepare supper and look after their mother.

In spite of Juliette's grumbling and mumbling about
being too tired to help, she and Colette actually managed to paint two wall-length bookshelves a crisp, clean
cream color. The shade did wonders for brightening up
the store. It had always bothered Colette that it was so
dark in her father's shop, for how was anyone supposed
to peruse or read books in such a dimly lit space?

After months of penny-pinching, she had finally gathered enough money to buy the paint and supplies she needed and had set to work on her plans. With the cream-colored walls and shelves, the store was becoming a place in which one would want to sit and read comfortably. Once the shelves were dry enough, she intended to rearrange the way the books were traditionally displayed. She would place some of the books with the front covers facing out, making the titles easier for customers to read. She smiled at the prospect her changes would create.

The three sisters worked for over an hour together, pausing only when Juliette tripped backward over some rolled canvas and fell flat on her bottom. It had taken a good five minutes before she and Paulette had stopped laughing at the ridiculous image of Juliette on the floor and got back to their painting.

"What do you think, Colette?" Paulette proudly held up two small wooden boards, with elegantly printed letters in black paint. One read "Philosophy" and the other "History."

Colette clapped her hands together in glee. "Oh, that looks lovely, Paulette!" She took one of the signs from her little sister and held it up. "It's perfect!"

When all the signs were completed, they would designate the different areas for various subjects of books throughout the shop. Again, the signs would allow customers to search with ease for books. Paulette's neat and uniform lettering added an element of sophistication to the plain wooden placards. The gilt-edged trim did the same as well.

"They will look wonderful when we hang them with that green ribbon," Juliette announced in rare accord.

The green ribbon had been a wonderful stroke of genius on Colette's part. While at the dressmakers being fitted for their new gowns one afternoon, she saw rolls of the most beautiful green grosgrain ribbon. Instantly knowing just how to use them in the shop, she quietly asked the dressmaker to include the rolls in their purchases. Saying a silent thank-you to an unwitting Uncle Randall for purchasing the yards of ribbon, she smiled at how tasteful and elegant the shop would look when she was finished.

"I have to admit, Colette, that I thought you were batty to try to change this old place. But it's beginning to look beautiful. The new paint makes it look as if it were a completely different store."

"Thank you." Colette was starting to believe it, too. Her father's shop was actually going to change. That she was the one who was making those changes thrilled her. Ever since she could remember, working in the bookshop was all she ever wanted to do.

After years of assisting her father, Colette had discovered ways to make the shop better, more attractive, more efficient. Her father had always disagreed with her, shaking his head in a patronizing manner, dismissing her modern ideas as the silly whims of a little girl. Now that her father was no longer alive to deny her innovative proposals, Colette was finally free to do everything she had ever wanted to improve the store. The first order of business was a new coat of paint. That was, of course, after she and Paulette had thoroughly scrubbed and polished the dusty store from top to bottom.

Pleased with the look of the wooden placards, which had turned out better than she had hoped, she hugged her little sister in gratitude.

Just then Yvette strode into the room. "Heavens! Look at this place!" she cried in astonishment. "It looks so different!"

"Doesn't it?" Paulette agreed, her sweet face beaming. "And we're not even finished yet!"

"Well, supper is ready, so come upstairs now," Yvette

said, already losing interest in the progress of the family shop. "Lisette made popovers!" She and Juliette, who needed no extra encouragement to head up to supper, left through the door immediately.

Paulette turned to go as well, then looked back at Colette. "Are you coming up?"

"In a few minutes," Colette answered, placing a paintbrush back into the bucket of paint. "I'm not hungry, so I'll just do a few more things down here and clean up a little bit."

Paulette nodded with an understanding smile. "I'll bring you down something to eat when I come back to help you."

"Thank you." Colette and Paulette shared a love of Hamilton's that their other sisters did not. In fact, it was little Paulette who for days on end had painstakingly helped her sort through, reorganizing and cataloguing, all of the books in the shop.

Wishing the paint would dry faster so she could begin reshelving the books, but knowing she would have to wait at least until tomorrow, she began to clean up the pots of paint and the sheets of canvas. Stretching her back and wiping the paint from her hands, she recalled the strange encounter with the extraordinary man who had come into the shop earlier that afternoon.

Lucien Sinclair, the Earl of Waverly.

As soon as she laid eyes on him she knew his type, for she had come across them in the shop many times before: entitled, arrogant, idle young noblemen who had no need to earn a living and looked down upon those who did.

His self-assured manner, his look of cultured breeding, and the fine cut and style of his expensive suit told her all she needed to know. He was predictably aristocratic and spoiled. Although as long as he continued to

purchase some expensive books, she did not care who or
what he was.

But oh, the way he looked!

He was unmistakably handsome. His patrician features were striking, and his dark green eyes lingered on
her for longer than anyone would deem proper. His
mouth had a charming dimple when he smiled, a smile
that changed the hard lines of his face, warming him,
and making him seem infinitely more attractive. She had
had to catch her breath at the sight of him. He must lead
women on a merry chase, indeed.

And she could have sworn that he wanted to kiss her.

That fact alone was startling enough, but what shook
her to the core was that she had actually wanted him to
kiss her. Well, not completely. To be fair, she had never
been in such a position before. The man was a complete
stranger. The most handsome stranger she had ever
seen, but a stranger nonetheless.

Yet there was something about him that unnerved her.
He was condescending, of course, showing blatant disapproval of her doing what he thought should only be
a man's job, but there was something else she could not
easily put to words or explain. They had stared at each
other for the longest time, and for the first time in her life,
she felt . . . Well, she didn't know how she felt, but she had
never felt that way before. He left her breathless and shaky
and with a fluttery feeling in her stomach. She did not like
it. Not one bit.

She reminded herself that in spite of how he looked,
Lord Waverly was an arrogant nobleman who looked
down upon her, just like all the men she would meet
next week at her first ball.

That thought caused a flutter of a different kind in
her stomach as well.

She was fraught with worry over the coming Season.

Having to please her aunt Cecilia and uncle Randall. Socializing with people she had nothing in common with. Needing to find a husband.

And marriage itself troubled her. Many nights she lay awake wondering if she would be able to find a husband who would condone her working in the bookshop. Most men outright frowned upon the idea of a woman managing a store, and some even found it mildly amusing, but all of them disapproved and automatically assumed she would refrain from working in the shop once she became a wife. But Colette had no intentions of quitting, of ever giving up something that she loved in order to please a man. She loved the bookshop too much.

And she knew she could make Hamilton's more successful than her father ever would have dreamed. Yet she knew her family was depending on her to support them.

If only she had more time.

Chapter Three

Well, Look Who It Is

Lucien Sinclair, the Earl of Waverly, entered the Hayven-hursts' massive townhouse with a heavy heart and a forced smile on his face.

Usually he enjoyed the London Season. Nights spent socializing with his good friends, playing cards, going to the theater, attending parties and balls, and critiquing the latest crop of debutantes had always put him in jovial spirits. The start of a Season was exciting and he had always looked forward to it before. But this year would be different. This Season meant business. His father was ill and dying, and the inevitable could be delayed no longer.

As much as he hated the thought of it, he had to find a wife.

He had put it off for too long as it was. Not that he hadn't tried over the years to find a suitable bride. Well, perhaps that thought was not quite true, he admitted to himself. In all honesty, since his disastrous relationship

with Virginia Warren, he had been avoiding the thought
of marriage altogether. And for good reason.

"Lord Waverly!" Countess Hayvenhurst welcomed him
with a glorious smile, her long, white-gloved arms outstretched in his direction. "We haven't see you in ages!
I'm thrilled you could come to our little party."

"Our little party" consisted of over five hundred guests,
an army of liveried servants, a dining room filled to bursting with rich foods and drinks of every type imaginable,
two orchestras, and enough flowers to fill a cemetery for
a few years.

Lucien smiled at her warmly. "I'm happy to be able
to attend, Lady Hayvenhurst. It seems you have outdone
yourself yet again."

"Oh it's nothing." She dismissed his compliments with
an airy wave of her hand. "I simply adore parties. Now
you must tell me, how is your father getting along?"

"He is much improved," Lucien lied, not wishing to di-
vulge the grim details of his father's illness to his hostess.
After years of his family being the favorite topic of gossips,
he was reticent to share private information with anyone.

"I am so relieved to hear it," she said. Lady Hayvenhurst,
a matron with four grown children, had to be over fifty but
still maintained a svelte figure with a considerable bosom,
which she showed off to great advantage. Her laughing
eyes and genuinely kind nature had won Lucien over years
ago. "You must give him my very warmest regards."

"I will be sure to, Lady Hayvenhurst."

"There are some pretty new faces here this evening,
Lord Waverly. Please try not to break all of their hearts in
one fell swoop," she admonished him with a merry wink.

"I'll do my best." As the heir to a marquis, Lucien knew
he was considered to be "a catch" by most of society, but
so far he had successfully eluded capture.

"It's about time you found yourself a lovely wife," she

said with a knowing grin. "You're too handsome to stay a bachelor. I think I may know just the perfect young lady for you. Would you like me to introduce you?"

"Thank you, but I think not. However, I'll be sure to let you know when I'm ready to settle down," he said, evading her usual matchmaking plans. Finding a suitable bride was a task he intended to accomplish without any assistance from well-intentioned matrons. "Where is Lord Hayvenhurst this evening?"

"Oh, he's about somewhere." She laughed carelessly. "He managed to lose me over an hour ago."

"If I find him, I'll send him your way."

"Thank you, my dear!"

As Lady Hayvenhurst greeted yet another guest, Lucien made his way forward, pressing through the heavy crowd. Judging from the large number of people, all of London had turned out for the ball.

"Waverly!"

Lucien turned as his name was called. Lord James Buckley, one of Lucien's closest friends and an inveterate gambler, stepped toward him. "How are you, Buckley?" Lucien asked.

"Just fine! We're starting up a poker game in Lord Hayvenhurst's back drawing room. Come join us and give me a chance to win back some of what I owe you."

Lucien shook his head. "I've only just arrived. Perhaps I'll join you later."

"Right, then." Buckley hesitated, his hands in his pockets, looking sheepish. "I haven't seen you in a few weeks, Lucien, and I'm sorry about your father's illness. And I know I owe you money. I haven't forgotten and I would really like to pay you back tonight. But the thing is, I owe Crandall some also, and he's pressing me for the money now, and as I'm rather short on funds at the moment . . ." He trailed off awkwardly.

"It's all right, Buckley," Lucien said. "Get it to me when you can."

Absolute relief showed all over his freckled face. "Thanks, Lucien. I will pay you back. I'm good for it, I promise."

"I know you are." Lucien then added, "But perhaps you should forgo any games tonight."

"Good idea!" Buckley nodded in understanding and headed off hastily. Lucien hoped his friend heeded his advice, but unfortunately sensed that he would not.

Continuing through the crush of people in the Hayvenhurst ballroom, Lucien paused now and then to acknowledge the familiar faces that greeted him. Above the growing din, he heard a very distinctive voice calling his name.

"Lucien!"

Lord Jeffrey Eddington, a tall, dark-haired gentleman with a wide grin on his face, waved in his direction, motioning for Lucien to join him. Still making his way through the mass of guests, Lucien finally reached his friend.

"It's a madhouse in here tonight," he commented when he reached the alcove where Jeffrey was standing. "I've been here forty-five minutes and still haven't been able to get a drink."

"Well, you can't have mine." Jeffrey held up a crystal tumbler half full of scotch. "I need it too much."

"Rough evening already?" Lucien asked with a wry look.

"I have been cut down by the most beautiful creature." After making a tragic face, he took a long swig from his drink.

Lucien laughed out loud. Lord Jeffrey Eddington, the illegitimate son of the wealthy and influential Duke of Rathmore, had a reputation only slightly worse than Lucien's own. Women, young and old, swooned at Jeffrey's feet.

He and Lucien had known each other since their days at Eton, becoming instant friends at the age of eleven when Lucien punched the arrogant and irritating Walter Brockwell in the face for calling Jeffrey a bastard. At the time Lucien wasn't even entirely sure what that word meant, but judging from the stricken expression on Jeffrey's face, he knew it signified something terrible, so he had hauled off and given Walter Brockwell a black eye, earning Jeffrey Eddington's loyal friendship.

Each suffering the effects of a shattered home life and without the need for further explanations, the two young boys turned into fast friends from that day on. They even attended Oxford together. Over the years Jeffrey became one of the very few people in Lucien's life whom he trusted implicitly. Lucien did not have a brother, but he felt that Jeffrey Eddington was as close to having a brother as he was ever going to get.

"I'd like to meet the lady who cut you down," Lucien remarked with a laugh.

"I've only just been introduced to her myself. A Miss Juliette Hamilton. You know I never go after the debutantes on the marriage mart, Lucien, but this one is a stunner—"

"What name did you say?" The words sounded eerily familiar to Lucien's ears. Hamilton with a French name. It could not possibly be the same name of the beautiful girl in the bookshop he had just met. *Could it?*

"Juliette Hamilton. Do you know her?" Jeffrey asked in surprise.

Lucien shook his head in wonder at the coincidence. "No, but I've heard the name before. Where is she now?" His eyes narrowed and scanned the room searching for a luscious brunette with stunning blue eyes.

"She was dancing with Lord Sudbury a short time ago.

But I don't see her any longer. She must be in the dining room." Jeffrey shrugged carelessly.

"Who is she here with?" Lucien could not help asking, still searching the faces in the crowd.

"An uncle, I think."

Interesting. Lucien believed she must be the sister of the bookshop girl, for how many Juliette Hamiltons could there be? At the possibility of seeing Colette Hamilton again, he felt his pulse quicken.

Jeffrey resumed his story. "As soon as I laid eyes on her, I wrangled an introduction through Lady Hayvenhurst, who made me promise not to tempt the girl. I don't wish to marry the chit, for heaven's sake, I just wanted to meet her. Being the bastard son of a duke has its perks."

Jeffrey gave him a rueful smile, but Lucien knew his illegitimacy was a sore spot with him, for all that he was raised as Rathmore's own son.

"Just as I got to her side," Jeffrey continued his tale of heartbreak, "I heard that stuffy prig George Bickford ask her to dance and she answered, 'I am honored, but I am not interested.' Can you believe that? Well, her honest remark made me only like her all the more! Bickford went off in a huff and I winked at her. And by God, she winked right back at me! She didn't stammer and blush, like all the others would have. Greatly impressed, I told her that I thought she had discriminating tastes. She said that she certainly did. Then the uncle came marching over, to scold her, I would imagine. As he was dragging her off, she turned her head back, and I swear, Lucien, she poked her tongue out at me! Unbelievable! And a lovely little tongue it was, too."

Lucien laughed at the idea of the girl acting so audaciously. Well-bred ladies did not behave that way. And if they did, they certainly did not do so in public. This one must be a firebrand, all right. "She sounds like a bit of trouble to me."

"She more than likely is, which is what intrigues me. You know I like a woman who can stir things up a bit. But enough of her." Jeffrey turned and leaned back against the wall in a careless manner. "Now you, my friend, you are here tonight on a matter of serious business."

Lucien nodded reluctantly. Indeed he was.

"And you're still determined to go through with this godawful idea before the Season is over?"

"I owe it to my father. He's dying, Jeffrey. I cannot deny him this. He's had too much sadness in his life as it is. I can at least let him see me married before he dies. He deserves to know the family line will continue."

The image of his father, Simon Sinclair, the Marquis of Stancliff, lying frail and weak in his darkened bedchamber, chilled him. The weakened muscles, the pallid complexion, and the dull, lifeless eyes haunted him. He owed his father more than he had given him over the last few years. His father needed him desperately now. And Lucien had vowed to himself to be there for him.

From the moment his father had been stricken with the strange paralysis, Lucien had been at his bedside night and day, and when he wasn't there, he was in Simon's office. He had actually taken over the duties of his father's estate, and to his great surprise he found that he actually enjoyed it. For the last few years Simon had been trying to get Lucien more involved in managing the marquisate, but Lucien's heart and mind had been involved elsewhere. Now it was different. Now he focused on the issues that needed his attention and he had begun making changes. As soon as he felt he could leave his father, he would travel to all the Sinclair estate holdings and see for himself how matters could be improved.

Lucien had learned more during the last few weeks

than he had in all his years at the university. Through working assiduously and dealing with the day-to-day financial issues of the massive estate that he was marked to inherit, Lucien finally found a sense of purpose within himself that no amount of gambling and pleasure-seeking had ever been able to assuage, no matter how diligently pursued. For the first time in years, he felt useful and hopeful of a meaningful life, even with his father's inevitable demise looming over him.

"I guess you would have to marry eventually anyway." Jeffrey pointed out the obvious. "I can't imagine you would see the whole estate go to that idiot cousin of yours."

Lucien nodded in agreement. "I can promise you that Edmund will never inherit my father's estate."

"Have you any prospects on the lucky woman who will be your bride?"

"None yet," Lucien answered with a heavy sigh. "I just know I want a sweet, biddable chit. One who is virtuous, kind, and good-tempered. One who will do as I ask and not cause difficulties. One who would be happy to stay quietly at home at my country estate, not here in town caught up in the social season. One who will be content enough with raising children."

"You didn't say she had to be beautiful."

"No, I did not." Beauty was definitely not a requirement in a wife for Lucien. In fact, he would prefer anything but beautiful. Beautiful women caused only trouble and misery. He knew that from firsthand experience.

Jeffrey laughed at the hard look on Lucien's face. "Any wife of mine would have to be a beauty. I couldn't bear anything less. If I'm going to be leg-shackled, I'd prefer a very attractive shackle. But what you're seeking won't be a challenging task. Simply look over there." He gestured across the immense ballroom.

There along the opposite wall amid the potted plants

and elderly matrons sat the plain, ignored young ladies who had not been asked to dance all evening, except perhaps for the obligatory dances required by their male family members. These were the ladies who had been passed over Season after Season but were still paraded about each year by their parents in hopes of finally snaring a husband. Never having given such females a second glance before, Lucien now stared at them with a critical eye.

One of those sad ladies would certainly make a suitable wife for him. Yes, he admitted to himself, some were rather decidedly on the plump side and a few were quite unfortunate looking, but all in all they were not repulsive. Perhaps they were not the most fashionable or the most sociable of women, but he was sure they had other admirable qualities. They just needed a closer look to find their less obvious nonphysical attributes.

No, these ladies certainly would not turn heads, but Lucien didn't want a wife who could turn heads. He wanted a woman who would behave, such as the small one with the blond hair in the plain dress, for example. She had a sweet expression on her face in spite of her dull attire. She would certainly be grateful to have a man like Lucien for a husband. Grateful enough to conduct herself as a faithful and obedient wife.

"You're not seriously considering one of those when you have your choice of the most beautiful and elegant women in London?"

Jeffrey's seductive words shook him, but Lucien would not be swayed. He knew what would be best for him, and he would not be deterred in his quest to marry an obedient and well-behaved woman. If that meant she would be plain as well, then so be it. Beautiful women were not worth the misery they were capable of causing. He had experienced all too painfully the heartache and damage they caused. No, he was quite right in his thinking. A plain, biddable wife. That was the way to go.

"Yes. What about that sweet-looking one on the end there," Lucien said in a quiet tone, pointing out the blonde.

Jeffrey shook his head in disbelief. "Well, I wish you luck, for I think you'll desperately need it. As for me, I'm fortunate enough not to have the pressure to marry placed upon my shoulders. Having no name to carry on has its benefits—" He stopped abruptly as a predatory gleam appeared in his eyes. "Well, well. Look who is coming this way . . ."

At Jeffrey's instruction, Lucien turned his head to see to what his friend referred. Two stunning women approached them, but he had eyes only for one, and she literally took his breath away. *Good God.* It was the beautiful woman from the bookshop. The very same woman he had been so tempted to kiss.

Even more enchanting than she had been that afternoon, Colette Hamilton stood before him. Gone were the dirt smudges and bits of dust in her hair. Gone were the shapeless navy dress and large work apron. Gone was the little shopkeeper. Even in that dark and dingy shop, he had recognized her as a beautiful woman, but now he could not take his eyes off her. One would never guess that she worked in a bookshop. Dressed in a fitted gown of pale blue silk, she displayed a lush and shapely form that aroused him immediately. Her rich, dark hair was arranged in a sophisticated style upon her head, baring her long, elegant neck. She now appeared a graceful and serene angel.

"Hello again, Miss Hamilton," Jeffrey said to the other woman standing beside Colette.

Lucien then noticed Juliette Hamilton for the first time. She looked like a darker version of her sister. Both were beautiful women, undeniably. However, Juliette could barely suppress the wildness in her eyes. Something about Colette's softer loveliness appealed to him more than her sister's daring beauty did.

"Please forgive me," Juliette Hamilton said with what closely resembled a smirk on her heart-shaped face. "But I do believe I have forgotten your name."

"You have forgotten me so soon? You have wounded me to the quick, Miss Hamilton," Jeffrey stated dramatically, his eyes full of mirth.

Juliette raised an elegantly arched brow at him. "Somehow I find that highly doubtful."

"I shall have to reintroduce myself to you, then. I am Lord Jeffrey Eddington and this is my friend, the Earl of Waverly." Jeffrey bowed gallantly.

Juliette's dark eyes raked over the both of them, but Lucien could only see Colette. He wondered if she was as surprised to see him as he was to see her.

"This is my sister, Colette Hamilton." Juliette introduced her to both men.

"There was not a doubt in my mind that you two were sisters," Jeffrey commented, greeting Colette. "You both look astonishingly alike."

"I am pleased to see you again, Miss Hamilton," Lucien said, with a polite nod toward the so far silent Colette.

"Good evening, Lord Waverly." She grinned cryptically.

"How do you two know each other?" Jeffrey asked him in confusion, while Juliette Hamilton's raised eyebrows conveyed her surprise that her sister already knew Lucien.

Enjoying the fact that he knew something about these two women that his friend did not, Lucien explained. "We met at her family's bookshop last week."

Taking in this bit of information, Jeffrey questioned, "Have you a bookshop?"

"Yes," Colette responded. "Hamilton's Book Shoppe. It's in Mayfair, just off Bond Street."

"I am a fortunate man!" Jeffrey grinned gleefully. "For now I know where to find two beautiful ladies!"

Both girls giggled at Jeffrey's words, but Lucien could not stop staring at Colette. "It's lovely to see you again, Miss Hamilton. What an unexpected pleasure to see you this evening."

Colette shook her head slightly. "I had not expected to see you either."

"Would you care to dance with me, Miss Hamilton?" Jeffrey asked, his eyes still on Juliette.

"I'm afraid that we cannot," Colette responded rather hurriedly, before her sister could answer. "It seems our uncle has already chosen our dance partners for this evening."

"Well, that is terrible news." Jeffrey gave a lamentable shake of his head. "I must see your uncle about getting my name on your list of partners."

"I would love to dance with you, Lord Eddington," Juliette said with a cool and defiant glance at her sister.

The silent interplay between the two women would have amused Lucien, but he sensed something wildly rebellious about Juliette. Colette clearly did not wish for her sister to dance with Jeffrey, which probably demonstrated good judgment on her part. Eddington and Juliette together could be an unmanageable and rather dangerous combination.

"Well, then. I can hardly refuse such a simple request, Miss Hamilton." Jeffrey grinned from ear to ear. "Shall we?" He offered Juliette his arm and the two of them moved into the throng on the dance floor before Colette could utter another protest.

Lucien stood there in awkward silence, Colette by his side, watching Jeffrey and Juliette waltz away together. He would love to take Colette in his arms and dance with her, but he knew it would be wiser to focus on his goal that evening.

"Are you enjoying the ball?" Colette asked, making a polite attempt at conversation with him.

"Well enough," he said, admiring the way her silky brunette ringlets framed her face. She was truly a beautiful woman.

"Did your 'friend' enjoy the book of poetry you bought?"

At first her question startled him, for he could not think to whom she referred. Then he recalled that he had led her to believe that he bought the poetry book for a woman. He gave her an answer to rattle her calm demeanor. "I decided to keep the book for myself."

She raised her blue eyes at him, as if expecting him to explain himself. The challenging look on her face elicited the same feeling he had for her that afternoon in the bookshop. He had come so close to kissing her then, and now that unexpected desire had returned with a vengeance. Her full lips simply begged to be kissed. He fought the urge to lift his hand and caress her face.

"I read page seventy-four and I'm afraid that I must disagree with you, Miss Hamilton." The look of surprise on her pretty face made him grin wickedly.

After their meeting in the bookshop, he had been intrigued by her referral to page seventy-four, and he made the effort to read the poem later that night. It turned out to be a ridiculous poem about love at first sight. Surprised that a business-minded and opinionated lady such as Colette would have a tender spot for fated love, he had laughed heartily at her romanticism. Love at first sight was for inexperienced young fools who did not know how love could wound a heart.

"Then you disagree with Christopher Marlowe's sentiments?" she questioned him with a curious glance.

"Of course," he scoffed. "There is no such thing as love at first sight."

"There you are, Colette!" A tall gentleman with a shiny bald head and bushy eyebrows strode purposefully toward them.

"Lord Waverly, may I present my uncle, Lord Randall Hamilton," Colette introduced him to her uncle. "Uncle Randall, this is the Earl of Waverly."

Lucien noted the sudden gleam in her uncle's eyes. "Good evening."

Randall Hamilton gave Lucien a polite nod. "Good evening, Lord Waverly." He took hold of Colette's arm. "If you would excuse us, please."

Pulling his niece aside rather forcefully, he moved her behind a large and leafy potted plant, but Lucien could still hear their conversation due to her uncle's harsh tone of voice.

"I have been looking for you for the last twenty minutes. Where is Juliette?" he demanded impatiently, his anger evident in his manner.

"She's dancing."

"With whom?"

Colette hesitated before answering. "With Lord Eddington."

"Good God! I should have expected something like that from her. Not only is Eddington a bastard, but he also has a notorious reputation. Did I not give you both explicit instructions that you were only to dance with gentlemen I approved of first? Did I not?"

"Yes, Uncle Randall."

"And yet here I find you with Lord Waverly, whose reputation is only slightly better than that of Eddington's."

Lucien cringed at that comment. He was not completely innocent of all the feats ascribed to him, but the talk about him was highly overexaggerated. For the first time, the idea that he was someone a young woman might be warned away from left him feeling slightly unsettled. Would this hinder his search for a prospective bride?

"If you expect to marry well, you must be extremely careful. Lord Eddington and Lord Waverly may flirt with you, but they will never marry you."

The uncle continued to berate Colette, yet maddeningly his voiced lowered into a fierce whisper so that Lucien could no longer make out what he was saying.

He fought an impulse to intervene and protect Colette from her pompous uncle, yet he knew that with his reputation, to have him defending her would do little to help her cause. And though he was loathe to admit it, he agreed with Randall Hamilton, for he was absolutely correct. If he wanted his nieces married, then Colette and her sister should not be seen flirting with the likes of Eddington and himself. Lucien felt some relief that there was a male relative looking after the pretty Hamilton sisters after all. Colette was managing a bookshop on her own, which in itself was problematic. She needed her uncle to watch over her. And Lord knew that the reckless Juliette desperately needed someone to take her in hand.

No, Lucien did not care for the way Colette's uncle treated her, but had the Hamilton sisters been in his charge, he would be giving them similar orders.

He glanced toward the potted plant and watched as Randall Hamilton marched off with Colette firmly in his grip. Ignoring the niggling sense of unease in his chest when he thought of her, Lucien forced his attention back to the quiet ladies sitting along the wall.

He had a job to do. He needed to find a wife. And he knew without a doubt that his search for a woman who met his list of requirements would not involve love at first sight.

In fact, it would not have anything to do with love at all.

Chapter Four

Business or Pleasure?

"I don't even care for Jeffrey Eddington in a romantic way," Juliette declared hotly in her defense. "I just wanted a bit of fun. I thought balls were supposed to be fun. None of the other gaseous windbags I met last evening were any fun at all. And I just wanted to show Uncle Randall that I don't have to do everything he says."

Colette fought the urge to snap at her sister and instead slammed the small stack of books she had been holding onto the table in front of her.

She had spent the entire evening at the Hayvenhursts' ball being lectured by her bombastic uncle, while Juliette flirted outrageously with or scorned any male that came within distance of her. Colette had been so angry by the time they got home, she didn't trust herself to speak civilly. Here it was the next day, and she was still having a difficult time of it.

"But right now we do *have* to do everything he says, Juliette!"

"I know that," Juliette conceded ruefully, "but I just cannot bear all his orders and proclamations."

"And you believe that I do?" Colette snapped in response. "Do you think I liked dancing with those stodgy men he partnered me with? Do you think I enjoyed being dragged about by Uncle Randall all night, listening to his ranting about your behavior?"

"No," Juliette admitted, her defiant attitude somewhat deflated. "But you just seem to bear it all better than I do. You're the responsible one."

Colette stared pointedly at her sister. "Do you have any idea how important this is to us? It's not just you and me. Our marrying well is important to Mother. And to Lisette, Paulette, and Yvette. Everything we do now affects them and their futures, as well as our own."

Juliette glanced down in shame. It was the first time she showed any remorse for her behavior. Colette felt that maybe she had finally gotten through to her.

"This is not a game, Juliette. If you damage your reputation by acting recklessly and foolishly just to spite Uncle Randall, you will not only ruin your own chances of finding a husband, but you may very well ruin mine, too."

Her sister still said nothing.

"Do you want to end up on the street if we lose the bookshop? Or worse yet, do you want to have to live with Uncle Randall and Aunt Cecilia? Because that is just what will happen if we don't marry well and I cannot make a go of this shop. Our whole family and our way of life are depending on you and me."

Juliette looked up, her face contrite, and whispered, "You are right. I'm sorry you had to bear the brunt of my actions, Colette. I promise I will try to behave better next time."

"Thank you," Colette said with a sense of relief. "We'll

be going to Lady Hutton's ball next. I expect you to make more of a pointed effort to please Uncle Randall then."

"I will."

"I'm not saying that you have to marry anyone he suggests, just try to comport yourself in a manner that satisfies him, all right?" Colette began shelving the books she had slammed onto the table a few moments before.

"I will try, I promise."

Now that she was no longer in disgrace, Juliette's disposition lightened with a flashing smile and Colette marveled at the mercurial quickness of her moods. Her sister could change from anger to laughter in mere seconds. Her ability to do so always astounded her.

Colette rolled the tall library ladder that allowed her to reach the higher shelves of the philosophy section into position and began to climb the wooden rungs. "Hand me those books, please." She pointed to another stack on the table that she had already alphabetized and categorized.

Juliette languidly passed two volumes of Rene Descartes up to her sister. "You have to admit that all the men Uncle Randall suggested were hideous. Each one was a disaster. A disaster with deep pockets, but a disaster just the same. The only handsome men who even got close to us were Lord Eddington and his somewhat humorless friend, the Earl of Waverly."

At the mention of Lucien Sinclair, Colette's foot slipped from the ladder rung and she dropped one of the books. She righted herself quickly and took a deep breath.

"Be careful up there!" Juliette admonished, retrieving the fallen book.

"I'm fine," Colette said shakily.

Juliette continued, "Lord Eddington was great fun, though. A girl has to be on her toes when she's with him. But that Lord Waverly seemed so proper and so very lord-of-the-manor stiff, for all he has a reputation as a rogue. I didn't care for him."

Colette wondered what her sister would think of Lucien Sinclair if she knew that he'd almost kissed her in the bookshop last week. She had kept that little secret to herself, though. Last night Lord Waverly had possessed a cool seriousness that made her more uncomfortable than his attempted kiss. Frankly, she had been stunned to see him at the Hayvenhursts' ball and had been unsure how to approach him. He had not asked her to dance as Lord Eddington had done with Juliette and he had seemed uninterested in her, almost distant. And still he managed to occupy Colette's thoughts for the remainder of the night.

However, Juliette's astute observation could not be denied. Lord Eddington and Lord Waverly were indeed the handsomest men in attendance. And apparently the most wicked, according to her uncle's claims. She found that information about Lord Waverly easy to believe after their sensual encounter in the bookshop last week, when she thought he wanted to kiss her. Yet if Lord Waverly's reputation was that of a rogue, she could not help but wonder why he did *not* kiss her that day. Wasn't that how rakes behaved?

Even though he had irritated her with his condescending attitude, for some reason she had spent the remainder of the evening trying to imagine what it would be like if he *had* kissed her. Perhaps it was his mention of page seventy-four.

The poem by Christopher Marlowe she had recommended to Lord Waverly that afternoon had always been her favorite. She didn't even know why she told him about it, but the words had escaped her mouth before she could stop them. The poem was one of many she had committed to memory over the years, and its romantic meaning had always resonated deeply within her.

Who Ever Loved, That Loved
Not at First Sight?

It lies not in our power to love or hate,
For will in us is overruled by fate.
When two are stripped, long ere the course begin,
We wish that one should love, the other win;
And one especially do we affect
Of two gold ingots, like in each respect:
The reason no man knows; let it suffice
What we behold is censured by our eyes.
Where both deliberate, the love is slight:
Who ever loved, that loved not at first sight?

Deep within Colette's practical and responsible being lurked a yearning romantic soul that she kept well hidden from others. As much as she understood and agreed with her uncle's reasons that she and Juliette must marry for money, such a mercenary approach went against her warm core. She held out a slim hope that she would meet the perfect husband during this Season. A man she could love and be loved by in return. A man who would support her work in the bookshop, yet still take care of her and her family. A man who would be a partner to her in all ways. She felt in her heart that she would know this man at first sight, just as in the poem.

Recalling that Lord Waverly had said he wanted the book as a gift for a female friend, Colette wondered who this friend was, and if he had read page seventy-four with her. But more importantly, she wondered why he mentioned the poem to her at all.

The jingling of the bells above the front door brought her back to the present.

"My, my," Juliette muttered below her. "Look who the cat dragged in."

Colette glanced around from her perch on the ladder and froze in place.

Lucien Sinclair, the Earl of Waverly, stood there in the shop as if her very thoughts had conjured him to appear.

"I'll take care of this," Juliette whispered low, while Colette remained immobilized.

"Good afternoon, Miss Hamilton," he said rather lightly, as Juliette moved forward to greet him. "It's a pleasure to see you again."

Colette's heart raced erratically and she clutched the sides of the ladder tightly in her palms. She took a deep breath to steady her nerves. *Honestly, what am I so nervous about?* More than likely he was just there to purchase books.

"Good afternoon, Lord Waverly," Juliette said.

Colette detected a slight sarcastic quality in Juliette's voice as Lucien Sinclair stopped beside the front counter. She suddenly realized he had not noticed her clinging to the ladder near the back of the shop, but she had a clear view of him. And that view was quite nice. In his long black cape and black hat, he appeared extremely tall and imposing. The misty drizzle outside had covered him in little spots of water and he seemed to shimmer. His handsome male presence demanded all of her attention.

"Did you enjoy the Hayvenhursts' ball, Miss Hamilton?" he asked her sister politely.

"As a matter of fact, I had a lovely time," Juliette said with forced pertness. "Did you?"

"Yes."

"How odd," she remarked carelessly at his response. "I had the distinct impression that you were not enjoying yourself."

"Why would you think something like that?" Lord Waverly questioned her, his dark brows furrowed.

"Because, to be quite frank, you had a rather serious

look on your face." Juliette was simply being perverse, but Colette clapped her hand over her mouth to keep from laughing out loud at the audacity of her sister's words.

His eyes widened at Juliette's bold statement, but he retaliated quickly. "I suppose seeing a young lady behave scandalously might have that effect upon me."

"You would not be referring to my behavior perchance, would you, Lord Waverly?" Her voice positively dripped with sweetness.

With a disapproving glare, he countered evenly, "What do you think, Miss Hamilton?"

"I'm sure it must be quite difficult for you to recognize it in someone else, since it's obvious that you don't know how to do it yourself, Lord Waverly, but I was merely enjoying myself."

"By flirting outrageously with every gentleman present?"

Colette listened to their conversation with a growing sense of fascination. Lord Waverly was chastising her sister for the very same reasons she had done earlier. On the one hand she felt disheartened that Lord Waverly had noted her sister's scandalous behavior last night, but on the other hand she was grateful to have an ally.

"Oh, not every male, Lord Waverly," Juliette stated with an arch look. "Only the handsomest ones with the most charming manners." While clearly implying that he did not fall into that category, Juliette changed the topic with deft ease. "Did you come in here simply to escape the rain, or is there perhaps a purpose to your delightful visit today, my lord?"

Proving himself a gentleman of restraint by not responding to Juliette's taunt, he stated the obvious. "I am here to purchase books."

"Well then, Lord Waverly, how can I be of assistance to you today?" Juliette asked with false brightness.

"I don't believe you can help me at all, Miss Hamilton.

I was hoping your sister would be available to select some books for my father. And what better place to find something interesting than at Hamilton's Book Shoppe."

"Yes, interesting would be the word to describe it." Juliette gave him a challenging look.

Ignoring her sarcasm, he asked, "Is your sister here?"

"All of my sisters are here. To which one were you referring, I wonder?"

He tilted his head in acknowledgment of her little game and to indicate that he was not amused by it. "I was referring to Miss Colette Hamilton."

Juliette smiled triumphantly. "Well, why don't you ask her yourself? She's right there." She gestured with an elegant wave of her hand to Colette.

In surprise Lord Waverly turned to find Colette perched on the ladder, his eyes raking over her. Colette suddenly wished she were not wearing her dusty old work apron and had taken the time to fix her hair nicely that morning. She knew she looked like a disheveled mess.

Glancing up at Colette, he called to her. "Good afternoon, Miss Hamilton."

"Good afternoon, Lord Waverly," she murmured in response. Carefully she forced her shaking legs to step back down the ladder one rung at a time. Running a hand over her mane of dark hair to smooth it as best she could, Colette faced him.

"I was just having an interesting discussion with your charming sister," he commented, his sarcasm unmistakable.

"Yes, I heard." She nodded toward the ladder.

"Apparently." He smiled at her, softening the lines of his face and causing her heart to flutter. "Are you able to assist me today?"

"Of course." Trying to sound more businesslike,

Colette asked, "Are you seeking a book as a gift for a special occasion?"

"No. Unfortunately, my father is not well and confined to bed. I thought I would bring him some new reading material."

"I'm so sorry to hear about your father," she murmured. She could not help but wonder what was wrong with him. "What does he like to read?"

"Well, your father had chosen a collection of fiction books for me last time. I ended up reading them to my father and he enjoyed them. But I believe he would like something a little more historical."

Juliette groaned audibly and made a face of pointed disgust.

"Don't you like to read about history?" Lord Waverly asked her.

Juliette shook her head adamantly, her dark black curls shaking. "I'd rather have my fingernails pulled out."

A faint smile tugged on the corners of Lord Waverly's sensuous mouth, yet his expression remained serious. "That's a rather drastic alternative, Miss Hamilton. Are you afraid that by reading history you may actually learn something that might benefit you?"

Juliette's face grew scornful at his condescending words. "I have read enough and learned enough to know that men have caused all the misery in this world—"

Recognizing the tone in Juliette's voice that meant she would soon fly into one of her little tirades, Colette quickly intervened. "Juliette is not the scholarly one in our family."

"That much is obvious." Lord Waverly turned his eyes on her, and Colette had to catch her breath at the force of his green-eyed gaze. "I suppose that the title of the 'scholarly one' falls to you?"

"Only by relative comparison," she explained lightly.

At that moment Paulette entered from the backroom

of the shop, carrying an armful of her hand-painted placards. The violet dress she wore carried the evidence of the black paint she had used, and much of her long blond hair had been loosened from the thick braid down her back.

"This has to be another sister," Lord Waverly declared with some astonishment.

Startled, Paulette looked up at the sound of a male voice. "Good afternoon."

Intensely proud of all her sisters, Colette made the introductions. "Paulette, this is Lord Waverly. We met at the Hayvenhursts' Ball last night. This is my younger sister, Paulette Hamilton."

"It's a pleasure to meet you." He held out his hand to Paulette, who seemed more than awestruck by his handsome presence.

"It's a pleasure to meet you," Paulette echoed in a faint whisper, awkwardly balancing wooden placards in her left hand in order to take his with her right.

Lord Waverly smiled at Paulette's nervousness and gallantly took the signs from her and shook her hand. He turned back to Colette once again, his expression astonished. "It's uncanny. Do you all look this much alike?"

Colette nodded, accustomed to this type of question when people met her sisters for the first time. "I'm afraid so. We have varying shades of hair and eye color, but we do tend to resemble each other a little."

"That's an understatement." Lord Waverly could not stop glancing between her, Juliette, and Paulette.

"The rest of the signs are dry now," Paulette announced excitedly, regaining her composure and pointing to the stack that Lord Waverly held.

"What are they?" he asked, his expression curious.

"New signs for the shop. They will help customers know where to find books," Paulette explained, her face flushed with pride. She took a sign from him, one at a time. "This one says 'Science' and we shall hang it over there, where the scientific books are shelved. And this one, 'Divinity,' and this one is 'Geography,' and this one is 'Literature,' and this one—"

"We all know how to read, Paulette," Juliette interrupted in exasperation. "You needn't recite each one for us."

Fifteen-year-old Paulette stuck her tongue out at Juliette. "You are merely jealous because I actually know how to spell these words and you're lucky if you can read them."

"I think you're exactly right about her, Miss Paulette. Your sister seems to dislike the very things she knows the least about," Lord Waverly said with a slight wink. "However, I think your signs are splendid."

Paulette's stunned expression turned to one of utter delight at finding an unexpected ally against her antagonistic sister in the handsome gentleman she just met. Colette laughed to herself as Juliette received the slight comeuppance she deserved. Juliette's personality was such that she provoked most people by either her comments or behavior. Colette enjoyed seeing Lord Waverly give Juliette a little taste of her own medicine.

Juliette rolled her eyes in disgust, keenly aware at this point that she was outnumbered. "I shall not even dignify that remark with a response, and I shall take my leave of you all now. Good day, Lord Waverly."

"Good day, Miss Hamilton," he said, amusement twinkling in his green eyes.

Juliette flounced from the bookshop with an exasperated air, exiting through the door that led to their living quarters upstairs, slamming it behind her for emphasis.

Paulette declared to Lord Waverly, with a beaming smile, "I like you!"

"Thank you," he responded quietly. "I like you, too."

Colette noted that he seemed taken aback by Paulette's

compliment and thought she detected the hint of a blush on his clean-shaven cheeks.

"I've worked on these signs all week and we're going to hang them with this cunning green ribbon. Won't that look wonderful?" Paulette chattered excitedly. "Colette and I are redoing the entire shop!"

"So I've noticed." Lord Waverly gave Paulette a charming smile and then turned his attention to Colette. "Are you responsible for all these changes?" he asked her.

Colette nodded with pride, thinking of all the late nights that she and her little sister had sorted and alphabetized every book in the store while Colette created an extensive inventory list. For as long as she could remember, her father had arranged the books in some sort of system only he understood, making it almost impossible to find a particular book without his help and guidance, which was most likely the reason he would allow no one to learn his secret system. Some books were grouped by size, some by color, and some by topic. He even had a section filled with books he considered unfairly criticized or discarded by the reading public. There was no rhyme or reason to their categorization. Her father's disorganization was a never-ending source of frustration for Colette. With her new freedom, she was finally able to arrange the books by subject area, and then alphabetically by author. A system that made complete sense to her.

"Yes, but Paulette helps me the most." Colette beamed.

"But we practically have to tie Juliette up and drag her down the stairs to get her to help us," Paulette couldn't help but add.

Lord Waverly laughed, and the smile lit up his face, making him appear even more handsome. A charming dimple at the corner of his mouth softened the graveness of his face. The result was astonishing.

"Why am I not surprised to hear that? What about the other sisters?" he asked.

Recovering from the effect of Lucien Sinclair's smile, Colette caught her breath and explained, "Lisette is busy taking care of our mother, who is ill, and Yvette is too young and uninterested to be of much help."

"So Colette and I do most everything in the bookshop on our own," Paulette confided, obviously thrilled with her newfound friend.

"And your uncle I met at the ball?" he asked.

"What about him?" Colette questioned.

"Doesn't he have anything to do with the shop at all?"

Uncle Randall would rather be caught dead than to be seen working in a bookshop. Colette shook her head. "No, my uncle would love nothing better than to see Hamilton's Book Shoppe sold."

"Then why does he allow you to have the shop?"

"Allow me?" Colette echoed in disbelief.

"Yes," he said simply, as if his question were acceptable.

"He has no right to sell it because it is not his shop to sell. It is my mother's. And someday it will belong to me."

"I see," Lord Waverly stated carefully. With an interested expression, he looked around the shop as if seeing it for the first time. "You have made some definite changes since I was here last."

"Good or bad?" Colette asked somewhat anxiously, not sure why his answer mattered so much to her.

"I first came to this shop a year ago and I remember it being rather dark and cluttered. And now, well, the light color certainly brightens up the place. It's much more organized with the books neatly arranged. And the signs designating the different areas are an excellent touch." He gave a warm grin to Paulette. "I could probably find the books I needed without any assistance at all. I would have to say that is a positive change."

Thrilled with his response, Colette felt all her hard work had been validated. "That was exactly my intention! A customer should be able to wander about and peruse the shelves if he wants. Or ask for assistance."

"You make a good point, Miss Hamilton, but I still think you should not be managing the shop without a man's help."

Colette folded her arms across her chest. "I'm doing just fine without one."

"So far," he challenged her. "But this is not work for a woman alone. A man is better qualified for making rational business decisions."

"That's ridiculous!" she declared hotly. Statements like his made her furious.

"That's outrageous!" Paulette chimed in, coming to her sister's defense.

With a smug expression, Lord Waverly stated very calmly, "Men are better at business. It is a proven fact, ladies."

"Proven by whom? Men?" Colette protested against his ignorant belief and rolled her eyes. "As if that means anything! I'm running this shop better than my father ever did, and if I just had more time I could—"

He peered at her inquisitively. "If you had more time, you could do what?"

"Nothing." She pursed her lips and shook her head. If she had more time she could make all the changes she instinctively knew would increase profits. If she had more time she could pay off her father's debts before the store had to be sold instead. If she had more time she and Juliette would not have to marry for financial reasons. But she needn't go into that with Lord Waverly.

Colette took a deep breath to steady her nerves. "I shall not waste my breath explaining what I could do when you obviously have a preconceived notion about the capabilities of women, and you are not open to any new ideas."

"In that case," he said, bowing gallantly and flashing a heart-melting grin, "Perhaps you could help me choose some books that would appeal to my father?"

"I would love to," she said in answer to the sudden change in his demeanor. Caught off balance by the contrasting personalities of the condescending nobleman and charming rogue that he encompassed, she felt her cheeks warm under his regard. "You mentioned that your father likes historical works, so we should begin our search over here."

He followed her toward the history section of the shop with Paulette trailing behind them, listening avidly to their conversations and anxious to hang her hand-painted signs.

Chapter Five

Surprise, Surprise

Lucien finished reading aloud to his father one of the books Colette Hamilton had chosen for him during his last visit to the shop and realized that not only was his father pleased by the story *The Count of Monte Cristo*, but he had thoroughly enjoyed the book by Alexander Dumas as well. The woman had excellent taste. Normally such a thing would surprise him, but somehow with her it didn't. She would have a fine sense of literary style. It suited her image.

Lucien's father smiled lopsidedly at him and slurred his words. "Thank you."

"You're welcome," he said wearily and closed the book, placing it on the polished cherry table. He stood and poured his father a glass of water from the Wedgwood china pitcher on the sideboard. He had been spending a great deal of time in his father's massive bedroom suite lately and felt somewhat confined.

Seeing his father bedridden and ailing had shaken Lucien. While he was growing up, his father had not always been the strong athletic type, but he had not been an invalid either. However, this apoplectic attack drained Simon Sinclair, the Marquis of Stancliff, of all life, and the doctor had confirmed Lucien's fears. There was no indication that he would recover the full use of his right leg, right arm, or his speech. In his weakened condition, his father seemed to have lost the will to live.

"You should rest now," Lucien suggested, holding the glass of water to his father's lips.

Simon took a small sip and then shook his head in a feeble gesture. "No . . . I t-talk."

"Of course we can talk if you like." Over the last months Lucien had learned to understand his father's garbled speech. And in spite of Dr. Garver's pessimistic predictions of recovery, Lucien believed Simon's pronunciation was improving. Slightly. He sat back down on the leather armchair and waited patiently for his father to speak.

"Y-you . . . d-don't . . . h-have . . . t-to . . . marry."

Racked with guilt, Lucien said, "Father, I have already made up my mind." He owed it to his father to be married and settled down while he was still alive to see it happen.

Ever since the debacle of his engagement with Lady Virginia Warren five years ago, Lucien had lived his life like a bat out of hell, earning a notorious reputation for himself, taking no responsibility for anything, not caring about anyone but himself, and causing his poor father more stress than he deserved to bear. His father's illness opened his eyes to how selfish he had been behaving.

Yet his father had never reproached him. Not once. And at times Lucien more than deserved to be reproached.

Again, Simon shook his gray-haired head in protest, his wrinkled face furrowed. "N-n-no! D-don't . . . m-mar-ry . . . f-for . . . me-e."

"I've already chosen someone suitable," Lucien stated calmly. "It will be fine."

His father became more agitated and shook his head again. The watery blue eyes that had seemed vacant suddenly flashed with a spark Lucien had not seen in years. "No. F-for y-you, y-yes. F-for m-me, no!"

"Father, it is beyond time that I was married and had a family of my own. I realize that now."

A single tear dripped down his father's wrinkled and withered cheek. "M-motherrr . . ."

Good God! They had not spoken of Lucien's mother in years because his father could not bear to have her name mentioned. Lucien's stomach churned at the thought of his mother. Hazy images of a dark-haired woman with sparkling eyes, a lilting laugh, and the scent of roses washed over him. Childhood memories of his mother were few and far between, but he distinctly recalled that Lenora Sinclair's presence lit up any room she entered. Elegantly gowned and sweetly perfumed, she would visit the nursery in a dramatic fashion and gather Lucien in her arms and smother him with kisses before leaving for whatever fabulous party she was attending that evening. Although he'd rarely spent time with her, Lucien had adored his mother and so had his father. Apparently that was not enough for Lenora, who wanted more from life than either Lucien or his father could give her.

She left them when he was only ten years old, and the crushing pain of losing her had devastated both of them.

"P-please, don't. D-don't do it," Simon managed to sputter. "N-not, n-not like your mother." The effort it took to articulate those few words drained him. He closed his eyes and breathed heavily, wheezing and hoarse, but he continued to shake his head in protest. "Don't."

Lucien did not want to talk about his mother now, nor ever, truth be told. She had made her choices and she was gone from their lives for good. He had buried his grief with her when he was a child. His father, unfortunately, had not been able to do the same even after all this time.

"It's all right. I think I've finally found a lady whom I believe will be perfect for me," Lucien explained in a calm and rational tone, attempting to ease his father's stress. "You will like her, Father. I promise that I'll marry her before autumn. You will attend my wedding, and we shall have children, your grandchildren. The Marquisate of Stancliff will not end up in the hands of cousin Edmund. I give you my word on that."

"D-don't do it f-for m-me."

Lucien could not fathom why his father kept repeating this when Lucien was finally giving him what he wanted at long last. He realized it was time to settle down and take up the reins of responsibility and manage the estate, especially because his father could no longer do so. Lucien's marriage would give his father a modicum of peace, knowing the family line would continue with the Sinclairs and not end up with the Blackstones.

Simon made a feeble attempt at a dismissive wave with his good hand.

Lucien recognized the weary signal as the time to leave his father, who was obviously exhausted. His furrowed brows indicated his frustration at not being able to express himself clearly. Simon seemed to have aged twenty years in the last few weeks, becoming almost unrecognizable from the man he once had been.

"Yes, I'll go now and send Nurse Fiona up to help you. You should get some sleep," Lucien said, patting his father on the shoulder. "I'll see you in the morning."

He left with a heavy heart and an increasing sense of unease.

Later that evening, as Lucien arrived at Lord Hutton's party, he still puzzled over his father's vehement protests to his plans for marriage. The illness must have affected the old man's thinking. Left him slightly unbalanced. Of course Simon wished his only son to marry. Every noble patriarch's ambition was to continue the family line, and Lucien was determined fulfill that dream for him.

He glanced about the crowd as he made his way through the receiving line, but did not yet see Jeffrey Eddington. Which was a good omen. Jeffrey would only try to dissuade him from his mission that evening.

Lucien had made his decision at the Hayvenhursts' ball which young lady he intended to pursue. He had spent the evening doing his homework, finding out all he could about her. She came from a well-respected and dignified family. Not a hint of scandal had ever touched her. She possessed clear blue eyes, a smallish nose, and light blond hair, done in simple curls. But most importantly in his view, a general air of steadiness and earnestness surrounded her, indicating she would eventually make a fine wife and mother.

He went in search of Lady Faith Bromleigh.

Not even an hour later, Lucien learned that it was quite a challenge to maintain an interesting conversation with a paragon of virtue. He had asked her about the weather, her general health, the various guests at the party, the music being played, the food being served, and the intricacies of the steps being danced. Lady Faith Bromleigh murmured simple yesses and noes with alarming regularity and did not venture an opinion on anything. There was only so much a fellow could say in response to such banal replies, and he had run out of topics upon which to question her. Especially with her mother hovering around them like a hawk, giving him sharp looks.

Lucien needed a drink. A strong one.

"Are you thirsty?" he asked her, if only to have an excuse

to escape for a little while. "May I get a glass of champagne for you?"

"No, thank you," she murmured demurely, her eyes downcast. "I would prefer punch or lemonade, please."

This was the type of woman he wanted, so why did he find her behavior so irritating? She was exactly what he had prescribed for himself. She did not argue, but bowed her head in deference to him. She smiled sweetly and possessed a calm and serene manner. She would never cause him a moment's worry.

Then, across the ballroom, he saw Colette Hamilton, and completely lost his train of thought.

Waltzing in the arms of Jeffrey Eddington, of all people, Colette laughed at something he was saying to her and her face lit up with merriment. In that moment the differences between Faith and Colette were glaringly exposed to him. Colette's exquisite beauty was infinitely more appealing than Faith's plain looks, but the beautiful and lively Colette was too modern and opinionated, full of passionate ideas and determination. Her strong, spirited nature, although nowhere near to that of the impetuous Juliette, filled him with apprehension. Other emotions, some best unmentioned and under control, flooded him at the thought of her.

He would definitely be better off with Lady Faith Bromleigh.

Yet Lucien felt an unexpected tightening in the pit of his stomach at the sight of Colette with his best friend. *Strange.*

He went to get Lady Faith a glass of punch, and for himself something much stronger.

"You are a delightful dancer, Miss Hamilton," Lord Jeffrey Eddington said with a seductive grin.

"Thank you very much," Colette replied, unable to resist his genuine charm. "You are a very fine dancer yourself."

Lord Eddington had somehow managed to finagle a dance with her before her Uncle Randall could protest. And Colette had been thrilled. She found that she liked Lord Jeffrey Eddington very much, in spite of his scandalous reputation. She agreed with Juliette's appraisal of him. He had a warm and easy manner about him. He also had a way of making a woman feel as if she were the only woman in the room.

They waltzed together quite easily, and for the first time all week Colette was actually enjoying herself. Lord Eddington made her laugh. He was irreverent and lighthearted, ignoring all the stuffy social rules that had been pounded into her head by Uncle Randall and Aunt Cecilia.

As the last strains of "The Blue Danube" came to an end, the orchestra began readying for the next dance. Lord Eddington escorted her from the floor.

"Would you care to rest for a bit?" he asked.

"That would be lovely. Thank you."

A footman walked by with a tray of glasses and Lord Eddington took one for Colette and for himself.

"Have some champagne," he offered with a gleam in his eye.

"Thank you again, Lord Eddington." Taking the glass from his hand, she glanced nervously around the room, but did not see her aunt and uncle. They must have cornered Juliette somewhere. Relaxing somewhat, Colette sipped the bubbly liquid, feeling its coolness slide down her throat.

Colette could not help but notice that Jeffrey Eddington was very handsome. His facial structure was noble and elegant, with an angular jaw. He had deep azure eyes, which were fringed with long, dark lashes. He had an attractive mouth, too, warm and quick to smile. Lord

Eddington's charm was just as powerfully attractive as his good looks, and she found her pulse quickening when he gazed at her.

"You are much sweeter than your sister," he commented in a light tone.

"Yes, that is true. Juliette is somewhat impulsive."

"Somewhat?" he asked incredulously.

"Point conceded. She can be quite a trial at times," she corrected herself.

"But that's what I love about Juliette, her spirit," he explained. "No one could, or should, ever tame her."

Something in his voice caused Colette to look closer at Jeffrey. She could not help but ask him, "Have you feelings for her?"

"I'll admit that at first I was attracted by her beauty, but I now feel that Juliette and I are too much alike and more suited to be just friends."

Admiring his honesty, she acknowledged his good judgment. "You are more than likely right about that. But I am curious about you, Lord Eddington. Tell me about yourself." Colette had heard of his illegitimate birth and scandalous reputation from her uncle, and wondered what he was doing flirting with her. Marriage was definitely not on his agenda, yet quite obviously on hers.

"Oh, that's a dull tale."

"Surely not!" she encouraged him. "I highly suspect that anything in relation to you would not be dull."

"I'm just a man." He held his hands out in mock helplessness.

"Just a man?" Colette laughed at his false humility. "Well, my lord, could you please tell me why a man such as yourself is so interested in ladies such as Juliette and myself?"

"Honestly?"

She tilted her head in his direction. "That would be nice."

He seemed slightly embarrassed. His gaze lowered before he glanced back up at her. "I like you both. I have no sisters of my own and I feel a little protective of the two you."

"That's very gallant of you, Lord Eddington, but what makes you think we need protecting?"

Jeffrey flashed her a charming smile. "Isn't it obvious? Your sister is trouble just waiting to happen, your uncle is intent on selling you both to the highest bidder, and it seems someone should be protecting you from those like myself."

Colette smiled then. "Ah, but who will protect us from *you*?"

Jeffrey laughed loudly. "You are a wise lady, Miss Hamilton."

"And you would be wise to remember that," she challenged him.

At that moment she spotted Lucien Sinclair crossing the room, carrying two crystal glasses. After spending that afternoon with him in the bookshop, she felt even more intrigued with the man. He had sparred with Juliette as if he'd known her for years, befriended and gained the undying loyalty of Paulette in an instant, and had left her feeling completely unlike herself. Although they had laughed and talked easily together selecting a few books she thought his father might enjoy, she felt an impossibly strong and magnetic undercurrent of feeling between them that left her quite breathless when she was near him.

Now curious to see where Lucien Sinclair was going, and for just whom he was carrying a glass of champagne, she craned her head, but could not see through the crowd of guests. She lost sight of him as he entered one of the withdrawing rooms. A pang of disappointment shot through her.

"Watching someone in particular?" Jeffrey asked with a meaningful glance.

Although she sensed that Lord Eddington knew full well whom she had been staring at, she was embarrassed to be caught doing so. Colette blushed. "I thought I saw Lord Waverly across the room, but I must have been mistaken."

Jeffrey regarded her carefully before saying, "You were not mistaken. That was Lord Waverly. He's a very good friend of mine. We've known each other since we were boys."

Here was a perfect source of information for Colette's burning questions. "Does he always behave so maddeningly?"

"I'm not sure what you mean."

"Well . . ." she began, "sometimes he seems so disapproving, close-minded, and stuffy, and then he can suddenly be lighthearted and charming."

"You find him charming, do you?" Jeffrey gave her a questioning glance.

"Perhaps," was her noncommittal response. She supposed Lucien Sinclair was charming in a maddening way.

"Well, I shall only say that Lucien has suffered in his life and he is often harder on himself than he needs to be."

Colette so wanted to know more about Lucien Sinclair, but bit her tongue so as not to seem like she was prying.

"Uh-oh," Jeffrey muttered low. "I'm afraid we are in for it now."

"What is it?"

"Here comes your aunt, and she looks decidedly unhappy."

Aunt Cecilia swooped down upon them in a flurry, her pale face pinched in disapproval, obviously dismayed to discover Colette with Lord Eddington, a man not inclined to enter into matrimony.

"Colette, I have been looking for you everywhere. Good evening, Lord Eddington." She gave a brief nod in his direction, her thin lips pursed in silent displeasure of his dallying with her niece.

"Good evening, Lady Hamilton," Jeffrey said with a most polite stance. "That shade of lavender complements your eyes most attractively."

Colette was stunned to note that her prim aunt actually looked flustered by Jeffrey's compliment.

"Why thank you, Lord Eddington." The faintest hint of a smile quickly vanished from Aunt Cecilia's face as she turned to her niece. "Now you must come with me, Colette. Your uncle wishes to introduce you to Baron Sheffield."

"Yes, Aunt Cecilia." She turned back to Jeffrey and smiled at him. "Thank you for a lovely time."

As her aunt dragged her away, she felt sure Jeffrey was winking at her.

Chapter Six

A Kiss Is Just a Kiss

"With your face, you should have every eligible bachelor falling at your feet. Instead I see you with Lord Eddington, and everyone knows he will never settle down." Uncle Randall scolded Colette with an impatient wag of his finger.

Aunt Cecilia added quietly, "For all his charm and good looks, Jeffrey Eddington is a complete waste of all our time and effort."

Uncle Randall continued to rant his disapproval of her behavior. "You need to focus your attentions on the proper kind of gentleman. Wealthy but suitable gentlemen very interested in marriage. The ones I choose for you."

"But the men you see as potential husbands for us are old enough to be our father," Colette retorted heatedly. And the most unattractive, she added to herself.

Aunt Cecilia snapped, her tone bitter, "Because they are the ones with the money, Colette. And the ones desperate enough for a wife to put up with you and your appalling lack of any kind of a dowry. Marriage is a serious business, and if you are still harboring any romantic illusions, you can just forget about them."

Groaning inwardly, Colette remained silent. She had no romantic illusions where marriage was concerned. She had learned that from watching her own parents.

Uncle Randall took hold her arm with greater force than necessary and pulled her close to him, stating, "I'm going to introduce you to Baron Sheffield now and you will be polite and flattering to him. He's extremely wealthy, having invested wisely in the textile market, and looking for a young bride to bear his children. He's been out of the country for some months and just returned. I've spoken to him about you, and he has watched you all evening and thinks you are quite lovely. He is also under the misguided impression that you have a disposition to match your looks. Don't you dare disappoint him with your modern ideas until after the wedding! Can you do that?"

Nodding, Colette glared at her uncle but did not respond, however much she longed to do so with a cutting remark. Somehow she managed to pull her arm from his grasp and took a step away from him.

"Now, here he comes. This is could be a very profitable venture, Colette. Smile and behave," Uncle Randall whispered sharply through the clenched teeth of his forced smile.

Colette looked up and her heart sank at the sight before her. Lumbering in their direction was a very large man who had to be at least forty if he was a day. He was younger than some of the doddering old fools she had met earlier, but his manner immediately repulsed her. With heavily pomaded black hair and a thick black beard, he smiled crookedly as he neared them, revealing tobacco-stained teeth.

"Ah, Baron Sheffield," Uncle Randall began with a feigned tone of happiness. "I would like to introduce you to my beautiful niece, Miss Colette Hamilton. Colette, dearest, this is Baron Chester Sheffield."

The distasteful man presented a gloved hand for Colette to take; yet she shuddered at his touch just the same.

"I have been most anxious to meet you, Miss Hamilton," he said, with an obvious leer down the front of her peach silk gown.

Colette gritted her teeth and pasted a smile on her face, wishing she could slap the lascivious expression from his face. At that moment she hated her uncle. "It's an honor to meet you, too, sir."

"I regret I cannot ask you to dance, Miss Hamilton. I have never been fond of dancing and prefer other entertainments."

"That's quite all right," she answered, very relieved, but not surprised, that dancing did not appeal to him. The man could hardly walk. She gathered that most endeavors that required any sort of physical exertion repelled him.

"Shall we go out on the terrace for a breath of fresh air?" he asked, his relentless gaze piercing her.

"That's a wonderful idea," Aunt Cecilia chimed in cheerily, ignoring the blatant look of disgust on Colette's face. "We shall leave you with Baron Sheffield for a few moments while we see to your sister." Aunt Cecilia's sharp eyes told her in no uncertain terms to not refuse the baron's invitation.

Before Colette could utter a protest, Baron Sheffield had a firm hand on her arm and he led her through a pair of French doors to the terrace. An enormous full moon glistened high in the sky, and the night air felt cool upon her skin. Colette breathed deeply of it so she did not have to smell Baron Sheffield.

"So, tell me about yourself, Miss Hamilton," he suggested amiably, as they made their way across the slate stones.

Ignoring the stench of stale cigar smoke around him,

she responded, "I fear there is not much to tell. I am sure my uncle told you everything you need to know about me." *That we are desperate for money and I am apparently available to the highest bidder?*

"Ah, such modesty. I admire that trait in a woman. It's such a rarity nowadays. Nevertheless I'm still curious as to why a lovely young lady such as yourself is not yet married. Why is that?"

Did she imagine that his hand clutched her arm tighter? Or that he was deliberately leading her from the gaslit terrace onto the darkened brick pathway to the more shadowy garden beyond? Did he actually think to make a romantic overture to her? She almost laughed in his face.

Fed up with men pulling her this way and that all evening, Colette stopped walking before they reached the tall shrubbery that blocked their view of the house. Her abrupt movement catching him off guard, he turned and glanced at her shrewdly.

"You haven't answered my question, Miss Hamilton."

"Perhaps you should first tell me why you are not yet married, sir."

His squinty eyes peered at her more closely. "Well, you do have a bit of spark in you after all. From your uncle's descriptions I thought you would be a meek little kitten."

"Well then, please let me rid you of that notion right here and now," she declared, staring back at him. She was not about to go off in the dark with this man, no matter what her uncle said. And there was no way she was going to marry him either. They were not *that* desperate. "If it is an obedient wife you seek, then I am afraid you have been greatly misled by my uncle where I am concerned."

"I know how to handle a disobedient wife, Miss Hamilton. Make no mistake about that." He grinned, lowering his face close to hers, and the stench of his breath made her head spin. "But I do indeed intend to find out if what I am about to purchase is worth my good money."

"Purchase?" she echoed with indignation. But then again, wasn't that what her uncle was doing? Selling her and Juliette? In essence, wasn't that what the marriage mart was all about in the end? A simple exchange of property?

Before she realized his intent, Baron Sheffield's clammy lips were pressed against hers as he pulled her tight against his barrel chest. She was no match for his large size, and he swung her around easily enough, lifting her off her feet and moving her farther into the shadowy area behind the bushes. As she struggled against the suffocating girth of him, she did not know which was worse, his rough whiskers scraping against her face or his fetid breath assailing her nostrils. She managed to pull her mouth from his, but his hands were still locked on her upper arms, holding her in place.

"Let go of me!" she cried, not caring at this point who saw them together or that her reputation would be ruined in the process. She simply wanted the odious beast to release her. Then at least she could outrun the man.

"Ah, the little kitten has claws!" He breathed hotly against her neck. "I think you might just be worth that much money after all."

"Let me go!"

Colette kicked her slippered foot against his leg as hard as she could, but it had no effect upon him. With her eyes tightly closed, she swung her head from side to side to avoid his wet fish lips and struggled to try to pull herself away from his forceful grip.

Suddenly she was free.

Stunned, she opened her eyes, trying to catch her breath.

"I believe the lady asked to be released."

Lord Waverly had Baron Sheffield's arm twisted behind his back. In spite of Baron Sheffield's unwieldy size, Lord Waverly seemed to loom over him. Colette did not recall Lucien Sinclair being quite so tall, but she was only too grateful for his height and strength, as well as his unexpected and quite timely appearance. The baron had the gall to look affronted, while the murderous expression on Lord Waverly's face left little doubt of his feelings on the situation.

"Unhand me, man!" Baron Sheffield sputtered in abject indignation, his round face puffed with outrage.

"First, you will apologize to the lady for taking liberties with her that were quite obviously unwanted. Second, you will leave this house immediately. Third, you will never come near Miss Hamilton again, or I shall not be so forgiving," Lord Waverly said. His voice had an edge that brooked no argument. To emphasize his point, he twisted the man's fat arm even tighter. "And if you apologize very nicely, I won't knock your teeth down your throat."

Aware of his weakness, the corpulent baron glared angrily at Colette and muttered with undisguised resentment, "My deepest apologies, Miss Hamilton. Please forgive my lack of control and excessive infatuation at your charms."

Lord Waverly released him with such force that the man stumbled forward and nearly fell flat on his face. Colette practically had to jump out of his way to avoid him, instinctively moving closer to Lord Waverly.

As he got to his feet again, the baron spat, "This won't be the end of it, Waverly." To Colette he spewed, "And you can tell your uncle that the deal is off." He turned and lumbered, huffing and puffing, as quickly as he could manage back to Lord Hutton's townhouse.

Still trying to catch her own breath, Colette finally raised her eyes to Lord Waverly's and felt a little lost looking in them. "Thank you."

"There is no need for thanks. Did he hurt you, Colette?" he asked, his voice full of concern.

She shook her head mutely, stunned at his use of her given name.

"Would you care to go back inside now?"

"No, not yet," she answered without hesitation. She was in no hurry to rejoin her aunt and uncle. "I think I should like a moment."

As if he understood her motivation, he said, "There's a bench over there. Come sit and pull yourself together a bit before going back to the ballroom."

For the first time all evening, she did not mind in the least that a man placed his hand on her arm. Lord Waverly gently guided her to a white marble bench set in an enclosure of leafy hydrangea bushes along the brick pathway, where some moonlight spilled through the trees above. The faint sounds of the orchestra playing from the ballroom drifted around them.

"Are you sure he did not hurt you?" he asked again, once they were both seated. His eyes quickly roamed over her body, as if he was assuring himself that she was unharmed.

Colette's pulse quickened under his scrutiny and her stomach felt suddenly full of butterflies. "I think he may have bruised my arms, but other than that I am quite well. I'm fortunate you came along when you did."

"It wasn't good fortune. I followed you."

"What do you mean?" she asked in surprise.

"I saw you leave the ballroom with him. You had a decidedly . . . unwilling look on your face. When I saw him take you from the terrace, I just—"

"You just . . . ?" She prompted him.

"I just had a feeling he was not going to behave with you as a gentleman should."

"Well, your instincts about Baron Sheffield proved quite accurate. He was horrid."

"Please don't tell me that your uncle thought that man was a prospective husband for you," Lord Waverly said.

Colette looked directly at him, once again thrown off balance by the stark handsomeness of his face. And the intensity of his gaze. And the fullness of his lips. Something about this man made her feel giddy, light-headed even. A delicious shiver ran through her. So different from the repulsive shiver she felt earlier with the baron.

"Apparently Baron Sheffield had been given the impression by my uncle that I would make a good wife for him."

"And you disabused him of that assumption?"

"Quite successfully." She couldn't help but grin. "With your help and persuasion, of course."

"You are most welcome," he said affably before his expression turned serious. "But why would your uncle choose such an unlikely prospect for you? Surely there must be a gentleman more to your liking than that rude beast?"

"My uncle expects my sister and me to marry very well. Baron Sheffield possesses all the required assets for a husband as far as my uncle is concerned."

"And those assets would be what?"

"Pots and pots of money. In addition to his baronial estate, he is apparently very wealthy from textile investments."

"Ah, I see," he stated quietly, his handsome face thoughtful. "Money is the key component of this marriage?"

"Unfortunately, yes."

"You are quite candid."

"It is my uncle's decision," she tried to explain, realizing how mercenary it seemed. "The reality is such that my father left my mother, my sisters, and me a less than modest amount to live on. Women have very little recourse in situations like this, Lord Waverly. Juliette and I need to marry well to support our family."

He nodded his head in understanding. "But what of the bookshop? Does that not bring in income for you?"

"Unfortunately, not enough."

"Why don't you simply sell the shop, then? It must be worth a good sum."

She shook her head determinedly. "No. Selling the shop is not an option."

"It means that much to you?" He could not mask the surprise in his voice.

"More than anything. I shall never sell Hamilton's."

Recognizing the resolve in her tone, he shook his head slightly. "If you insist upon keeping the shop, then perhaps it is best that you should marry soon so you can have the proper support and guidance of a husband, Miss Hamilton."

Ignoring his words, which disparaged her ability to manage the shop on her own, she simply said, "You called me Colette earlier."

"I did?" His voice was threaded with surprise. "I had not noticed. Forgive me."

The man seemed to be a study in contrasts. "For an earl with a well-known reputation, you are behaving like quite the gentleman, Lord Waverly."

"Ah, you have heard of my reputation, then." He looked at her without a shred of embarrassment. In fact, he appeared amused by her comment.

"Yes, but just vaguely, of course. My aunt and uncle have warned me against rogues like you. And your friend, Lord Eddington."

He gave her a searching glance. "And what do you think of Lord Eddington?"

Did she detect a note of jealousy in his voice? "I think he is a delightful man. I very much enjoyed dancing with him this evening."

He rubbed his hand across his chin. "Yes, well, I suppose we have both earned a certain standing in society's eyes."

She could not help herself from asking, "Have you really been with so many women?"

The corners of his mouth turned up slightly. "What a question from a lady!"

"So then it is not true what they say about you? You are not a rake?"

"Why do you ask that?"

"Because you have rescued me from the lecherous baron, showed concern for my well-being and safety, and have not once tried to kiss me."

"You are not my type," he explained with succinct ease.

"And why is that?" she asked. She could not help feeling slightly insulted by his remark.

"Because you are a virtuous young lady, one that a gentleman would hope to marry."

Now she was surprised. "That's not your type?"

"Decidedly not. I do have some standards. I prefer to dally with more experienced women who are not interested in marriage."

She dared a direct glance at him. "But you wanted to kiss me that day in the bookshop."

He held her gaze, but did not respond.

She would not let him off that easily. She knew she had not imagined what she had felt between them that afternoon. "You did want to kiss me, though, didn't you?"

He lowered his eyes. "Yes, I did."

His admission thrilled her. "But you didn't."

"Why? Did you want me to?" he asked, gazing directly at her.

His question turned her stomach upside down and she suddenly couldn't think. "Perhaps . . ."

He grinned wolfishly at her, a grin that lit his eyes from within and caused her stomach to somersault again. "Did I disappoint you?" he whispered, his voice as smooth as velvet.

"I'm . . . I'm n-not sure," she stammered, finding it difficult to breathe normally, lost in the look of his eyes, which glittered hypnotically in the moonlight. A thrill ran through her, as if something special were about to happen.

"I would hate to ever disappoint you, Miss Hamilton . . ."

He leaned in nearer to her, his face so close to hers she suddenly could not breathe at all. He waited there, hovering. His eyes searched hers. He smelled clean and so very masculine and infinitely appealing. She could see the faint stubble along his chin and wondered what it would feel like to run her fingers across it. His nearness unnerved her and left her trembling, while her stomach felt as if it had just plummeted to her toes. Unable to bear the intensity any longer, she closed her eyes.

"Look at me," he demanded in a hushed whisper, his hand cupping the back of her neck in a gentle movement.

Her heart pounded wildly in anticipation as her lids fluttered back open. She took a shaky breath. His green eyes pinned her in place as his lips touched hers lightly, teasingly. He kissed her as if she were the most delicate, the most fragile of crystal. His touch was soft, featherlike. His mouth was warm, his lips smooth. The hand on the back of her neck pulled her closer, his fingers caressing the sensitive skin there, sending shivers down her spine. The feel was so exquisite she thought she would faint.

"Colette," he breathed her name into her mouth and suddenly his lips became more insistent, more demanding. They possessed her, seared her in a kiss so all-consuming she could not breathe.

She closed her eyes in spite of what he said and lost herself completely in the sensation of his mouth covering hers.

His mouth became possessive, virtually ravenous over hers. She felt devoured. To her own surprise, her lips parted, instinctively responding to his. His tongue entered her mouth. Shocked and thrilled by the sensation, her heart raced. Heated and slick, his tongue swirled with her own inside of her mouth. *Good heavens!* Was this what made women swoon in the gothic novels she had read? And that was her last rational thought as his kiss overwhelmed her with its blatant intimacy and intensity. He was strength and gentleness combined, and she could not get enough of him. A hunger grew within her as they kissed. Never had she felt something so completely and utterly satisfying, yet it left her yearning for more, desperate for more. She didn't want it to end.

Lucien's mouth on hers wasn't enough.

When did she place her hands on his shoulders? His quite broad and firm shoulders. *What possessed me to do such a thing?* And when did his other hand find its way around her waist?

And still they kissed.

And kissed.

She could no longer hear the music from the ballroom, nor the chirping of the crickets, nor the usual noises of the cool evening around them. Only the rapid thumping of her heart and the sound of their breathing echoed in her ears.

Then he pulled her closer, and she clung to him with no resistance whatsoever. She found herself sitting across his lap, a position that was at once so intimate and possessive. It was as if she had been designed to fit perfectly there, with his arms around her, holding her securely against his chest. The feel of his muscled thighs beneath her left her light-headed. It seemed they could not get close enough to each other. They melted into each other, as if they were the only two people in the world and where they were did not matter. Time seemed to disappear.

And still they kissed.

His hands cupped her face, his fingers threaded through her hair, loosening it from its upswept style. Lucien's touch made her feel cherished and adored. Colette had never experienced anything like it. She had never been kissed before, but she knew, just knew, she would never be kissed like this again. This was wild, reckless, and passionate. She had read about passion, of course. But now she was fast learning what the word truly meant.

She was kissing and being kissed passionately.

By a man who held her on his lap. By a man who touched her with infinite tenderness and unmistakable desire. By a man who . . .

Abruptly, he turned his head away from hers, and she collapsed into the crook of his neck. They both panted heavily, and he stroked her hair. For a long while they did not speak, but simply tried to regain their breath.

His voice was ragged when he finally spoke. "I'm sorry, Colette."

She knew why he was apologizing; yet she still wished he had not done so. The apology made their kiss seem wrong, and his mouth on hers felt more right than anything she had ever known. Reluctantly she lifted her head, feeling very groggy, as if she had just awakened from a most delicious dream. Her lips felt heavy and swollen and the thought of leaving his embrace made her want to cry.

They stared at each other, and she tried to read his unfathomable green eyes. Did he regret kissing her? Did he think she was angry? *God, but he is stunningly handsome.* Lightly, she touched his face with her fingers, tracing the strong cheekbones and the masculine line of Lucien's jaw. *Lucien.* For of course, she could not think of him as anything but Lucien now.

Lucien. Lucien. Lucien.

"Colette?"

"Hmm?"

"Are you all right?"

"Yes," she whispered when she was capable of speaking coherently again. "Is kissing always like that?"

"No. No, it's not." His husky words thrilled her. He took her hand in his large one and pressed a sweet kiss to her palm, and then he gently closed her fingers, as if saving the kiss for her.

Her heart fluttered wildly at the tender gesture.

"Which is why this cannot happen again between us."

Then she could only nod in agreement with him as she slowly came back to her senses. It certainly could not happen again. What was she thinking? Kissing the man in full view of whoever happened to be walking through the garden! She had just behaved more scandalously than Juliette had ever done! No, this could never happen again!

What had come over her?

Gently Lucien slipped her off his lap and onto her feet, which were none too steady at that point. Suddenly flooded with embarrassment, she could not look at him.

"We must get you back to the house unseen. You should enter first and I'll stay outside a while longer."

Her hands went intuitively to her hair; she knew it must look a fright. Everyone would know just by looking at her what she had been doing. Kissing the Earl of Waverly in a moonlit garden while she sat in his lap! She had behaved disgracefully, yet oddly enough, she did not regret one minute of it.

As she attempted to put her hair to rights, Lucien leaned over and kissed her cheek. The kiss was soft and gentle, and sent another thrill through Colette's body.

"You are a beautiful woman, Colette. You can have any man you want, and so you must promise me that you won't allow your uncle to force you to settle for any man you don't wish to marry."

She stared at him, feeling confused by the deep emotions Lucien stirred within her heart. "I promise," she whispered before turning and making her way along the brick pathway back to the house.

Her heart pounding, Colette gulped deep, filling her lungs with air to calm herself. The comparative glare and the noise from the ballroom made her want to hide her face, which she knew had to be flaming scarlet. She inhaled another long breath and pressed her hands to her heated cheeks, suppressing the urge to look back in the garden. Would Lucien be standing there, watching her? How long would he wait before returning to the ball? Torn between wanting to run back to his side and never wanting to face him again, she ventured hesitantly into the ballroom, wishing she could hide somewhere quiet and relive what had just happened to her.

Juliette found her first.

"I've been looking for you everywhere! Where have you been?" her sister demanded.

"For a walk in the garden."

"Alone?" Juliette's sharp eyes missed nothing.

"No," Colette attempted to explain. "The repulsive Baron Sheffield dragged me out to the garden with him and then had the nerve to try to kiss me!"

"He did no such thing!" she exclaimed in shock.

"Unfortunately, he did." She recoiled at the memory of the baron's mouth on hers.

"Oh, Colette!" She laughed nervously, her expression aghast. Juliette grabbed her hand in comfort. "How perfectly awful! What did you do?"

"I kicked him." Colette described the events in a whisper as the two of them hid behind a marble column. "He was not very happy with me, quite angry really, and stalked away. By now I'm certain he has told Uncle Randall that I am an utter hoyden."

"Well, at least you won't have to bear his company again."

"No. But I've no doubt Uncle Randall will find someone equally detestable to court me."

"Are you sure that is all that happened to you?" Juliette questioned.

Colette flushed, unsure why she did not want to tell Juliette that she had just kissed Lucien Sinclair passionately. "Why do you ask?"

"I'm not sure. You just have a look about you, excited or happy. You look different somehow."

"I suppose I'm still just upset about Baron Sheffield." She shifted the topic. "What have you been doing while I was gone?"

Juliette's expression was not one of total belief, but she obviously had something she wanted to share with her.

"I've been disappointing Uncle Randall also. He found me playing cards with Lord Eddington in the drawing room and he just about had an apoplectic fit! Aunt Cecilia wants to take us home immediately."

Colette shook her head in despair. It would be a miracle if either of them were to come out of this Season with their reputations intact, let alone with husbands.

Chapter Seven

A Male Point of View

A few days later Colette continued to work in the bookshop as evening approached. The books had now all been placed neatly on the shelves, and the signs that Paulette had painted hung from the ceiling held with dark green ribbon. Also, a new sign with "Hamilton's Book Shoppe" printed in elegant writing hung above the counter. The major changes were now completed. Colette stepped back to admire the place and felt an incredible sense of accomplishment at her progress. The store looked completely different from when her father was alive. A few months ago she had only her ideas. Now the shop was generating much talk in the neighborhood, and people were coming in to take a look for themselves at what the Hamilton girls had done to their father's shop. They had marveled at the changes and congratulated her.

And, most importantly, they bought books. Her sales had doubled from the month before. Which was still a pitiful amount, but better than nothing. Business was picking up slowly but surely.

Colette arranged a few wooden chairs in a circle as the tinkling of the bells above the door caught her attention.

A thin woman, about thirty, wearing a neat gray bonnet and dress, asked shyly, "Hello. I hope I am not too late. This is when the reading group meets, isn't it?"

"Yes, it is," Colette responded with an encouraging smile. Just the day before Colette met the woman, who worked as a governess for a family in Mayfair, and had encouraged her to attend. "Please come in and have a seat, Miss Rutan. I'm so happy you decided to join us."

The woman nodded and situated herself on one of the chairs that Colette had just arranged. "This is so exciting!" Miss Rutan exclaimed. "I've never been part of a reading group before! Thank you for inviting me."

"You're quite welcome."

The door to their quarters upstairs opened and Paulette and Lisette entered the bookshop. Lisette carried a tray with a blue flower–patterned china teapot, creamer, and sugar bowl, and Paulette followed with another tray filled with matching cups and saucers and a plate of cookies.

"We've brought some refreshments," Lisette declared as she efficiently set up a serving area on a table covered with a pretty chintz cloth. "Would you like some tea?" she offered their first guest.

The bells jingled again and Colette greeted two more women, who also took seats in the circle. The taller of the two, Miss Benson, wore a bright yellow scarf around her neck and spectacles, while the shorter one, Mrs. Cornell, clutched a book tightly to her chest.

The Ladies' Reading Circle had been Colette's idea, too, knowing that the women would have to buy the books in order to join the group. Paulette had made a sign advertising that Hamilton's would hold a monthly book discussion group for women. Their first book was Mary Shelley's *Frankenstein*. A little dark, perhaps, but it was daring and much talked about. And Colette thought it important that they begin with a female author. She had hoped for a larger group, but three women, along with her sisters, was at least enough to start.

The three ladies, Colette, Lisette, Paulette, and a most reluctant Juliette had just begun their discussion of the work when the bells above the door signaled another entrance. Colette turned her head to see Lord Jeffrey Eddington enter the bookshop. He held a copy of *Frankenstein* in one hand and a small bouquet of flowers in the other. He was grinning mischievously from ear to ear.

"Good evening, ladies," he said grandly. "Would you mind if I joined you?"

Stunned speechless, Colette stared at him in confusion. Juliette suddenly developed a case of the giggles and laughed surreptitiously into her hand, which was held tightly over her mouth. Paulette and Lisette looked as stunned as the other ladies did.

"Lord Eddington, what on earth are you doing here?" Colette finally managed to ask, after he breezily swept into the room, placed the flowers—a lovely assortment of hyacinth and lily of the valley—on the table, and seated himself upon an empty chair, looking extremely comfortable. He acted as if this were the most ordinary of occurrences, when as far as she knew he had never set foot in Hamilton's before. Or any bookshop, for that matter!

"Isn't it obvious? I'm here to discuss *Frankenstein*. It's one of my favorites." He smiled winningly around the group.

"But, Lord Eddington, this is a *women's* discussion group," Colette explained, wondering why he had suddenly appeared in the bookshop. Judging from the highly satisfied look on Juliette's face, she must have had something to do with this.

"Yes, I know that, but I thought you might benefit from a male point of view. You don't mind if I participate, do you, ladies?" He asked so charmingly; Colette watched as each woman, including Paulette, nodded in acquiescence. It was impossible for the man to be denied.

"It *would* be interesting to have a man's opinion," Mrs. Cornell volunteered.

The sight of the matronly Mrs. Cornell batting her eyes at Jeffrey amused Colette. "Juliette?" she questioned her sister with a single word.

"I may have mentioned to Lord Eddington in passing that we were meeting here this evening," she said, still attempting to suppress the laughter that bubbled within her.

With a serious expression on his handsome face, Lord Eddington questioned the group, assured of his acceptance with the women. "Did you know that Mary Shelley was only nineteen when she wrote this novel?"

Without missing a beat, Paulette jumped right into the discussion. "Yes, and her parents were revolutionaries. That must have had a strong influence on her writing, don't you agree?"

As the conversation swirled around her, Colette sat back against her chair, helpless to keep Lord Eddington from participating. This was not how she imagined her first book discussion group. She tried to keep up with the dialogue but was disconcerted by Lord Eddington's strong presence. She never would have suspected him of participating in such a way. What was he doing there? Did he really have feelings for Juliette? *Or, even more incredibly, me?*

Of course that thought led her thoughts to Lucien Sinclair.

As much as she tried to block that night from her memory, she had not been able to think of anything but their world-altering and seductively sensual kiss. The feel of Lucien's lips on hers, the caress of his strong hand at her waist, the huskiness of his voice when he whispered her name. And how she had not wanted it to end.

Oh, she was not completely ignorant of the ways of men and women. Years ago she and Juliette had secretly read one of the thick medical textbooks she had found on a dusty shelf in the shop. *A Complete Study of the Human Anatomy and All Its Functions by Doctor T. Everett* even had pencil sketches to accompany its explanation of sexual intercourse. The two of them had been shocked, appalled, and fascinated by the information the book contained, which really created more questions for them than it answered.

Now Colette had stunned herself with the realization that she might actually want to do what came next.

With Lucien Sinclair.

She wanted to feel his strong male body against hers. And heaven help her, had he taken further liberties with her that evening in the garden, she doubted if she would have had the resolve to stop him. And if she were truly honest with herself, she knew she would have willingly done anything he wanted.

Sleepless nights and tormented dreams had plagued her ever since he had kissed her. She had not seen Lucien since that night and almost felt relieved. Almost. What would she do when she saw him next? Surely they would meet again. She had been half hoping he would visit the bookshop to see her. But he had not come. So she was left on needles and pins wondering what would happen when they saw each other again.

Suddenly noticing the puzzled looks on her sisters' faces, she recalled that she was expected to participate in the discussion, and she dragged her thoughts from the seductive Lucien Sinclair and forced herself to focus all her attention on the group. An hour later, after much conversation, debate, and laughter, Miss Benson, Miss Rutan, and Mrs. Cornell declared the group a success and promised to come again next month and more importantly, to bring their friends with them.

"Will you be joining us again next month when we discuss Jane Austen's *Sense and Sensibility*, Lord Eddington?" Mrs. Cornell asked him with a flirtatious batting of her eyelashes that astonished Colette.

"I would never pass up an opportunity to spend an evening in the company of such beautiful women." His good looks and magnetic charm had enraptured the women and left them giggling as they exited the shop.

Now alone with the Hamilton sisters, Lord Eddington commented, "My God, you four girls look remarkably alike."

"We know," they all stated in unison.

Lord Eddington laughed in amusement. "There is one sister missing, is there not?"

"Yvette. She's the youngest, and Mother said she was not old enough to join us. Not that she would understand the discussion anyway, even if she did attend," Paulette explained with the sophisticated air of a sibling only slightly older yet far superior to her younger sister.

"I would like to meet your youngest sister," Jeffrey said, still staring at them in amazement, "as well as your mother sometime."

"Perhaps you will," Colette said, somewhat confounded by his sudden interest in her family.

Lisette spoke up. "It was a pleasure meeting you, Lord Eddington. You made our first book group discussion quite memorable."

"I enjoyed it myself. You ladies definitely gave me some ideas to ponder."

"Come, Paulette, it is past time we went upstairs," Lisette suggested. "Good night, Lord Eddington."

"Good night, Miss Hamilton, and Miss Hamilton."

Giggling at Jeffrey's teasing, Paulette helped Lisette gather up the remains of the refreshments and headed back upstairs. Colette began to remove the chairs from the circle.

"Here, allow me do that." Lord Eddington took a chair from Colette's hands. "Just tell me where you want this. Against the wall?"

Colette nodded as he went to work, then she and Juliette exchanged curious glances.

"You're not impressing us," Juliette called to him.

"I'm simply being a gentleman." He grinned slyly. "I can be one when it suits me."

Juliette rolled her eyes at him, but admitted grudgingly, "I did not think you would have the nerve to actually join us."

"How could I possibly turn down an invitation from you, my lovely Juliette? Besides, I wished to take a look at your shop for myself, and what better way is there than to spend the evening with beautiful women?"

"Well, you did lend an air of excitement to our little group," Colette admitted, surprised by the success of her first literary discussion.

"I thought so, too," he boasted with a devilish grin. "Excitement is my specialty, you know. Now, ladies, how else can I be of help to you?"

"There is nothing else to be done, but thank you for offering," Colette replied.

"Well, then, I should be going. Thank you both for a most interesting evening. I rather enjoyed myself more than I thought I would. Shall I see you next at Lady Boswell's party tomorrow night?"

"I suppose so," Colette murmured.

As he gathered up his coat and hat, they bid him good-bye and watched as he left. Colette locked the shop door behind him and pulled down the shade.

"Now why do you suppose he came here tonight?" she asked her sister.

Juliette laughed and crossed her arms over her chest. "To prove me wrong."

"What do you mean?"

"At Lord Hutton's party I made a remark to him that I didn't think he ever took anything seriously. So when he learned of the book group, he stopped by to show me that he could be serious."

Pondering this, Colette shook her head. A man like Jeffrey Eddington did not attend a ladies' literary discussion group without a good cause for motivation. "No, I don't think that's it. I think he is a little sweet on you, Juliette, and he's trying to win you over."

Juliette laughed outright. "No one tries to win me over! If anything, he's sweet on you, and he's trying to win *you* over!"

Now it was Colette's turn to laugh. "That's ridiculous!"

"Is it?" Juliette gave her a knowing look, turned, and made her way upstairs, leaving Colette stunned.

Chapter Eight

Let the Games Begin

Lucien smiled good-naturedly as he laid his cards on the table. Four aces. His friends groaned when they saw his winning poker hand. "And that's the game."

"Doesn't that beat all?" Lord James Buckley complained with a desperate frown. "How do you always manage to win, Waverly?"

"Just born lucky, I guess." Lucien grinned as he collected his considerable winnings from the center of the table. It wasn't as if he needed the money. Lucien just liked to play cards and spend time with his friends. Not since his father's apoplectic sickness began had he hosted a night of cards.

"He gets all the cards and all the women," Buckley muttered to the others, his thin face narrowed in dissatisfaction. "It's not fair."

"Fair enough," Jeffrey Eddington responded cryptically, collecting the cards from the table. He shuffled them effortlessly and they began another hand.

They had recently learned to play poker, a distinctly American card game, from their friend Harrison Fleming, who had visited New Orleans the year before, and they had been playing it ever since.

"I think Waverly's luck may have just run out," Eddington continued, dealing the cards with efficient speed and practiced skill.

"What do you mean?" Thomas Hargrove asked eagerly, puffing on his cigar, the smoke filling Lucien Sinclair's study with a tangy cloud.

Eddington turned to Lucien and raised an eyebrow. "Are you going to tell them or should I?"

Lucien shrugged, picking up his cards from the table. He honestly didn't want to discuss the matter, but now that Jeffrey brought it up, he was sure to have no peace until he confessed his plan. "It seems I'm finally going to settle down and choose a bride."

Buckley and Hargrove's riotous questions erupted in the smoke-filled room.

"You're jesting!"

"Why would you do it now?"

"Who is she?"

"Yes, who is the lucky girl?"

Lucien breathed deeply. "I have a young woman in mind and have not asked her yet, but I plan to. I'd like to be married as soon as possible."

Buckley cried out in surprise, "Good God, man, you can't mean to leg-shackle yourself so soon!"

"You're serious, aren't you, Lucien?" Hargrove questioned, his face full of astonishment.

"Yes, I am." Lucien left it at that.

"So tell us who she is," Eddington said with a distinct gleam in his eye.

Lucien offered, "You'll know when the time comes."

"He's being mysterious," Eddington declared.

Lucien shrugged as the poker game continued, ignoring the continued requests for more information. They would learn it all soon enough. In the meantime, Lucien intended to pursue Lady Faith Bromleigh in the proper manner.

After another two hours, he collected his considerable profits and the game ended for the night. Before Buckley could leave, Lucien discreetly slipped him his winnings.

"This is the last time I will play with you, Buckley. Use this to pay off some of your debts." Lucien could not bear the grateful look on his friend's face.

"I can't take this from you, Lucien," Buckley mumbled. "I owe you money."

Yes, Buckley owed him money. A great deal, actually. But Lucien also knew that Buckley was in very deep trouble and in danger of losing his house. He hated to see his friend, whom he had known for years, in such dire straits, even if it was due to his own weakness and poor judgment.

"Stop gambling," Lucien told Buckley in a tone that left no doubt as to his feelings on the matter. "You can no longer afford it."

"Thank you. I will pay you back, I swear it." Looking abashed, Buckley nodded sadly. He did not hesitate as he pocketed the money before he exited the room.

With just Eddington left, Lucien walked to the sideboard and poured them each another glass of fine scotch whisky from a crystal decanter.

"You shouldn't give him any more money, Lucien," Jeffrey stated simply, accepting the glass of whisky Lucien handed him.

"You saw that, did you?"

"Yes, and it's a waste of good cash."

Lucien sat in the rich brown leather wingchair opposite Jeffrey in front of the fireplace. The orange flames crackled and cast shadows across the room. "I realize I shouldn't. But I also know he needs it."

"Don't misunderstand me, I like Buckley, too, but he owes money all over town. He's a grown man, for Christ's sake. He should know better. If he can't afford to lose, he shouldn't play. You're only prolonging the inevitable by helping him out."

Lucien nodded, knowing that Jeffrey was correct in his assessment of Buckley. Still, Lucien couldn't help but feel bad for him. Buckley was in for a humiliating downfall one of these days. And more than likely sooner than he expected. Lucien shook his head before taking a sip of the whisky. "Have you been given a new assignment yet?" he asked.

Behind Jeffrey's indolent and womanizing reputation, there hid a strength of character few would ever suspect him of possessing. For the past few years he had taken on a position with the British government. Aside from Lucien, no one had any idea of Jeffrey's clandestine work for his country. And Jeffrey wanted it that way.

"Yes. They're pretty quiet at the moment, at least on my end of things. A war between Prussia and France will stir things up inevitably, I suspect," Jeffrey explained.

"Are they sending you to Paris?"

"More than likely before the end of summer."

Lucien nodded, thinking that he might very well be engaged by the end of the summer, while his friend would be aiding his country in Paris.

"So please tell me you're not seriously considering the dull Bromleigh chit."

Lucien gave him a steady glance, unwavering in his meaning. "I am."

"I'm disappointed in you, Lucien. Of all the wonderful girls out there for you to marry, why her?"

"Faith Bromleigh will suit just fine."

"Fine? Fine?" Jeffrey scoffed with indignation. "Can you even have a conversation with her?" In response to Lucien's tight-lipped silence, Jeffrey said disparagingly, "I knew it! I'm sure she's a nice enough girl, but do you really want to spend the rest of your life with someone who has a personality like wall paint?"

Again, Lucien could not respond. Jeffrey had a valid point. Still, he knew he was making a sound decision. It was very important that he marry the right type of woman. And the biddable Faith Bromleigh was the best example of what he was looking for in a wife.

"And can you picture yourself bedding her?"

Lucien remained silent again at Jeffrey's questioning. Faith Bromleigh did not arouse passion in him because she was not a passionate person. That was why he'd chosen her.

Jeffrey continued, "If you feel you must marry before your father dies, then at least choose a woman with some life in her, like one of those Hamilton sisters. Juliette and Colette are both beauties with enough wit and charm to last a lifetime."

At the mention of Colette Hamilton's name, Lucien's entire body tensed. He had been attempting to block her from his thoughts all week. Since he kissed her that night in the garden, he had been tortured with images of her. He could have kicked himself for kissing her, but at the time he had been powerless to prevent it. He simply had no choice but to finally taste those berry-sweet lips for himself. If he were totally honest, he had been dying to kiss her since the moment he set eyes on her in the bookshop.

But even he, he who had kissed countless women over the years, had been completely unprepared for the effect Colette had upon his senses. Good God, she had left him reeling and desperate for more. So much more . . . He had wanted to take her there in the garden, to tear that

silky gown from her body and feel her naked skin pressed
against his, to caress her plump, ripe breasts, to kiss every
inch of her, to drive himself into her warm, seductive
little body.

Yet even he knew better than to trifle with a girl like
that. Colette wasn't one to be taken lightly. She was the
type of girl that a man married. Unfortunately, she was
not the type he must marry. Someday Miss Colette Hamilton would lead her husband into a merry hell, with her
stubborn ways and modern notions. He could not afford
to risk a marriage with a wife like that. After a childhood
racked with nothing but scandal, he wished for some
measure of peace in his life, with a wife he could trust to
behave and who would be faithful to him.

"If you think they would make such perfect wives, why
don't you marry one of them?" Lucien questioned with
a challenging look.

Jeffrey countered pragmatically, "I'm an undercover
operative for our country, the illegitimate son of the
Duke of Rathmore, a notorious and well-respected rake,
and I'm about to leave for Paris. Yes, I'm an ideal candi-
date for any woman to marry."

"Well, don't try to foist them on me, then. Especially
Juliette. That one is a holy terror."

"She's fantastic!" Jeffrey defended Juliette with an eagerness that surprised Lucien. "I have had some of the
most entertaining conversations of my life with that girl.
And believe me, I've had some great ones." He paused
thoughtfully. "But what about Colette? She would appeal
more to your tastes."

"I hardly think a woman who runs a bookshop and
handles business like a man would be suited to be a marchioness. Besides, what is your interest in these two particular sisters?"

"I think they're amazing. I've never met women

quite like them. I spent some time with them the other night—"

Lucien almost choked on his whisky. "You did what?"

"Easy, old man," Jeffrey cautioned as Lucien continued to cough. "As I was saying, I went to their bookshop—"

"You went to Hamilton's?"

"Yes, and would you mind not interrupting me?"

"Fine, but why on earth would you go to their bookshop?" Stunned by the realization Jeffrey had been to Hamilton's Book Shoppe, Lucien could not come to grips with his own reaction. He felt a strange, overwhelming possessiveness about Colette, her sisters, and the shop, and did not like the thought of Eddington visiting them. He didn't like to think of him dancing with Colette either, though he would be hard-pressed to explain just why he felt that way to Jeffrey.

"I wanted to see where they came from, these fascinating sisters. I've met all but the youngest now. And they are all quite lovely, intelligent women. Besides, Juliette practically dared me to come visit. I could hardly disappoint her."

"The two of you together would be a devastating combination," Lucien quipped, shaking his head at the thought.

"Yes, wouldn't we, though?" Jeffrey agreed amiably. "But Juliette and I are much better suited to be good friends, if that makes any sense."

"I don't know if you should even be friends." Shaking his head in mock horror, Lucien grimaced.

Jeffrey laughed. "Ah, but she's fun."

Curious, Lucien couldn't help but ask, "And what about Colette?"

"What about her?"

"What are your feelings for her?"

Jeffrey gave Lucien a very hard look. Lucien found himself turning away, his eyes lingering on the orange flames in the fireplace. He watched the golden light dance and flicker wildly across the charred wood.

"I think Colette is an amazing woman," Jeffrey declared without hesitation. "She would be a credit to any man she marries. And that man would be a very lucky one. She's just twenty years old and supporting her family. Did you know that?"

"Yes," Lucien admitted reluctantly. The thought had weighed on him. "We should see if we couldn't send some business her way."

"That isn't a bad idea," Jeffrey admitted. "The poor girls could use a break."

After a long pause, Lucien stated, "I received some news that will take your mind off the Hamilton sisters. I received a letter from my mother today."

"You're not serious?" Jeffrey asked, incredulous. "Good God! After all this time. What did she say?"

"It seems she has returned to London and has learned of my father's illness. She wants to see him. And me."

Jeffrey remained speechless for some time before asking, "What do you intend to do?"

"I don't know yet."

"Imagine hearing from her after all these years."

Lucien had imagined it hundreds of times when he was younger. He had dreamed of her returning, declaring she missed him too much to stay away and promising to never leave again. But those childhood fantasies had ceased by the time he was twelve and his mother had not written him a single word. Since then he had hardened his heart against ever being hurt by her again.

"Have you told your father yet?"

Lucien shook his head in regret. "No, I'm afraid hearing about my mother might cause him more pain than he's in already."

"Maybe it would help?" Jeffrey tossed out the suggestion casually.

"How?" Lucien demanded. Tormenting his father with news of his faithless wife's return could hardly aid in his recovery.

Jeffrey leaned forward in his chair, his elbows resting on his legs. "Maybe seeing your mother again after all these years might give your father a bit of peace. They probably have a lot to say to each other."

"The man can barely speak, Jeffrey. It wouldn't be fair to him."

"Perhaps. But is that for you to judge or decide?"

Lucien shrugged, unsure. "I just wonder what she wants after all this time. What could she possibly have to say to either of us?" He had a bad feeling about it. His mother had destroyed their lives once before when she abandoned them, running off with another man. The pain and the scandal devastated his father. He could not bear to see her hurt Simon like that again. Lucien shuddered to think of the scandal her unexpected return would certainly create.

Jeffrey asked, "Isn't that exactly why you should see her? To find out?"

Lucien was not sure he wanted to know.

Chapter Nine

Cry Uncle

"It's the only way, Genevieve," Randall Hamilton pleaded with his brother's widow. "The bookshop is worthless, but the building itself would bring quite a handsome sum of money."

"I don't know . . . *Je ne sais pas quoi faire* . . ." Genevieve hesitated. "Colette loves the shop so much. I could not sell it without breaking her heart." She sighed wearily, distressed by the subject of the conversation.

Randall attempted to quell his mounting frustration with the feeble woman. Her steady decline over the years astounded him, for Genevieve La Brecque had once been stunningly beautiful. So stunning that Randall had even fancied himself in love with her at one time. But she had ended up marrying Thomas. How his half brother had managed to wed a woman like Genevieve always eluded him.

Thomas had been a weak and studious child who had become an even weaker and more bookish man. Although they shared the same father, Thomas and Randall had turned out as different as night and day. Where Randall was driven by the desire to be powerful and rich, Thomas had been motivated only by his love of books.

Even when they were children, Thomas was content to sit in their father's library and read for hours on end, whereas Randall had spent his time riding his horses and avoiding the schoolroom at all costs. Their old tutor doted on the studious Thomas but despaired of ever teaching the recalcitrant Randall anything. They both ended up attending Cambridge, but while Thomas actually went there to learn, Randall attended merely to placate their father while having as good a time as he could carousing with his friends.

When their father died, Randall inherited the title of Lord Hamilton and little else, discovering how worthless and empty that inheritance was. Their father seemed to have squandered a great deal of the family fortune over the years. Highly disappointed at that unexpected turn of events, Randall pursued a wealthy wife to bolster the family coffers. He married the passably attractive Cecilia Brewton, a minor heiress, but the best he could do under his dire financial circumstances. It proved to be a good choice after all, for he and Cecilia agreed upon what was important in life and they both made it their goal to obtain that end. Cecilia spent wisely and always made sure that Lord and Lady Hamilton showed their best side to the public. Together they had risen as far as they could socially, making only the highest connections, attending only the elitest parties. They had been doing well financially until this year, when Randall had made some very unwise shipping investments in which he took a terribly costly blow. Sending money to help support his brother's family was bad enough, but then he discovered his son Nigel's staggering gambling debts. Randall was in danger of losing everything.

It galled him to no end that all of the success that he and Cecilia had worked so long and so hard to achieve now rested precariously on the shoulders of two of Thomas and Genevieve's daughters.

His younger half brother and his family had always been the bane of Randall's existence. While Randall worked to raise the family's social position, Thomas opted to open a little bookshop near Mayfair, much to Randall's great humiliation. Randall didn't know which he despised most: his miserable half brother, the beautiful Genevieve, and their ever-growing passel of daughters; or the dilapidated bookshop that bore his family's name.

That Randall's financial security now depended on the whims of his flighty nieces rankled him. For weeks before the start of the Season, Cecilia had done her best to school Colette and Juliette in the correct mode of behavior, but it appeared to be a lost cause. Now he was through wasting his time with them and their fickle ways.

"It's not Colette's broken heart that concerns me at the moment, Genevieve. It is our survival."

A pained expression crossed her pale and faded features.

"I've been very patient with you," he began again in an attempt to remain calm. "When Thomas first died, I left everything to your discretion, did I not?"

She nodded weakly. "*Oui*, but—"

"Well, it has been almost a year now. The bookshop barely brought in enough money to support the seven of you when Thomas was alive, and it is bringing in even less now. Colette has shown me the books. As your nearest male relative, I am honor bound to assist you. And I have, but I cannot continue to support you. I have graciously outfitted the girls for a Season and introduced them to eligible prospects, but they are not cooperating with me, Genevieve. Juliette especially."

He frowned at the memory of Juliette slapping Lord Trenton across the face in the middle of Lady Deane's musicale. He had been furious with her because Trenton had been perfectly willing to take on a willful spirit like Juliette, and he had agreed to settle quite a large sum on her. How a weak man such as Thomas and a pathetic creature as Genevieve managed to create a daughter as strong-willed and obstinate as Juliette astounded him. Actually, all of their daughters had more backbone and gumption than both of their parents combined.

Life played odd and often cruel tricks on families, for how had he and Cecilia created a son as disappointing and weak as Nigel?

"Juliette is a special girl." Genevieve's chin went up. "*Elle est extravagante. Elle n'écoute que son coeur.* From the start I told you she would never let you choose a husband for her. She will need to—"

"She will need to control herself, that is what she will do," Randall interrupted angrily. "I've exhausted every prospect for her. She's a hellion and no man will have her, mark my words. Not as a wife anyway!"

"Randall!" Genevieve cried out in shock, blinking back tears. "She is my daughter!"

"We have to sell the building. There is no other alternative."

The building's value had more than quadrupled since Thomas purchased the property twenty years ago, but his sister-in-law didn't need to know that. Hell, Randall had just learned of it himself. If he had known he certainly would not have spent so much on his nieces' wardrobe for this charade of a Season. He needed that extra money. And then some. And he needed it now.

"What of Colette? *Elle sait ce que l'on attend d'elle.* She will behave. Surely she can marry well?"

Randall rolled his eyes in frustration. "Colette is almost as bad as her sister."

Genevieve shook her gray head in protest. "*Non*, Colette is a good girl. She knows what to do. She will not let us down. She will marry well for us. A kind gentleman will want her as his wife. And she will be happy."

"Are you listening to me?" He struggled not to shout at his dim-witted sister-in-law. "We are a month into the Season. Your daughters have blatantly ignored every bit of advice and guidance that Cecilia and I have given them. They have turned down a dozen suitable prospects between them, they are seen in the company of notorious rakes, and Juliette has given herself quite a little reputation as a firebrand already. I don't know if there's anything more I can do to remedy the situation."

Rendered speechless by his anger, Genevieve covered her face with her long, elegant hands, as if believing her problems would disappear if she could not see them. Randall had frightened her. As well he should.

"I have given your two daughters the opportunity of a lifetime. If they refuse to marry whom I choose for them, I cannot be blamed. And I can no longer continue to support you financially, since I am in a financial bind of my own. If we sell the building, I can recoup my losses with the girls and you will have a tidy sum to live on. Do you understand what I am saying to you, Genevieve?"

Slowly she removed her hands from her face. "Yes, I understand. *Bien sûr, je ne suis pas une imbécile.*"

"You could buy a little cottage by the sea. You'd like that, wouldn't you? The girls wouldn't have to work in the bookshop anymore. You would be happy there."

She pressed her fingertips to her temples and sighed melodramatically. "I do not know," she wailed, her

French accent becoming more pronounced. *"Je ne sais pas quoi faire . . ."*

The French always had to act with histrionics, Randall thought with disgust. He pressed his advantage, knowing he was close to her capitulation. "It's the right thing to do and you know it. And we don't have to tell Colette. We can tell her after it's sold. She will most likely to be grateful to be relieved of the burden of managing the shop. We shall inform her of the sale after it is completed."

The last thing Randall wanted to do was let Colette know he wanted to sell the shop. She was too smart and would fight him tooth and nail on that point. And she would find out the actual selling price and demand what was rightfully hers. He couldn't allow that to happen. He deserved most of the money for all the trouble his brother and his family had caused him over the years. Besides, he needed the money to pay off the mountain of debt that Nigel had accrued this year.

"Oh, Randall, *je vous en prie.* Please do not make me do this!" she cried.

"I'm not making you do anything, Genevieve. I am simply guiding you to make a wise financial decision. If you give me the deed to the building, I will sell it for you. You will make a substantial sum of money, which will support you in your old age in a lovely cottage by the sea. You will not have to depend on me anymore. We would both like that, would we not, Genevieve?"

"You have never cared for me," she sniffed with an injured air.

Ignoring her pout, he continued determinedly. "That is neither here nor there, my dear. I am offering you a chance to be self-sufficient and to take the burden of that pathetic bookshop off your daughter's shoulders. Come now, Genevieve, admit it. You hate the bookshop almost as much as I do." It was a stab in the dark, but he had had his suspicions over the years.

"*Oui,*" she confessed, almost relieved by the admission. "*C'est la vérité.*"

She looked at him with her wide azure eyes. Genevieve had been beautiful once, just as beautiful as her daughters, and what she ever saw in the insipid Thomas, Randall never understood, but now she was a mere shadow of her former self. Randall felt an overwhelming sense of pity for her.

"Thomas spent all his time down there. He was never here with me."

"So sell the building. There is nothing to keep you here but sad memories. Move to the seashore with the girls."

"Do you really think it will bring a good price?" she asked, and he had to contain his elation at her question. She was wavering.

"I know it will bring a fair price. The real estate in Mayfair has at least doubled over the years," he lied easily.

"Truly?" she asked, unable to hide the glimmer of hope in her eyes.

"Yes. And didn't my brother use your inheritance to buy the building in the first place?"

"*Oui,* without even consulting me when my mother left that money to me! It was my money!" she cried, the years of anger and resentment evident in her furrowed brow and pained expression. "*C'était mon argent.* I never wanted to live here." She gestured in disgust toward the shabbily furnished rooms with a wave of her elegant hand.

"Then sell it. Give the deed to me, Genevieve."

"I will," she said, her eyes ablaze with emotion, murmuring rapidly in French. "*Que Dieu me protège mais je dois le faire. Je vendrai donc ma librairie.* I will sell the bookshop, Randall."

He exhaled in relief at her answer. "I will take care of everything, Genevieve. But don't tell the girls. It will only upset them. Especially Colette," he warned.

"No, I shall not tell her." She called in the direction of the other room, "Paulette! Paulette!"

A bedroom door opened and one of his nieces appeared. "Yes, Mother?" she asked, as she entered the parlor where he sat with her mother. "Good afternoon, Uncle Randall."

"Good afternoon, Paulette," he said to her. With her honey-colored hair and blue-green eyes and angelic features, she would be a beauty to match her older sisters when she was grown. It never ceased to astound Randall. He would give his brother credit for that at least, if nothing else. Thomas had somehow managed to produce five stunning daughters, each one lovelier than the next. They were fortunate in that. Randall shuddered at his plight had his nieces been homely . . .

"Go into my room, *ma petite chérie*, and in the top right drawer of my bureau are some papers. Will you bring them to me, please?" Genevieve asked.

"*Oui, Maman.*"

As Paulette ran to do her mother's bidding, Randall wondered whether his French sister-in-law was truly incapacitated or simply acted that way for effect. He had not seen her outside the house in years, with the exception of Thomas's funeral last year. She relied heavily on an ornate gilt cane and the assistance of her daughters, but she seemed mobile enough. He believed she rather enjoyed the attention her "infirmity" gave her.

"You are making a wise decision," he reminded her encouragingly, as Paulette returned with a sheaf of papers and handed them to her mother.

"*Merci, ma petite,*" she kissed her daughter on the cheek. "You can go now. I shall call you when I need you."

Paulette nodded obediently and left them. Genevieve shuffled through the papers in front of her. She squinted at them, her face puzzled. Sighing heavily, she finally handed them all over to Randall with a helpless look. "I do not know what it is I am looking for."

Thrilled at his success, Randall flipped through the documents until he found the deed of ownership to the building. He gave the rest of the papers back to Genevieve.

"Remember, do not mention this to Colette, or any of the girls."

"I shall not speak of it until it is over and done with." Her mouth trembled slightly when she spoke.

Randall nodded his approval, pocketing the precious deed carefully in his coat. "I will sell only at the highest price, and you will have your little cottage soon enough and be rid of this place."

"*Je vais finalement m'en débarrasser.*" Sadly she wiped a tear from her eye and sniffled. "Yes, I will be rid of this place," she echoed him woodenly.

With her heart pounding rapidly and holding her breath so as not to be heard, Paulette Hamilton listened stealthily at the door to the parlor where her mother sat talking with Uncle Randall. She knew how wrong it was to eavesdrop, and she truly tried her best not to listen to her sisters when they were speaking privately, but she could not help herself from listening when Uncle Randall had unexpectedly knocked on their door earlier that afternoon. Colette was working downstairs in the shop and her other sisters were out, so Paulette was home alone taking care of their mother when he arrived. Immediately her mother dismissed Paulette from the parlor when Uncle Randall said he wanted to speak with her privately. She noted that Uncle Randall had entered their home though the private entrance, not through the shop, indicating that Colette was unaware of his visit. Alarmed by the situation, she had lingered on the other side of the closed door, listening.

Her mother was going to sell the shop! Not only was she selling the shop, she was selling the entire building and moving them to the seashore!

And her mother wasn't telling Colette or any of them about it.

What did that mean? And more importantly, what should she do about it?

She should tell Colette. Colette would know exactly what to do.

Paulette felt a sharp pang of remorse. Poor Colette worried about everything. Ever since their mother had become ill, Colette had taken care of the family. And when their father died, she had taken on the entire responsibility of the bookshop, working endlessly to make it support them. When Uncle Randall offered to give Colette and Juliette their debut, she had gamely agreed, knowing that she was being sold in marriage for their benefit. She took so much upon her shoulders.

Paulette heard Uncle Randall leave and she sighed heavily, her head resting against the back of the door. Now she waited for her mother to call her. Her mother had a fear of being alone, and one of her daughters always had to be by her side. Minutes ticked by on the little clock on her dresser, and still her mother did not call to her.

She wondered at the significance of that as she waited and thought of what to do.

Even though she never intended to, Paulette overheard lots of conversations that she shouldn't be privy to, but sometimes it was the only way to learn what was going on in her family. She had overheard Colette and Juliette talking about money and how dire their situation was and how worried they were. Paulette knew how hard Colette worked and how she never complained when she was tired or scared. Juliette handled things differently. She would laugh or act as if she didn't care, but Colette made everything safe for her and Lisette and Yvette. Colette never wanted them to worry.

Paulette felt a pang of sadness at the thought of all her own hard work in the shop and all the lovely little signs she had carefully painted and tied with green ribbon.

As much as Paulette loved the bookshop with all her heart and would be sad to lose it, maybe selling it and moving to the seashore would be for the best. Of course, Juliette would be thrilled by the news of leaving the shop. And Lisette would support any decision their mother made, while Yvette was too young to care what they did. If they sold the shop and moved, they would no longer have to worry about money, and Colette would not have to work so hard.

Maybe Uncle Randall was right.

Maybe she wouldn't tell Colette after all.

Chapter Ten

How May I Help You?

"Do we have a deal, then?" Colette asked, holding her breath in anticipation and fervent hope while staring at the barrel-chested man with wire spectacles standing in front of her. His impassive expression made it difficult for her to read his thoughts.

Mr. Kenworth paused, considering and weighing his options. Then he nodded slowly. "Yes, I believe we do, Miss Hamilton." Still he did not smile. "As I have said before, I'm not used to doing business with a woman. But I am impressed with your changes to the shop thus far, so we shall begin on a trial basis. I shall have the rest of the stationery delivered to you tomorrow morning. It has been a ple"— he stopped himself before saying "pleasure"—"interesting doing business with you. I look forward to a successful partnership with your shop."

"Thank you, Mr. Kenworth." Colette could not help but grin, thrilled with the deal she had just negotiated to sell Mr. Kenworth's fine stationery in the bookshop. He had been disinclined to work with her at first, but she finally won him over. She had already displayed some samples of his high-quality paper under the glass on the counter. Now her customers could order pens, ink, envelopes, and writing paper through her, and she would get a percentage of the profits from the Kenworth products.

They shook hands across the counter, and when he placed his top hat on his head and turned to leave, she saw Lucien Sinclair standing behind him. As the bells jingled above the door signaling Mr. Kenworth's departure, Colette stared silently at Lucien, her heart in her mouth. She had not even heard him enter the store. How long had he been standing there watching her? Her heart pounded at seeing him for the first time since she had kissed him with such reckless abandon, and her cheeks flushed profusely at the memory.

"You do drive a hard bargain, Colette," he stated, his eyes on her. "You'll make a success of this shop yet."

"That is the general plan," she managed to say, feeling an enormous sense of pride at his compliment.

They both stared at each other. Lost in the depths of his green eyes, she knew instinctively that he was thinking about their wildly passionate kiss as well.

"What are you doing here?" she finally blurted out.

He laughed at her bluntness, his smile nearly knocking the wind out of her. "Isn't the usual greeting in a shop, 'How may I help you?' Or do you greet all your customers this way?"

Colette flushed, her stomach fluttering with nervousness. "You know what I meant."

"Yes, I did," he admitted, "and in answer to your question, I've come to purchase more books from you."

"Oh, forgive me. I thought because of the other night . . ." she stammered weakly in sudden mortification, wishing the wood plank floor would swallow her up whole.

"Yes. About the other night," he began, his voice growing serious. "I owe you an apology for my behavior."

"You have already apologized for kissing me," she whispered, feeling even more humiliated by his words.

"You misunderstand. I'm not sorry I kissed you, Colette. In fact, I enjoyed our little interlude more than I care to admit. The fact is that I should not have taken such liberties with you in the first place."

"I think I asked you to kiss me."

He reached out a hand and tenderly brushed a stray curl from her cheek. His fingers massaged her skin, sending a thrill through her at his touch. "Perhaps," he acknowledged with a slight nod of his head and a grin that melted her heart. "But I am a man who should know better."

"Your gallantry in helping me with Baron Sheffield was most appreciated. The least I could do was offer a kiss in return." She managed to smile back at him.

He was about to reply when the door to their quarters upstairs flew open and Paulette entered the shop.

"It's time for supper, Colette—Oh!" She stopped abruptly upon seeing Lucien Sinclair standing beside the counter. A wide smile lit up her young features. "Hello, Lord Waverly."

"Hello, Miss Hamilton." He grinned warmly at her.

"I'll be up in a few minutes, Paulette," Colette said, coming out from around the counter. "I just have to get some books for Lord Waverly."

"I have a wonderful idea!" Paulette exclaimed brightly. Giving Lucien an endearing glance, she asked, "Would you please do us the honor of dining with us this evening, Lord Waverly?"

Horrified at her sister's invitation, Colette exclaimed, "I'm sure he has other plans for the evening."

"Please?" Paulette asked, her eyes silently pleading with Lucien. "It would be lovely to have you dine with us."

Lucien eyed Colette briefly, as if assessing her opinion, before he turned his gaze back to Paulette. "I could not refuse such a persuasive invitation. And since I have no plans until later this evening, I would be honored to join your family for supper."

Stunned speechless, Colette stood frozen on the spot. Lucien Sinclair wanted to have dinner with her. And her sisters. And her mother. *Why?*

"Oh, that's simply wonderful!" Paulette declared with a jubilant toss of her blond head. "We hardly ever have visitors. Let me run up and tell the girls." With that Paulette disappeared upstairs, leaving them alone once again.

Colette looked at Lucien. "You are being very kind, but you really don't have to stay to please my little sister."

"I'm not simply being kind to Paulette. I'm curious. Will I meet all of your family if I venture up those stairs with you?"

"I'm afraid so," Colette admitted with a rueful grin. "I can only imagine the furor going on up there when Paulette tells them the news. There's still a chance for you to make a hasty exit while you can."

"And miss my first occasion to meet all five of the Hamilton sisters at once? Not on your life!"

Colette felt an odd little thrill race though her at his use of the word "first,'" which to her implied there would be more occasions to be with her family. Unable to ponder the meaning of that thought now, she said, "Just remember that you were fairly warned and you squandered your only opportunity to escape." Colette stepped past him, intending to turn Paulette's hand-painted 'Open" sign on the front door of the shop to read "Closed."

"Please wait," Lucien called out to her, placing a hand on her shoulder.

She spun around in surprise, feeling breathless at the closeness of him and reeling from the contact of his hand upon her body. His eyes rested on hers, and her stomach flipped wildly. The flecks of black in the green of his irises made his eyes appear dark and mysterious. His face inched closer to hers and the crazy sensation that he wanted to kiss her again raced through her. God help her, but she wanted him to kiss her!

"May I do that?" he asked, pointing to the sign. "I've always wanted to."

Relief and disappointment rushed through her, but she laughed at his unexpectedly playful attitude. "You may." She stepped aside and watched as he flipped the sign with an extravagant flourish.

"Now what do we do?" he asked excitedly. With a look of delight on his face, Lucien appeared even more attractive, if such a thing were possible.

"You have to pull down the shade and lock the door. There, with that key." She pointed to a large skeleton key hanging from a long green ribbon on the wall.

After locking up, he declared, "I've never closed a shop before."

"Well, congratulations," she said and closed the large leather-bound ledgers on the counter top, wondering at Lucien's behavior. She had thought him a proper, stuffy lord, as Juliette called him. But he had handled Baron Sheffield like a prizefighter and kissed her as a thorough rogue would. Then appeared in her shop, acting as excited as a little boy playing a game. And now he would join her family for supper. Nothing he did made any sense.

He followed her as she dimmed the lamps around the shop, helping her reach the higher lamps. As the light faded, her heart raced. *Why is he staying? Why does he want to meet my family?*

"Is that it?" he whispered close behind her, his voice as smooth as velvet.

Slowly, she turned around to face him. "Yes, that's it. The shop is officially closed."

In spite of the dimness she could see the angles of his face, the strong lines of his jaw, the planes of his cheekbones. He was so tall she had to tilt her head back to look at him. He made her feel incredibly small. He smelled good, of something clean but spicy. She suddenly found it hard to breathe as she stood with him in the growing darkness.

"Colette?"

She could feel his breath on her cheek as he whispered her name. With her heart pounding wildly, she carefully licked her lips, fighting a yearning desire to wrap her arms around his neck and pull him close to her. Tilting her head toward him in case he did intend to kiss her, she whispered in response to his saying her name, "Yes?"

"Shouldn't we go upstairs now?"

Lucien followed Colette up the narrow staircase that led to the family's living quarters above the shop. Not for the first time he wondered what the hell he was doing there. He had simply stopped by to purchase new books to read to his father. Now he had willingly consented to have supper with all the Hamilton women. What was he thinking?

That was just it. He wasn't thinking. *At all.*

He'd been so tempted to kiss her just a few moments ago that he had to steel himself from doing what every nerve in his body cried out for. The feeling was even more overpowering now that he knew the delight of kissing her. He knew the feel of her sensuous lips, the seductive curve of her mouth, the taste of her sweet tongue. God, he wanted to taste her again.

And he sensed without a doubt that she wanted it, too.

She was truly a stunning woman. With her hair pulled

back from her face and dressed in a businesslike shopkeeper's attire, she was even more seductive than in the low-cut ball gown she wore the other night. Her high-necked dress only made him want to strip it off her, while loosening her long dark hair from its tight constraints and watching it tumble in silky waves to her waist. He wanted to crush her to him and . . .

"Mother, I'd like you to meet a friend of mine, Lord Waverly. Lord Waverly, this is my mother, Genevieve Hamilton."

Lucien shook himself from his indecent thoughts of Colette as he stepped forward into a warm and inviting room to meet Colette's mother. She seemed a frail woman and by all appearances, a neglected beauty. He immediately sensed a profound unhappiness within her as she gazed up at him from her place on the divan with the saddest eyes he had ever seen.

"Good evening, Lord Waverly. Thank you for joining us, but you must excuse our simple meal, since we were not expecting guests this evening." Her voice held the trace of a French accent and she gave Paulette a meaningful look, as if to say she did not approve of unexpected visitors being asked to dinner.

Lucien smiled charmingly at her. "Thank you for having me, Mrs. Hamilton, but I could hardly refuse an invitation to dine with such lovely ladies. And if I may be so bold, it is quite apparent that your daughters inherited their beauty from their mother."

A smile lit her face, and for an instant Lucien could clearly see the beautiful woman she had been in her younger days. "Ah, you are a rogue, are you not, Lord Waverly? *Tu es bien le plus beau, Monsieur le Comte*," she asked, somewhat flirtatiously.

"Oh, he's worse than that, *Maman*," Juliette declared boldly from the small dining room. "He's a gentleman!"

Lucien turned to her. "Good evening, Miss Juliette. How lovely to see you again." His tone clearly stated the opposite.

She laughed, sticking her tongue out at him.

"Juliette Sara! *Tiens toi bien. Ne me fais pas honte!*" Immediately Genevieve scolded her daughter. "Behave yourself! Lord Waverly will think you are ill-mannered."

Juliette flashed him a wicked grin. "He already knows that, don't you, my lord?"

Placing a gentle hand upon Lucien's arm, Colette interrupted them, preventing Lucien from flinging a deserved retort back at Juliette and requiring him to focus his attention back to Colette.

"I don't believe you have met my sister Lisette."

Another Hamilton sister stood in the doorway to the kitchen. Again Lisette possessed the same facial structure as her sisters, yet there was more of an innate sweetness about her than the others had. She smiled shyly at him, her eyes full of friendly warmth. At least this one wouldn't be throwing daggers at him.

"It is a pleasure to make your acquaintance, Miss Lisette."

"It's wonderful to meet you also," she answered. "I hope you like roasted chicken, for that is what we are having for supper."

"If that is what smells so delicious," Lucien said, suddenly aware of the grumbling of his stomach, "then I am surely in for a treat this evening."

Colette continued the introductions, presenting yet another sister to him. "And this is the baby, Yvette."

"I'm not a baby," the youngest of the Hamilton sisters protested indignantly. "I'm thirteen!"

A smaller version of Colette, but with blond hair in long braids, stood before him. Yvette, too, would be a stunningly beautiful woman. Lucien could not help comparing all of them to Colette. In his mind, she was the original. The other sisters were all copies.

Yvette curtsied elegantly for him, stating with a dignified air, "It's a pleasure to meet you, my lord."

He took her tiny hand in his, making a grand fuss over her. "The pleasure is mine, Miss Yvette. It's an honor to make the acquaintance of such a lovely young lady."

Yvette preened and swished the skirts of her pink and white striped dress.

Paulette rolled her eyes at her little sister's antics and took Lucien by the arm, dragging him toward the small dining room. "Lord Waverly, you can sit at the head of the table," she declared possessively, "right next to me."

Undoubtedly, Lucien had won over a devoted admirer in little Paulette.

As he stood at the head of the table, it occurred to him that this was most likely their father's place, and a disconcerting twinge of melancholy pinched at his heart. But then a flurry of movement surrounded him as the girls each took on a responsibility. Lisette and Colette helped their mother from the divan to her seat at the opposite end of the table, while Juliette, Paulette, and Yvette scurried to bring steaming dishes of chicken, roasted potatoes, and fresh bread to the table.

Feeling rather useless, Lucien again wondered dazedly what he was doing there in this house with these six women. He really had no business being there at all. But there was no help for it now. In for a penny, in for a pound, as the old expression went.

When all the ladies were seated, Lucien took his seat. With Colette to his right and Paulette to his left, he was well situated and surprisingly more comfortable in this female gathering than he would have ever imagined. Yvette said a short prayer of grace and the food was served and passed around without preamble. He had never been a part of such a simple, homey meal in his life, with not a single servant in sight. Lisette popped up to the kitchen now and then to get more of something, but everyone just helped themselves. And the food tasted even more delicious than it had smelled.

"*Monsieur le Comte*, Colette has been rather reticent with the details on how you two met. Would you please enlighten me on how you happened to befriend my daughter?" Genevieve asked while moving the food around on her plate with her fork, but barely eating a bite.

Lucien found six pairs of eyes in varying shades of blue staring at him. They were an amazing family and he felt somewhat beguiled by them. Here in their small rooms above a London bookshop they had created a haven in which he felt unexpectedly at home.

"I had the good fortune of meeting your daughter one day in the shop while buying some books for my father, and then we became reacquainted at Lady Hayvenhurst's ball, where I was introduced to Juliette as well." He turned to Colette with a knowing smile. "And we seem to keep running into each other. We most recently met again in the garden at Lord Hutton's." He could not help but notice that Colette blushed at his secret reference to their kiss. He had wanted to see if he could get a reaction out of her and was pleased to see that he had.

"Do you know Lord Eddington?" Paulette asked him, her sweet face full of curiosity.

"Yes, he's a very good friend of mine. Have you met him?"

"Yes, he is a member of our ladies' reading circle."

Lucien almost choked on the mouthful of wine he had just taken. "Is he now?" *How very interesting.* Jeffrey had only mentioned visiting the bookshop. The thought of Jeffrey as a member of some sort of reading group was ridiculous! What was he up to? And just which sister was he after?

Paulette explained animatedly, "Yes. At first the reading circle was supposed to be just women, but we all voted unanimously to keep Lord Eddington in our group."

Yes, Lucien just bet it was unanimous where Jeffrey was concerned.

"He's a remarkable man and very knowledgeable about literature," Juliette said without glancing up from her plate.

"I had no idea," Lucien remarked sardonically, detecting a suppressed smile on Juliette's face.

"Yes," Colette added, nodding. "Lord Eddington brought some valuable insight to our discussion."

"Do you have any brothers or sisters, Lord Waverly?" little Yvette asked, looking at him with wide eyes.

"No," Lucien responded to her question. When he was growing up he had always wished for a brother or a sister. "I am an only child."

"I cannot even imagine not having siblings," Lisette marveled.

"I imagine it all the time," Juliette commented dryly.

"Oh, you do not!" the other four cried in protest at her remark, causing Lucien to laugh at their demonstration of family togetherness.

"All right, all right," Juliette conceded, placing her hands up in defeat. "Having four sisters is the joy of my life. Let's change the subject, shall we?"

"Yes, let's," Colette agreed readily, but her eyes were merry.

After a pause, Lucien volunteered a question. "Mrs. Hamilton, have you named all your daughters with the '-ette' ending on purpose?"

Genevieve smiled lightly. "*Oui, mais bien sûr*, I did not know at the time that I would have five daughters. Although once I started, how could I not continue, *eh, monsieur*? I just wanted them to have something in common to unite them. I gave them French names, but their middle names are English."

Lucien turned to Colette with an inquiring look.

She responded, "Elizabeth."

Juliette said, "Sara."

Lisette stated, "Annabelle."

Paulette said, "Victoria."

With a proud little nod Yvette added, "Katherine."

"Well, they are all lovely names for very lovely ladies," Lucien said, enchanted by this charming little family of women. Something about them touched him.

"Oh, Lisette, tell what happened to you today!" Yvette squealed with excitement. "We've been waiting for every-one to come home to share the news."

Lisette blushed prettily and shook her head with a shy glance. "No, Yvette, not now, we have an important guest."

"He's not a guest, he's just a man!" Juliette declared with a challenging look toward Lucien. "Tell us what happened."

"Tu peux nous le dire. Tout ira bien, ma chérie. You can tell us, Lisette. It will be fine," Genevieve encouraged her with a faint smile.

Lisette again protested, but before she could utter a single word, Yvette called out, "Henry Brooks finally asked her to go to the Willoughbys' tea dance next week!"

Amid a chorus of squeals of excitement and shouts of congratulations, Lucien looked to Colette. "I gather this was a long-anticipated occurrence?"

"Yes." Colette nodded, the happiness for her sister evi-dent in her expression. "We've all known Henry Brooks for years, and he and Lisette have had feelings for each other for almost as long. We've just been waiting for Henry to make the first move. And it seems he finally has!"

"I see." Being privy to a scene of intimate family life he had never experienced before, Lucien felt he belonged. The feeling of being part of a loving family was so unfa-miliar to him, yet he found himself irresistibly drawn in by them, fascinated. As the commotion died down,

Lucien offered his best wishes to Lisette. "Henry Brooks is an extremely lucky fellow."

"Thank you, Lord Waverly," she said with a shy glance in his direction.

"I received a letter from Christina Dunbar today," Juliette said with more enthusiasm than Lucien had witnessed before in her. "She arrived in the United States and absolutely adores living there. She said that New York City is the most exciting place in the world, and that I would love it as much as she does."

"Christina is a dear friend of Juliette's," Colette explained for Lucien's benefit. "She's newly married to an American gentleman."

Juliette's eyes sparkled. "She invited me to visit her."

"You are not going to New York, Juliette!" Genevieve exclaimed with a vehement shake of her gray-haired head.

"Why can't I?" Juliette challenged her mother, her face full of youthful determination. "It's not as if I'm asking to go to Africa or India, for heaven's sake!"

Genevieve gave her daughter a certain look that said in no uncertain terms that she would not engage in such a discussion with her at that moment.

Ignoring her mother, Juliette immediately turned to Lucien. "Have you ever been to New York, Lord Waverly?"

"No, I haven't, but I too have a good friend who lives there."

"I shall go there someday," Juliette declared, her eyes flashing, defying her mother.

"And just how do you think you are going to manage that?" Paulette scoffed at her.

"I don't know yet, but mark my words, one day I will!" Juliette's statement left them all quiet.

Attempting to lighten the mood, Colette asked, "Did anything else interesting happen to anyone today?"

"No," Paulette said slowly with a pointed look at Colette, "but Uncle Randall stopped by earlier."

Lucien knew he did not imagine the pall that immediately fell over the table at the mention of their uncle. Genevieve's face blanched, if it were possible for her to become any paler. Lucien had only met Randall Hamilton on a few occasions and had no particular liking for the fellow. Apparently, neither did his five nieces.

"What did Uncle Randall want, *Maman*?" Colette asked, her brow furrowed in concern.

"*J'ai très mal à la tête*. I have a terrible headache," Genevieve whispered, her voice thin. "Lisette, help me to my room. *Excusez moi, s'il vous plaît.*"

"Why didn't you mention Uncle Randall was here?" Colette persisted in asking. "What did he want?"

"He . . . he wanted to update me on your progress this Season," Genevieve managed to say as Lisette helped her to her feet. She leaned on her cane and began to shuffle from the table.

Colette glanced hurriedly at Juliette, then back at her mother. "But what did he *say*?"

"He said that you are both misbehaving," Genevieve admonished with more vigor than Lucien had thought her capable of: "*Tu ne te trouveras jamais de mari à ce train là. Je ne veux pas en parler avec toi maintenant.* You need to listen to your aunt Cecilia and uncle Randall's advice. I shall speak no more of it in front of our guest. *Bonsoir, Monsieur le Comte.* Good evening."

Both Colette and Juliette stared mutely at their plates, their heads down. Lucien would have laughed at seeing Juliette so chastised, but he did not care for the worried and anxious expression on Colette's face. He rose to his feet to assist Lisette with her mother. Genevieve gratefully accepted his help, thanking him, as they both escorted her to her bedroom.

He returned to the dining room and the girls still sat speechless. Lisette followed close behind him.

"I suppose I should be going now," Lucien said to the subdued group still seated at the table.

"Oh, no, Lord Waverly, I've made a lovely apple tart for dessert! You must stay and have some!" Lisette pleaded. "We would be terribly disappointed if you left now."

"Yes, please stay!" Yvette and Paulette echoed.

Juliette and Colette remained noticeably silent.

Lucien glanced to Colette in question. She nodded, wishing for him to remain, and he felt oddly relieved that she wanted him there. Without a word, he returned to his place at the table. Lisette abruptly began clearing plates from the table and exited to the kitchen. Yvette followed her lead and began to help.

"Did you hear that Charles Dickens died yesterday?" Paulette blurted out.

"Yes," Lucien said with interest. "I just read it in today's *Times.*"

"What terrible news," Colette murmured at the loss of the prolific writer.

"We must place all his books on the front shelf, Colette, because everyone will want to buy one now," Paulette suggested.

"That's a brilliant idea, Paulette!" Colette exclaimed, her eyes lighting up at the prospect of selling more books.

Within moments the conversation grew animated and the mood lightened.

By the time Lucien finished his delicious apple tart, he had confirmed that although the Hamilton sisters looked alike, they were decidedly different in personality. Sweet Lisette possessed a caring and unassuming manner, but seemed to be the one foremost to comfort the others. Paulette had a thoughtful and intelligent mind and a kind heart. Little Yvette was high-spirited and quick to

laugh. Juliette, of course, rankled him endlessly, but he
had to admit that she had her finer qualities. Even
Genevieve Hamilton could be quite charming. The sisters were all endearing and amusing, and somehow they
seemed to win him over with their candid honesty and
good humor, while their strong sense of camaraderie and
devotion to each other fascinated him. The only relation-
ships Lucien had really experienced with women were
with his mother, with Lady Virginia Warren, and with the
type of pleasure seeking woman who shared his bed.

Never had he met women like the Hamiltons.

And then there was Colette . . .

Above all she intrigued him. He noted how she cared
for her younger sisters. How she patiently tended to her
ailing mother. How she worked in the bookshop to support the family. With their father deceased and their
mother obviously incapable, Colette, in essence, had
taken over the role of parent to the other girls. They all
looked to her to make their decisions. But at twenty
years old, Colette should be enjoying parties and balls
and being courted by suitors.

Ah, but she was being forced to find a husband, wasn't she?

As much as he hated the idea, it would probably be for
the best. A husband would take her away from toiling in
the bookshop and would look after her properly. But then
what of her sisters if Colette married? He watched the four
pretty girls laughing as they cleared the dishes. Any man
who took Colette as a wife would undoubtedly undertake
the responsibility of her sisters. And their ill mother as well.

And there was her uncle, parading Colette before a lot
of ridiculous old fools. None of the men he had seen her
dance with were half good enough for her. He made up
his mind then and there to introduce Colette, and Juliette as well, to more suitable candidates for a husband.

As he took his leave from the charming Hamilton sisters,

Lucien realized he had felt more relaxed and more at home with this little family that evening than he had in a very long time. In fact, he could not recall feeling that way ever, at least not as an adult. Colette walked him to the front door of the house and down the front staircase, which was a different entrance than through the bookshop.

When they reached the bottom landing, he said, "Thank you for a lovely evening."

"Thank you for being patient with my sisters," Colette said, tilting her head up to look at him. "And I apologize for the awkwardness with my mother."

"There is no need for apologies." He paused before asking, "Is everything well with your uncle? I couldn't help but notice that you seemed very worried that he had come to see your mother."

She hesitated slightly. "As you have seen, my uncle does not always have my best interests at heart when choosing a prospective husband, and I was just worried that he would try to convince my mother to persuade me to marry someone I had already refused to. . ."

"I understand now," Lucien whispered. "You need not explain."

She gave a half-smile as she gazed up at him. "You are very chivalrous."

"No. No, I am not," he said honestly, thinking that at the moment his thoughts of her were far from chivalrous. "Remember what I said to you, Colette. Make sure you choose a husband you want. Don't let your uncle choose for you."

"Thank you, Lucien," she whispered. She nodded obediently and looked up at him in expectation.

The sound of his name on her soft lips and her beautiful face lifted to his in anticipation of a kiss sent a flood of desire coursing through him that was almost unbearable. Lucien craved nothing more than to pull her against him and place his mouth over hers, branding her in a searing kiss. He ached to push her up against the wall, right there in that tiny little vestibule, lift the skirt of her gown, and drive himself into her over and over again. God, but he wanted her. Unable to stop himself, he touched her cheek softly, tracing the line of her jaw to her chin. Knowing without a doubt that even one kiss, the lightest kiss, would push him over the edge of a dangerous precipice from which there could be no return, Lucien took a step back from her, his body trembling with torment.

"Good night, Colette," he whispered, his voice hoarse and edgy with unquenched desire.

As he walked home that June evening, he wished the night air were much cooler.

Chapter Eleven

Pillow Talk

Exhausted, Colette snuggled under the pale yellow gingham quilt that covered her bed and closed her eyes tightly, but it was no use. She kept reliving the evening with Lucien Sinclair and the kisses that had almost happened.

Juliette entered the bedroom they had shared their whole life. It was a cozy room for all that it was small. Pale yellow wallpaper dotted with sprays of colorful flowers lined the walls, and a well-worn patterned carpet in shades of green and gold covered the floor. Four gilt-framed scenes of tranquil country life hung from ribbon above the mantel and a small writing desk stood in the corner. Juliette dimmed the light that rested on the nightstand between their two beds.

"Yvette needs new shoes," Juliette said, climbing into her own bed. "She's completely outgrown the ones we just bought her."

Colette yawned. "I know. I already left money for Lisette to take her for a new pair tomorrow. Paulette will simply have to stay with Mother again while they are out, because I'll need you in the shop with me tomorrow to help with the first delivery of the stationery."

The empty silence declared Juliette's ambivalent feelings of having to help in the shop. She would never shirk her share of responsibilities, but she made it very clear that she would rather be doing anything else but working in the bookshop.

"What do you think of Lisette and Henry Brooks?" Colette asked.

"I think Lisette will marry him eventually, but I don't think she'll be happy with him in the end."

"Why do you say that?"

"It's just a feeling I have. Henry is a nice enough man, but not quite right for her. But Lisette, just like Mother did in marrying Father, will settle for him because she is afraid to try for something better, and she will end up miserable. Which is something I for one don't ever intend to do."

No, Juliette would never settle for less than exactly what she wanted. She would never change or try to be something she wasn't to please a man. Which made Colette wonder about herself. In attempting to marry to save her family and the bookshop, would she too be settling? How far would she go to save them? Up till now she had refused her uncle's choices because she had found his choice of men unacceptable, indeed quite repulsive. But how long could that go on? She *had* to marry at some point.

"Why do you think Lord Waverly stayed for dinner?" Juliette asked in the darkness.

"Because he was hungry?" Colette answered with her eyes still closed.

A down-filled pillow landed smack on her face. Sputtering indignantly, she sat up and hurled it back at Juliette. "Go to sleep already!"

Catching the pillow, Juliette laughed before asking

again, "Aren't you the least bit curious as to why he was here tonight?"

"No," she pronounced firmly. Colette did not want to think about it anymore. In fact, her head throbbed from puzzling over Lucien's actions and wondering at his motivations.

"There is something you're not telling me about Lord Disapproves of Everything Fun, isn't there, Colette?"

"No," she murmured guiltily, hiding her face in the blankets.

"Yes, there is. I know it. He suddenly shows up at the shop and joins us all for dinner for no reason? And we know it's certainly not me he is interested in!" Juliette paused thoughtfully before asking, "Has he kissed you?"

"What makes you think such a thing?" Colette attempted to sound outraged by her sister's question.

"He looks at you like he wants to kiss you. And your face was flushed all night."

"Is it that obvious?" Colette whispered, grateful for the dark.

"So you did kiss him! I knew it!" Juliette declared triumphantly, and Colette knew she was smiling. "When did it happen?"

"That night in Lord Hutton's garden."

"Tell me everything," Juliette demanded.

Relieved to finally share the experience, Colette confessed all.

Upon hearing the details of Colette's romantic encounter with Lord Waverly, Juliette was almost speechless. "Aside from being appalled that Baron Sheffield thought he could have his way with you, I am very impressed with Lord Waverly's rescue techniques."

Colette said nothing.

After a tense silence, Juliette asked, "Did you like kissing him?"

"Yes," she replied with an anguished sigh. "And, Juliette, I cannot forget about it, and I don't know what to do."

"About what?"

"That I liked kissing him and I want him to kiss me again. He wanted to kiss me tonight, I'm sure of it."

"Did he?"

"No, but we came close a few times." *Achingly close.* "What do you think it means?"

"I haven't a clue." Whatever was happening between her and Lucien left her very confused. Colette had begun to anticipate his unexpected visits, found herself yearning to talk to him, and felt a desire to be near him. He seemed to care for her, seemed interested in her life and her family, and from the way he kissed her, he obviously found her attractive, but she did not know how he felt about her.

Juliette said with a superior air, "I've heard things about him."

"Don't tease me, Juliette. What do you know?" Colette had heard rumors of Lucien's wild ways, but the stories seemed incongruous to the Lucien she knew. Well, except that night in the garden. Once again, nothing about Lucien made any sense.

"Well, I've heard that he has avoided marriage for years." Juliette seemed reluctant to share this news. She sighed heavily. "But I think you should know that now he wants to settle down and marry before his father passes away."

"I haven't heard that," Colette cried in disbelief. Lucien had never said a word to her about marriage. "Who told you such a thing?"

"Jeffrey Eddington."

"Oh," Colette murmured softly as realization dawned. "He would know better than anybody."

"And Lord Waverly already has a lady in mind."

Colette's heart suddenly beat frantically in her chest.

Lucien already knew whom he intended to marry? And he kissed her passionately only last week? She dared to ask, "Did Lord Eddington say who she was?"

Juliette hesitated before answering her. "Lady Faith Bromleigh."

Colette mentally checked off a list of names of women she had met during the Season, but the name did not ring a bell. "I have never heard of her."

"She's a plain, quiet little thing. Her father is a known for being very protective of her." Juliette was quiet for a moment. "Are you very disappointed?"

Ignoring the sinking feeling in the pit of her stomach, Colette responded weakly, "Why should I be disappointed?"

"Because he kissed you, but he is interested in marrying another girl."

Colette put up a brave front. "Just because I kissed him doesn't mean that I've lost all my senses. I have no desire to be a countess or a marchioness someday. You know that means nothing to me. Yet I'm well aware of Lucien's reputation and that he can have his choice of women. I don't expect anything from him."

"You call him Lucien now?"

"I suppose so," Colette admitted quietly, surprised that she had referred to him that way to Juliette.

"He was engaged once before, you know, a few years ago," Juliette continued. "To Lady Somebody or Other, but she broke off the engagement after some sort of scandal and left for Europe."

Colette sat upright in bed once again. "How on earth do you *know* all these things?"

Juliette stated with a self-evident tone, "Because I ask."

Colette wondered what type of woman this other lady was whom Lucien had wanted to be his wife. Was she prim and proper? And what had happened to end it?

"Colette, has Lord Waverly said anything at all to you about marriage?" Juliette asked in a thoughtful manner.

"He told me not to allow Uncle Randall to force me into marrying someone I didn't want." Her words echoed hollowly in her ears. If Lucien had been interested in marrying her, would he not have said something else to her?

"Well, it seems that absolutely nothing that stuffy lord does makes any sense. He disapproves of your working in the bookshop; he saves you from the likes of the fat baron, kisses you passionately in the moonlight, shows up at your house unexpectedly and dines with your family, but intends to court another girl. I think I might slap him if I see him again."

Colette finally laughed. "He's no more confusing than Lord Eddington."

"At least he hasn't kissed me! Or you, for that matter." She gave Colette a sharp look. "Has he?"

"No! Lord Eddington is very charming and sweet, but I don't think of him that way."

"Me either. But I think he may have feelings for you, Colette."

They were both quiet, each settling down among the covers, lost in her own thoughts. Juliette's words spun around in Colette's head. Did Lucien truly intend to marry Faith Bromleigh? Did Jeffrey Eddington have feelings for her?

"I don't like that Uncle Randall was here today," Juliette said ominously.

"Well, I don't like that Mother didn't tell us about the visit," Colette added. "It makes me nervous."

"I'm sure Uncle Randall is upset that we haven't made suitable matches yet. What do you think he said to mother?"

"That he's at the end of his rope with the pair of us."

"Would you marry Lord Waverly if he asked you?"

Colette's heart flipped over in her chest at the mention of Lucien's name and marriage. Would she marry him if he asked her? "That's a ridiculous question. He would never marry someone like me."

"But it would solve your problems. He'd be a good husband. He's powerful enough to tell Uncle Randall to go to the devil. He would take all us girls in, and we wouldn't have to worry about money. And he is handsome, and by your own account, a very good kisser."

"And he'd sell the bookshop right out from under me."

"Oh, who cares about the stupid shop? It's just a pile of moldy old books! I don't know why you love it so much."

The undisguised scorn in her sister's tone of voice caused Colette to flinch. "I just do. You needn't make fun of me simply because you don't understand. Do I make fun of you for wanting to go to New York?"

Juliette remained oddly silent in response. Colette did love the shop and felt proud of the work she had put into redoing it. No one could take that away from her. And she would never settle for a man who wanted her to give it up either.

Chapter Twelve

For Sale

The bells above the door jingled as Lucien walked into Hamilton's Book Shoppe a few days later. Surprised by the large number of customers in the shop, he glanced about, searching for Colette.

He caught her eye as she was helping a woman with a ridiculously feathered hat choose a picture book for her grandchild. Colette's beautiful face registered her surprise at seeing him, and he felt a secret thrill at knowing he disconcerted her. He nodded to let her know that he would wait until she was finished.

Lucien was astounded by the changes Colette had made in the shop. A month ago it was a dismal mess. Now bright and airy, with the books attractively arranged and organized, the shop bustled with people eagerly buying books. Comfortable chairs were arranged for customers to sit in and read at their leisure. Fine stationery and pens were elegantly displayed in a glass-fronted cabinet. Fresh wildflowers filled a china pitcher, adding a cheerful splash of color on top of the counter. Colette had transformed the place. The old dark bookshop had changed into a friendly and inviting place to be. He watched as she sold books to six different customers, wrapping their packages with bright green ribbon.

When there was finally a lull she turned her attention to him, asking, "Back so soon?"

"You really must work on your greetings to customers."

"Forgive me." Colette shook her head and smiled ruefully. "How may I help you?"

"Now, that is more like it!" He grinned at her.

"Is there something you need?" she questioned him suspiciously.

"I never purchased any books the last time. You and your siren sisters distracted me."

Her sweet laughter floated around him. "In that case, how may I help you today, Lord Waverly?" she asked in her most efficient shopkeeper tone.

Following her lead, he played the typical customer. "Well, Miss Hamilton, I would like to purchase more books for my father. I was thinking of some of Charles Dickens's work."

"Oh, I've just sold my last one! A copy of *Bleak House*," she explained. "His books have been so popular since he passed away. I've ordered more, but they won't be in for a few more days."

"How unfortunate. I suppose I must wait and return when they arrive."

Colette guided him to the counter and gave him a small white card. "If you fill this out with your address, we can have the books delivered to you."

"You now provide a delivery service?"

She nodded with a look of pride. "Yes, I've hired a local boy. I am teaching him how to read, and in return he will run errands for me. In the meantime, I can help you choose something else to tide you over until the Dickens books arrive."

He agreed to her suggestions as they made their way among the shelves. They were still selecting books for his father when the clock chimed four. Colette cried, "Good heavens! I'm late for my appointment with Mr. Kenworth! I must hurry."

Hurrying to the door to their quarters upstairs, she called up to her sister. "Paulette? Can you come down here now?"

Lucien watched in fascination as Colette quickly grabbed her bonnet and gloves from the peg hanging on the wall. Tying the ribbons of the bonnet securely under her chin and tugging her gloves onto her hands, Colette murmured with a worried frown, "I really mustn't be late. I promised I would be there at quarter past the hour."

"Oh, Lord Waverly! I didn't know you were here!" Paulette cried in delight as she entered the shop. "How nice to see you!"

"Good afternoon, Miss Hamilton." Lucien couldn't help but smile at her sweet face; she was so obviously happy to see him.

"Paulette, can you manage the shop by yourself until Juliette returns?" Colette asked, hastily gathering a sheaf of papers and placing them in a leather case. "She should be back shortly."

Paulette, thrilled at being given such an important responsibility, stood straighter. "Of course I can!"

Uncomfortable with a fifteen-year-old girl alone in the shop, Lucien volunteered, "I can keep an eye on her until Juliette returns."

Colette's blue eyes widened at his words. "Thank you! Oh, and Paulette, make sure you wrap up Lord Waverly's purchases. Tell Juliette I'll be back before we close. Good-bye!"

With a little wave of her hand, she rushed from the shop. A strong sense of disappointment filled him at Colette's departure. Lucien shook himself at the feeling, not liking it.

"Your sister works very hard, doesn't she?" he remarked quietly to Paulette, who had gone to stand behind the polished counter, trying her best to appear professional.

"Yes, but it's because she loves it."

"Do you think she works too hard?" Lucien handed her the two books he had selected for his father.

As she slowly began to wrap the books, Paulette looked thoughtful. "Sometimes I do think she works too hard, and that's why I'm in a terrible situation."

Intrigued by the girl's somber expression, Lucien took it upon himself to question her. "What terrible situation?"

"Can I trust you to keep a secret?"

"Absolutely."

She gave him a measuring look as she weighed whether she would confide in him or not. Glancing nervously around the room to ascertain that no one was lurking nearby and listening to their private conversation, she dropped her voice to a faint whisper. Lucien had to lean in closer to hear her. "Well, I've learned something that will help Colette to not worry so much or work so hard, which is good. But it will also make her very sad, which leaves me rather torn. I don't know if I should tell her or not."

"Will she learn of the situation eventually?" he asked.

"Yes, but there is nothing she can do to prevent it, and it will only cause her pain to know about it beforehand."

Touched by Paulette's devotion to her sister, Lucien said, "In the meantime, this indecision is causing you some pain as well."

She nodded sadly, her sweet face anguished. Her remarkable resemblance to Colette left him disconcerted.

He wanted to help her. "Does anyone else know of this? Juliette?"

"No. No one knows. I only know because I was listening—that is, I overheard my mother and Uncle Randall talking the other afternoon."

Recalling the strained and charged emotions at the dinner table when their uncle's visit was mentioned, Lucien could only imagine what had occurred. He felt oddly concerned by Paulette's dilemma. "Perhaps if you share this information with me, I could help you decide what to do. Also, I have found that sometimes just telling another person can make you feel better. And as an older and wiser adult, I can give you a more knowledgeable point of view upon which to base your decision."

"If I tell you, you must promise me that you won't go and tell Colette behind my back. You will let me decide what to do?"

He could tell that she was truly concerned about her sister and wanted his help, but was fearful of confiding in him. Her quandary pulled at his heartstrings. "As a man of honor, I vow to keep your secret. I will only offer my advice to you, which you may use as you see fit. I promise I will leave the final decision up to your discretion."

Again, she looked him over as if weighing whether he were trustworthy enough and then glanced around the shop, which fortunately for them was still devoid of customers at that moment. "I shall tell you, then."

"I am honored by your confidence in me."

Rapidly the words rushed from her mouth, as if she feared she might change her mind before she could tell him. "My mother gave Uncle Randall the deed to sell not just the bookshop but the entire building, and she does not want Colette to know about it until after the sale is completed."

Even Lucien, who instantly understood the financial

and societal motivations Colette's mother and uncle would have in selling the building and heartily agreed with them, could not help but grasp the devastating emotional impact such a sale would have upon Colette. And just when it seemed that the bookshop might actually be profitable. Colette would be heartbroken, and indeed, even if she knew about their plans, she could do little to prevent her mother from selling the shop. Mrs. Hamilton and their uncle had made a wise decision in not sharing the information with Colette, for she would surely try to change their minds about selling the building.

Paulette continued to explain her reasoning to him. "I know it would hurt Colette if they sold the shop, especially without telling her, because she loves it so. I love it too, but Colette lives for it. And it is beginning to make a small profit. But Colette works so hard, too hard. Uncle Randall and my mother think it's the reason she won't accept a husband. So maybe it would be good for her to not have the bookshop to distract all her time. Perhaps it would be better for her not to have all of us as a burden."

"First of all," Lucien finally interrupted her, "although I've only known her for a short time, I feel I know enough about Colette to tell you that you and your sisters are not a burden to her. She loves you. And she loves this little shop. And yes, I agree, she works entirely too hard, but I think your mother and uncle have only her best interests at heart. If I were you I would keep this information that you were not supposed to be privy to in the first place, to yourself. They are right. Do not tell Colette. If your mother is determined to sell the shop, and it is in her name, then she has every right to do so and there is nothing Colette can do about it."

Paulette nodded sadly. "But I feel I should tell her. She's made so many changes and put so much of herself into this bookshop. I can't bear to think of how she will feel when she discovers that she has lost it."

He patted her hand in comfort. "You're a very good sister, Paulette."

"I don't feel like one." She sighed heavily, as if the weight of the world were on her small shoulders.

"What do you think you shall do?"

"I'm not sure yet, but you don't think I should tell her?"

"No. I believe it would be wiser not to."

Once again she nodded thoughtfully. "Most likely."

"Yes," he agreed quietly.

She finished wrapping his books and he paid for them. As she handed him his change, Paulette's youthful brow furrowed with worry and she whispered quickly, "You promise you won't tell Colette?"

"I promise. I am a man of my word."

"I thought you were a rake!" she blurted out, quickly covering her mouth with her hand.

"Eavesdropping again?" He gave her a knowing look, and from her flushed cheeks he knew he had guessed correctly. "But if you thought me such a scoundrel, why would you confide in me?"

"Because I like you, and I think you are a fine gentleman, no matter what Juliette says about you," she declared fervently.

He laughed loudly at her comment. He definitely had a devoted little friend in Paulette Hamilton.

Juliette entered the shop then. She immediately took in their conspiratorial stance and their laughter and assumed the worst. With her arms folded across her chest, she eyed them suspiciously. "I heard you say my name and I just know you both are saying dreadful things about me."

"Not every conversation is about you, Juliette!" Paulette responded and gazed back at Lucien with serious eyes. "Thank you, Lord Waverly."

"I think you may call me Lucien at this point."

Her thrilled grin lit up her face and Lucien felt rewarded.

"What have the two of you been up to?" Juliette asked curiously.

"I've told Paulette my deepest, darkest secrets and she has promised not to tell anyone. Good afternoon, ladies." Taking his prettily wrapped books, Lucien winked at Paulette, placed his hat on his head, and left the shop, leaving a bewildered Juliette and a smiling Paulette behind.

As he walked toward his carriage, he lost himself in thought. Colette had put a tremendous amount of work into improving the store, and from personal observation the changes seemed to be profitable. She had expanded business and skillfully promoted the shop to increase sales. For a woman, she had made incredible strides in a short amount of time. Hell, even for a man! He had to admit he was impressed by her remarkable innovations. It would be a shame to see all of her hard work wasted.

Suddenly it occurred to him what he could do to help, not just Colette but all the Hamilton sisters.

Although he couldn't prevent Genevieve Hamilton from selling the building, there was definitely something he could do to make sure Colette did not lose the bookshop. He had the means at his disposal and he could have his solicitor arrange the transaction anonymously. Yes, the more he thought about it, the better his idea seemed. Although he did not dare examine why it was so important to him to help Colette Hamilton.

Chapter Thirteen

Biting the Bullet

Utterly uncomfortable, Lucien sat in the dimly lit drawing room in the home of Lord Cedric Bromleigh. He had just stated his intentions toward Lord Bromleigh's only daughter, Faith.

"Quite honestly, I am taken aback by your interest in my daughter," Lord Cedric Bromleigh said, looking Lucien up and down in confusion. "You are not what we had in mind for her."

Not what they had in mind for her? Bloody hell! Lucien knew he was one of the best catches of the year. Most families would be thanking their lucky stars to have their daughter chosen by him. And just who did they expect was going to marry Faith, anyway? She barely opened her mouth and no one took notice of her because she blended into the wallpaper. Which is exactly why Lucien chose her.

The older man looked down his long nose at Lucien and continued his speech. "Lord Waverly, I'm a typical father in that I love my daughter more than anything on this earth. But I must tell you that I'm not typical in other ways. I allow my daughter to have her own opinions. As for myself, I would be more than happy to have you as my son-in-law. But this is not my decision to make."

Lucien bit his tongue. After his drastic decision yesterday to help Colette Hamilton and his questionable motivation for doing so, he needed to be safely wed to Faith Bromleigh as soon as possible. Or at least be engaged to her, before he did anything more impulsive over Colette Hamilton again.

Before he did something even more dangerous.

As he sat in the chair across from him, Lord Bromleigh continued, "My daughter is an angel, pure of heart, and as good as gold. Her sweet, obliging nature and unsullied character would make any man proud to call her his wife. Faith knows how to run a home perfectly. She is intelligent and well read. I freely admit, she may not be the finest rose in the garden, but she is special and beautiful nonetheless. I would say she is a daisy. Plainly pretty, hearty, and constant. There will be no thorns from Faith, of that a man can be sure. Now, my fine Lord Waverly, you have a grand estate, a noble lineage, and great wealth. But if you have serious intentions of wedding my cherished and only daughter, you must prove yourself to her first."

"Prove myself?" Lucien shook his head in disbelief. He had to prove himself to Faith Bromleigh? Was the man unbalanced? What was there to prove? By all accounts he was handsome, charming, wealthy, and an earl. And would be a marquis when his father passed on. Why wouldn't she want to marry him?

"Yes," Lord Bromleigh explained further. "You have proven yourself to be a good judge of character already by choosing Faith in the first place. Only a very wise man can see past the exterior façade of beauty to the true beauty within a human being's soul, and I give you credit for being able to discern that Faith would make an admirable marchioness for you. I have no doubt of that. Now I need to know that you are her choice."

"Her choice?" Again Lucien echoed Lord Bromleigh.

He gave Lucien a very serious look before saying, "Unlike most fathers, I do not intend to hand over my most prized possession to a man my daughter has no desire to marry, no matter how lofty his rank or title or how grand his wealth. I need to know that she cares for you, that marrying you is her choice."

Suddenly relieved by that bit of news, Lucien relaxed. *Well, that was different.* He would have no problem on that score! Of course Faith would want to marry him. There were very few women he couldn't persuade to marry him.

Lord Bromleigh tilted his head to one side and nodded. "You may court her if she wishes. But I will not force her hand on this issue."

"Of course not," Lucien agreed heartily, more at ease than he had felt a moment ago. "And I have no indication that she would be disinclined to such a match with me. Although I should inform you that I wish to marry her soon. By the end of the summer."

"Why is that?" the man asked, his eyebrows narrowed in suspicion. "Why would you rush?"

"I am sure that you are aware of my father's illness, but I've kept quiet how seriously ill he truly is. I would like him to attend my wedding, but I don't think he will last much longer . . ." *And I will surely do something I regret with Colette if I don't get married soon.* That temptation motivated him to marry just as much as his father's illness.

"Ah, I see." Lord Bromleigh's head bobbed up and down. "Yes, that is a very commendable reason, but I would prefer to see you court my daughter steadily and seriously. I wish for her to know you well before she

WHEN HIS KISS IS WICKED   147

makes the decision. She should be sure you are the one she wants to spend the rest of her life with."

Lucien was sorely tempted to walk out and forget the whole thing. To spend months and months courting? To marry a girl who should be thrilled at the chance to marry him, the Earl of Waverly and heir to the Marquisate of Stancliff? The situation was laughable. He had no doubt he could sweep Lady Faith Bromleigh off her feet in an afternoon. Or less. Besides, he hadn't the heart to sort through wallflowers again. He just wanted the whole issue to be settled as soon as possible.

"I shall court your daughter. But as soon as she agrees to marry me," Lucien said to Lord Bromleigh, "I must insist that we have a very short engagement. And in the interest of time, I will procure a special license."

"I have no objections to a quick and quiet wedding, but again, Lord Waverly, that would be Faith's decision to make. Women set such a store on weddings. In the meantime, you may only escort my daughter to functions at which I will be present," Lord Bromleigh stipulated.

"Of course."

"My wife and I shall be attending the opera tomorrow evening with Faith, and you are welcome to join us."

"Thank you. I would be honored to join you."

"Good luck, and good day to you, Lord Waverly." Lord Bromleigh shook Lucien's hand.

Ignoring the tightening sensation of a noose around his neck, Lucien shook Lord Bromleigh's bony hand. In two months' time, the man would be his father-in-law. As Lucien left their house, a strange feeling settled in the pit of his belly.

He climbed into his waiting carriage and instructed the driver to take him home. When he arrived at Devon House, he went straight into his private study, shutting the door behind him and pouring himself a glass of scotch. Seated at his polished cherry wood desk, he stared out the window, not really seeing the people that walked by outside as his mind warred with his heart.

He had made the right decision, he told himself over and over. Why didn't he feel better about it? Ignoring the images of Colette Hamilton that kept intruding on his thoughts, he turned his attention to the stack of letters waiting for him on his desk. Maybe work would take his mind off the hollow feeling welling up inside.

As he leafed through the letters, he could not concentrate on any of them and gave up, tossing the pile aside in frustration. One letter fell to the floor. He glanced at it and stopped cold. He recognized the handwriting immediately, for he had received a letter from her once already. The feminine script was elegant and dramatic, just as she had been.

His mother.

Good God, she had sent him yet another letter. He sighed, his heart heavy with trepidation. What more could she have to say? His hand shook slightly as he broke the wax seal.

> *My Dearest Lucien,*
>   *You have not responded to my last letter, which I can only assume means that you do not wish to see me. But I implore you, as your mother, to relent and allow me to visit. I don't ever expect you to understand or forgive me for what I have done, but please give me this one opportunity to see you. I am aware your father is ill and perhaps has not much time left. Please, Lucien. I must see you both.*
>   *I am, as always, your loving*
>   *Mother*

Unmoving and staring at the words, Lucien clutched the note in his hand. When he had ignored her first missive, he assumed that would let her know that he did not wish to see her and she would not contact him again. Now it seemed he would have to respond to her in some way. His father did not have the strength to see her, of that he was sure. But what if what Jeffrey suggested proved correct? Perhaps seeing his mother again would give his father some small measure of peace before he passed away.

And what about himself? Did he want to see the woman who abandoned him when he was ten years old? What could she possibly have to say for herself after all that time? How could she justify leaving her husband and son and running off with another man? Did she expect their forgiveness? Their understanding? As far as he was concerned, there was no excuse for her behavior.

Lucien crumbled her letter in his hand. Taking a clean sheet of paper from the desk drawer, he dipped his pen in the inkwell and began to write.

Chapter Fourteen

A Night at the Opera

As guests filled the theater, Colette sat with Juliette, Jeffrey Eddington, Uncle Randall, and Aunt Cecilia in the private box of the Duke of Rathmore. She and Juliette giggled with delight when an invitation had been sent to Uncle Randall requesting that he and his two nieces join the Duke of Rathmore and Lord Eddington at the opera. Unable to turn down a coveted invitation from the powerful and influential duke, Uncle Randall and Aunt Cecilia accepted eagerly, anxious to elevate their social standing. When they arrived at the theater they were a bit disappointed when Lord Jeffrey Eddington begged their forgiveness at the fact that his father had suddenly taken ill, and offered his deepest regrets.

Even without the duke actually present, Aunt Cecilia still preened ridiculously, giving herself airs with the fact that she at least was sitting in the duke's private box. She missed the sly wink Jeffrey gave to Colette and Juliette. Juliette could barely suppress her amusement at Jeffrey's little trick that enabled him to spend an evening at the theater with her and Colette.

Once again Colette found herself wondering just what Lord Jeffrey Eddington's intentions were in pursuing them in such a way. In any case, she was content to be out with him for he was such fun, and her uncle could not reprove her for this night at least.

Colette leaned over the railing to peer at the audience members below, admiring the lovely gowns and fancy attire. The theater overflowed with guests eager to see the latest Italian opera that evening. Elegant lords and ladies tried to appear important and acted as if they truly cared about the opera but were really only there to see and be seen. Heavy matrons and elderly noblemen sat looking bored in their seats. Giddy debutantes, preening in their newest fashions, surreptitiously attempted to flirt with handsome young men under their mothers' watchful eyes. The chatter reached a fevered pitch but no one was talking about the opera. It was a typical night in London.

As her gaze drifted up to the boxes across from where they sat, Colette's breath caught as she noticed a familiar figure. Lucien Sinclair. He appeared to be with an older couple and a young lady in a green silk gown, while he sat rather impassively, making polite conversation with the older gentleman.

Juliette leaned close to her and whispered in her ear so their aunt and uncle could not hear. "Do you see who Lord Waverly is sitting with? That is Lady Faith Bromleigh, the one I told you about. Those are her parents."

Colette mumbled, "They make a nice pair together."

Juliette shrugged as if she did not agree. "You must be blind. Do you think he kisses *her* in dark gardens? I doubt it."

Colette shook her head, ignoring the sudden nauseous sensation in her belly. Although she could not picture

Lucien Sinclair kissing Lady Faith the way he had kissed her, she did not like to picture him kissing anyone else.

Had she only imagined the feelings between them? Perhaps she had read too much into his attention to her. He had not made any formal overtures to her or asked to court her, as he had obviously done with Lord Bromleigh's daughter. He had not asked her to the theater. He had not asked her to go riding in the park. He had not formally called on her in any way.

No, he had just kissed her passionately. And his kisses left her weak, shaking, and hungry for more.

Yes, it was the kissing that gave her pause. Others might say that he kissed her because he was a rake, but somehow, deep down, she knew there was something more between them. It was the *way* he had kissed her. The way he held her in his arms. And how he said to her afterward that kissing did not always feel that special. She believed him.

Or was she simply a fool who wanted to believe him?

Her heart sank as she watched Lucien sit with Lady Faith at his side. She was a true *lady*. And not just because of her title either. Colette knew that Lady Faith Bromleigh, with her modest clothes and shy demeanor, would never deign to work in a bookshop as Colette did. She would never dirty her hands working for a living. She was the perfect earl's wife. Something Colette could never be. And that was why Lucien was sitting in the theater with Lady Faith Bromleigh and not Miss Colette Hamilton.

"Would you care to borrow my opera glasses?" Jeffrey asked her with an innocent grin. "You would be amazed at how much clearer everything is with these."

Unable to stop herself, she murmured, "Thank you."

She took the small brass binoculars from him and held them to her eyes, peering at the people below, attempting to gaze nonchalantly around the theater, as she gradually

moved her line of vision to the Bromleighs' box. She took
a closer look at Lady Faith Bromleigh, the woman whom
Lucien intended to marry.

The girl was passably attractive. With her pale blond
hair parted severely down the middle, she could not
quite be called pretty for she had not enough light in
her blue eyes or a hint of a smile in her expression. It was
difficult to imagine her doing anything but sitting with
her hands folded primly in her lap.

No, she was not fashionable nor elegant in the least.
Faith's dark green gown was high-necked and plain,
quite different from Colette's off-the-shoulder gown in
a delicate shade of blue, edged with a darker blue lace.
Earlier Juliette had remarked that the color emphasized
her eyes as well as her bosom and Aunt Cecilia had said
the gown was the height of fashion, so Colette had felt
quite flirtatious wearing it. Now however, seeing the
somber way in which Faith Bromleigh was attired, Colette suddenly felt overexposed and flashy. Obviously
Lucien preferred women who dressed modestly, without
drawing any attention to themselves.

Very slowly, without attracting attention, she moved
her line of vision to peer at Lucien, who sat beside Faith
Bromleigh.

Her heart nearly stopped beating and she suppressed
a horrified squeal as she found him staring directly at her
with his own pair of opera glasses. Startled and embarrassed to have him catch her spying on him, she hurriedly dropped the glasses in her lap just as the house
lights dimmed. Grateful for the dark, she wished she
could crawl under the chair and hide. How mortifying to
be caught looking at him! It was not until the orchestra
began playing that it suddenly occurred to her that she
had caught him looking at her, too. She smiled.

Colette did not know Italian, but it hardly mattered,

for she became lost in the beautiful singing. Able to discern the poignant love story, she became riveted by the action on the stage and was startled at the drawing of the velvet curtains at intermission.

Jeffrey and Uncle Randall left the box to bring the ladies some refreshments.

"Which one of you does he fancy?" Aunt Cecilia hissed as soon the men were gone. Almost as tall as Uncle Randall, Cecilia possessed severe facial features that only accentuated her haughty demeanor: a long pointed nose, sharp cheekbones, and thin lips that pursed into a perpetual frown. Her wheat blond hair was pulled tightly from her face.

"What do you mean?" Colette asked, knowing full well to what her aunt referred.

"You know exactly what I mean," Aunt Cecilia said flatly. "Lord Eddington is obviously interested in one of you enough to extend an invitation to your uncle and me tonight. I would simply like to know which one of you it is." Her keen eyes flicked back and forth over them.

"I have no idea." Colette told the truth.

"Well, perhaps he is still making up his mind between you," Aunt Cecilia ruminated aloud. "If either of you can bring him up to scratch, that would be something! For all that Lord Eddington was born on the wrong side of the sheets, his father is still the Duke of Rathmore. Imagine marrying into that family! Has he said nothing to indicate interest in either of you?"

Colette shook her head. Juliette kept her mouth closed, oddly enough.

Aunt Cecilia continued, "He's a charmer, that one. And quite handsome, too."

A look came over her aunt's face that Colette had never seen before. A little sparkle appeared in her eyes and she almost smiled.

"Perhaps your uncle will be able to get some information out of him while they are alone," she continued, wrapping her shawl tightly around her shoulders. "Still you must be careful with a man like Eddington. People can easily get the wrong idea."

Before Colette could respond, Lucien Sinclair opened the curtains to their box. Looking more handsome than ever in his fine evening clothes, his virile presence engulfed her.

"Good evening, ladies. I happened to notice you from across the theater and thought I would stop by to say hello."

"Hello," Colette said. She could barely breathe at the sight of him and she did not imagine that his gaze rested on her longer than necessary. The stunning emerald green of his eyes and his thick lashes startled her.

An actual smile appeared on Aunt Cecilia's face. "Why, Lord Waverly! What a pleasant surprise to see you here."

Lucien said, "You ladies look lovely this evening."

Aunt Cecilia beamed at his compliment while Juliette rolled her eyes in an unladylike manner, but Colette felt he was looking only at her.

"How is your father, Lord Waverly? Is he well?" Aunt Cecilia questioned him.

"Thank you for asking, Lady Hamilton. He is much recovered."

"I am delighted to hear it."

"Have you enjoyed the opera so far?" Colette asked, hating how ridiculously nervous she felt in his presence. The strange tension between them seemed more heightened than usual.

"Not particularly," he said, his expression unreadable.

"No?" Judging from the subdued demeanor of the Bromleigh family, Colette could not help but believe he referred to the company he kept rather than the opera performance itself.

Lucien explained, "I do not seem to be in the mood for opera this evening." He paused before looking directly at Colette. "Are you enjoying the view from here?"

Colette did not know whether to cringe or laugh at his reference to their little exchange with the opera glasses. "The view has been quite lovely," she managed to reply.

A seductive smile swept his face and Colette felt her pulse quicken in response.

"How are the Bromleighs?" Juliette asked pointedly.

Lucien turned to her with a direct gaze, although he seemed almost surprised to hear the Bromleigh name mentioned. "They are quite well, thank you."

"How is Faith enjoying the opera?" Juliette pressed him, possessing a talent for goading people.

"She adores it. In fact, I must return to her now. I wish you ladies a good evening." Lucien bowed elegantly and took his leave of their box. To Colette, it suddenly felt as if the sun hid behind a cloud.

After he left and the red velvet curtains swung back into place, Aunt Cecilia declared, "Now that man would be a feather in our family cap indeed."

"I thought you disapproved of him!" Juliette exclaimed.

"Of course not! He is the heir to a wealthy marquisate," she said with calculated practicality, her hard eyes glittering at the prospect. "For all his scandalous reputation, any girl would consider herself lucky to land him. Although I too have heard rumors he is about to settle down with that quiet Faith Bromleigh and his presence with them this evening does lend credence to that rumor, I do wonder at his visit to us. He certainly did not stop by to chat with me. I wonder which one of you has captured his interest?"

Colette could not answer her, for she honestly did not know what to say to her aunt in response. She dared not tell her that she had captured Lord Waverly's interest while kissing him in a secluded garden.

"Hmm," Aunt Cecilia pondered, her eyes still on them. "That would be something if he were to marry one of you. On the other hand, you must guard your reputations. Oh, here is Lord Eddington now. I must say, I do so enjoy his company."

Their conversation came to an abrupt end as Uncle Randall and Jeffrey returned, bringing them each glasses of lemonade. As Colette sipped the sweet liquid, she could not stop herself from glancing across the theater in Lucien's direction. He had returned to his seat beside the staid Faith Bromleigh and Colette found him staring blatantly back at her. His gaze unwavering, Colette forced herself to look away from him, a strange feeling in the pit of her stomach.

As the second act began, she could feel his eyes on her, even in the dark.

Chapter Fifteen

Special Delivery

The doorbell rang at Devon House, but to Lucien, preoccupied with balancing accounts for the estate in his study, the sound of the bell barely registered in his consciousness. Fully immersed in adding up figures and comparing his sums to those of Mr. Kirby, his estate manager, he moved his pen with quick precision across the paper as his mind calculated the large sums with skilled ease.

A knock on the door of his private study prompted him to call, "Come in," but he did not look up from his books. There was an error in Kirby's accounting, and Lucien was determined to find it.

"My lord, you have a visitor."

"Mmm-hmm," Lucien murmured in response to Granger, the Devon House butler. He continued to work at the long column of numbers on the sheet in front of him.

"It's a young lady."

Lucien still did not respond, his head bowed over the ledger in front of him.

Granger cleared his throat rather loudly. Having been with the Sinclair family since before Lucien was born, he felt he had certain privileges within the house. "My lord, there is a young lady here to see you. A Miss Hamilton."

"Who do you say?" The name had finally penetrated Lucien's preoccupied brain. He immediately closed the leather-bound ledger and placed his pen back in the inkpot on his desk. "Miss Hamilton? Why didn't you say so in the first place? Is she alone? Where is she now?"

What on earth is Colette doing at my house?

Granger seemed taken aback by Lucien's sudden barrage of questions. "She's waiting for you in the front parlor. And yes, she is alone. Apparently she has come to deliver some books you ordered from her shop."

A sudden excitement racing through him at the thought of Colette at Devon House, Lucien rose to his feet in front of the great mahogany desk where his father once sat. He had immediately assumed it was Colette who was waiting in his parlor, but perhaps it was one of her sisters. "You say it was Miss Colette Hamilton?"

"Yes, I believe that is the name she gave. She's quite a pretty lady, my lord." Granger grinned, obviously understanding Lucien's interest in the young woman.

"Yes, well, that she is." Lucien smiled ruefully. "Thank you, Granger. I'll see to the lady now."

As Lucien made his way to the front parlor, he realized his heart was beating faster than usual. Surprised by and annoyed with himself for the obvious sign of excitement at seeing her, he tried to relax and breathe calmly before he saw her.

Colette stood waiting by the large window overlooking the street, with her back turned partially to the room. She had not heard him come in. Her profile, the elegant outline of her face, was visible under the pretty yellow bonnet that covered her rich hair, and he thought how beautiful she was simply standing there. She wore a simple dress the color of pale daffodils, which only emphasized the blue color of her eyes and set off her figure to perfection. A figure that would make any healthy man's blood boil. She was gut-wrenchingly attractive. He recalled what it felt like to hold her in his arms and kiss her senseless, touching her and kissing her.

He did not like how she made him feel.

She haunted his thoughts night and day.

Lady Faith Bromleigh did not inspire such feeling within him, which was exactly why she was the perfect choice to be his bride. There would be no pain, no drama, and no heartache with that marriage. With Faith, he would be safe.

Unlike Colette, who left him feeling off balance, somewhat vulnerable, and always so damned aroused. Yet he had never met a woman he'd wanted to learn more about. A woman he wanted to talk to, wanted to kiss, and wanted to make love to and hold on to. A woman he wanted to pull into his arms that very moment and crush her to him— *Bloody hell!*

The object of his lustful thoughts and sensual fantasies turned to look at him. For a moment all he saw were her incredible blue eyes, and he could not breathe.

"Good afternoon," she said hesitantly, unsure of her welcome. She gestured to a bundle wrapped in brown paper resting upon the side table. "Your Charles Dickens books arrived. You haven't been by the shop recently, so I thought I would bring them to you myself."

"Thank you, Colette," he managed to say. "That was very thoughtful of you."

"You're welcome. It was no trouble, really. I needed to go for a walk and get out of the shop for some air anyway."

"You brought no chaperone with you?" he questioned.

"No," she responded crisply. "I am a businesswoman

conducting business, and I do not require the presence of a chaperone. This is not a social call."

"I see." But he did not. She should not be venturing out unescorted no matter what her reason. He searched for something to say to her. "Did you enjoy the opera the other evening?"

"Yes," she said, her face lit from within. "It was my first time at the opera and I found it quite lovely."

"You and Juliette were there as guests of Lord Eddington?"

"Yes, his father invited my aunt and uncle."

"I see," he said. She seemed to withdraw from him at the mention of the opera. An awkward silence ensued for a few moments.

She began to walk toward the door, as if to leave the room. "Well, I should be returning to the bookshop now. I—"

"No, please stay," he protested, placing his hand on her arm to stop her, suddenly loath to see her leave. He had barely recovered from the shock of seeing her in his home, and now she wanted to leave before he'd had a chance to talk to her.

Startled by his words, she froze and looked up at him, her expression confused. "Why?"

Realizing his hand was still on her arm, he still did not remove it, relishing the warmth of her skin through the soft yellow material of her dress. An image of him sliding that dress from her curvaceous body flashed through his mind, causing him to shake himself back to the present. He should send her home, safely on her way. After that night in the garden, he was too tempted by the sweetness of her mouth. For both their sakes, he would be wise to have her leave.

"Because I have wanted to show you our library and I would like your advice about what books might be a good addition to our collection," he heard himself saying.

She hesitated. "I'm not sure if I should . . ."

"I could really use your help," he cajoled.

"Well," she murmured, a shy smile appearing on her face. "I suppose it would be all right. Shall we bring the new books to the library?"

"Absolutely." He retrieved the package from the table.

Ignoring the little thrill he felt that he had successfully persuaded Colette to stay, he escorted her from the parlor and down the main hallway of Devon House to the library. He swung open the heavy double doors.

"Well, what do you think?" he asked her.

Thick, dark wood shelves lined the walls of the massive room, while tall arched windows framed the fourth wall. Half the shelves were completely empty. A white marble fireplace flanked by bookshelves dominated the main wall. A few leather chairs were scattered about and a wooden ladder rested against one of the shelves. The floor and windows were bare, devoid of carpet and draperies. The heavy odor of fresh paint lingered in the air.

He watched her expression as she inspected the shell of a library.

"It will be an impressive room when it is finished," she remarked bluntly, "but it is definitely in dire need of more books."

"Yes, it is," he admitted with a chuckle, and then explained. "We used to have a full library with some wonderful first editions. But apparently there was a leak behind one of the walls. A very slow leak. With my father so ill, I didn't notice it until the damage was done. The shelves had buckled and the books became wet and molded, especially after that bad rainstorm we had last fall. They had to gut the room, rip out the old shelves, and repair the walls. Now that the library has been completely redone, we are in the process of restocking the new shelves."

"What a sad loss! I hate the idea of books being de-

stroyed. It's as if a little part of history is being erased."
A shadow crossed her face.

"You do love books, don't you?" he asked, oddly touched
by her statement.

"I do," she acknowledged readily. "And I envy you the
freedom of stocking your personal library full of books
that you love. In the shop I have to stock books that
other people might like. But to have your own library,
and one as lovely as this, that is a special treat."

"Yes, but I have no idea what to choose, how to
choose, or how to arrange and organize the books that
I do have. As you can plainly see, I am in desperate need
of assistance, and who better to help me than you?"
What the hell was he doing? He'd just given Colette
Hamilton leave to come to his house again. He needed
to stay away from her, not invite her in!

The smile that she gave him lit her face from within.
Her blue eyes sparkled with excitement. "I would love to
arrange your library and select the books! Provided," she
paused and eyed him levelly, "provided that you buy all
the books through Hamilton's. What we don't have in
stock I can order for you."

Admiring her determination to succeed, he had to admit,
"You are an astute businesswoman, aren't you, Colette?"

She gave him a challenging look. "Are you just realizing that?"

"I think so. You drive a hard bargain, but it's agreed. I
admit that I am relieved to have help. This is a rather
large library, and I've been at a bit of a loss with what to
do with it."

"Oh, it's a perfect room!" she cried, hurrying to the
shelves. She ran her hand across one empty shelf, testing
its weight and durability. She moved to the books that
were stacked rather haphazardly on one shelf. Picking
up a few, she read the titles and set them back down. She

backed up and eyed the room carefully, turning in a slow circle, sizing up the room through a professional eye.

"You will need a vast amount of books to replace your collection." She pointed to the shelves one by one, her mind moving quickly. "We'll put fiction on those shelves, beginning with the classics. That area will house the books on history and art. Over there we'll put scientific and reference materials. And you will definitely need a thick carpet to warm up the room and to muffle the noise. A wide desk should go there, as well as a seating area with large comfortable chairs near the windows to take advantage of natural reading light. And yes, more lighting needs to be addressed. I can have Paulette do the lettering on small cards we can place in brass-plated cardholders to label the different subject areas, just like we do in the shop, only on a smaller scale. Oh, and I know a wonderful printer who makes the most elegant bookplates, and I can have them engraved with Devon House—" She suddenly stopped mid-sentence and turned to him with a sheepish look in her face. "I'm talking too much, aren't I?"

"Not at all." Lucien had found himself enjoying her enthusiasm for the venture. The woman loved what she did. A little thrill raced through him at seeing her so obviously happy. He was also impressed with her expertise, recognizing the fact that she seemed to know exactly what to do. In a matter of minutes she had elegantly refurbished the entire room.

"Well, I shall draw up a list of essential books that you should begin with and have some sent over as soon as possible."

"I believe," he said slowly as an idea formed in his mind, "that this could be a lucrative sideline for you to have, Colette. Helping people stock their private libraries."

She looked at him curiously. "You are serious, aren't you?"

"Yes. You could use me as a reference."

"I thought you didn't approve of women working?"

"I don't," Lucien quipped. "But you are working, whether I approve or not—"

"My lord?" Granger asked, standing hesitantly in the doorway.

"Yes?" Lucien responded rather brusquely.

Granger explained his interruption. "Your father has been ringing for you. It's your usual reading time. Shall I tell him that you are otherwise engaged?"

"That is not necessary, Granger. Please tell him I will be up directly."

The butler exited the room, and Lucien turned his attention back to Colette. "Would you like to come with me?"

"To where?" she asked.

"To read with my father. I would like to introduce you to him." The words were out of his mouth before he could consider what he was saying. He felt as if he were completely incapable of controlling himself when he was in her presence. *Why does that happen with Colette?*

As she wavered with the decision to go with him or not, he realized just how much he wanted his father to meet her.

"I would be honored to meet your father."

"Thank you," he whispered, pleased by her response.

"Is he very ill?" Concern crossed her beautiful features.

Lucien nodded. "He has suffered an apoplectic attack. It was rather severe, causing him to lose control over the right side of his body. He cannot move his right arm or leg, and he has difficulty speaking since the right side of his face is paralyzed. His speech has improved somewhat since it first happened a few months back. I've learned to understand what he is trying to say."

"Oh, how dreadful for him. Is he terribly depressed?"

"Yes, I believe so. That's why I try to spend as much time with him as I can. I read to him, talk to him about current events, and attempt to entertain him a little. His mind is still quite sharp. It's just that his body does not do what he wants it to do."

A look of sympathy swept her delicate features. "I can imagine that must be quite frustrating for him. Are you sure he will not mind my intrusion?"

"No, in fact, I believe it might cheer him. He has not had visitors since this happened, and has refused to see anyone he knows. But he has not met you, so how can he refuse your company?"

Colette nodded in helpless agreement with his winning logic. Then she paused. "And what of your mother?"

Since the age of ten Lucien had learned to deftly answer that particular question. With his cool and calm manner, he never revealed the devastation his mother had inflicted upon his life. But now when Colette asked, his gut clenched and he gave her a rather flippant response. "Surely you've heard the story of my mother from someone by now. It's infamous."

She regarded him intently, her gaze full of concern. "You needn't tell me, if you don't wish to."

Something in her manner calmed him, and for the first time in his life Lucien wanted to share what happened to him that day when the world as he knew it ended. "For all the scandal it caused, it's a very short story. Of course, I didn't learn the truth until later. My mother ran off with another man when I was ten. One morning I woke up and my father told me she had gone away. We never saw her again. As I'm sure you can imagine, the social and emotional ramifications were horrendous."

"Do you still miss her?" she asked quietly.

He sighed heavily, running his hand across his chin. "I used to. For years I used to pray for my mother to come home." He paused thoughtfully. "Over the years I suppose I simply grew accustomed to life without her."

Her eyes grew softer as she watched him. "Oh, Lucien, I'm sorry," was all she said.

Her use of his first name almost undid him. The softness, the tenderness, the aching compassion in the way she whispered his name almost brought him to his knees.

"Let's go upstairs now, shall we?" he suggested abruptly. The tightening sensation in his chest made him uncomfortable.

Colette seemed surprised by the sudden end to their conversation but nodded her assent. Lucien took her arm and led her from the library and down the corridor. Silently she followed him up the wide and curving front staircase and along the upstairs hallway until they reached the doors to his father's suite of rooms.

Colette gave him a nervous glance and he squeezed her arm reassuringly before he guided her to where his father sat huddled in a large leather chair beside the mantel. In spite of the warm June weather, a blazing fire roared in the grate and a gray woolen blanket was wrapped around his thin shoulders. His rheumy eyes narrowed at the sight of Colette.

"Father, I have brought a visitor to meet you. This is Miss Colette Hamilton. She is the lady who has been choosing the books I've been reading to you. Colette, this is my father, Simon Sinclair, the Marquis of Stancliff."

"Good afternoon, my lord," Colette said warmly, taking his outstretched left hand in hers. "I'm honored to meet you, for your son has told me such wonderful things about you."

His father nodded in greeting and there was a hint of amusement in his eyes as his gaze flicked in brief question to Lucien and then back to Colette.

"Miss Hamilton's family owns a bookshop and she has graciously agreed to advise me on how to restock our library."

"Oh, Lucien!" she cried suddenly, turning to him. "We left the Dickens books in the library. You were going to read one to your father!"

"I'll go get them," he said, grateful for a moment to himself to regain his footing. "I'll be right back."

As Lucien returned to the library to retrieve the books, he wondered how his world had suddenly turned upside down since the doorbell rang. How did he end up inviting Colette to restore his library? She would be visiting the house regularly. It was insanity. Then he confided in her about the day his mother left, when he had never discussed that with another soul. Now she was upstairs with his father! How had he allowed this to happen? He should have simply accepted the books and let her go on her merry way.

He knew the decisions he had just made regarding Colette were going to be grueling and thorough tests of his strength and self-control. He had just allowed the woman who tempted him above all others into his home.

Good God, what was he thinking?

When he returned to his father's room, he stopped short at the scene before him. Colette had pulled up a small damask-covered chair beside her father and sat talking to him. The two looked rather comfortable together. Due to the extreme warmth in the room, Colette had removed her little yellow bonnet and her light summer shawl. The firelight glistened on her rich brown hair, and her creamy skin looked as if it were fine alabaster. The soft cadence of her voice drifted through the room as she spoke.

Lucien's heart constricted strangely at the sight of Colette and his father together, but he stood silently so as not to interrupt them. Leaning against the door frame, he just watched. And listened to her as she spoke cheerfully about her beloved bookshop. Her face was animated as she described her work at Hamilton's. Her warmth and charm brightened the dim room to which his father had been relegated these past months in a way he had never been able to lighten them, and he felt immensely grateful to Colette for doing so. His father smiled crookedly, but not disapprovingly, at the fact of her managing a business on her own. With a surprising sense of ease, she conducted a perfectly intelligible conversation with a man who could not speak clearly and whom she had just met.

Colette never ceased to amaze him.

Something made her glance back and spot him in the doorway. "Oh, hello, Lucien. I was just telling your father about my little shop. Come and join us." She smiled invitingly.

Once again he felt an unusual sensation in his heart. "Would you care to read to him this afternoon?" he asked her. "I think my father is tired of hearing my voice and would enjoy a change, wouldn't you, Father?"

Simon nodded as enthusiastically as he could, obviously agreeable to this suggestion.

"I would be honored to read to you, Lord Stancliff," Colette answered graciously, looking into his eyes as she did.

Lucien handed her one of the books they had chosen. His fingers brushed hers lightly as she took it from him, sending a thrill through him. Their gaze held for a moment and he felt that special something pass between them again. That something that had been there from the very first. Something he could not describe. A feeling. A knowing. An understanding. An attraction. Shaken by the fact that he instinctively knew that she felt it too, Lucien held his breath. Colette quickly averted her eyes and settled back in to her chair, opening the leather-bound copy of *David Copperfield*.

"Lucien tells me that you have never read any of

Charles Dickens's work before, my lord," she said with a bright eagerness. When his father shook his head, she continued, "Well then, you are in for a wonderful treat, because Mr. Dickens was an amazingly gifted storyteller."

Her eyes briefly glanced in Lucien's direction over the rim of the open book and he smiled at her in encouragement. She then focused all her attention on the task at hand as if she read to his father every day. Without interrupting her, he took a seat near them and listened intently. As she read with genuine inflection and emotion, Lucien found himself caught up in the story, which he had never read either. Now he began to understand why Dickens was so popular. But perhaps it had more to do with the reader than the author who had him spellbound.

He could not keep his eyes off Colette.

Her graceful neck arched forward, and her full lips moved enticingly as she read the pages. Her lips fascinated him. Now that he knew the sweet taste of those lips, they tempted him all the more. He imagined them pressed heatedly against his mouth, nibbling along his jaw, leaving a trail of heavenly soft kisses across his chest, moving lower . . .

Good God! The woman is reading to my father!

Lucien forced his lustful thoughts to the back of his mind only by closing his eyes and losing himself in the story.

Colette read five chapters before Nurse Fiona, the capable and kind Scottish woman Lucien had hired to look after his father, entered the chamber. "It's time for Lord Stancliff's supper," she announced, her soft Scottish burr evident in her speech.

Simon made an erratic motion to them with his good hand. "S-supper, supper."

"Yes, it's time for supper now." Colette grinned at him, closing the book and placing it on the end table. "And it is time for me to be on my way."

"S-stay for supper," Simon Sinclair uttered rather clearly. Lucien was impressed.

"Oh, thank you very much for the invitation, Lord Stancliff, but I really ought to be going home now." Colette began, rising to her feet. "I've intruded long enough."

"Nonsense," Lucien declared decisively. "We've taken advantage of your kindness this afternoon. The least we can do is offer you some refreshment. Please stay and have supper with us."

"It's rather late," she said hesitantly, glancing between him and Simon. "I only meant to drop off the books, and here I am still, hours later. My sisters must be worried about me."

It was oddly comforting having her there with his father and it surprised Lucien how much he wanted Colette to stay. He had already joined her family for dinner, and now he wanted her to spend time with his family. Such as it was. "That is easily remedied. I will have a footman send a message around to inform them. Surely you can have a light supper with us?" He gave her his most persuasive smile.

He saw the indecision on her face, and she clutched her bonnet and shawl tightly against her chest. "I don't know . . ."

"Then it's settled," he said. "Nurse Fiona, please have Granger send a footman to Hamilton's Book Shoppe, just off Bond Street, to let Mrs. Hamilton know that her daughter is dining here this evening with my father, and that I shall escort her home later. And please arrange to have supper for the three of us served up here in my father's sitting room."

"Very good, my lord." The tall nurse exited the room to follow Lucien's instructions.

Lucien turned back to look at Colette, who had not

moved an inch. A mix of emotions crossed her features, and he was thrilled to note that pleasure was one of them.

"There," he declared with a wave of his hand. "You see? It's all taken care of. You can stay for supper. And then I shall take you home in my carriage afterward."

The early summer sun set with long golden rays that reached into Simon Sinclair's sitting room, bathing the chamber with warm hues. A simple meal was served at a small but elegantly set table near the fire, so Simon would not get too chilled. They dined on roasted lamb and fresh green vegetables, Lucien having discovered early on that very rich meals had a deleterious effect upon his father. He poured a glass of wine for Colette and himself, and a small amount for Simon, whose eating skills had improved somewhat over time as he learned to use his left hand instead of his right. Simon still needed some assistance now and then, which Lucien provided.

Once she conceded to stay for supper, Colette immediately relaxed.

"Father," Lucien began the conversation, "Colette is the oldest of five daughters."

Simon's lopsided grin appeared on his gaunt face. "A-all p-pretty, too?"

Lucien caught Colette's embarrassed glance and enjoyed causing her more embarrassment. "They all look remarkably alike, and yes, they are more than pretty. In fact, they are beauties. And they all have French names as well. One day we must have the Hamilton sisters over for a visit, Father. I'd hazard to guess they would cheer up the place."

Colette's light laughter warmed him. "Or we would give your poor father a dreadful headache!"

"I recently had the good fortune to dine with Colette's family. Their mother is from France."

Simon's eyes lit up. "Ah," he sighed. "T-the F-french."

"My father loves France and anything French," Lucien added.

"My mother was born in Paris and came to London to visit her cousins when she was eighteen," Colette told them. "She met and married my father and never went back to France."

"She swept your father off his feet?" Lucien asked.

Colette remarked, "It seems that way."

Simon grinned gleefully. "French women!"

Lucien and Colette exchanged amused glances.

"Do you all speak French?" Lucien asked her.

"*Bien sûr, je parle français de temps en temps lorsque je suis en famille,*" Colette uttered with flawless ease. "But my father did not speak a word of French. My mother still speaks French to us from time to time."

"Father spent a year in France when he was younger, and he has never recovered," Lucien explained for his father. "He fell in love with their language and culture. And I daresay the women, too."

Simon surprised them both with a very hearty growl, leaving no doubt in their minds how he felt about the females in France.

Colette's sweet laughter brightened the room. "Why, Lord Stancliff," she said in mock innocence and gave him a sly wink, "I'm shocked!"

Simon actually winked back at her as Lucien watched the affectionate interplay between them with undisguised amusement. His father genuinely liked Colette, and Lucien couldn't help the profound pride he had in her at that moment.

"Enough about my family," Colette said. "Please tell me about Devon House."

"It's been in our family for years," Lucien said. "It was designed and built by my father's grandfather, Henry Sinclair, back in 1780."

Over the years Devon House had become something of a local landmark, and many an aspiring artist, intrigued by the beautiful design, had sketched the magnificent home. Five stories high and almost a block long, the white Georgian-style building had tall Palladian windows on the first floor, leading up to gabled windows on the top floor, and possessed a grand and symmetrical sophistication. A black wrought-iron fence with intricate scrollwork intertwined with delicate vines and leaves outlined the perimeter of the house and a curved marble staircase led up to the front entrance of double doors of polished mahogany with a fan light window above them. The classic and well-designed structure graced the quiet lane with its elegant lines and columns. But to Lucien, it was simply his home.

"Why is it called Devon House?" she asked.

"Because it was named after Henry Sinclair's mother, Margaret Devon."

Simon interrupted, his eyes alight with amusement. "G-grandmother's m-money!"

"Yes," Lucien nodded, surprised at his father's blatant honesty about a fact he usually liked to keep quiet. "It was Margaret Devon's money that saved the Sinclair family from financial ruin years ago."

"It was money well spent," Colette remarked with unabashed warmth. "It's such a grand and lovely house."

"Once the library is complete," Lucien added, with a pointed look at Colette.

They then began a lively discussion of books and their plans for the library. After a light dessert of glazed pears, Simon made a weak gesture with his hands. Before Lucien could explain what it meant, Colette knew instantly.

"I see we have tired you, my lord," she said quietly. "I shall take my leave now."

His father struggled to speak, his watery eyes staring intently at Colette. "C-come b-back?"

"You would like me to come back?" she questioned him.

He nodded with a lopsided smile.

"I would be honored to come read to you again, Lord Stancliff."

His father looked toward Lucien and again struggled to speak. "M-marry her?"

Lucien jumped to his feet. *Damn.* His father thought Colette was the woman he intended to marry. "No, Father," he said hurriedly, shaking his head and hoping that Colette had misconstrued what he said. But judging from her downcast eyes and flushed cheeks, he feared she had heard quite clearly. "You're tired and need your rest, Father. Miss Hamilton will visit you again when she is able."

"Of course I shall," Colette said brightly, eager to change the topic of conversation. "We have the rest of the book to go yet! And so much more happens in the story! I'll return in a few days to help with the library, and I shall come read to you then. I've so enjoyed your company, Lord Stancliff."

She reached out her hand to him, and his father grasped it weakly in his own gnarled one. "Th-thank y-you."

"Thank *you,*" she returned, giving his hand a squeeze.

With a trembling motion, Simon brought Colette's hand to his lips, placing a light kiss upon her fingers.

"Now I shall definitely return, for how can I resist such a gallant and handsome gentleman?" Her flirtatious tone brought another half-smile to Simon's face.

Lucien silently blessed her for being so good with his father. He hadn't seen Simon so alert and alive looking in a long time. Her vibrant and lovely presence had truly brightened his father's spirits.

Colette gathered up her things, thanked them both

for a wonderful evening, and with another affectionate farewell to his father, followed Lucien from the room.

Together they walked the length of the elegant, Persian-carpeted corridor. It had been a memorable evening. The last time Lucien had enjoyed himself this much was the night he spent with Colette and her sisters. He had not felt such a strong sense of home and belonging since before his mother left.

Before they reached the top of the staircase, Lucien placed his hand lightly on her shoulder. She paused and faced him. "You were wonderful with my father, Colette. You made him feel good today. I cannot recall seeing him so happy. We owe that to you. Thank you."

Her loving smile caused his heart to turn over in his chest. "He's a sweet and charming gentleman, Lucien. It was my pleasure to read to him."

"It was our pleasure to have you with us."

"I truly had a lovely time this evening."

Their gazes locked as she tilted her head up to look at him, and they stared into each other's eyes. Neither moved. Neither blinked. Lucien suddenly found it difficult to draw breath into his lungs.

"I really should be going now," she whispered so softly he could barely hear her. Fascinated by the way her lips moved, he knew she spoke, but the words had no meaning for him. The silence in the long, empty hallway echoed deafeningly in his ears. They were completely alone.

"I should go," she murmured again, her aquamarine eyes still on his.

"Don't go yet."

He stepped closer to her, causing his heart to pound in his head. Every single nerve in his body tensed at the closeness of her. Maybe it was the wine he had with supper. Maybe it was her light, sweet violet fragrance that surrounded him, enveloped him. Maybe it was inevitable. But he had to kiss her just once, and then he would send her home.

Just one kiss.

In one quick movement, his arm reached out and encircled her, pulling her up against his chest, and his mouth came down over hers possessively. As he lost himself in the feel of her seductive lips, the soft silken touch of her mouth responding wildly to his, he held her even tighter, the length of his body pressed intimately against hers.

He had Colette Hamilton in his arms just feet away from his bedroom.

He knew then with a dreadful certainty that this would not end with just one kiss.

Chapter Sixteen

Once a Rogue

Colette couldn't breathe. She couldn't move. She couldn't think. She could only hang on and kiss him back. Her knees trembled and she doubted she had the strength to stand if she did not wrap her arms around his neck for support. The scent of him, something clean and spicy and distinctly male, enveloped her and she lost herself in the sensation of his insistent mouth on hers.

As she had when he kissed her the first time, she instinctively opened her mouth to him in invitation. His low growl of approval excited her almost as much as the feel of his warm tongue penetrating her mouth. Filled with satisfaction at having pleased him, she pressed closer to him, loving the contact with his broad chest. His lean, muscular arms encircled her easily, pulling her closer still.

Oh, God, she should not be doing this . . .

But how could she not?

Lucien's warm hands cupped her face and he continued kissing her. Her world seemed to tilt and spin crazily around her as she clung madly to his broad shoulders for support. Her legs shook. His long fingers threaded into her upswept hair, gently loosening the pins that held her wavy locks in place. As her long hair fell like a dark curtain around her, his kiss deepened. His mouth locked on hers, devouring her, with a hunger that matched her own. His kiss demanded all of her, and she surrendered on a sigh, giving herself to him freely, eagerly.

Slowly he backed her up until she found herself against the wall, her hips pressed against the wainscoting. And still his lips never left hers. A crazed and ravenous sensation overtook her, until all she could think of was Lucien. Lucien's seductive lips, hard and insistent on her mouth. Lucien's rough stubble, rubbing the tender skin on her face, branding her. Lucien's strong hands—caressing her cheek, entwined in her hair, locked around her waist, now moving around the curve of her hips.

Still linked tightly around his neck, her hands found their way into the soft mane of his hair. Marveling at the feel of the softness of his dark curls, she splayed her fingers around the curve of his head while his hand slid up higher and cupped her breast. She sucked in her breath at the intimate contact. He gently squeezed her, kissing her lips even harder.

Suddenly he pulled his mouth away from hers, and her arms fell reluctantly to her sides. Without his support, her head fell gently back against the wall. An overwhelming sense of loss encompassed her at being deprived of his touch.

"Open your eyes and look at me," Lucien whispered, his voice ragged and out of breath.

Pressing her bruised lips together and soothing them with her tongue, she could still taste him. Her lips felt full and heavy. Again it felt as if she were waking from a deliciously warm dream on a cold winter morning, and slowly she opened her eyes. His face was so close to hers, his green eyes intent, urgent. She blinked at him, her own breath coming in short gasps, and glanced away.

He took her chin in his hand and tilted her head to face him. His fevered eyes pleaded with her. "Leave now, Colette. Leave now while I can still let you go."

Lucien was right, of course. She was inexperienced, to be sure, but she was not dim-witted either. She knew this was treacherous territory for a female and instinctively felt that her heart, her reputation, her future were all at risk. Logic and good sense demanded that she leave that instant and run all the way home as fast as her feet could carry her, locking the door behind her.

Yet here she stood. Still. With this powerful man who made her heart race. With this man she could not resist. With this man who elicited feelings in her she'd never felt before. She was tingling with life, every sense in her body heightened when she was with him, her nerves stretched taut with anticipation and desire. Oh, yes, she should definitely run.

Yet Colette could not move a muscle. She stood perfectly still, rooted to the floor, holding her breath.

"Please . . . Colette . . . please . . . go . . ." He leaned in nearer once more, his mouth brushing ever so lightly against her cheek, hovering near her lips, so close she could see the fine dark stubble along his jawline. The stubble that she had felt scratching against her own skin just seconds ago. The sight of it excited her. He nudged her lightly with the tip of his aquiline nose. "Colette." Her name became a plea and a caress against her cheek. Her heart pounded wildly.

"I don't want to leave," she breathed, her voice a mere whisper. Unable to resist being with him, she reached up and put her arms around him again, and she kissed him.

She brazenly kissed him, disregarding every ounce of good sense she possessed.

"Oh, God, Colette," he growled into her mouth, kissing her hotly. He suddenly lifted her from the floor, sweeping her into his strong arms.

Surrounded by Lucien, she gasped. The sensation of being held by him left her breathless. Resting her head against his massive wall of a chest, she clung to him as he walked, knowing exactly what his intended destination would be.

Colette surrendered herself willingly then. And God help her, completely.

He carried her on long strides to his bedroom, the sound of their heartbeats echoing wildly in her ears. Once inside, he kicked the door closed behind them. Fleeting images caught her eye as they crossed the expanse of his chamber. High windows covered in long drapes. A thick woolen carpet, dark paneled walls. One very large four-poster mahogany bed. He laid her on the heavenly soft bed, her head cradled by downy pillows. It smelled deliciously of Lucien, warm and masculine. Lying beside her, he sought her mouth hungrily, as if they hadn't just been kissing madly moments before. She relished the taste of him on her tongue once again and sighed, wrapping her arms around his neck. With a swift and sure movement, he eased on top of her, his long male body covering the length of hers.

The magnificent weight of him above her left her feeling light-headed. She was in Lucien Sinclair's arms. She was in his enormous bed. *His bed!* This was how wayward girls got into trouble, she thought, suddenly sympathetic to their plight. Lucien had her in his bed. And he was about to do things to her that no man had ever done before. The enormity of what she had just consented to washed over her in a tidal wave of emotion.

He must have feelings for her. He must. He could not do this with her if he did not. *Could he?* Oh, she wanted him to have feelings for her! Her own heart felt close to bursting with the roiling emotions contained within. But God help her, even if he did not love her, she wanted this moment with him. Wanted to be with him any way she could.

If she ended up marrying some dreadful old nobleman to save her family, then at least she would have had this one night with Lucien Sinclair.

Unconsciously she arched her body against his, wanting something, yearning for something only he could give her. His swift intake of breath encouraged her untutored movements and she writhed restlessly beneath him. Wanting more, she pulled him tighter to her, while his mouth still kissed hers relentlessly. Lost in their melting lips, he rubbed himself against her, his legs intertwined with hers. At the intimate pressure, she gasped into his mouth and he caught her breath with his. *Heaven help me!* Her body turned to liquid as the intense sensation poured from her waist to the tips of her toes. He pressed himself between her thighs again and she felt faint at the pleasure he caused and eagerly lifted her hips to meet his. Their frantic movements increased their pace, and still they kissed.

His hands ran over her body, feeling her curves through the cover of her daffodil yellow gown. Then he eased his body from hers, and very gently, he turned her over onto her stomach, Colette's body pliant to his demands. Undoing the buttons down the back of her bodice, his fingers worked effortlessly and rapidly, until the dress was loosened and tugged from her overheated body. Her petticoats followed rapidly until she lay back on the bed with nothing but her sheer undergarments covering her, grateful for the dimness in the room. Practically naked, she looked up at him, feeling shy, but at the same time surprisingly at ease with him.

"No corset?" he whispered, leaning back over her, his eyes pinning her in place.

She despised corsets. "Only when I'm wearing a ball gown."

"Thank God." He placed a light kiss on her cheek, another on her lips.

She reached her hands around his neck and pulled him to her, yearning to continue where they left off.

He bent his head and took her mouth savagely, kissing her lips in with all the power in him, and she matched him. If she kissed him ceaselessly for years, she doubted she could get enough of him. Their tongues twisted together in the wet heat of their mouths, exploring and plundering each other in a frantic dance. They devoured each other, each taking as much as they could.

Coming up for air, he suddenly pulled away from her mouth, panting heavily. Her eyes flew open in protest at the loss of his kiss but fluttered closed in relief after she saw the impassioned look in his face. Cradling her face in his hands, he gentled his assault on her senses and touched his lips to hers, softly, ever so tenderly. He then rained feather-light kisses all over her face, as if he needed to taste every inch of her. Lucien's delicate kisses fell on her forehead, her cheeks, her eyelids, the tip of her nose, the curve of her ears, and the point of her chin, along her jawline. He kissed and nuzzled the soft length of her neck down to the hollow of her throat, moving lower to her chest, licking a burning trail of languid pleasure. The exquisite caress of his skilled tongue on her hypersensitive skin left her shaking.

Her breathing became more frantic as he slowly inched the thin material of her chemise even lower, exposing her bare breasts to his gaze. The heavy rise and fall of her chest only emphasized their rounded weight. She watched as he cupped one breast firmly with his warm hand, pressing his lips to the soft flesh. *Oh God.* Stroking her heated skin with his amazing tongue, he traced a swirling path around her nipple, teasing the sensitive peak until it hardened in his mouth.

Colette closed her eyes in quivering pleasure and lost herself in the mind-numbing sensation of Lucien's lips and tongue on her breasts. Drowning in a deliciously intimate sea of warmth and kisses, her very flesh tingled and her body ached with a growing need. She yearned for more of him, to be closer to him. Her fingers wrapped in his thick hair again, breathing in the scent of him as his dark head bent over her chest.

"Lucien," she whispered, feverish for something she couldn't define, opening her eyes again to look at him.

Sensing her need, he lifted his head and gazed at her wordlessly, his eyes heavy lidded and dark with desire. She had to feel him against her, to feel his bare skin pressed to hers. He rose above her and she tugged at the buttons of his white shirt until the wide expanse of his chest was open to her. His body, perfectly muscled and toned, reminded her of a statue at a museum. She raised herself to press impassioned kisses against his warm flesh. The pounding of his heartbeat echoed through his chest and she held herself tight to him to listen. Never had she felt this close to someone, and the power of the contact had her reeling.

Together they lay back among the fluffy pillows before he rolled over on top of her again, positioning his still-trouser-clad body firmly between her legs. As before, Colette gasped at the exquisite feel of his hardened body pressed so intimately to hers. Looking into her eyes, he rubbed against her, and as she quivered, his mouth covered hers in a searing kiss. *Good heavens!* It was all too much. She felt a hot, yearning ache pooling deep within her, and her body trembled with unexplored need and untamed desire.

And still he kissed her as if she were his very reason for living.

Mindlessly her hands caressed the bare planes of his back, feeling corded muscle tense with exertion under soft skin. The male body fascinated her; he could be so strong and hard and still feel smooth and soft. His mouth left hers again and she wanted to cry with the loss of it. He murmured hoarsely, "God, you're beautiful."

She thought her heart would burst with the emotions it contained. Pressing kisses into the hollow of his shoulder, Colette clung to him, not entirely sure what would happen next or how it would make her feel. But she trusted him, trusted him to take care of her and guide her where she needed to go.

"I want you," he whispered in her ear before he rose from the bed. Feeling cold and bereft as he left her, she watched while he unfastened the ties at his waist. As he removed his trousers, her eyes were riveted to the bottom half of his body. The sight of his fully aroused male form made her mouth go dry and left her dizzier than she had been from his kisses.

Once more he covered her body with his in a way that now seemed achingly familiar, and she almost cried out with the intimacy and tenderness of it. In this sacred position, she instantly grew warm again, heated by the contact of skin against skin. His soft, full lips began their sensual magic on her eager mouth, his tongue delving within and dancing with hers. He positioned himself between her legs, and the sensation melted her mind completely. She could not think a single coherent thought. All she could do was feel, feel Lucien above her, around her, touching her, kissing her, caressing her.

And still it was not enough.

She wanted more of him. Her hands seemed to move of their own volition, for she certainly did not consciously make them, running up and down his back, pressing her fingers into him, in an attempt to bring him closer to her. She squirmed beneath him, and he ground himself against her, causing her to stop breathing for one heavenly moment. Ripples of pleasure slid up her body, leaving her yearning and aching for more. He did it again. And again.

"Lucien . . . I want . . . Lucien . . ."

He pressed his forehead against hers, his breath coming in heavy pants. They stared at each other in the shadowed light, the evening darkness covering them. Then he took her hand in his and slowly guided it lower, between them, to grasp the hard length of him. Stunned by the heated silkiness of his skin, she gently traced the tip, and down the thick shaft, growing bolder as her touch became firmer, more controlled. His eyes closed and his head fell back. Fascinated by the shape and feel of his body, she stroked and caressed him, her fingers moving up and down, gently squeezing, but his sharp intake of breath caused her to stop. With a soft kiss on her lips, he drew her hand away from him and settled himself on the bed beside her, his head propped up by his arm, and he stared at her with a wicked grin. She clung to him, in protest, wanting him, the weight of him, above her again.

Tenderly he kissed her cheek and wrapped one arm around her waist to calm her. Waiting nervously for she knew not what, she gazed back at him. Then the hand at her waist began to move. Lazily he stroked the flat length of her quivering stomach, with gentle, easy motions. His fingers worked a sensuous path across the curve of her hip, down her thigh to her knee, and back up, across her stomach and down the other leg. Warm, soothing caresses continued, up and down, back and forth, down and up, veering ever nearer to the present center of her being. Unable to move, to think, to speak, and barely able to draw a breath, she was weak with anticipation. All feeling, every nerve in her body, focused on the growing all-encompassing need within her. Closer and closer, he teasingly massaged her skin. Oh God, this, *this*, was unimaginable, unbearable, unstoppable. Never had she dreamed *this* . . . When Lucien's fingers finally touched the soft curls between her thighs, and with infinite tenderness, delved within the slick, aching folds, Colette practically flew out of her skin. One intent finger sank into the depths of her, the core of her, and she thought she would shatter into a million pieces right there on the bed.

"More?" he breathed in her ear, his voice raspy and low.

Unable to speak, a faint little sigh escaping her, she nodded in assent to make sure he knew she was definitely agreeable to more. With his face close to hers, his mouth sought her lips in a heated kiss while he pressed another finger deep within her. Enflamed by the exquisite pleasure of Lucien touching her that way, her body burned. She clung to him frantically, for he was the only solid thing in her spinning world. He *was* her world. The all-encompassing, all-consuming need that racked her body could only be assuaged by Lucien. She needed him. All of him. More of him.

"Please, please . . ." she whimpered softly as his fingers moved within her, making every bone in her body melt.

With his kisses hot on her fevered cheek, he continued to stroke her. The sensations created by his fingers within her caused her hips to move in unison with him. An intense longing built within her, and she pressed herself against his hand, searching for a release. On and on it went, until she thought she would go mad from it all. Time lost all meaning. All that mattered was his mouth on hers, his naked body beside her, and his exquisite fingers. Just when it seemed she could not endure another moment of waiting, a sudden intense burst of pleasure spread through her with such fervor that she cried out for him.

Lucien held her close to his chest then, cradling her in his arms, kissing her hair, soothing her as she regained her senses. She breathed him in as she lay in his arms, wondering at her own body. No one had ever explained *that* to her. Then again, how could they? What had just happened between them defied words. It had been heavenly. Yet strangely enough, that exquisite release had left her still wanting more.

Her mouth sought his and he responded to her overture with an eagerness that excited her. Their lips clung to each other ravenously. In a sudden and swift motion, he rose above her, separating her legs with his knee. Colette thrilled at the inevitability of what would come next, the anticipation almost too much to bear. He pressed himself against her, and her breath came in shallow pants. Waiting. Wanting. Wishing.

"Colette?" he asked in an anguished voice, his green eyes heavy with desire for her.

Looking up at this man poised above her, his handsome face looking intently at her, his voice saying her name, his breath mingling with hers, the broad expanse of his chest touching the tips of her breasts, and his legs interlocked with hers, there was only one reply she could give. Fear, shame, shyness, and regrets were feelings for another time. Right now, right here, with this man, she wanted this. She wanted him. All of him.

"Yes." The word escaped her mouth in a hiss, and she pulled him to her, pushing her body toward him at the same time.

A throaty groan tore from his mouth and he plunged into her with a quick and sure motion.

Colette cried out, not so much from the pain but from the surprise. The surprise of how he felt inside her, of the physicality of being so close to a man. This man.

Lucien stilled at her cry, sheathed within her.

Not wanting him to stop, instinctively she thrust her hips against him. That was all it took before he continued this dance. Slowly and gently he moved within her, rocking her in a steady motion. The sensation took her breath away and began to build in intensity. She wrapped her arms around him, gripping him tightly, knowing he was taking her into the unknown, but she felt safe going with him. As his thrusts grew more urgent, deeper, more forceful, she welcomed them with a fervor that matched his.

Once again she sought the blossoming sensation of pleasure that grew insatiably within her body. Her movements mirrored his, arching her back and meeting him thrust for thrust. Her mind lost all sense when he placed his hand between them, right where their bodies were joined. He touched her expertly, and the ache that had built to a fevered pitch finally exploded in a burst of pleasure so exquisite, so blissful, and so enrapturing it felt as if a million little sparkling stars fluttered around her. As she called his name, he called hers, and continued to drive into her.

Over and over again.

Reeling from the assault on her senses and overwhelmed by the tremendous emotions that flooded her, Colette felt molten tears spill down her cheeks.

She loved him. The complete sense of peace and rightness and belonging enveloped her being. She belonged to Lucien. Nothing in her life had prepared her for this feeling with Lucien. Nothing she had read in books compared to the intense emotions that surged within her heart for this man.

Lucien's movements became more frantic and a fine coating of sweat covered him as he labored over her. She kissed his face, his neck, clinging to him, urging him, tears flowing from her eyes.

"God, Colette," he exclaimed in a growl as he gave one final, deep thrust, before he shuddered and collapsed above her. They both panted and gasped for breath for some time, their arms and legs wrapped around each other.

The room was now in complete darkness and hushed in quiet. Lucien finally lifted his head and moved off her, kissing her cheek tenderly as he did so. He pulled her into the crook of his arm, pressing kisses in her hair.

"Are you crying?" he asked, his voice soft and remorseful. He touched a gentle finger to her cheek, following the path of tears.

"No." She sniffled a little and gave a nervous laugh, wiping at her tears with her hands. "I'm fine."

"You *are* crying, Colette."

"But not because I'm sad or hurt," she explained hurriedly. "I'm just crying because . . . I don't know. I suppose because it was just so beautiful and I never knew anything could be so special."

"Ah, Colette."

She shrugged, feeling awkward and suddenly shy with him, as if she had angered him somehow. "I'm sorry I cried."

He rested his head on the pillow beside her, taking her hand in his and placing it on his chest. "You have no reason to be sorry. I am the one who should apologize."

"Apologize for what?" Her heart resumed its frantic pounding pace. *Oh God, he regrets being with me already.*

Mortification and an alarming sense of humiliation overwhelmed her being.

"Apologize for what?" he echoed her question in disbelief, frowning. "For what just happened here between us."

After a sickening pause, she managed to ask, "Are you sorry it happened?"

He paused for a thoughtful minute. And another. She waited, holding her breath, her heart in her mouth.

Finally he muttered, "I don't know."

"Well, I'm not," she said in a small voice.

He said nothing else. An uncomfortable silence settled over them. *What happens now?* Suddenly she did not know how to act with him. He did not seem like the same Lucien who had kissed her senseless and just made love to her. A distant, cold stranger had taken his place.

"I should go," she murmured, with the forlorn thought that she wished she were already at home in bed with him right here. How heavenly to be able to curl up next to him in this very bed and sleep with his strong arms about her all night long. A dream that would never come true either.

At her words he did not let go of her, but neither did he encourage her to stay. "Colette?" Her name sounded like a cry of pain.

She waited for him to continue, wishing she could see his face in the darkness. *Oh, Lucien,* her heart cried, heavy with raw emotion. Was he angry with her? Sad? Regretful? The room seemed too silent, too full of shadows.

"Colette . . ." he began again, his voice tinged with bitter remorse. "You deserve so much better from me. I shouldn't have let this happen. It was wrong and I knew it when I kissed you the first time. I shouldn't have taken advantage of you—"

"Stop," she interrupted him as stinging tears threatened anew. Sitting up, she clamped her hand over his mouth. She could not bear to have the most incredible and beautiful experience of her life with the man she loved reduced to nothing more than a mere lack of willpower on his part. How could he not feel the way she did about it?

"Don't say any more and listen to me. You did not take advantage of me, Lucien Sinclair. When I said I wanted to stay, I meant it. I wanted this as much as you did, if not more. So please don't be sorry, because you did not make me do anything I didn't wish to do. I don't regret it, not one minute of it. It was heavenly. The most thrilling, and most wonderful, and most amazing, and . . . and . . . I . . . I need to go home." The last words were uttered on a sob as she pulled away from his embrace and rose from the bed as quickly as she could.

"Colette," he called after her as she fumbled in the dark to find her clothes.

I will not cry again, she instructed herself, taking a deep breath as she found a bundle of her clothes on the floor. *I will not cry.* Feeling for her chemise, she flung it over her head hurriedly. She had to leave before the tears began. And this time the tears *would* be because she was sad and hurt.

Lucien had followed her off the bed and lit a lamp on the bedside table. The dim light cast a yellow glow in the room. He pulled on his trousers and Colette turned her back to him and continued dressing as fast as she could, thankful once again that she did not wear a corset regularly, for it would only have slowed her down. Still, she needed him to fasten the back of her dress.

He came up behind her and wrapped her in his arms, pulling her against his chest. "Wait," he whispered in her ear.

At his touch she almost melted in his arms, dangerously close to crying in great, wrenching sobs.

"Listen to me." He spun her around gently, so she faced him. His green eyes bored into her as he spoke. "I did not mean that I was sorry I made love to you. This was different for me, too. That's because it was with *you*." He paused and placed an emphatic kiss upon her lips. Pulling back, he looked at her meaningfully. "But you have to understand the great mess we've just created."

Her head swam with what he said. *He felt something, too.* "What do we do now?" she asked, her heart racing.

"What do we do now?" He blinked. "I don't know yet."

He doesn't know! The man who always had an answer for everything suddenly had no answers when it came to her. Her tears dissolved instantly. Irritated with him, she demanded, "Well, what do you usually do?"

"What do I usually do?" he echoed her in confusion.

"Yes, you're the one with the reputation. What do you usually do in these situations?" she questioned him harshly, and then added, "And stop repeating everything I say."

He loosened his hold on her, and she took a few steps away from him. She bent to retrieve her shoes. Angrily shoving her foot into her low-heeled slippers, she snapped, "Well?"

"In spite of your lurid imagination, I am not usually in 'these' situations. In fact, I have never been in a situation like this before."

"Because now you're expected to marry me?" She challenged him with her directness.

"Yes," he admitted quietly, but did not look at her.

"And you won't?" The stinging behind her eyes returned and she blinked rapidly.

He did not answer her, and in an instant her heart, brimming with tender new emotions, shattered like fine crystal upon a slate floor. She had been a complete and utter fool. He didn't want her, and he certainly did not love her.

His inability to respond to her question was more than answer enough.

Chapter Seventeen

Regrets Only

"Where have you been?" Juliette demanded when Colette finally arrived home later that night.

Juliette had been given the responsibility of closing the bookshop, not a task that that she relished with great joy. When Colette had gone out earlier that afternoon to deliver books, Juliette had counted on her returning right away. Instead Colette had been gone far longer than necessary and then sent the surprising message that she would not be home for supper at all, which irritated Juliette even further.

The night had grown late. Their mother had retired for the evening, complaining of her usual headache. Lisette, Paulette, and Yvette were already in the room the three of them shared, but Juliette had waited up for Colette. Now she followed Colette into their bedroom, wanting some answers as to why her sister had been gone so long and why she looked so oddly disheveled.

"You received my message, didn't you?" Colette

asked, carelessly tossing her bonnet and shawl on the chintz-covered chair in the corner.

Juliette's eyes narrowed. Her very meticulous sister never threw her belongings. She always hung everything neatly in the wardrobe, taking great care of her possessions, especially with their new clothes their uncle had purchased. Juliette continued suspiciously, "Yes, but that does not answer my question."

"You knew I was at Lord Waverly's house. He just escorted me home in his carriage."

"But that doesn't explain why you are so late coming from his house. Or why you left to deliver a few books and returned over six hours later."

"How did you fare in the shop tonight?" Colette changed the subject.

"Fine. We had quite a few customers, and two more ladies signed up for the reading circle. Everything is taken care of and properly locked up for the night."

"I know," Colette admitted. "I checked before I came upstairs."

"I never doubted you wouldn't." Juliette flopped down on her quilt-covered bed and curled her legs under her lawn nightgown. Colette never trusted her alone in the shop for long, and she wondered why she had done so this evening.

With a weary sigh, Colette sat on her own little bed across from Juliette's and removed her shoes, kicking them across the room. "How are Mother and the girls?"

Juliette noted her sister's actions with a growing sense of unease, but answered calmly. "They are fine. We had stew for supper. Lisette still had nothing to wear to go to the dance with Henry, but I gave her that pink gown of mine. You know that new one with the little puff sleeves? It never suited me anyway. Paulette annoyed me all evening long. Yvette is getting a cold. And Mother is suffering from her usual headache. There. That's all there is to tell. Now, stop evading and tell me what you've been up to this afternoon."

Ignoring her sister's demands, Colette asked, "Did Mother ask where I was?"

Juliette shook her head. "Of course not. Does she ever? She assumed you were working down in the shop all evening." Noticing Colette's red-rimmed eyes and haunted expression, she suddenly had a feeling that more had happened at Lord Waverly's than she suspected. And that something was not good. "Did Lucien kiss you again?"

Colette buried her face in her hands.

Juliette jumped off the bed and flew to her sister's side. Placing a consoling arm around her, she asked, "What happened?"

"I don't know if I can talk about it yet," Colette confided in an anguished whisper.

"Why not?"

"It's too dreadful, and I don't know what to do about it."

"Well, then you had definitely better tell me. Honestly, Colette, I can't imagine you doing anything that's so bad that you couldn't tell me about it."

"I've made a terrible, irrevocable mistake."

"Take a deep breath, and start from the beginning," Juliette instructed soothingly.

She listened while Colette haltingly began to explain the events that occurred after she delivered the books to Devon House. It all seemed perfectly fine. "So you met his father and dined with them. Agreeing to refurbish his library was a brilliant stroke of business genius. The shop will make a mint of money from his book orders alone! Even I can see the sense in that. So far, I see no problems. Supper is over, you said good-bye to his father, you're on your way out the door, and what? He kissed you?"

Colette nodded imperceptibly and whispered, "Yes."
Her cheeks flamed scarlet.

"You kissed him before, so that can't be what you're
upset about. What else happened?"

"We did more than just kiss." Once again Colette hid
her face in her hands after her guilty admission.

Stunned by the news, Juliette pondered what "more"
referred to exactly. Over the years she had had her share
of fleeting romances with eager boys who fancied themselves in love with her. She had let them kiss her once or
twice and she had been unimpressed by them, and
therefore had never ventured on to "more" than kissing.
Now her imagination raced.

"What *did* you do?" Juliette asked in a hushed tone,
fearful their sisters might overhear their conversation.
Especially Paulette, who possessed exceptionally keen
little ears.

"I cannot even say it," Colette whimpered, her voice
muffled in her hands.

Juliette thought for a moment, her imagination running wild. "All right, then, if you can't tell me what you
did, then at least tell me *where* you did it."

Colette mumbled something unintelligible through
her fingers.

"Say that again?"

"In his bed."

Her sister's voice was so soft Juliette thought she had
not heard correctly. Surely Colette didn't mean that! For
Juliette knew what those words implied. Years ago she
and Colette had hid behind a back shelf in the bookshop and furtively read about human reproduction in
one of the large, leather-bound medical texts in the
shop. *A Complete Study of the Human Anatomy and All Its
Functions by Doctor T. Everett* had explained the act in
detail and she and Colette had thought it all quite

bizarre and cold, definitely not something one would engage in willingly.

"Oh, Colette," Juliette whispered. "Are you okay?"

Colette groaned with a sheepish expression.

"I'll take that as a yes," Juliette advised dryly.

"I feel sick to my stomach."

Alarmed, she asked her, "Was it that terrible?"

"It's not like the book at all," Colette murmured under her breath.

Stunned by that bit of information, Juliette could only wonder, "Is it worse?"

Colette lifted her head, wiping stray tears from her red-rimmed eyes. She sniffled. "No. It was actually wonderful."

Left speechless, Juliette stared wide-eyed at the implications of this development. "He didn't . . . He didn't force you to do it, did he?"

"No!" Colette responded so vociferously that Juliette was taken aback. "Lucien would never do that."

She regarded her sister with a sense of wonder, having no frame of reference to guide her. "Well, what happens now?"

Colette's face clouded with sadness. "That's what I asked him."

"And what did he say?"

"He won't marry me."

"He said that?" Juliette asked.

"Well, not in those exact words, but that's what he meant."

"But, Colette, do you want to marry *him*?" That was the more important question to Juliette's way of thinking.

"Yes, I suppose," she sighed. "But it's pointless. He will never marry me. He wants a traditional wife. He disapproves of my working in a bookshop. I could never give up the shop, and he knows that."

"You and the shop!" Juliette muttered in scorn. "Sell

the shop and marry Lucien. It's obvious that you're in love with him."

Colette's tears began. "That's the thing, Julie, I think I am in love with him, but he's not in love with me."

"But he should marry you. He's a gentleman and it's the right thing to do." Growing angry, Juliette wanted to throttle Lucien Sinclair. How dare that man take advantage of her sister in such a way and then not have the decency to offer for her!

"He won't," Colette sniffled. "He'd rather marry that Faith Bromleigh."

"He's afraid of you, Colette!"

Colette shook her head. "No, I don't think that's it. He's been with so many other women and I'm simply another one on his list. In any case, I would more than likely not make a good countess or an eventual marchioness. I don't think he loves me. If he did, none of the other things would matter all that much."

"Maybe he loves you and just doesn't know it yet?"

At Colette's dire look of exasperation, Juliette continued, "Men often have difficulty recognizing their own feelings. Perhaps Lucien is just slow to warm up."

"After what we just did this evening, I don't think warming up is his problem."

Juliette giggled helplessly at her sister's little innuendo. "What was it like?"

Colette had always been forthright and honest with her. They had shared confidences about everything since the time they could talk. But ever since she met Lucien Sinclair, Juliette had sensed a reticence, a preoccupation, about Colette. She was not her usual self. It was as if Lucien had placed a spell over her, changing her somehow. Falling in love must have something to do with it, Juliette surmised. It seemed that Colette felt her feelings would be tarnished in some way by sharing them with her.

Looking at her bright eyes and flushed cheeks, one would think she had a fever. Juliette knew instinctively that she would get no details on the subject of male and female sexual interaction from her.

"I can't talk about it." Colette's voice filled with anguish. "Oh, Juliette, what am I going to do? He doesn't want to marry me, and who will want to marry me the way I am now?"

"This is a problem." Juliette nodded sympathetically. "Yet I'm still a little surprised that it's your problem and not mine, quite frankly."

Colette laughed a little and gave a halfhearted smile. "Me, too."

"Well, I think you need to marry someone who may not know the difference or who would not really care that you've already been with someone else."

"There is no such man," Colette scoffed.

"Yes, there is."

"Who?"

"Jeffrey Eddington." Juliette's words had an instant impact on her sister.

"That's impossible!" cried Colette. "He would know right away if a woman was experienced or not, because he is so experienced. And a man like Jeffrey, just like any other man, would expect his wife to be a virgin."

Juliette shook her head. "Not Jeffrey."

"How would you know such a thing?"

"We talk about a lot of different things." Juliette truly adored Jeffrey and they had become rather good friends over the last few weeks. It was nice to have a male who was completely candid and honest with her, who spoke his opinion and did not sugarcoat everything for her like other men did. Jeffrey was not in love with her, nor she with him. Most men of her acquaintance panted after her, trying to persuade her to marry them. But not Jeffrey Eddington.

Juliette knew she was beautiful and that men fell in love with her easily, but she had no use for most of the men she met. They bored her. They treated her as if she were made of glass and the slightest upset might shatter her. They didn't understand her or believe that she had a brain and thoughts and opinions of her own. When she let loose her caustic wit, they did not know how to respond to her and fled. Now she had earned herself a reputation as a heartless flirt.

It was why she appreciated Jeffrey Eddington. He treated her like an equal, while always behaving as if she were a lady.

"You talk about such things with him?" Colette asked, her mouth gaping wide, scandalized at the idea.

Juliette gave her a meaningful glare. "I only *talked* with him about intimate activities between men and women. Unlike you, I have not engaged in those activities."

At Juliette's riposte, Colette could say little in her own defense. Deflated, she said, "You are right. Forgive me. I have no room to criticize you after my own behavior. Please tell me what Jeffrey said."

Feeling justified and somewhat superior to her older sister for the first time, Juliette explained, "He is of the opinion that a woman's past is her own business."

"That is surprising."

"Not once you get to know him better. It must have something to do with his mother and her affair with the Duke of Rathmore. Jeffrey has had an unconventional family life, and that has opened him up to a wider range of thinking. I think you should marry him."

"*Jeffrey Eddington?*" Colette's voice almost rose to a screech.

"Yes. I believe he has some tender feelings for you. And he'd be a wonderful husband."

"Tell me how he would feel knowing I have been intimate with his best friend?"

"Yes," Juliette acknowledged with a frown, "that might be a little tricky."

"And you are forgetting that I don't love him."

"Love has little to do with anything in many marriages, Colette. You know that as well as I do. And you have precious few options as it is. For all that he is an illegitimate rogue, Jeffrey is young and handsome, in addition to being wealthy, smart, humorous, and kind. You couldn't do much better than him."

Colette was silent for a few moments. "Do you really believe he has feelings for me?"

Nodding, Juliette suddenly realized what she had to do to save her sister. She needed Jeffrey's help, but she was not certain she would get it. Given the right opportunity and timing, this idea could work . . .

Chapter Eighteen

A Cottage by the Sea

Colette sat frozen in place, not believing what she heard, too stunned to move. The pretty cabbage rose–patterned wallpaper in the parlor blurred in front of her, forming a hazy sea of red before her eyes. Her heart hammered wildly and her hands shook in her lap. Staring numbly at her mother and Uncle Randall, she could barely make her mouth form the terrible words. "You sold it? You sold the shop? Our home, the building, everything?"

"We had no choice, Colette. Money had to be gotten from somewhere. You and your sister turned down half a dozen offers of marriage. Selling this building was the most logical solution." Uncle Randall's voice seemed hollow and surreal to her. The spider veins on his nose seemed more prominent and his bushy eyebrows narrowed over his cold eyes.

"Who bought it?" Colette could focus on nothing but the fact that she'd lost the bookshop. Her mother and her uncle had betrayed her. She had suddenly lost everything she had ever worked for. They had not even consulted her before ripping her heart out.

"That is the strange part," he explained, sitting back in the armchair near the mantle. "It was bought, for a higher price than we asked for I might add, under the strict condition that the buyer remain anonymous."

"What in heaven's name does that mean?" Colette cried in confusion.

Uncle Randall shrugged. "It's none of my business why, but someone wishes to keep the fact that he bought this building a secret. So for the time being there is no rush. The contract stipulated that the new owner was not interested in occupying the space anytime soon, so no changes are necessary right away. Ample notice will be given before they even require you to vacate the premises, which means that your mother can choose a new house with ease. Isn't that right, Genevieve?"

Swallowing against the wave of nausea that flooded her, Colette could not look at her mother. Genevieve had sold the shop without a word to her eldest daughter, knowing how much it would hurt her. After all Colette had done to support the family. The feeling of betrayal knifed her heart deeply. Her mother had given Uncle Randall her consent to sell, when she had promised Colette that she would not.

"*C'est pour le mieux.*" Her mother's weak voice wafted over from the velvet chaise where she reclined in her usual debilitated pose. "It is all for the best, Colette."

Ignoring her, Colette asked a question of her uncle. "Does that mean I can at least keep the shop open until I hear otherwise from the new owner?" If the new owner had no imminent plans to occupy the building, then perhaps Colette had a chance to try to buy or even rent the shop back. However remote such a possibility was.

"I suppose so, although why you are spending your time

there baffles me," her uncle said gruffly. "You need to put your energies into finding a husband, not managing a bookshop. You should be grateful to be rid of the place."

"Your uncle is right." Again her mother chimed in. "It is high time you were married and had a husband to look after you."

Colette still refused to look at her mother or even acknowledge that she had spoken. An anger, a white-hot rage, that she had never before experienced flooded every fiber of her being. Suddenly unable to speak for fear she would begin screaming, she stood without a backward glance to her mother or uncle and left the room, slamming the door behind her. She raced down the steps and out the front door.

Once out on the street, she was not sure where to go. She stood looking up at the small dark green building she had loved her entire life. The sight of the elegantly scripted letters that spelled out "Hamilton's Book Shoppe" above the front window brought the sting of tears to her eyes. She stood there for some minutes, staring until she could bear it no longer. But the pent-up anger and frustration within her compelled her to go somewhere. Anywhere but where she stood.

Turning hurriedly, she walked ahead blindly, blinking back tears, not seeing the ladies and gentlemen strolling by or hearing the large omnibuses loaded with passengers clambering along the street. The dusky sun lowered behind a cloud-strewn sky. Shops closed their doors for the night. Lamps were being lit in the windows of the houses. Colette kept walking, oblivious to where she was going. Her steps became more hurried as she went. She had to think what she would do next.

Mother sold the shop. Mother lied to me. Mother sold the shop. Mother lied to me. The words repeated over and over in her head, becoming louder and louder. She'd lost everything,

everything she had worked so hard for, all for a little cottage by the sea. Not only had she lost the bookshop, but she had made a complete fool of herself over Lucien Sinclair. Now she would be reduced to an old maid in a cottage by the sea, spending the rest of her life living with her mother. Tears ran down her face as she made her way along the street.

Her mother, her bitter mother who carelessly dropped the responsibility of raising her children on Colette's shoulders, who could not be bothered with the tedious task of paying the bills or managing the bookshop, suddenly felt she knew what was best for Colette and sold the shop. The woman who cried, fainted, and pleaded a headache at the slightest inconvenience, the woman who avoided financial matters, the woman who had not left the confines of her house in years and was content to let her daughters manage everything on their own— now she knew how to make a business decision without consulting Colette?

Her anger at her mother seethed and roiled within her.

In one calculated move, her mother had swept away the one part of Colette's life that she had made her own.

She ignored the strange looks she received from passersby, not caring what anyone thought of her. She simply needed to get away. Away from her mother. Away from her uncle. Her sisters. The shop. But where could she possibly go? It did not really matter as long as it was not home. For an instant she thought of walking to Devon House to see Lucien, and then just as quickly as she considered it, she dismissed the idea. She had not seen Lucien since their passionate night together, and her pride would not allow her to go crawling back to him. She would not go back to Lucien, however much she longed to be held in his arms.

She crossed the crowded street and continued up the avenue, just walking.

"Miss Hamilton! Miss Hamilton, over here!"

The fact that someone was shouting her name slowly registered in her angry fog-shrouded brain, and she turned to see who had called to her.

His black top hat perched jauntily on his head, Lord Jeffrey Eddington waved to her from inside his fine carriage, smiling broadly. Pulled by two ebony horses, the shiny black-lacquered carriage came to a stop before her. Jeffrey's charming grin disappeared and his handsome face clouded with concern as he drew closer. In an instant the door flew open and he bounded to the sidewalk beside her.

"Here now, Colette. What's happened? You look dreadfully upset."

She hastily wiped the tears from her eyes, suddenly aware that she had fled the house without a hat or gloves. She must be a sight! "I'm fine, thank you," she whispered.

His keen eyes missed nothing and he shook his head. "No, you're not fine at all. Come with me."

Before she knew it, Jeffrey had whisked her into his carriage and they were moving down the road. Not caring where they were going, she allowed Jeffrey to take over. She sat opposite him, and he stared at her, his longs legs stretched out in front of him.

"What's wrong?" His light blue eyes peered at her intently. "Has something happened to you or one of the girls? Juliette?"

She thought about saying nothing. She thought about telling him it was none of his business. She thought about making something up. Her pride almost kept her from revealing the truth, but she was suddenly too tired.

"My mother sold the bookshop." The words hurt as she said them aloud, but they still did not seem any more real.

"What do you mean?" His shocked expression conveyed more emotion than his words did.

Colette nodded sadly and her voice cracked as she explained. "She sold it without even consulting me. It no longer belongs to us, and she's moving us all to the seashore."

In a quick motion Jeffrey moved to sit beside her, wrapping his arm around her shoulder and pulling her against his broad chest before Colette could even make protest, had she wanted to. In actuality she was more than a little grateful for his comforting presence.

"That's terrible news. Surely there must be something we can do."

She shook her head. "It's already done. My mother and my uncle just told me about it this afternoon. I was so upset I simply ran out of the house. I didn't even know where I was going, but I had to get away, and that's when you found me. I've lost everything, Jeffrey. Everything."

He continued to hold her, his hand gently patting her back with long strokes. The swaying of the carriage rocked them back and forth in a gentle motion, and Colette relaxed against him. *How odd to be held by Jeffrey Eddington!* Yet the oddest part was that it was very nice. More than nice. There was a good, clean scent about him, and his arm felt strong and protective around her, giving her a wonderful sense of calm.

Usually cheerful and full of amusing stories and laughter, Jeffrey now seemed grave and serious. She had not witnessed this side of his personality before, and it surprised her.

"You haven't lost everything, Colette. You still have your sisters and your friends."

"Yes," she agreed wearily. "It's not the same, though. I love the bookshop. I was the one who worked in it every day. I was the one who took care of everything. I made it mine, and she had no right to sell it."

"Your mother is just looking out for you," he said soothingly, his expression kind. "That's what mothers do."

"She's looking out for herself," Colette couldn't help but snap, feeling small and petty as she uttered the words.

"Perhaps," he conceded. "But I'm sure she did not reach the decision to sell the shop easily. She had to know that doing so would hurt you. Did you talk to her about why she didn't tell you?"

"No," she admitted. "I was too angry to speak with her after I found out the shop had been sold."

"Maybe you should try."

"I suppose." Colette nodded weakly, before tears suddenly spilled down her cheeks. Overwhelmed by all that had happened and Jeffrey's unexpected kindness, she wailed, "What shall I do now?"

Without a word, he reached into his jacket pocket and retrieved a linen handkerchief. Handing it to her, he pressed a light kiss to her forehead. Almost stunned enough by the kiss to stop crying, Colette accepted his monogrammed handkerchief, which smelled pleasantly like Jeffrey, and wiped the tears from her face, sniffling.

"What do *you* wish to do, Colette?" he asked, his voice soft and full of concern.

She gave a half laugh, half sob, shaking her head. "I don't know anymore, and it doesn't matter anymore. I've lost everything I care about. Everything."

"This isn't just about the bookshop, is it?"

No, Colette's tears were not just about the bookshop. The tears were the ones she had not shed when her father died. They were the tears she had kept locked inside over the frustration of dealing with her self-absorbed and bitterly dramatic mother, of handling the responsibility of caring for her younger sisters, of the strain of knowing she

had to make a financially successful marriage, and over
the constant worry of managing the bookshop on her
own. She was crying about everything that had occurred
over the last few months. But most of all, the mortifying
pain of what had recently happened with Lucien hurt
more than anything else. Now, at the first sign that someone seemed to care about her enough to ask what she
wanted in her life, hot tears flowed down her cheeks.
Overwhelmed by emotions too numerous to name, she
simply told Jeffrey the truth.

"It's about losing the bookshop after working day and
night to make it a success. It's about my mother thinking
only of herself. It's about my uncle pressuring me to
marry."

"I see." Again Jeffrey was surprisingly quiet. For a man
who was usually quick with a wicked retort or a joking response, he was oddly reticent to say anything to her.

"I know I ought to be married by now, but I don't wish
to have a husband look at me merely as someone he can
order about."

"Has your uncle found someone suitable for you?" He
eyed her carefully.

"Not yet. He's still looking, although I'm sure he de-
spairs of anyone marrying me or Juliette."

"I understand his concern for Juliette. Her fierce in-
dependence and sharp tongue would scare off even the
heartiest male. But you, on the other hand, you should
have had a multitude of offers by now from suitable gentlemen."

"Not as many as you would think."

"That's because your uncle is an idiot."

She could not help the laugh that escaped her. Leave
it to Jeffrey to make her laugh. She dried her tears, then
clutched his handkerchief tightly in her palm. Colette
settled into the feel of Jeffrey's arm around her. How

heavenly it would be to have someone to hold her like this whenever she was upset or worried. What a luxury that would be!

If only that someone could be Lucien Sinclair.

When Lucien had held her, she felt as if nothing bad could ever happen to her. Being in his arms had been absolute heaven. But he did not want to be with her. He had made that abundantly clear on that dreadful night. Lucien would marry a proper, traditional woman who did not enjoy running a business. He wanted a woman whose virtue was not so easily given away. A woman who would not be overcome by passion, as she was.

She cringed at the memory of the few words they had exchanged after an awkwardly tense silence in the carriage the night he took her home. Now days had passed since she had seen or heard from him.

The conversation that she had with Juliette flashed through her mind. Juliette believed Colette should marry Jeffrey Eddington. Could that even be a possibility when her heart longed only for Lucien Sinclair?

Jeffrey was a good man. Undoubtedly he would be a kind husband and would always treat her well. Handsome, witty, and fun, he also cared for her and her family. Marrying him would not be the worst decision she could make in her life. She had never been the type of woman driven by a desire to marry into an elevated social position. Even though she sensed that deep down it bothered Jeffrey, and some women would not even consider marrying him because of it, the facts of his illegitimate birth meant nothing to her.

But what would Jeffrey think of her if he knew the truth of what she had done with Lucien? For all that Juliette described him as understanding and forgiving of women's indiscretions, Colette did not believe he would easily overlook such an intimate past between his best friend and his wife.

Jeffrey was being so sympathetic and comforting that for an impulsive moment she considered telling him about what happened with Lucien. Although she would love to hear his thoughts on the matter, she could not bring herself to say the words aloud. What she had done with Lucien was too humiliating. Too ruinous. And Jeffrey did not need to be burdened by such information about his closest friend.

While she sat with this wonderful man's arms around her, she longed for the arms of another man. She felt dreadful.

"Jeffrey?"

"Yes?"

"I'm sorry . . . I . . ." she stammered awkwardly. "I . . . Forgive me. You have been very sweet to me, and here I am burdening you with all of my problems. You must have been on your way somewhere this evening, before you saw me running down the street like a complete madwoman. You were very kind to stop and help me, but I've taken up enough of your time. Could you please take me home now?"

Jeffrey nodded and gave instructions to his driver to go to Hamilton's. He then turned to her, demanding her attention with a glance. "I didn't stop to help you simply to be kind, but because I care about you very much, Colette. You are a special woman. I admire all that you have done with the bookshop and I am terribly saddened to see you lose it. I am not giving up hope that there still is not something we can do to rectify the situation."

"Thank you, Jeffrey."

"Does Juliette know about the shop being sold?"

"I suppose she does by now, and she is probably out of her mind with worry, wondering where I am."

"Yes, I'm sure she is worried. However, before we get you home, I wish to say something to you."

Sensing a seriousness in him, she nodded to let him know he had her full attention.

"I want you to know that you can count on me for anything you need. You can come to me any time of day or night and I will help you."

When Colette looked at him he was staring at her with a look on his face that puzzled her. He really was a handsome man. Oh, not handsome in the same way Lucien was. Lucien was more—oh, Lucien was just Lucien.

At Jeffrey's gallant offer of assistance she could only murmur once again, "I will. Thank you."

He was very close to her and he used that to his advantage as he leaned even closer to place a kiss her lips. It was a sweet kiss, gentle and tender. His lips felt warm and inviting. If Lucien had not passionately and thoroughly kissed her a number of times already, Colette might have enjoyed this lovely little kiss from Jeffrey. Slowly he pulled away from her. She gazed at him in the dim light of the carriage.

"I'm sorry," he said, easing his head back against the seat. "I shouldn't have done that."

"Why do men insist on apologizing after they kiss me?" she blurted out before she could stop herself.

He turned, eyeing her curiously, the glimmer of a smile on his mouth. "Well, well, well. Just how many men have you kissed, Colette?"

Nervous laughter bubbled from her and she shook her head. "Not that many."

The carriage came to an abrupt halt, jostling the two of them.

With his arm still around her, Jeffrey asked softly, "Would one of those men happen to be Lucien Sinclair?"

Feeling her cheeks warm in mortification at his question, Colette merely nodded and whispered a faint, "Yes."

"I thought that might be the case. It seems you are quite the irresistible woman."

She gave an inelegant, helpless shrug.

Suddenly Jeffrey cupped her face in his hands and kissed her again, this time a more aggressive kiss, a more demanding kiss. His mouth covered hers heatedly, his arm pulling her tighter against his chest. Inexplicably, she kissed him back, her hands reaching around his neck. They clung to each other, their lips locked together. Just as she realized how breathless and dizzy she felt, he released her. Stunned by the impact of his kiss, she stared helplessly at him. Although his kiss was wonderful, she knew that something was lacking. The special connection she shared with Lucien had made their kisses more powerful, more intense, and so overwhelming. She forced herself to suppress the feeling that she had somehow betrayed Lucien by kissing Jeffrey.

Lucien does not care whom I kiss, because Lucien does not want me.

Giving her a crooked smile, he uttered in a low voice, "And I'm not apologizing for that one."

Completely sympathetic now to all the women who had ever swooned at Jeffrey Eddington's feet, she returned his smile. "I don't wish for you to."

He chuckled deep at her remark. Removing his arm from around her, he sat up straighter. "You should go back inside now and talk things out with your mother."

"Thank you, Jeffrey." She reached for his hand and squeezed it affectionately. "For everything."

"You are very welcome. I may have to leave for France in a few weeks, but please remember that I am always here for you if you need me, Colette. You simply have to send word to me."

Thinking it a somewhat odd statement for him to

make—although very sweet—she could think of nothing to say but, "I will."

With that he escorted her out of the carriage, helping her to the ground. He gave a little wave to her as he climbed back inside. Before Colette entered the shop, she turned back toward him with a heavy heart and watched his carriage drive away.

Chapter Nineteen

Mama Mia

Lucien ascended the wide curving staircase of Devon House and headed to his father's suite to read to him. He had returned home earlier than he had expected and thought he would use the time to begin their reading session. Just as he approached his father's room, he heard the murmur of a soft female voice. Immediately ruling out the voice as Nurse Fiona, for she possessed a rather gravelly voice and this one was definitely pleasant, he wondered who had come to visit his father. The realization dawned on him before he actually saw her.

His heart pounding like thunder in his chest, Lucien stared at Colette Hamilton. She sat before the fire with his father, her head bent over the copy of *David Copperfield*. Reading aloud softly, her dulcet voice filled the room. In a lovely day gown of deep rose, with a matching jacket and her lustrous sable hair swept artfully off her neck, revealing smooth white skin, she looked incredibly beautiful. He fought a crazy impulse to kiss the back of her elegant neck.

What was she doing there? Why was she reading with his father, as if it were the most natural thing in the world for her to be doing? How could she sit there and act as if nothing had happened between them just days ago in this very house? In his own bed, for Christ's sake!

Lucien had not slept since the night of their earth-shattering encounter. He had not decided if his sleep-lessness was caused by his blatant stupidity in having bedded her or by the haunting memories of the exqui-site passion they had shared together. In truth the deci-sion hardly mattered. He had made a terrible mistake with her and he did not know how to correct it.

Yes, he ought to marry her. She deserved that much respect from him. She had been an innocent and he had pressed his advantage with her, no matter how willing and enticing she had acted that evening. He had told her to leave and yet she had only pushed him further beyond his limits of self-control by willingly agreeing to continue.

Just what was she doing visiting his house unchaper-oned that afternoon anyway? This was what came from women being independent and was exactly why he be-lieved women should not be running their own business. It was simply wrong. There was no reason for her to be traipsing around town, visiting men in their homes! A beauty like Colette could wreak havoc upon the city. She was a walking temptation.

He still could not believe that it had even happened.

She had been astonishingly uninhibited and eager, kiss-ing him passionately and relishing every caress. She had loved it just as much as he had, and her heartfelt words haunted him. "*I don't regret it, not one minute of it. It was heavenly. And the most thrilling and most wonderful, and the most amazing . . ."* And he had humiliated her afterward.

He let her believe that she meant nothing to him.

Letting her believe the worst of him was easier than facing the truth himself. In all honesty, being with Colette had been like nothing else in his life.

And now she hated him. Her icy silence in the carriage when he took her home that night had been cold and final and told him in no uncertain terms what she thought of him.

The ironic part was his reputation as a rake. He had earned such status a few years ago when he had quickly and effortlessly taken any woman who glanced at him in encouragement. His affairs had been meaningless and heartless, as he desperately struggled to satisfy the aching void within him to forget his disastrous relationship with the beautiful Lady Virginia Warren.

He conceded that he had a very public but brief affair with a famous opera singer, a fling with a lovely and talented actress, a few weekends in the country with a sweet tavern wench, and a rather long stint with a widowed duchess. And for the most part that was it. Which in his mind did not signify him as a rake, for he never seduced innocents. But after his well-known break with Virginia Warren the word spread, apparently from the young widow, who was not happy when he ended their affair, that Lucien Sinclair, the Earl of Waverly, had a way with women. Because his close friend was Lord Jeffrey Eddington, and Jeffrey *did* dally with scores of women, and being that society loved to suspect the worst of people, they readily believed that Lucien was more of a scoundrel than he actually was. Granted, his penchant for enjoying himself did nothing to quell the rumors either.

All had been done in an effort to rid his memory of Virginia Warren.

Now there was a woman he never should have gotten involved with. Virginia spelled trouble right from the start, but he had been blinded by her sultry beauty and his own ardor.

And he would not let that happen to him again. Which was why he could not let down his guard with Colette. Especially the modern, forward-thinking, independent, and beautiful Colette. If someone like Virginia could devastate him so thoroughly, then Colette Hamilton would surely destroy him for good.

Now debating whether or not to let his presence be known, he observed the scene for a while longer, oddly enjoying Colette sitting with his father. Perhaps she sensed him, but she suddenly glanced toward the doorway and stumbled over the words on the page, losing her place. His father turned toward him and offered a lopsided half-smile.

"Good afternoon," Lucien said.

Colette nodded at him and closed the book, directing her gaze toward her father. "I would so love to stay and continue reading with you, Lord Stancliff, but I should be going now, for it is later than I realized. I shall return again next week."

Simon held out his hand to her and Colette took his gnarled hand in hers, smiling at him. Touched by the affection between them, Lucien muttered, "I did not mean to intrude. You may continue reading if you wish, Miss Hamilton."

Without meeting his eyes, Colette rose from the chair and gathered her things. "I'm sorry, but I really must be going home now."

She brushed by him as she passed through the doorway. Lucien stood immobile for a moment, gave an apologetic glance to his father, and then hurried after her. Colette had continued walking at a brisk pace along the corridor but he managed to catch up with her at the top of the staircase. Reaching out, he touched his hand to her shoulder. She paused, but still did not look at him.

"What are you doing here?" he asked softly.

Colette flinched away from him, shrugging her shoulder to avoid contact with his hand. Taking a step down the stairs, she finally looked back up at him. "I was not expecting you to be home, but I was here doing the job I agreed to do."

What was she talking about? *What job?* His perplexed look annoyed her.

"Your library, remember?" she prompted him, her tempting mouth frowning.

He shook his head in blank puzzlement.

"I was working in your library this afternoon, and I thought I would visit with your father before I left since I promised him that I would the last time . . ."

Stunned, Lucien stared at her in mute surprise. He had completely forgotten about his hasty invitation to help select books. Given what they had shared later that night, he would have expected her to disregard their earlier agreement about his library. Besides, he did not think he could bear the temptation of having her in his house. "After what happened between us, why would you do such a thing?"

"Why?" she echoed in affronted outrage.

For a moment he thought she might slap him, but then she squared her petite shoulders and held up her chin proudly. God, she was gloriously beautiful. Standing there on the staircase, poised to defend herself, she was a woman unlike any he had ever known. The overwhelming desire to pull her into his arms and kiss her once again washed over him in staggering waves. The memory of being buried deep within her and the sound of her voice crying out his name called to every nerve in his being. He clenched his hands tightly to keep himself from grabbing her and doing just that.

"Contrary to what you believe about women," Colette began, her voice laced with passion, "I gave you my word that I would help with the library, and I committed to read to your father. What kind of businesswoman would I be if I let my emotions guide me? Since you seem incapable of answering, I shall answer for you, Lord Waverly. If I allowed myself to cry and wail anytime my feelings were hurt by a man, I would not remain in business very long. However, no matter how fervently I wished never to see you or set foot in this house again, I did not let my emotions overrule my business decision."

Impressed by her argument more than he wanted to admit, he remained silent as she stared at him, her incredible blue eyes flashing with anger.

"With Granger's consent this afternoon, I have arranged for the library furniture to be delivered next week, and I shall return in a day or two to oversee the stocking of the shelves with the first book delivery. Good day, Lord Waverly." She turned with an imperious toss of her silky curls and began to descend the stairs.

Lucien stood motionless, watching her go; fighting the urge to reach out and grab her, to stop her from leaving by carrying her back up to his bed and making love to her for days and days.

"Colette, wait, please," he called after her.

She was midway down the long winding marble staircase when Granger hastened to answer the doorbell. Colette had just reached the last step as Lucien caught up with her and Granger opened the front door.

"Colette," he began again. "Just give me a moment. I'm sorry—"

Lucien stopped abruptly at the sight before him, his mouth frozen in mid-sentence.

Lenora Sinclair stood in the doorway. Lucien recognized her instantly, for his mother had barely aged in fifteen years. As beautiful as ever but smaller than he remembered, she entered the house that had been her home for the first eleven years of her marriage to Simon Sinclair.

It had been a decade and a half since the venerable Devon House butler had opened the door for Lenora Sinclair, the Marchioness of Stancliff. Unruffled by this dramatic turn of family events, Granger calmly waved his arm to allow her entrance and closed the front door as if serving his long-absent mistress were an everyday occurrence.

"Hello, Granger," Lenora Sinclair said, with an unsure smile, staring up at the tall, craggy-faced butler whom she had known since before Lucien was born. "I hope you have been well."

"Welcome, my lady. It's wonderful to see you again," he murmured in his usual dignified tone. "Shall I bring you some tea? No cream, with two sugars?"

"Oh, you remembered . . . How thoughtful! Thank you, Granger, that would be lovely." As Granger made a dignified exit and left them standing in the marble entrance hall, Lenora turned to her son. Her eyes softened and she uttered faintly, "Hello, Lucien."

Her anxious expression and tentative smile made her seem fragile, not at all the forceful whirlwind of stylish glamour and sparkling brightness he remembered from his childhood. She stood about as high as his chest, the dark hair piled upon her head and hidden by a frivolous bonnet adorned with a peacock feather. A gown of deep blue draped over her still slender form. Her face had grown fine lines, but the porcelain creaminess of her skin had not faded over the years. Lucien figured his mother had to be closer to fifty than forty by now. Her upturned nose and wide emerald-hued eyes, the same shade as

Lucien's, had always been Lenora's most praised features, and they had held her in good stead over the years. She was still a very attractive woman.

"Hello, Mother."

How odd to say those words after so many years. Hello, Mother. *Mother.* He had imagined her return thousands of times when he was a young boy. His favorite fantasy consisted of his waking one morning to find his mother sitting calmly beside his father at the breakfast table as if she had never left, asking brightly, "What would you like to do today, my darling boy? Shall we go riding together? Or go on a picnic?" The very ordinariness of that domestic scene had been such a perfect antidote to the empty chaos his life had become when she left. Of the various scenarios of his mother's grand return he had alternately prayed for and wished for over the years, none of them ever involved him as a grown man standing awkwardly with her in the elegant hall of Devon House.

He had absolutely no idea what to say to her. She was his mother, but he did not know the woman in front of him.

"I was not expecting you today," he said woodenly, for lack of anything better to say.

"I'm sorry for calling unannounced like this. I know we planned for next week, but I . . . I just couldn't stay away any longer."

"Yes, fifteen years is a long time to stay away from your husband and son." The sarcastic remark escaped his lips before he could stop himself. Honestly, what was her impatience to see them after all those years? She couldn't wait a few more days to arrive at the time he had agreed to meet her? When he could have been more prepared to see her?

His mother stared pleadingly at him while an awkward silence descended upon them.

A sudden poke in his ribs jarred him back to his

senses. He had completely forgotten about Colette. She stood quietly beside him observing the entire Sinclair family drama unfold. Colette's face, now devoid of her earlier anger, possessed a look of surprised interest and even concern. Lucien's infamous mother had finally come home. No doubt all of London society would hear of the news by sundown.

"Excuse my rudeness," Lucien said, noticing the curious looks between the two women. "Mother, may I present Miss Colette Hamilton, a very good friend of mine. Colette, this is my mother, Lenora Sinclair, the Marchioness of Stancliff."

"I am very happy to meet you, Lady Stancliff," Colette said with a polite smile.

His mother gave an eager nod, seemingly relieved to hear a kind word. "And I am pleased to meet you, too."

Another awkward pause lengthened between the three of them. Lucien could not help but note the very odd trio they made: himself and the two women who ironically tortured his thoughts.

"Lucien, why don't you escort your mother to the parlor now where you can sit comfortably and Granger can serve tea?" Colette proposed softly.

More grateful for Colette's calming presence and sensible attitude than he realized, Lucien instantly agreed to her suggestion. "Yes, let's do that, shall we?"

Colette shook her head and stepped away from him, her motive clear. "I really should be going. It was lovely meeting you, Lady Stancliff."

He reached out and took her hand in his. Wrapping his fingers around hers, he squeezed her hand in appreciation, his eyes lingering on her. "Thank you, Colette." To his surprise, she squeezed his hand back before pulling away from him.

"I'll see myself out," she said as she walked to the massive front door. As always, her graceful movements mesmerized him. He watched the door close softly behind her.

"She seems to be quite a lovely young lady." His mother's voice interrupted his errant thoughts, which had magnetically followed Colette from the house.

"Yes, she is," he agreed. "Shall we?" Without another word she followed him to the front parlor. He wondered idly if it felt strange for her to be back inside the house which was once her home. He certainly knew it felt strange for him to have her here.

She seated herself on a burgundy velvet divan, nervously arranging her trailing peacock blue skirts flecked with golden thread. Choosing a high-backed brown leather chair across from her, Lucien waited patiently for her to explain herself.

"Is Miss Hamilton a close friend of yours?"

"I don't wish to discuss her with you."

"Fair enough." She smiled anxiously at him, her hands twisting the gold-colored gloves in her lap. "My, but you've grown so much, Lucien. You've become a handsome man. You've definitely got the look of your father about you."

He merely nodded.

Her voice became soft. "You're not going to make this easy for me, are you?"

"Make what easy for you, Mother?"

"My return. The fact that I wish to see you again and try to explain some things to you, now that you are old enough to understand—"

He interrupted her more heatedly than he wished to. "Understand what? Why you left us? Why you abandoned your ten-year-old son? No, I don't understand, but maybe you can understand why I don't wish to make this little tea party easy for you, because it sure as hell isn't easy for me."

After a pause, she looked back up at him. "Yes, you

have every right to be angry with me. You were so young when I left, and couldn't possibly understand my reasons at the time, but I am terribly sorry for what happened. You have no idea what a painful decision leaving was for me to make. And I know that you must have suffered dreadfully, Lucien. I know because I suffered, too. I lost all those years with my little boy, just as you lost them with me. I realize nothing can make up for the choices I made or replace the years we've lost together. I do wish for you to know that I missed you every minute and thought about you and worried about you. And that—"

Again Lucien interrupted her. "So worried about me that you never once wrote me a letter or a note in all this time? Do you know what that would have meant to me?"

"Yes, I . . . It's just that . . . You see . . ." she stammered awkwardly.

Granger chose that moment to enter the parlor with the tea. As the butler silently busied himself preparing their refreshment, Lucien seethed with years of hurt and anger at his mother. How dare she waltz back into his life and expect him to make it easy for her! Did she think he could suddenly forgive her, just like that? Welcome her home with open arms?

Lenora's hands shook as she picked up the teacup, spilling tea down the front of her gown. She gasped and dropped the cup on the carpet. Granger fussed over her, helping to clean up the mess, as the black liquid seeped into her peacock blue dress.

"I should go," she murmured hastily, rising to her feet. "Perhaps you are right. I should not have come."

"Sit down, Mother, and tell me why you are here." Lucien's tone of voice brooked no argument.

Slowly sinking back to the divan, his mother stared at him. After an uneasy glance between the two of them, Granger wisely left the parlor, closing the door behind him.

"You've written me three times in the past month, and you came here unexpectedly today because apparently you could not wait another minute to see us. After over fifteen years, what could be so damn important, Mother?"

She breathed deeply and looked as if she might cry, which Lucien fervently hoped she would not. How much was he to bear?

"There is no excuse for what I've done. None at all, so I will not try to make one. I only wanted to see you again, and to say that I am sorry, Lucien. I bitterly regret leaving you and your father. I owe you both at least that small offering. That is all."

"Where have you been?" He had heard all the rumors, of course. Everyone had. Yet he wanted to hear the truth from her.

"In Europe. Italy mostly. I only returned to England last month. That was when I first wrote to you."

"Have you always been with him?"

She had the decency to look embarrassed at his reference to the man she ran away with. "Yes, for many years."

"And now?"

"Now he is dead. And I am alone. Although he left me a very wealthy woman."

"Father was not wealthy enough for you?"

"Money was never the issue, Lucien . . ."

"Then what issue was strong enough to lure you away from your husband and child?"

A pained expression crossed her face. "That is between your father and me." She paused. "Which I can now deduce that he never explained to you."

"I didn't need Father to explain to me. I didn't need anyone to explain to me when every socially aware person in London knew what happened. You ran off with Count Acciani, breaking Father's heart—"

"Breaking your father's heart?" She rose abruptly to

her feet, her face full of sorrow. "Breaking your father's heart?" she echoed in disbelief. "There are two sides to every story, Lucien, and you have only ever heard your father's side. He left me no choice. He forced me to go with Antonio!" She paused and asked breathlessly, "Is he still in his room?"

Lucien stood, and put out a hand in an attempt to calm her. "As I informed you in my letter, Father is not well. You cannot just barge in on him without warning. He has no idea you've returned. An upset like this would—"

Interrupting him again, her voice rising in pitch as she cried, "I don't care! He is *still* my husband and I have a right to see him. He cannot keep me away this time. I came all this way to see Simon and I will see him!" She pushed his arm away and rushed from the parlor, running along the hallway. Stunned by his mother's outburst, he followed her up the stairs and down the corridor to his father's room.

With Lucien close behind, Lenora flung open the heavy doors intent on her mission to confront her husband. She suddenly halted, stopping in her tracks. Her eyes widened. She stared in shock at the drastically changed sight of a wizened Simon Sinclair sitting hunched before the fire with a shawl around his shoulders.

"Oh, Simon," Lenora whispered, her expression one of utter devastation. Tears welled in her eyes. "I had no idea . . ."

Startled by the commotion, Simon glanced up, his expression one of confusion. If he was surprised at his wayward wife's sudden presence in his bedroom, he did not show it. They both simply gazed at each other in silence, until tears began to trickle down his gaunt cheeks. Slowly and with great care, he stretched out his good arm to her. With a little gasp, Lenora fairly flew across the room to him, sinking to the floor at his feet. She buried her head in his lap. Simon's hand stroked her hair.

Shocked by the scene in front of him, Lucien was speechless. Somewhere in the far reaches of his mind, he realized his mother was right. Whatever happened to cause her to leave her husband all those years ago was between the two of them, and only they understood why. Obviously his father forgave more easily than Lucien, and for his part, he did not know if he could ever forgive his mother. Feeling as if he were intruding, he softly closed the doors to his father's suite, allowing them some privacy.

For some time Lucien stood motionless outside his father's room, unable to move.

Chapter Twenty

What Are
Friends For?

"Come now, Jeffrey, please tell me you'll do it," Juliette cajoled with her most winning smile as she stood behind the counter of the bookshop. It was rather late in the afternoon and the bookshop was devoid of people beyond the two of them.

"I don't know if such a scheme will work." Jeffrey smiled back at her even though he disagreed with her plan.

"Of course it will work!" she exclaimed in defense. A plan of her creation would not fail. "It's obvious. Don't you see they just need to be nudged in the right direction?"

"And you think jealousy is a tactic that will work on Lucien Sinclair?"

She arched an elegant brow at him and gave him a knowing look. "Jealousy works on every man, Jeffrey, no matter what his status or rank. Haven't you learned that by now?"

He gave a low whistle. "You are a dangerous woman, Juliette Hamilton." He shook his head in amazement, a helpless smile on his handsome face.

Ignoring his comment, she continued, "If Lucien thinks that you are seriously pursuing Colette, he will certainly want her enough to realize Faith Bromleigh is the most ridiculous choice for his bride."

"How do you know I don't seriously want to pursue Colette myself?" he challenged her.

Juliette scoffed at him with a laugh. "I would tell you that you are wasting your time. Colette is head over heels in love with Lucien Sinclair."

"I don't think she's quite as far gone as you claim," he said, his eyes not meeting her gaze. "She's not immune to my charm, you know."

Juliette observed him carefully. "No one is immune to your charm, darling Jeffrey. I cannot deny that. Except of course for myself, that is. I have the power to resist you, just as I can easily resist most of the male population."

He rested his chin on his hand, flashing her a devastating smile. "Now why is that, Juliette?"

"For the reason that all of the men I've met border on complete stupidity, utter dullness, or total lecherousness. I've been unimpressed with them." She amended agreeably, "Present company excepted."

"Oh, I am honored to make your short list," he gestured gallantly. "So then explain why you can resist me, since I am neither stupid or dull? Although I must admit to having some lecherous tendencies." He gave her a sly wink.

Juliette laughed lightly at him. "Because, Jeffrey, you are not the type of man I wish to marry."

"And what type would that be?"

"I'm not entirely sure," Juliette answered thoughtfully. "Someone different and unconventional. Perhaps even dangerous. When I meet him, I'll just know he's the one."

"You are dreaming of a romantic highwayman, Juliette." He paused before adding, "I hope you find who you are looking for."

Juliette was surprised with his sincere tone. Perhaps she did have the makings of a highwayman in her mind. "Well, thank you, but we're not talking about me. This is about Colette."

"And your plan is for me to court your sister to make my best friend jealous?"

"Yes."

"Are you sure he's in love with her?"

She nodded with conviction. "Of course he is. Who wouldn't be in love with her? But he's afraid of her and that's why he'd rather have the insipid Faith Bromleigh, because she's safe. He will be doomed to a life of utter dreariness if he marries her! Am I wrong?"

Jeffrey shook his head. "No. I've tried to talk him out of this alliance with Faith Bromleigh from the beginning, but he's determined to go through with it. Lucien wants to marry while his father is still alive to see it happen, and he wants a wife who won't upset his tea cart."

"That's exactly what he doesn't need and why it's up to us to wake him up before it's too late. If he thinks there is a serious contender for Colette's hand, he might realize what he stands to lose."

"How do you know Colette is in love with him?"

"A sister knows these things, so believe me when I say that she's besotted with him."

"Shouldn't we let Colette in on this little plan of yours?"

"Heavens no! If she knew, she'd have no part in it! She must not suspect you are pretending with her, Jeffrey. Neither of them must ever suspect what we're doing."

"I love that this is now 'our' doing. How are you so sure what 'we're' doing will work?"

"I just know." Juliette watched Jeffrey's face closely as

he considered her words. She needed Jeffrey's help. Her plan would not work without him.

"I have a feeling I may regret this, but I'll do it."

She leaned across the counter and placed a soft kiss on his cheek. "You are a true friend."

"That's what I'm afraid of," he uttered, his smile rueful. "I just hope this crazy scheme of *ours* doesn't come back to haunt *me*. What about your uncle?"

"He has lightened up on us somewhat since selling the shop."

"So he's given up on you and your sister snaring rich husbands, has he?"

"For now, anyway." Juliette shrugged carelessly. "At least until he needs more money."

"Well, I can only help you for a little while. I'll be leaving for France before the summer is over."

Curiosity got the best of her. "Why are you going to France? Have you a secret love hidden there?"

"Yes, more than one actually." His rakish grin disappeared and he added, "I have some important business to attend to."

Juliette's light laughter bubbled forth at his explanation. "Business? What kind of business? Following a pretty actress or a young widow to Paris is not business, Jeffrey."

He gave her a deep look. "It's business and it is very private."

She tried to imagine Jeffrey working at something important and could not quite do it. He enjoyed pleasure too much to take anything seriously. She highly suspected there was a woman involved. "You are not going to tell me, are you?"

"No, I'm not."

"Very well then, Mr. Mysterious. You may keep your little secrets to yourself. Just remember to uphold your part of the bargain."

The door to the upstairs opened and Colette entered the shop. After exchanging a complicit glance, Juliette and Jeffrey immediately stood up straighter and guiltily assumed an air of feigned innocence.

"Good afternoon, Colette." Jeffrey grinned at her broadly.

"Good afternoon," she greeted them as she came closer. Juliette noted an enigmatic look on her sister's face. Luckily Colette seemed too distracted to notice their sudden jump in posture and awkward expressions.

Colette announced, "You'll never guess whom I just met."

"Who?" Juliette and Jeffrey asked in unison.

Unable to keep the news to herself, Colette did not encourage them to name any possible contenders. She blurted out, "Lucien Sinclair's mother!"

"You're jesting!" Juliette cried. Of course she, like everyone else, had heard the scandalous stories of Lenora Sinclair, but had believed that the woman lived on the continent somewhere with her lover, the count of something or other.

Jeffrey responded more calmly than one would expect at hearing the news of his best friend's mother. "I was aware that she had been in contact with Lucien recently, but I did not know she had arrived so soon."

Colette began, "She surprised him and simply showed up unannounced at his door as I was about to leave. I was introduced to her just a short while ago."

"Why were you at Devon House?" Jeffrey asked. Juliette did not miss how his blue eyes narrowed at the idea of Colette at Lucien's house.

"I was reading to Lucien's father and working in their library." There was a defensive tone to Colette's words that surprised Juliette. Her sister's sensitivity to any mention of her and Lucien Sinclair was quite obvious.

"What was she like? Lucien's mother, that is?" Juliette asked.

"She is beautiful, and I could definitely see a resemblance between them. I only stayed a short time because it was very tense between them. Lucien did not seem happy to see her."

"Do you blame him?" Jeffrey questioned.

"Not in the least," Colette responded. Her fine brows narrowed. "I actually felt sad for the two of them."

"I wonder what caused her to return after all this time," Juliette ruminated aloud. "Do you have any idea why she came back?"

Colette shook her head. "No, nor am I sure how Lord Stancliff will react to seeing her. If Lucien was not overjoyed, I doubt his father will be happy when he sees her. He's so frail, I worry about him." Colette paused and glanced between Jeffrey and Juliette, suddenly sensing something between them. "And what have you two been up to while I was gone this afternoon?"

"Oh, the usual," Juliette answered carelessly. "We've been giving away kisses to anyone who buys a book. I kissed the male costumers and Jeffrey kissed the females. You wouldn't believe how many books we've sold!"

Jeffrey held up his hands in mock seriousness. "But I only kissed the pretty ones, I swear."

Colette shook her head in exasperation. "I don't know what to do with the pair of you."

"Well, I have no idea what you should do with your rapscallion of a sister," Jeffrey began good-naturedly ribbing Juliette, "but I, on the other hand, am another matter altogether. I propose you join me at the theater tomorrow evening."

Colette's startled expression at Jeffrey's invitation turned to one of seriousness as she considered his request. She glanced briefly at Juliette and then said, "Yes, Jeffrey, I would love to go with you."

"Wonderful." A warm smile spread across his face. "I shall come by with my carriage to pick you up then, around seven."

"Thank you."

Looking for all the world like the cat that ate the canary, Juliette grinned at her sister.

Chapter Twenty-One

Still Waters
Run Deep

Lucien stifled another yawn as Lord Bromleigh droned on about the type of trees he had recently planted on his estate in Sussex. Lord Bromleigh had told this exact same story two nights ago, and Lucien still could not fathom what the man was talking about. He had been invited to dine with the Bromleighs for the second time that week and he was having difficulty keeping his eyes open. Good Lord, but the man was an utter bore.

Faith nodded eagerly as her father continued his dull discourse on the advantages and disadvantages of maples and oaks. "Yes, Papa. The trees will be lovely and I shall greatly enjoy the shade they will provide."

Lucien's intended bride was seated across from him and had worn another dull and serious gown of an inde-terminate shade of taupe. The odd thought that once they were married he might suggest that she visit a more flattering dressmaker crossed his mind. She might actually be pretty in a light shade of blue or pink, to bring out some color in her face.

But then again, it did not really matter what Faith looked like.

What mattered most now was banishing Colette Hamilton from his mind. He had not seen her since his mother returned to Devon House, but she continued to haunt his thoughts every waking moment. Lucien had no need to be haunted by a woman. He had had quite enough of that in his life, thank you. The sooner he married Faith Bromleigh, the better off he would be. A peaceful coexistence would suit him best. He could not bear a tumultuous marriage like his parents had.

Nor could he explain the strange reconnection the pair was experiencing now.

The change in his father since his mother's return had astounded Lucien. It seemed as though the man suddenly became ten years younger. His speech had improved dramatically and he was attempting to walk. In spite of Lucien's fears, Lenora's return seemed to have had a healing influence on Simon. Now his mother and father were inseparable, closeted in his room for hours at a time, talking and crying. Lucien supposed they had a great deal to discuss, but unlike his father, he was not so ready to forgive his mother.

"Lord Waverly?"

Lucien was startled to discover that Lord Bromleigh had addressed him directly.

"Yes?"

He eyed Lucien sharply. "I asked if you would like to escort my daughter for a short walk in the garden?"

Ignoring the knot forming in the pit of his stomach, Lucien nodded at Lord Bromleigh's question, and turned to Faith, whose face had turned a remarkable shade of pink. "Yes, I would love some fresh air, wouldn't you, Lady Faith?"

With her eyes downcast, she merely lowered her head in acquiescence. Lucien dutifully escorted Faith Bromleigh from the formal dining room and out the French doors to the patio and garden beyond.

The awkward silence grew as they walked the neat flagstone path; only the sounds of their shoes on the stone echoed around their ears. Lost in his own thoughts, Lucien was content to walk in wordlessness for as long as he could.

"Did you enjoy supper, Lord Waverly?" Faith asked.

Surprised by her attempt at conversation, he answered, "Yes. It was delicious."

They continued walking slowly.

"My father said you wish to marry me."

Now completely stunned by her, Lucien stood still and stared at the plain woman beside him. "Yes. Your father spoke the truth."

"May I ask you a frank question?"

"Of course." Wondering what the timid miss would ask him, he felt somewhat bemused by her. For the first time since he met her, she looked directly into his eyes, and he was taken aback by the intensity he saw within the pale blue depths.

"Why?" she asked.

"Why what?"

"*Why* do you wish to marry me?"

"Why do I wish to marry you?" he questioned her in return.

Faith gave him a look that bordered on exasperation. "I may be shy, Lord Waverly, but I assure you that I am not stupid. I am quite aware that I'm not the epitome of fashion or the wittiest or prettiest female out this

Season. However, you are a most eligible bachelor and could have your choice of any of the beauties. So why would you care to marry me?"

For the first time they were alone together and actually having a conversation without either of her parents hovering over them. He had to admit he admired her candid approach, even though he would not have expected it of her. Perhaps there was more to her personality than he had given her credit for. "Since you wish to be forthright, let me ask you this question first, Lady Faith. Am I someone you would consider as a husband?"

She paused longer than he would have suspected, which irritated him. She should be jumping at the chance to marry him. She just said he was one of the most sought-after bachelors in London!

When she finally responded, her answer surprised him. "I'm not entirely certain. To all outward appearances we are quite different in our tastes and interests, and I'm not sure we have much in common. I have no idea what you would expect in a wife, nor if I could successfully fulfill the role of countess and eventually marchioness. I must admit, Lord Waverly, I harbor serious and grave doubts about whether we would suit each other as husband and wife."

The longest speech he had ever heard from her almost knocked him off his feet. Was the girl refusing his suit before he had even asked for her hand? The very thought boggled his mind.

"Would you please kiss me, Lord Waverly?"

Certain that he had not heard correctly, Lucien asked, "I beg your pardon?"

"You heard me," she said softly. "Please don't make me repeat myself."

He could not conceal the incredulousness in his voice. "You wish for me to kiss you?"

"Yes."

Lucien cleared his throat. "May I ask why?"

She gave him a funny little look, as if she had proven her point. "If you have to ask why, then it is evident that you have no desire to kiss me."

At her words, Lucien suddenly leaned down and pressed his lips to hers, catching her somewhat off guard. He held her close for a moment, feeling the softness of her body. There was no rush of feeling, no overwhelming passion possessing his body. He was in complete and utter control. Oh yes, he would be quite safe with Faith Bromleigh. Not a doubt about it.

When he released her, she took a little step back from him. Lucien stood straight and smiled at her, expecting her to be swept off her feet.

"Well," she said matter-of-factly, biting her lip. "It's just as I feared."

Confused, Lucien stared at her. She did not seem the slightest bit flustered by his kiss.

"That was nice enough," she continued, her expression serious, her brows drawn together. "But it had none of the magical feelings I would expect to have when kissing my future husband."

Left speechless, Lucien was dumbfounded by this unassuming young woman. No, he had not felt that wild flood of desire when kissing Faith, nor had he expected to experience that with her. But he never imagined that *she* would not feel desire for *him*.

"I should have felt something. Don't you agree?" she asked, tilting her head up to look at him.

"I suppose I do," he admitted reluctantly.

She shook her head slightly. "No, there was nothing special in that kiss. Do you believe it is possible that such a feeling might grow to be there between us?"

"I don't know," he stated, feeling quite foolish. He had

never been attracted to her, but never suspected that it especially mattered to *her*. Apparently it did.

"Lord Waverly, I am not a horse to be bought at auction," Faith declared fervently. "I have feelings and thoughts of my own. Before we pursue this relationship any further, I believe we should be honest with each other."

"Yes . . ." He waited to hear what she would say next, certain that it would not be something he wanted to hear.

"Perhaps we could give it a little more time?" she asked.

Not sure if he felt a sense of relief or disappointment at her suggestion, Lucien agreed with her. Maybe time could make things better between them. "Yes, I believe that might be a good idea."

Chapter Twenty-Two

Silence Is Golden

Colette still had not spoken to her mother. Ever since she discovered that the shop had been sold, she and her mother had maintained a cold silence in each other's presence. Colette had actually been surprised by her mother's tenacity because she had half expected to see her teary and apologetic when she returned home that first night and had been somewhat disappointed in her mother yet again that she had not expressed some remorse. Naturally the atmosphere in their little house had grown tense and strained, leaving Juliette, Lisette, Paulette, and Yvette caught in the middle of the acrimony between their mother and their sister. Colette continued to stay away from her mother as much as possible by keeping busy in the shop, where Genevieve never ventured.

Colette was satisfied by another day of brisk sales. The books seemed to fly off the shelves lately. Her ladies' reading circle had grown to over twenty members and had now become weekly meetings filled with quite lively discussions.

The stationery and writing supplies she stocked from Mr. Kenworth were selling even better than she had hoped.

After the last of the customers left for the day, she had sent Juliette and Paulette upstairs to have supper. Now she sat quietly at the counter, going over the accounts, and was thrilled to see that she had earned yet another modest profit that week. However, the joy came on a bittersweet wave in the knowledge that she would soon be losing the store.

Sighing heavily, she wondered when the new owner would contact her. Uncle Randall had said the buyer was not in a hurry to take over the store. Although she thought that somewhat odd, the fact that she had more time to make a success of the shop inspired her. Knowing that this might be the only chance she ever had to be in control of a business, as well as her own life, however long or short that time turned out to be, she was determined to leave on a triumphant note just to prove to herself that she could do it. And in spite of almost everyone being against her, the shop was becoming a success. She had attracted far more costumers than her father ever had.

"Colette?"

Her mother stood before her, clutching a shawl around her thin shoulders and leaning on her gilt cane.

"*Maman?*" She could not hide the shock at seeing Genevieve in the bookshop. When Colette had been younger, she recalled a vicious argument between her parents, in which her mother vowed never to set foot in the shop. Immediately after, Genevieve became ill and took to her room, and indeed had not entered the shop again. Until now.

Her mother did not speak at first, but gazed in amazement at the changes Colette had made to the store. She seemed like a small child, staring in wonder. "You have done all this?"

"Yes," Colette admitted proudly. "With help from the girls."

"I had no idea . . . None whatsoever. I never knew. I never dreamed the place could be transformed in such a way. *Je n`aurais jamais imaginé que la librarie puisse être aussi belle . . .*" Genevieve continued to look around at the attractively organized bookshelves, the charming signs hanging from green ribbons, the inviting arrangement of comfortable furniture, the gleaming glass cabinet full of beautiful paper and expensive writing tools. It was not the same shop at all.

"Did you not ever listen to Paulette and me discussing the changes we were making?"

"I suppose . . . I did not really pay attention . . ." Again her mother demonstrated her breathless and dramatic flair by waving her hand in a grand gesture and then placing her hand over her heart. "*C'est tout simplement ravissant, Colette.* Lovely."

"Thank you. It's a shame you have waited so long to see it."

The fleeting smile on her face disappeared. "I know you are angry with me for selling the shop."

"You did not even consult me about it, Mother."

"It is not your shop," Genevieve said with indignation. "It belongs entirely to me, not you. *C'était mon argent.* It was my inheritance, my money, which purchased it. I may do with it what I please."

The strength in her haughty demeanor surprised Colette, who had not witnessed this side of her mother's character in years. However, it did not dispel her anger either. "Out of courtesy to me, out of respect for all I have done, for managing every aspect of the business since Father died, I think you could have at least consulted with me about it first."

"*Non.*" Her mother waved her hand adamantly. "No.

You would only have caused a scene. I knew you wished to keep it. However, I did not. I have hated this shop since the day we moved in and I am thrilled to be rid of it."

After a long pause, Colette asked quietly, "Even though you know it breaks my heart to lose it?"

"It broke my heart to live here, year after year, watching my life pass me by. Your father promised me—" Genevieve stopped in mid-sentence, obviously thinking better of what she had planned to say. "*Ce qui est fait est fait.* That is between your father and me. As it is, I have had to live my life denied of anything I ever wanted and abide by the decisions made by others. Now it is my turn to decide. I am done with this little house, this dreadful bookshop, and this filthy city. I received more than twice what we paid for the shop, and now I wish to leave. With Randall's help, I have purchased a small house in Brighton and I have instructed your sisters to begin packing. We shall leave in two weeks."

Colette's head spun. *Leaving? Two weeks? Brighton? What is Mother thinking?* All this time Colette had been so concerned about losing the shop, she had not given any thought about where they would live. A cottage by the sea sounded vaguely pleasant, but now they had a small house in Brighton. A definite place. Their new home. Her mother planned to take the family away from London.

Colette had lived her entire life above Hamilton's Book Shoppe. As a little girl she had learned to read and write at her father's side in the back room of the shop. She and her sisters had played hide-and-go-seek among the bookshelves too many times to count. She loved the scent of paper and ink and leather-bound books. The shop was her home. She did not know if she could survive without it.

"Why Brighton?" Colette managed to ask, her heart in her throat.

Her mother said simply, "I wish to be by the sea and breathe fresh air for a change."

The woman who had not left the house in years suddenly craved sea air. Colette could not quite believe what she was hearing. "What about the Season?" Colette murmured, her mouth dry. Neither she nor Juliette had secured a marriage yet. Surely her mother did not wish to lose the chance of marrying off two of her daughters?

Genevieve gave her a hard look. "Randall said no one suitable has offered for you, and you have refused the matches he has suggested."

Colette wanted to protest, but Uncle Randall had spoken the truth. She and Juliette had spurned all the men he had presented to them, albeit they were all horrid and repulsive, but no one else had asked for either of their hands in marriage. They had both failed miserably on that count.

"He feels he has spent enough time and money on you and Juliette," Genevieve began irately, her French accent becoming more marked as she spoke. "He is frustrated with your progress and he is blaming me for letting you both run wild. Now that he has recovered his losses with a portion of the sale of the building, he washes his hands of both of you. I too am disappointed at your lack of effort in finding a husband. You have squandered a great opportunity in your life, Colette, the gift of a London Season. You had the chance to marry well and reside in luxury for the rest of your life. And what do you do? You throw it all away on this pitiful bookshop, for nothing. I ask you, how will you ever find a suitable husband now?"

Colette hung her head, unwilling to meet Genevieve's disapproving gaze. The anger she felt with her mother for selling the shop evaporated as a deep shame crept over her. If her mother even suspected what Colette had done with Lucien, she would die of humiliation. And her mother made a good point.

How *would* Colette find a husband now?

Even though Jeffrey Eddington had been more attentive

to her of late, it did not mean he had intentions of marrying her, and Colette could not in all good conscience
marry him, even if he did ask her. The only man she
wanted to marry was determined to marry someone else.
And the main reason the man would not marry her was because she ran a business, a business that was no longer hers
to oversee. The absurdity of the situation would have made
her laugh if she were not so distraught over it.

"If you wish to join us in Brighton, we shall leave two
weeks from today on the train."

"What do you mean, if I wish to join you?" Colette
asked in confusion.

"You have made your feelings for me quite clear, so
naturally I assumed you would not wish to stay with me.
Will you be coming with us?"

Colette grew silent at her mother's martyrlike stance
and wished she did have somewhere else to go. Two weeks.
She had only two weeks to do something to change her
life. "Of course I will. I could never leave the girls . . . or
you. Besides, where else would I go?"

"You are such an independent woman, I thought perhaps you would find a place for yourself."

Colette was stunned by her mother's cold words. "I
had no choice but to be independent, Mother. What
would have happened to us all had I not been?"

"I would have handled it," she spat back, stepping
closer to the counter where Colette sat.

Colette's outrage finally broke free. "Such as you did
handle it, *Maman*, with fainting and headaches and
hiding in your room, while conveniently leaving all the
responsibility of caring for this family to me?"

In a sudden move Genevieve reached across the
counter and struck Colette across the face with a stinging
slap. Shocked and breathless, Colette stared in horror at
her mother. In all her life her mother had never struck

her. She blinked back tears as Genevieve turned and left the shop without a single word.

Trembling, Colette rubbed her cheek and sat in stunned silence, staring at the glass window facing the front of the store. The blinds had been drawn, but she knew just outside, just beyond that thin pane of glass, the street beckoned. She could walk out that very door and do as she pleased. But how? Where would she go? What would she do? She might be able to obtain a position at another bookshop in town and support herself. The thought of her four sisters tugged at her heart and she knew without a doubt that she could never leave them.

With a forlorn little sigh, she wished she could talk to Lucien. Somehow she felt he would know what to do in this situation. He just had that way about him. He made her feel safe, secure. It was a shame things had changed between them since that night at his house.

Not that she regretted that night at all, not really. Since she had not been raised in a conventional manner, how could she be expected to behave conventionally? She ran a business. She took care of her family. Would she ever find a man who was comfortable with and accepting of her abilities? Would she ever find a man who was willing to marry her knowing she would not change who she was? More than likely not. So why not take her pleasure where she could find it?

And being with Lucien had certainly been a pleasure.

But it was more than that with Lucien. She felt an intense connection with him. She wanted to share her dreams with him. She loved him.

Unaware how much time had passed, she startled when Juliette quietly entered the room. She came right over and sat upon another stool beside Colette.

"She told you about the move to Brighton?" Juliette asked softly, her eyes full of concern.

Colette merely gave a sad nod in answer to her sister's question.

"She broke the news to us at supper." Juliette sighed in resignation. "I cannot believe I'm the one to say this, but I think I'm going to miss this old shop after all."

The comment was ridiculous enough to make Colette smile ruefully. "Whatever shall we do in Brighton?"

Juliette shrugged. "I suspect much the same that we do here, except we can swim in the sea."

"I had a terrible argument with Mother."

"I know," Juliette confessed. At Colette's questioning glance, Juliette explained, "Paulette was listening at the door and came and told me."

"I should have known."

"Are you all right?"

Colette merely nodded.

"Well, at least we have one more ball to attend before we leave. Jeffrey is escorting us both to the Hayven-hursts' party next week. It might be our last opportunity to meet the men of our dreams before we are forced to leave the city."

Juliette's comment was meant sarcastically, but Colette knew it to be true. Chances were good that Lucien would be there. It might very well be her last chance to see him.

Chapter Twenty-Three

Will That Be All?

Lucien entered Hamilton's Book Shoppe hesitantly, glancing around for Colette. He still had not been able to talk to her privately since that night in his bedroom, but felt safer seeing her at the shop. Since it was almost closing time, he hoped he would have a chance to talk to her privately.

Seated atop a tall stool behind the counter, Paulette lit up when she saw him and she gave a little wave. "Hello, Lord Waverly! I mean, Lucien."

"Good evening, Paulette." He returned her smile, intrigued by her animated little expression. "Are you minding the store alone again?"

"Yes." She nodded proudly, straightening her shoulders. "I'm quite accomplished at it."

"Where are your sisters?"

"Upstairs. Colette will be down in a minute to close up."

"I see." He looked around the shop, still marveling at the incredible changes Colette had made over the weeks. She had truly accomplished so much since the first time he had visited there. Her ability to make her dreams a reality impressed him.

"Are you here to buy books or to see Colette?" Paulette asked with an arch look.

The impish gleam in her pretty eyes caused him to smile in spite of himself. He had been fairly caught by a fifteen-year-old. "I confess. I am here for the sole reason of speaking to your sister," he admitted.

She grinned knowingly. "I thought as much."

"Do you mind if I wait here for her?" He placed his hat on the counter.

Paulette nodded affirmatively. "I must warn you though, you should hurry, you don't have much time left before we leave."

What was the girl talking about? "Time for what?"

"Time to ask Colette to marry you."

Stunned, Lucien could only stare at her for a moment. "However did you get that idea into your head?"

"Well, isn't that why you are here all the time, because you are in love with her?"

Lucien shook his head in mute silence. *Because he was in love with her?* He was not in love with Colette!

Giving him a skeptical look, Paulette uttered with complete confidence, "It's obvious to me that you are both in love with each other."

"Is it, now?" To think he had once believed Paulette to be a highly intelligent and reasonable child. Now she was talking complete nonsense. He was not in love with Colette, nor was Colette in love with him. *Was she?* Which led him to ask another question, "What do you mean before you leave?"

"Hasn't she told you yet? Uncle Randall finally sold the shop and my mother has purchased a house for us in Brighton. We're moving there soon, so it would be best if you proposed to Colette before we leave."

Ignoring her remark about proposing, he asked, "Brighton? Are you all really moving there?" It had never occurred to him that they would leave London.

She nodded, somewhat sadly. "That's where our mother wishes to live."

He was surprised Colette had not mentioned this to him, but then again, things had not been the same between them since the night at his house. She must be devastated. "Is Colette terribly upset about losing the shop?"

"Of course she is. I knew she would be. But she is handling it quite well."

"Yes," Lucien mumbled, lost in his thoughts. This was not turning out as he anticipated.

"Hello."

Turning around at the sound of her voice, Lucien faced Colette, looking lovely in a simple dress of dark burgundy, her full breasts outlined temptingly. Her long chocolate-colored hair was pulled loosely back from her face. Lucien found himself aroused just looking at her, amazed at the force of his desire. He took a deep breath. He'd been half expecting her to toss him from the shop on sight; her neutral greeting gave him hope that perhaps the evening might be pleasant after all.

With a warm smile, he nodded to her. "Good evening."

Colette turned to her younger sister, looking at her pointedly. "Run along upstairs, Paulette."

Putting up a protest, Paulette began valiantly, "I was just speaking to Lord Waverly and tell—"

"Go upstairs now, Paulette," Colette repeated, her voice edged with impatience.

"Fine," Paulette muttered with a beleaguered sigh, knowing she was defeated. She slid off the stool on which she had been perched and made her way reluctantly around the counter, bidding them both good night.

"It was lovely talking with you, Paulette," Lucien said kindly. "Good night."

"And don't listen at the door!" Colette called after her sister as she reached the staircase.

"I wouldn't dream of such a thing!" Paulette cried indignantly with her hands on her hips. With an affronted sigh, she closed the door firmly behind her.

"Oh, wouldn't she, though," Colette retorted as she silently raced back to the door and yanked it wide open. A flabbergasted Paulette jumped guiltily back from where she had been poised to listen.

"Aha!" Colette pronounced triumphantly. "Now go upstairs!"

As Lucien laughed out loud, Paulette fled up the steps and Colette closed the door behind her, locking it for good measure. "That should hold her for a while. It's a terrible habit she has," she explained as she made her way back to where Lucien had been waiting.

Still amused by the scene, Lucien had to come to Paulette's defense, for he had benefited from at least one of her eavesdropping sessions. "Yes, but she has good intentions."

"No, she doesn't!" Colette cried, and then laughed in spite of herself.

"Your sisters are all wonderful," he remarked earnestly. "You must know they love you very much."

She nodded in agreement. "And I love them."

"Your family is very important to you." He stated the obvious. To know Colette was to know she loved her sisters. Enjoying the easy moment between them, Lucien hesitated to bring up the reason for his visit, and suddenly held the vain hope that she would not ask why he was there in the shop.

"Speaking of family," she began quietly. "How was the visit with your mother?"

He sighed heavily, recalling the dramatic changes that had occurred at Devon House. A month ago he never would have thought it even a remote possibility. "It has not been easy for me. My mother and I are still working things through."

"I would imagine you have a lot to catch up on. She's been gone for a long time."

"It's strange to see her again," he admitted. "I don't know quite how to treat her."

"Of course it must be awkward between you. Has she seen your father?"

"Surprisingly enough, she and my father have reconciled."

Colette's eyes widened. "He forgave her for leaving?" she asked incredulously.

Lucien nodded. "Apparently there is more to their story than I had been led to believe all these years."

"I wonder what happened between them to cause her to leave a man like your father. Still, I don't think I could forgive my husband for leaving me for someone else for years," she murmured, shaking her head.

He looked at her curiously, intrigued by her comment. "Would you ever stray in your marriage, Colette?"

"Of course not." She hesitated, and then questioned him, her blue eyes inquisitive. "Would you?"

"No."

She glanced away and said nothing. They stood there in the empty shop, neither one addressing the issue that mattered most to both of them.

"I should close up now," she murmured.

Without a word, Lucien assisted Colette in the now familiar process of shutting down the bookshop for the night. They worked together in companionable silence and once the front door was finally locked and the lights dimmed, she turned to him.

"Thank you for your help, but I think it is time for you to go," she said, looking hesitant.

He did not want to leave. His desire to stay with her superseded all other feelings. "You haven't asked why I came by to see you," he stated in a low voice.

Keeping her eyes on his, she whispered, "Because I don't wish to know."

"Don't you?" On an impulse he reached out and took her hand. Her elegant fingers, so surprisingly soft, felt ridiculously small and delicate in his. It amazed him that such small, feminine hands could accomplish so much. But Colette's hands seemed capable of anything.

Colette shook her head, a silky tendril of her hair shaking loose, framing her face. She did not want to hear why he had come to see her, but she did not pull away, allowing him to hold her warm hand within his. Slowly his fingers threaded with hers, locking their hands together. An overwhelming sense of belonging settled over him. His thumb gently caressed her hand, stroking the soft skin of her palm.

She knows, Lucien thought, with a pang of remorse. Colette had sensed what he had come to say; that he was sorry for what happened that night at Devon House, and that he wanted to help her somehow and make it up to her. And she did not wish to hear it from him. *Could he blame her?* He realized then that he was a complete idiot. He needed to say those things to her simply to assuage his own guilt. It would only make him feel better, not her. Aside from asking her to marry him, there *was* nothing he could say to her. He should not have even come.

Their fingers still intertwined, they stared at each other in the dimness of the empty shop. The clip-clop of a horse's hooves on the cobblestone street outside echoed faintly through the room. Otherwise it was silent. Colette's beautiful face tilted up to him, the shadowy light falling across her flawless cheeks, her expression full of sorrow.

Feeling unbearably responsible for the sadness in her eyes, Lucien pulled her to him, enfolding her in the comfort of his arms. Again, she did not resist, but almost seemed to welcome his embrace.

With her head resting against his chest, she melted into him. She felt like heaven in his arms. Gently he stroked the length of her back. The floral scent of her hair flooded his senses and he could not help but press a tender kiss to the top of her head, holding her tight.

"I'm so sorry, Colette."

She looked up at his whispered words, her cheek pressed against his jacket. "Please don't say that to me again."

He looked down at her beautiful face, with her sensuous lips that beckoned to him, and his heart skipped a beat in his chest. He had never intended to hurt her. He wouldn't knowingly hurt Colette for the world. He wished he could take back what happened that night at Devon House. No, perhaps he wouldn't go that far. He reluctantly admitted to himself that he was glad he had made love to her. He simply wished he could take away the consequences of his impulsive actions that night. As he held this amazing woman in his arms, he marveled at how she made him feel.

And then he did it.

He leaned his head forward and covered her mouth with his. Unable to restrain himself, he kissed her with a heated intensity built up over days of not being able to see her or touch her except in his tormented dreams. He could not get enough of her. As his mouth took possession of her, a little sigh escaped her and he groaned.

Something about Colette stoked a need for her in him that was out of his control, out of his realm of knowing.

Everything about her was wrong for him.

Colette Hamilton was too beautiful and too independent and too full of modern ways and notions. She voiced her opinions and made business deals and managed to take care of her family. She was too passionate and unrestrained in her emotions. She blatantly refuted every single one of his beliefs about what constituted a woman's role in life. Still, he found himself irresistibly drawn to her. He felt strangely protective of her, even responsible for her. And yet, he desired her more than any woman he had ever known. *God, but he desired her.* Colette was a dangerous combination, and the truth be known, she terrified him.

And there he was kissing her. Yet again.

As his lips and tongue seared her, she responded eagerly, her hands snaking their way around his neck, her fingers splaying into his hair. She felt so good, so incredibly perfect in his arms, while her luscious tongue explored his mouth and her full breasts pressed against his chest. Her lithe little body beckoned to be touched and caressed and his hands ran the length of her, circling her slender waist and resting on the curves of her hips. He knew he was making another mistake in kissing her, but he could not rein in his impulses around her. He could not. He wanted to kiss her. Hold her. Touch her. Remove every shred of her clothing and kiss her all over. He wanted to drive himself into her sweet body over and over again until he couldn't think about anything else. He just wanted her.

Oh, this was dangerous, he knew. Very dangerous. But he was beyond caring.

All he could see, feel, hear, touch, and taste was Colette.

His hands moved lower over her the delectable curve

of her bottom. With his hands he squeezed and pressed her hips firmly against his. A soft moan escaped her and she rubbed herself against him and he caught his breath. Inflamed by the intimate contact, they kissed wildly, their passion for each other increasing with each gasping breath.

Colette tugged frantically at the collar of his jacket. At first he thought she grabbed him for support, and then the thrilling realization dawned on him. She was trying to remove his jacket. *God help him!*

They were surely lost now, for how could he resist her?

With an eager groan, he shrugged his dark gray jacket from his shoulders, dropping it to the floor without losing contact with the sweetness of her mouth. The brass buttons of his silk waistcoat were her next focus, and soon the waistcoat joined his jacket in a pile on the floor. The sheer excitement of having Colette in a frenzy to undress him aroused him beyond belief. With mounting impatience, she hastily unfastened the buttons of his shirtfront, spreading the white linen wide, her hands running over the smooth planes of his chest.

Practically bare-chested now, his shirt gapping open to his waist, he began to walk her backward toward the bookshelf. She took awkward steps, her hands clinging to his naked shoulders beneath his open shirt, her lips still joined with his. He walked her in reverse until her back was against one of the bookshelves. His body trembling, Lucien could not get enough of her mouth and the heady, sweet taste of her. Her kisses were all-consuming. It was almost as if they feared that losing contact would break the seductive spell they had fallen under.

What am I doing?

Feeling as if he were in a dream, there in the darkened bookshop in the history section with her family just upstairs, Lucien kissed Colette with a wild urgency and a desperate need that completely overwhelmed him.

Ignoring his pounding heart, he finally broke their prolonged kiss and cupped her face in his hands. Staring into her eyes, he knew he should end this. But the look of impassioned longing on her face, her dark, heavy-lidded eyes full of desire, and her heated body pressed eagerly against his weakened already thin resolve. Still breathing heavily, he murmured her name as a question.

For an endless moment she stared back at him, and he was mesmerized by her. Her lips, reddened and swollen from his kisses, trembled in hesitation. He should turn away, but he couldn't. He was rooted to the floor, fascinated by the passionate look of intent in her eyes. Was it sparked by desire? Was it daring? Without uttering a single word, Colette slid her hands ever so slowly from his shoulders. Her fingers, smooth and silky, glided with a feather-light touch down his chest. He dared not move a single muscle although every nerve in his body tensed with eager anticipation as the tips of her fingers gradually caressed the taut skin of his stomach. His skin burned where she touched him, inflaming his need for her. When she dared to lower her hands over his hips to the hardened bulge straining at the front of his trousers, Lucien sucked in his breath. *Christ!* She was not making this easy. He was already rock-hard with desire; the bold touch of her fingers through the fabric of his pants found him close to bursting.

With an anguished groan, he covered her mouth in another searing kiss just as her fingers firmly closed around him. He was lost. He pressed her up against the nearest shelf, her bottom resting on the edge. Leaning her back, his tongue still possessing her mouth, he lifted the skirt of her burgundy gown and ran his hand up the length of her stocking-clad thigh. Colette clung to him, breathing heavily. With one touch of his finger, he knew she was ready for him, wanted him. The thought drove him mad. She had already freed him from the constraints of his trousers, amazed at how easily something so illicit could be accomplished. Within a matter of seconds he had thrust himself deeply inside her. Losing himself in the incredible heat of her body, he could think of nothing but the woman who arched against him, wanting him as much as he wanted her. It was the most erotic moment of his life. As they moved against each other, their pace increasing, their movements grew more urgent as he sought to give her the pleasure she was giving him. Her head fell against his shoulder and the warmth of her breath heated the skin of his neck. She clung to him with both long legs hitched tightly around his waist as he thrust into her over and over again. Books fell to the floor around them, their pages carelessly tossed open, as he rocked against her.

For an endless while there was just the two of them, their hearts pounding, their mouths gasping, their bodies embracing. With no words to describe his feelings for her, Lucien just knew that he never wanted to let Colette go. She belonged to him. Suddenly Colette's breathing became more rapid, her movements more frantic until she cried out his name into his mouth. With a few more grinding thrusts, Lucien immediately followed her into bliss.

They held on to each other for some time, trying to regain their composure, each loath to let the other go.

In the dimness of the empty and silent shop, they slowly slid from their awkward position on the bookshelf and began to arrange their clothes into some semblance of decency amid an epic silence before facing each other. With his pants closed and his shirt buttoned once again,

Lucien collapsed into the nearest seat, an overstuffed armchair in the corner, and pulled a limp Colette onto his lap, wrapping his arms around her.

"Oh, God, Colette," he whispered, overwhelmed by his feelings for her and unable to define them. *What had they just done? Again.*

She rested her head against his, and he breathed in her sweet scent. She felt like heaven in his arms and he could not resist another kiss on her lips.

"This isn't the reason you came to see me tonight, is it?" she asked in a weak attempt to lend humor to their situation.

With a rueful half-smile, he gave his head a shake. "No, I must say, it was not."

She hesitated before saying, "But you did come to apologize for the last time this happened."

"The last time this happened at least I took you in a civilized manner, in a bed. Not a bookshop."

Seeming flustered and charmingly embarrassed by his referral to their erotically charged, and quite reckless, encounter, Colette hid her face against his chest. He shook her lightly and squeezed her in comfort, kissing her again. He could not kiss her enough.

With her soft voice tinged with regret, she whispered, "And you're going to apologize to me for this time, too?"

"No, I'm blaming you entirely for this one."

Unsure if he was teasing her or not, she gave him a puzzled look. On some level he wasn't joking. She had been rather bold with him this evening and he could not fight his desire for her. Not that he would have minded under normal circumstances. But this . . . this encounter, this madness, which had been more phenomenal and passionate and amazing than anything he had ever experienced in his life, should not have even occurred in the first place. He shouldn't be having sexual liaisons with Colette at all. Period. This was a godawful mess, this was.

He kissed her cheek, softening his words to her. "No, this was entirely my fault. But this can't keep happening with us, Colette."

"No," she murmured low in agreement. "It can't ever happen again. It won't."

He held her tightly, enjoying the feel of her body cradled intimately across his lap. He could hold her like that forever. "When were you going to tell me that you and your family were moving to Brighton?"

She pulled away from him, sitting up. "Does it matter?"

"Of course it does," he said soothingly, pulling her back toward his chest. He needed to hold her close. "Do you want to live in Brighton?"

"No," she admitted with a heavy sigh, relaxing against him once again. "But there is not much of a choice for me in the matter. It seems my mother, with Uncle Randall's help, sold the shop."

Lucien paused, his heart suddenly pounding. "Which brings me to the other reason I wished to speak to you tonight."

She looked at him curiously.

"I'm the man who bought the building, Colette."

Her shocked expression was not unexpected, but the scrutiny in her narrowed eyes caught him off guard.

"You?" she breathed. "You bought our shop?"

"Yes, to help you," he explained. "And your family." He had not intended to ever reveal his identity as the anonymous buyer, but then he had not anticipated her family relocating to Brighton either.

She stared at him in disbelief and something akin to horror shadowed her delicately formed features.

Lucien assumed Colette would be relieved, perhaps even delighted by the news. Her silence worried him.

When he'd purchased the building, he did it because he felt protective of the Hamilton girls. He did it anonymously so as not to cause them to feel indebted to him. With the unnamed buyer not requiring them to vacate the premises and allowing the bookshop to remain open, he felt he would be easing their financial burden while allowing them to maintain the status quo without ever knowing he was the one who helped them. He rather thought he had done a good deed and had been pleased with himself over it. Now, however, he had second thoughts about his little plan. Colette seemed strangely withdrawn and quiet.

"Aren't you relieved you can stay in London? And that you can keep the shop open now?" he suggested hopefully.

The slap stunned him, for he didn't see it coming. Her hand flew across his cheek in a stinging blow. He instinctively grabbed her wrist before she could hit him again, which she clearly had every intention of doing. Pulling her hand from his grasp, she sprang from his lap, scurrying away from him. She was furious.

"What the hell was that for?" he asked, frowning and rubbing his cheek in confusion. It was definitely not the response he had expected from her.

"Get out," she uttered with a coldness and finality in her tone that chilled him.

Wondering what the devil had gotten into her, he rose from the chair and followed after her. "Colette?"

She picked up his jacket and waistcoat from the floor where she had removed them so seductively only moments ago and flung them at him. "Get out, and don't ever try to see me again."

Catching the garments before they hit his face, he made another attempt to discover what was going on in her pretty head. He thought he had done something nice, but apparently he had offended her. "What is the matter?"

Colette saw his hat resting on the counter and threw that at him, too. She then marched determinedly to the shop door and reached for the key. Her hands trembled as she turned to face him. "I don't know who you think I am, but you cannot buy me off."

Incredulous at her words, he asked again, "What are you talking about?"

"Apparently I'm good enough for you to bed, but not good enough for you to marry. You have made that point abundantly clear to me, Lucien, and I accepted it. I am a working woman and you are an earl, and as the heir to a marquis you have higher expectations in a wife. Fine. I wish you luck with Faith Bromleigh. But I will not be paid for services rendered with my own shop like some wharf-side doxy so you can walk away from me with a clean conscience. You can keep the building and the bloody shop and let it rot for all I care. I'll be leaving with my family, and you need never trouble yourself over me again." She took a gasping breath before unlocking the door and swinging it wide open. "Now get out of here this minute."

"Colette, I—"

"Don't speak to me. I can't bear it."

"It's not what you think, Colette," he attempted to explain, unable to bear the pain in her expression. "I didn't buy the building to atone for sleeping with you at all. I bought it be—"

"Get out before I scream."

"Fine," he said as he stalked through the doorway. As he turned back to say one more thing, the door slammed in his face. Stunned, Lucien stood there, clutching his waistcoat and jacket in his arms, staring at the "Closed" sign swinging wildly in the door of Hamilton's Book Shoppe.

Chapter Twenty-Four

Table for Two

The next evening Lord Jeffrey Eddington escorted Colette and Juliette to their last ball before moving to Brighton. Once again, Lady Hayvenhurst was hosting the final of her lavish parties of the Season, and her many guests crowded the grand ballroom.

Colette had no desire to attend such an affair, but Juliette had cajoled her for hours until she had consented to accompany her and Jeffrey to the party.

"Really, Colette. This is our last chance for a bit of fun in town before we are relegated to the country. Who knows what can happen tonight? Forget about Lucien Sinclair and the bookshop and just enjoy yourself," her sister had suggested earlier that evening.

If only she *could* forget Lucien Sinclair. Colette had been unable to think of anyone or anything but Lucien Sinclair for weeks now. After their scene in the bookshop the night before, she truly never wanted to see him again. Not only did she cringe at the memory of her own behavior, but the impact of Lucien's words had left her sick to her stomach.

Dressed in her best gown of ice pink with a little bustle covered in baby rosettes, she had allowed Lisette to curl her hair in an elegant arrangement down one shoulder. Carrying a pink silk reticule and a lacy fan, she attempted a smile as Jeffrey handed her a glass of sparkling champagne.

"Are you smiling at me or the champagne?" he questioned her with a gleam in his eye.

She really did smile then, even laughed, for Jeffrey's lighthearted mood was contagious. "At the champagne, of course."

"Not me?"

He did look remarkably handsome in his black evening clothes. His dark hair was neatly combed and his clean-shaven face accented the masculine lines of his face. "I wouldn't wish for you to get an inflated head, my dearest Lord Eddington."

"I couldn't possibly," he scoffed easily. "Now drink up. We're going to have fun this evening! Let's celebrate your last evening out in London with a little style."

Jeffrey tipped his glass to hers and Colette mimicked his motions, taking a sip of the cool and sparkling liquid. She smiled brightly and made a concerted effort to have fun, even if it killed her. She scanned the crowded ballroom, wishing to see Lucien and yet dreading it at the same time.

"Where has Juliette wandered off to now?" he asked.

"My aunt and uncle have cornered her, wishing to introduce her to Count Someone. It's my uncle's last attempt to marry one of us off."

"Well, she is in good hands, and you are stuck alone with me. Now, let's go outside for some air, shall we?"

Placing her hand on his arm, and careful not to spill her drink, she followed Jeffrey out to the veranda. They found two unoccupied chairs arranged around a small, round wrought-iron table in a secluded section of the veranda and made themselves comfortable. A cluster of candles flickered in glass holders in the center of the table. A long reflecting pool at the edge of the veranda had been filled with floating candles and, as if Lady Hayvenhurst had ordered it herself, hundreds of stars glistened in the warm summer sky. It was a lovely spot. They could enjoy the night air and still hear strains of the music from the orchestra.

"You look quite stunning this evening," he said.

"You are very kind," she responded. She would have thought she might feel uncomfortable being alone with him after their kiss in his carriage, but he had a way of making her feel entirely at ease. He possessed the kind of charm that instantly won people over. She paused before saying, "There is something I've been wondering about you, Jeffrey."

"What is that?"

"Why is it you have not married yet?" Colette asked, suddenly curious.

He winked at her. "Are you asking me to marry you, Colette?"

She laughed at his teasing. "I asked you a serious question."

He inclined his head to her. "I've yet to meet a woman I cared to make my wife."

"Ah. So you are optimistic that a bride is in your future?"

"Absolutely. I'm just not ready to settle down yet."

"Lucien is ready, though, isn't he?" Colette could not help herself from questioning his friend.

"Supposedly," Jeffrey said. "But I for one think he is making a terrible mistake."

"A mistake in getting married or in his choice of a bride?"

"Faith Bromleigh is not the right woman for him."

Colette silently agreed with him, although she kept that

opinion to herself. "Wasn't he engaged once before?" She casually sipped her champagne, surprised to see that she had almost finished the glass.

"Yes." Jeffrey rolled his blue eyes skyward in disgust. "Now that engagement was an unmitigated disaster!"

"What was she like?" She had tried to imagine the type of woman Lucien might propose to and could not picture one.

"Virginia Warren was beautiful, witty, very sophisticated. Lucien was head over heels in love with her."

Even though she was still enraged over his callous treatment of her in trying to buy her off with the shop, her stomach knotted in reflex at the thought of Lucien in love with another woman. A beautiful, clever, and sophisticated woman, no less. She did not believe he was truly in love with Lady Faith Bromleigh and suspected that he was interested in marrying her only because Faith was everything Colette was not. *But head over heels in love? Lucien? How would he act? What would he say? How would one detect that he was head over heels in love?*

She questioned Jeffrey, "Why didn't they get married if they were so in love?"

"I said Lucien was in love. I didn't say Virginia was," he remarked cryptically.

"Oh . . ." Colette let that bit of news sink in before daring to ask, "Can you tell me what happened? Who broke off the engagement?"

Jeffrey glanced around the veranda at the various people milling about and lowered his voice, leaning his head closer to Colette's to avoid being overheard. "First tell me why you wish to know."

She sat up straight, blinking.

He placed his hand gently over hers, which rested on the table between them. "You're in love with him, aren't you?"

"I hate him."

He shook his head knowingly. "No, you don't."

"Yes, I do," she reiterated firmly.

"You can't fool me, Colette."

"Fine. Think what you like, but tell me what happened."

He gazed at her intently before resuming his story. "Virginia was a spoiled, malicious woman who was never satisfied with what she had. Nothing was good enough for her, not even Lucien. I tried to warn him, but sometimes not even your closest friends can save you from disaster."

Fascinated, Colette nodded for him to continue.

"Lucien will never talk about her, but I made no such promise myself." Jeffrey flashed her a wicked, secretive grin.

"Go on," she prompted, dying to know what happened between Lucien and this woman.

Jeffrey's smile disappeared and again his voice dropped to a low whisper. "At first there were rumors about Virginia's behavior, which Lucien flatly denied and deliberately ignored. I had heard from a reliable source that Virginia had entertained, shall we say, a certain gentleman who was an acquaintance of mine. I warned him, because I had sensed she was nothing but trouble from the start, but Lucien was blind to everything except the exotic and sultry Virginia. They scheduled the wedding, which was heartily approved by both families. The week before the wedding, he caught her with the aforementioned gentleman." He paused pointedly. "And I am providing you with the edited version of the events."

Colette gasped and covered her mouth hastily with her elbow-length-pink-gloved hand. "Oh, that's dreadful."

"Believe me, it was. I had the unfortunate honor of being present when Lucien discovered the truth. He would never have told me about it otherwise."

Colette sat unmoving. A part of her felt sorry for Lucien, but a bigger part of her was thrilled that Lucien had suffered the pain of heartbreak. It was only fair, since he had broken her heart. Still the entire story left her feeling oddly unsettled and conflicted.

"And being the gentleman he is," Jeffrey continued, "he let everyone assume he was the one who broke off the engagement. He protected Virginia. He took on the scandal, while Virginia's parents packed her off to Europe, ostensibly to mend her broken heart."

"I had no idea," she breathed. This glimpse into Lucien's past had surprised her. Lucien seemed so confident and sure of himself, it was difficult to imagine him wounded in such a way. If Virginia Warren's reckless passion had devastated him, what about her own reckless behavior with him? What must he think of her?

Jeffrey leaned in closer to her, his forehead almost touching hers. "Virginia broke his heart, and Lucien's never quite been the same since. Until he met you, Colette."

She glanced away from Jeffrey. *Until he met me? Is Lucien in love with me?* As she let all this sink in, she finished off the last of the champagne in her glass.

"Don't look now, but you will never guess who just stepped out on the veranda," Jeffrey whispered low.

Of course, Colette could not help but look. There was Lucien Sinclair, the Earl of Stancliff, with the pale Faith Bromleigh by his side. She had hoped against hope that Lucien would not be in attendance that evening. Apparently luck was not on her side. And Lucien looked stunningly handsome, his height and broad shoulders accentuated by his elegant black suit. Vivid images of those naked shoulders, the strong muscled arms, and the smooth planes of his chest assailed her, causing her to suck in her breath at the sight of him. Only last night those arms were around her, holding her, pulling her against him. Only last night he made passionate love to her. *Against a bookshelf, for heaven's sake!*

And then he thoroughly humiliated her by presenting

her with the bookshop to compensate for his unwillingness to marry her.

Desperately wishing she could simply disappear, Colette had no choice but to remain where she was, watching in utter dread as Lucien and Faith Bromleigh advanced toward the little wrought-iron table where she sat with Jeffrey. The air suddenly grew charged with a palpable tension.

"Good evening, Lady Faith," Jeffrey said, his hand still covering Colette's before he stood to greet her. "Hello, Lucien."

Lucien nodded to Jeffrey, but his dark green eyes remained locked on Colette as he made the introductions. "Faith, this is Miss Colette Hamilton. Miss Hamilton, this is Lady Faith Bromleigh."

With her heart flipping wildly in her chest, Colette could not look away from him. Lucien's eyes raked her body as if he could see through her pink gown, and she felt herself grow heated under his intent gaze. She could still feel his insistent lips on hers, his gentle hands caressing her, his hardened body moving within her, her legs wrapped around his hips. *Oh God.* Torn between wanting to slap his handsome face or throw herself in his strong arms, she could only stare helplessly back at him.

"It's a pleasure to meet you, Miss Hamilton," Faith said softly.

A wave of nausea so strong she feared she might be sick right then and there washed over Colette as she murmured a faint greeting to the woman Lucien intended to marry. Completely unsure of what she said and barely able to look at Faith Bromleigh, Colette could only endure the powerful force of Lucien's gaze on her as she struggled to maintain her composure.

"Miss Hamilton, I must admit that I have heard wonderful things about your bookshop."

"Oh?" Colette mumbled awkwardly, still staring at Lucien.

"Yes, perhaps I shall stop by."

"That would be lovely," Colette heard herself say. The thought of Lucien's future bride visiting Hamilton's left her cold inside. Yet it hardly mattered to her at this point who came to the shop, since she was leaving for Brighton.

"Are you enjoying Lady Hayvenhurst's party?" Jeffrey came to her rescue by asking Faith a question.

"Yes," she murmured. "Thank you."

"We were just coming out for a bit of air," Lucien explained hurriedly. "We did not mean to intrude."

"You weren't intruding," Jeffrey said in an easy tone. "Colette and I were simply discussing our futures."

Finally breaking his gaze with Colette, Lucien actually flinched at Jeffrey's cryptic remark. "Well, we shall let you resume your conversation, then. Good evening."

As Lucien and Faith made their way along the crowded veranda, Jeffrey sat back down, once again placing his hand over Colette's in a touching show of support. "Are you all right?" he asked, his eyes narrowed in concern.

The compassion in his voice made her feel even more like crying than she already did from Lucien's presence. Colette merely nodded, unable to speak.

"Have another glass of champagne," Jeffrey suggested. "You look rather pale." He motioned to a passing footman, taking two more crystal champagne flutes from his silver tray. He placed one glass in front of Colette. "Drink."

With her hand trembling, she sipped the cool liquid a little more quickly than she had intended to.

"Easy there." Jeffrey took the empty glass from her with a grim expression. "I didn't mean for you to polish off the entire thing."

Feeling dizzier than she had before but slightly calmer, she gave Jeffrey a blank gaze.

"Oh, my beautiful Colette. You have it bad," he said sympathetically, leaning his head closer to hers and patting her hand.

"I'm fine," she said, although it felt as if her tongue had suddenly grown heavier.

"I've known Lucien for a very long time," Jeffrey confided. "He's one of the most intelligent men I've ever met, and he's my best friend. Yet I can't help but think he's a complete idiot."

Colette raised her eyes to him. "Because of me?"

"Yes, because of you," he confirmed heartily. "He's a fool to let you go."

"It's most likely for the best," she said with a weary sigh. "We're so different, we probably wouldn't suit anyway. He would make me give up the shop. I'm not at all like Faith Bromleigh. She's a lady," she managed to say before a slight hiccup escaped her. She covered her mouth with her hand, hoping Jeffrey had not noticed.

"I hadn't realized you'd never met her before," Jeffrey remarked. "She's terribly wrong for Lucien. However, their engagement is not official in any way. Lucien has not even asked her yet, so there's still time."

"Time for what?" She felt so light-headed it was difficult to focus on what Jeffrey was saying to her.

"Time for him to come to his senses and realize that you are the woman he should marry."

Jeffrey was so sweet to worry about her, but he did not know the truth. She had to break the news to him. "Well, that is never going to happen, Jeffrey. Lucien practically told me so already." Colette picked up Jeffrey's full glass of champagne and took a rather large sip.

Jeffrey took the glass of champagne away from her, his look quite intent and questioning. "What have you discussed with him?"

Jeffrey was so easy to confide in because he really cared

about her. She suddenly felt she could tell him anything. The words rolled off her tongue quite effortlessly. "Lucien won't ever marry me, Jeffrey. Even after what happened with us that night at Devon House, he said so. Even after what we did last night . . ." She reached for his champagne again.

This time Jeffrey simply handed the glass to her. "Oh, Colette," he whispered, his expression unexpectedly somber. "This has gone further than I thought."

"What has?" Colette managed to ask before hiccupping loudly. She took another gulp of champagne.

"Good heavens, Jeffrey! Did you get my sister intoxicated?" Juliette cried in a shocked whisper as she joined them at the table.

Jeffrey gave Juliette a grim look. "Not intentionally, but she does seem headed that way. Although it proved to be a most enlightening conversation for me." He glanced back toward Colette. "Are you feeling well?"

"I am perfectly fine." Colette's words sounded slurred even to herself, but she felt absolutely wonderful. She lifted the glass to her lips and took another swallow, finishing off the last of the champagne.

"Oh, no, you don't!" With a swift movement, Juliette swiped the champagne flute from Colette's grasp, as well as the empty one from the table, and handed both to a footman, instructing him to bring glasses of water. Quickly. "Honestly," Juliette remonstrated them, "must I do everything myself?"

"Do what?" Colette murmured, vaguely irritated that her sister would not allow her to have any more lovely champagne. She blinked, her head spinning slightly.

"Never mind," Juliette instructed her, focusing her attention on Jeffrey. "He saw you together?"

"Most definitely." He nodded. "And he was not pleased."

"Then now is your chance. I just saw them saying their farewells, and their daughter was with them."

Although she felt rather woozy, Colette still grasped that something odd was going on. They were referring to someone she should know. "Whom are you talking about?"

Ignoring her question, Jeffrey stood. "You'll excuse me, ladies, won't you?"

"Of course we will," Juliette said, taking his seat at the table with Colette. "I'll stay here with my sister." She gave Jeffrey a disapproving glance. "And make her drink some water."

Chapter Twenty-Five

Green-Eyed Monster

Lucien intended to leave the Hayvenhursts' house after he bid the Bromleighs farewell, but first he needed to find out what Jeffrey had been up to, sitting so intimately with Colette on the veranda. The pair had looked quite cozy together, sitting alone in the shadows, whispering and drinking champagne. Almost romantic. Ignoring the strange pang of longing that gripped him, Lucien stood in the hallway and scanned the packed ballroom for Jeffrey and Colette, hoping they had finally come inside.

After last night in the bookshop Lucien could not get Colette out of his mind, nor had he recovered from the event. Tonight, she looked more beautiful than ever. He wished he had been the one sitting with her at that little table in the candlelight. He wished he could waltz with her, holding her body close to his as everyone watched. He wished he could escort her home, right into his bed, and make love to her all night long.

He had made a mistake with Faith Bromleigh. He

could barely summon the wherewithal to engage her in
conversation. Her somber expressions and calm manner,
which at one time seemed to be her greatest asset, now irritated him beyond belief. He could not continue his
courtship of her and she knew it, too. Faith had even
stated as much to him earlier in the evening. A life with
her might be calm and uneventful, but he doubted he
would ever be happy with her.

Colette made him happy.

The errant thought stopped him dead in his tracks.
Colette?

That woman had more of a hold on him than he realized. And it terrified him. He had to get Colette out of
his system. *But how?*

His mind spun with vivid images of her. Colette's
beautiful blue eyes. Colette smiling at him. Colette atop
a ladder in the bookshop, laughing. Colette teasing her
sisters. Colette reading to his father. Colette kissing him.
Colette naked in his bed. Colette unbuttoning his shirt.
Colette slapping his face. Colette whispering with Jeffrey.

He ought to warn Jeffrey away from her. She was too
fragile right now. Lucien had already hurt her enough,
and Jeffrey would only wound her even more with his
charmingly careless ways. Jeffrey should not be flirting
with her.

He decided to make his way back out to the veranda to
see what the two of them were up to, when Lord and Lady
Maywood, an older couple, stopped him to say hello.

"How is your poor father?" Lady Maywood asked, her
sharp gray eyes inquisitive.

Lucien had answered this question at least a dozen
times already that evening. He knew everyone was really
asking about his mother. Lenora Sinclair's unexpected
return to Devon House had caused quite an uproar.
Tongues had been wagging ever since the news got out,

although everyone at Devon House had attempted to keep it as quiet as possible for as long as they could. But typically, word had somehow managed to spread, and ever since then calls were made to the house for the first time in months as the curious and gossipy society matrons attempted to inveigle their way in to see the infamous Lenora Sinclair. They had been steadfastly turned away by an impervious Granger. The Marquis and Marchioness of Stancliff were not accepting calls.

Lucien had known Lady Maywood since he was a young lad and he had never particularly cared for her or her husband, finding them both to be overbearing and pretentious. As he had done all evening he responded to them coolly but politely, not wishing to invite more scandal on the family name. "My father is much improved, thank you." His eyes continued to scan the room for Colette.

"I'm so glad to hear it," Lady Maywood uttered in a tone that belied her words. She then asked pointedly, "And how *is* your mother, Lord Waverly?"

Lucien had been expecting this question, too. "My mother is quite well, thank you."

"Lenora Sinclair! What a shock to have her return after, what has it been? Fifteen or so years since she ran off?"

Lady Maywood's malicious and vindictive undertone suddenly enraged Lucien. He had spent his life in the shadow of his mother's notorious abandonment and was now expected to live down her equally scandalous homecoming. He had had enough.

"There is no need for you to feign concern regarding my family's well-being, Lady Maywood," he said pointedly. "So go ahead and spread your vicious rumors and gossip. I'm honored my family could provide you with enough scandalous fodder to keep you busy over the years. With any luck, there will be more to come. Good evening."

Satisfied with the expression of complete astonishment on her pinched face, Lucien stalked off toward the veranda, leaving a flabbergasted Lord and Lady Maywood utterly speechless.

Feeling somewhat lighter than he had a few moments earlier, Lucien finally caught up with Jeffrey at the entrance to the veranda. He stepped outside and Jeffrey joined him.

"Where's Colette?" Lucien demanded, his voice sounding edgier than he intended.

"She's with her sister." Jeffrey motioned a short distance away to the little table where Colette and Juliette sat together on the veranda.

Lucien then saw her, just as Jeffrey said. She and Juliette had their heads close together and were whispering. He felt relieved that she was no longer alone with his best friend.

Jeffrey casually leaned his shoulder against the brick wall of the townhouse, folding his arms across his chest, and countered with a question of his own. "Where is your future bride?"

"She has left with her parents already," Lucien responded hurriedly, dismissing the fact as unimportant. "Listen, Jeffrey, I saw you with Colette just now, and there are some things you need to know."

"Yes?" Jeffrey gave him an expectant look, almost challenging.

Lucien did not need to go into the intimate details about his relationship with Colette. He had to protect her reputation at least. "Well, it's personal, but I can assure you that she's been through quite a lot lately, and I don't think you should be trifling with her."

Jeffrey's eyes narrowed. "Who says I'm trifling with her?"

"You know what I mean."

"No. Actually I don't."

Put off by Jeffrey's attitude, Lucien grew agitated. "I am merely pointing out that Colette is a very special woman, and I wouldn't want to see her hurt in any way."

"I'm not going to hurt her," Jeffrey said smoothly. "I am going to marry her."

Lucien's laugh was loud enough to cause a few heads to turn in their direction. "You? You're going to marry her?"

"Yes."

At the seriousness of his friend's tone, Lucien's laughter died in his dry throat. Jeffrey marrying Colette was completely out of the question. It was unthinkable as far as he was concerned. "You cannot marry Colette."

"Of course I can. She has already said yes."

"Since when?" Lucien demanded in disbelief. It was impossible. Colette would never marry Jeffrey. *Would she?* He had made it more than clear to her last night that he wouldn't marry her himself. Why wouldn't she marry Jeffrey if he asked her? A sudden cold rush of fear washed over him. *Colette is mine.*

No. No, she isn't. Not really. He had given her away. Pushed her away. He felt sick inside.

"Well, I haven't actually asked her yet," Jeffrey explained. "Well, not formally, anyway. But she gave me every indication her answer would be yes if I asked her."

"She did?" Lucien was stunned, absolutely stunned, his heart suddenly beating rapidly. He'd just made love to Colette last night. Together they had made history in the history section of the bookshop, for Christ's sake! Had that encounter meant nothing to her? How could she possibly agree to marry another man, only one night later?

The same way he had introduced her to his intended fiancée only this evening.

Jeffrey responded matter-of-factly, "Yes, she did."

Jeffrey seemed so self-satisfied that Lucien wanted to knock him down. Instead he reiterated his main point. "I'm telling you now that you cannot marry her."

"Why can't I?" Jeffrey demanded angrily.

"Because she's mine!"

The words were out of Lucien's mouth before he realized what he had said. The thought of Colette, his beautiful, independent, passionate Colette, in the arms of his best friend almost stopped his heart cold.

"She doesn't belong to you, Lucien," Jeffrey uttered with a deadly calm. "She can marry whomever she chooses. As can I. Besides, what does it matter to you who Colette marries? You're going to propose to Faith Bromleigh. Aren't you?"

Lucien did not answer, although he had already made up his mind that he no longer had any intention of marrying Faith after all. In fact, they had parted that evening on good terms, but with the clear understanding that their brief courtship had ended. Taking a deep breath to calm himself, which did nothing to ease the anger building within him, he curled and uncurled his fists at his side.

Jeffrey's eyes narrowed in suspicion. "Do you have some prior claim upon Colette I should know about?"

"My claims on Colette are none of your concern," Lucien ground out between tightly gritted teeth. Did knowing the way Colette's heart-melting smile lit up a room demonstrate that he had claims over her? Did kissing her passionately? Did making love with Colette in his bed or in a darkened bookshop? Did knowing just where she liked to be touched to make her cry with pleasure constitute claims? Lucien believed they did, but he was not about to enumerate them to Jeffrey. Especially when the subject of their conversation sat a few feet away from them. Instead he demanded, "What is your interest in her all of a sudden? I thought you were not planning on getting married for years."

"Meeting Colette and her sisters has changed my mind."

"Aren't you leaving for France soon?"

"Yes, but not for two or three more weeks. I intend to wed Colette before I go. I'll set her up in my house and then she can have her family stay with her or she can go to Brighton with them until I get back."

Lucien shook his head in disbelief. This was a new Jeffrey. A Jeffrey that had made concrete plans with a woman for the future. "You're serious about this?"

"Yes. I've thought it all out," Jeffrey explained calmly. "I'm going to take care of her and her sisters. Once she's my wife, she won't have to toil in the bookshop any longer. Not that it matters now, since the shop has been sold."

"Yes, I know," Lucien said. "I'm the one who bought the shop."

Stunned by Lucien's comment, Jeffrey stood up straight, moving away from the wall. His lazy posture completely vanished. "You? Why would you buy the shop?"

"Because her mother was selling it and it would have broken her heart to lose it."

Jeffrey's voice lowered and he seemed preoccupied. "I hadn't thought of doing that."

"No. But I did," Lucien stated.

"Well, once she's my wife, she won't have time to work any longer. I'll keep her too busy."

Jeffrey never even saw the solid punch that landed him flat on his back on the slate floor of the veranda. Immediately a commotion erupted. Shocked gasps and startled cries filled the night air.

"She's fainted!" he heard Juliette cry.

Lucien turned around and saw Juliette kneeling over Colette, who lay on the ground also. Her aunt and uncle came rushing to their aid as some of Lady Hayvenhurst's guests began to help Jeffrey to his feet.

Well, he had given the gossips quite a show that evening. Too angry with himself and the entire situation to care, he ignored the calls to him. Without a backward glance Lucien walked from the veranda as a crowd gathered around Jeffrey and the Hamilton sisters.

Later that evening, Lord Eddington's black carriage pulled up in front of Hamilton's Book Shoppe. Juliette Hamilton sprang from the carriage and hurriedly unlocked the door while Jeffrey half carried Colette out of the carriage and inside the shop. The one lamp that Juliette carried cast a yellow path of light as the three of them stealthily made their way to the back room of the silent bookshop.

"Sit her here," Juliette instructed Jeffrey in a brisk whisper as she hastily removed a small stack of books from a tattered armchair in the corner of the room.

Jeffrey led a still-woozy Colette to the chair and let her fall limply onto it. Colette's head fell back and she closed her eyes with a muffled little sigh. She was sound asleep.

"I had no idea she could get so foxed so fast," he said in amazement, shaking his head at Colette's helpless form.

"It's all your fault, giving her so much champagne. Good heavens, Jeffrey! Your face!" Juliette cried, staring at the ugly purple bruise forming around his eye and upper cheekbone.

"I am a handsome devil, aren't I?" he asked with a wicked grin.

"Oh, it looks so much worse than when we left Lady Hayvenhurst's!" She reached out her hand and gently touched his swollen cheek with her fingers.

"Don't press on it!" he cried out, flinching away from her. "That hurts!"

"I'm sorry!" Pulling her hand back hastily, she shook her head and bit her lip. "It's going to look even worse tomorrow."

"But it can't hurt any worse than it does right now."

"I'm afraid I have nothing down here for you to put on it. I can't risk going upstairs just yet. Not with Colette like this," she said worriedly. If her mother or one of her sisters happened to be awake and saw Juliette, they would wonder where Colette was. And Colette was in no shape to be seen by her family.

"That's all right. My valet makes an excellent poultice. He'll fix me up when I get home."

"Can I offer a kiss to make it better?" Juliette offered with a mischievous smile.

"It can only help." His eyes twinkled at her, making the bruise almost disappear.

Juliette rose on tiptoe and placed a soft kiss on the bruised area of Jeffrey's face.

Crestfallen, Jeffrey frowned. "I thought you were really going to give me a kiss."

Juliette began to giggle. "You're so obvious, Jeffrey." She flashed him a grin. "It seems Lord Waverly has quite a punch."

"We both did a bit of boxing back at Oxford." Jeffrey tenderly moved his jaw and stiffened cheek. "I'm not a bad shot myself, but I didn't even get a chance to take a swing back at him."

Oddly intrigued by the thought of those two fine examples of masculinity battling each other in a test of strength, Juliette mused, *Which one would win that fight?*

Lucien and Jeffrey's little scuffle had caused quite a scene on the veranda. When a woozy Colette had jumped up to see what had happened, she tripped and fell. Due to Juliette's quick thinking, everyone assumed Colette had fainted because of the altercation. Aunt Cecilia and Uncle Randall did not suspect that Colette had had too much champagne, although Uncle Randall had given her a skeptical glance, as if to imply that Juliette had done something to cause the row between Lord Eddington and Lord Waverly. When everyone was assured that Colette and Jeffrey were fine, they bundled Colette up, and she and Jeffrey hurried from Lady Hayvenhurst's party and into Jeffrey's carriage. Juliette was sure the gossip would be quite rife with speculation over the cause of the fight between the two friends. "I'm confident you could knock the lights out of Lucien Sinclair," Juliette teased him.

"At times your considerable charm leaves much to be desired, Juliette," Jeffrey remarked dryly.

Laughing at him, Juliette glanced at Colette. Her sister had chattered incessantly the entire carriage ride home. Still suffering the ill effects of too much alcohol, she now slept peacefully in the chair. "At least we can talk without Colette hearing us."

"She's going to have a terrible headache in the morning," Jeffrey predicted with a regretful expression.

"The poor thing," she murmured softly. Colette rarely appeared vulnerable, and in this instance it left Juliette feeling more than a little anxious.

"Oh, fine. She gets your sympathy, but I take a punch in the face for following your little plan and I get laughed at."

"It's for a noble cause, Jeffrey." She smiled sweetly at him. "You know how much I appreciate your help."

He gave her a skeptical look, and then they moved to sit on two overturned crates. Usually Juliette avoided the back room of the shop as much as possible. The overcrowded, windowless space used to make her feel claustrophobic. But she had to admit that it was not as bad now as she recalled.

Colette had been unable to spruce up the back room as much as she had the main shop, but at least it was cleaner and more organized than when their father was alive.

"What a scene that was! What luck Lucien hit you when he did! No one noticed my intoxicated sister. If Lucien hit you, he must have been jealous," Juliette whispered excitedly. "What did you say to him?"

Jeffrey rubbed his cheek with an unconscious motion, obviously recalling the dreadful incident. "Oh, I hit a nerve all right. I told him that I intended to marry Colette and that she had practically said yes."

Thrilled by this development and the probable success of her plan, she laughed at the thought of Jeffrey taunting Lucien. "Oh, my! He must have believed you!"

"I don't think he was quite sure at first, but then I convinced him."

"Did you truly ask Colette to marry you?"

"Of course not. Even if I did, she would refuse me. She is head over heels in love with Lucien."

"I told you she was. And this evening simply goes to prove that Lucien is in love with her, too. If he didn't care about her, he wouldn't have hit you."

"They are quite serious with each other," Jeffrey ventured quietly with a knowing look at Juliette. "If you take my meaning."

Of course Juliette knew, but she was stunned that Jeffrey knew how intimate Colette and Lucien had become. "How did you find out?"

He motioned his head toward Colette with a wry look. "Apparently too much champagne makes your sister rather talkative."

"I can't believe she told you something like *that*." Knowing that Colette would be mortified when she realized what she had revealed to Jeffrey, Juliette cringed.

Jeffrey seemed a little offended by her remark. "I'm a trustworthy fellow."

Juliette apologized. "I didn't mean that as a slight against your character, Jeffrey. It's just that Colette is so private, I am shocked she told anyone besides me."

He nodded. "Lucien did not tell me, either, if that is what you were thinking. He's too much of a gentleman."

Juliette wondered how much of a gentleman Lucien was if he refused to marry her sister after taking her virtue.

Jeffrey quietly inquired, "Were you aware that Lucien purchased the bookshop?"

Blazes! If Jeffrey had told her that he had suddenly sprouted wings and had learned to fly, she couldn't have been more astounded. Unable to speak, Juliette simply stared at him.

An amused smile flickered across his handsome face. "Well, well, well. It seems I finally knew something before the infamous Juliette did."

"He didn't really buy the shop, did he?" she asked breathlessly, still in awe of the earth-shattering news he had just shared with her. "Lucien is the anonymous buyer?"

"That's what he told me, and I have no reason to believe that he'd lie about something like that."

"No, of course not. If Lucien told you, then I'm sure he did buy it. But *why* would he do such a thing?"

"To prevent Colette's heart from being broken," Jeffrey clarified. "Or so he told me when I asked him."

Juliette was stunned. "He said that? That he purchased the shop to protect Colette?"

"Yes, he did. If you did not know Lucien bought the shop, the real question is, does Colette know?" he asked.

"She would have told me something so important!" *Wouldn't she?* Perhaps Colette didn't know either. Although they now knew whom the anonymous buyer was, questions upon questions still niggled at Juliette. Why did Lucien keep it a secret? What had he intended to do with the building? Had he wished for the shop to stay in Colette's care, since she was the motivation behind his purchase?

"So what happens now, Miss Master Plan?" Jeffrey interrupted her thoughts.

"Now, we wait."

"Wait for what? For Lucien to beat the devil out of me?"

"No." She managed a wry smile. "But you do need to stay away from him for a while until he discovers that you have no true designs on Colette. In the meantime, I have a feeling things will happen rather quickly."

Chapter Twenty-Six

The Plot Thickens

About to begin their reading session, Lucien sat with Simon in his bedroom. Exhausted after a seemingly endless and sleepless night, Lucien found himself at loose ends the next day and wandered into his father's chamber.

For the past week his mother had spent much of her time with Simon. To Lucien's complete amazement, she had moved back into Devon House with his father's blessings. The two of them acted as if the years of separation had not happened. Lucien could not quite understand it. Too much had happened too quickly for him to absorb. "You and Mother seem to be getting along well. It's almost as if she never left," Lucien remarked to his father. Lenora had gone out shopping that afternoon and Lucien used the time to visit with Simon alone.

His father smiled brightly, appearing more alive than he had in months.

"You're not going to explain to me what happened with you and Mother, are you?"

Simon shook his head. "It's p-private. Sh-she knows the truth. I know the t-truth now."

Lucien tilted his head, feeling somewhat angry. Her devastating departure had affected him just as much as, if not more than, his father, and they did not see fit to explain to him why. "And am I never to know the reason my mother left me for most of my life?"

Simon actually looked embarrassed, his head hung low. "M-maybe Mother will tell you."

"Well then," Lucien picked up *David Copperfield,* idly running his finger across the golden embossed lettering. "I suppose there is nothing left to say, is there?" With a heavy heart he held the book that Colette had been reading to his father, suddenly feeling her absence like a knife in his side.

"Marry her."

Startled by not just the clarity of Simon's words but their implications, Lucien glanced up. He knew his father referred to Colette, but it seemed he was under a misguided impression.

"She's going to marry Jeffrey Eddington." Lucien still could not believe it. If he had not heard the words directly from Jeffrey himself he would not have believed the story at all. The very idea of the two of them together made him feel like hitting Jeffrey again. Apparently last night's pummeling of his oldest friend did not quite satisfy him.

Lady Hayvenhurst's had been a disaster. He had caused a scene and enough gossip and speculation to keep society wagging its tongues for weeks.

At least he had finally seen through the folly of thinking he could spend his life married to someone like Faith Bromleigh. She was a sweet girl, to be sure, but completely wrong for him. He simply couldn't do it.

But learning that his best friend intended to marry the woman who tempted him above all others left him still in shock.

"No." His father shook his head adamantly. "No, she won't. She loves you."

Granger stepped into the room. "Excuse me, my lord, but there is a Miss Hamilton waiting to see you downstairs. She's in the blue drawing room."

Stunned, Lucien stood up with a jolt, the copy of *David Copperfield* falling to the floor at his feet. *Colette has come to see me?* The sudden pounding of his heart startled him. He felt like a giddy schoolboy at the mere thought of seeing her.

His father's broad smile lit up his face. "Hurry. G-go to her," he instructed with a wave of his good arm.

Leaving his father in Granger's care, Lucien wasted no time in getting downstairs, yet the whole time his mind was spinning with questions. *Why has she come? What does she want from me?* Admittedly he still felt angry with her for her bitter reaction to his buying the bookshop. And he was none too pleased with her for practically agreeing to marry Jeffrey Eddington less than twenty-four hours after they had been so intimate in the bookshop.

Yes, he had quite a few things he wanted to say to Miss Colette Hamilton.

He eagerly opened the door to the blue drawing room and stopped dead in his tracks when he saw Juliette Hamilton seated calmly upon the velvet sofa, regarding him with something akin to amusement.

"Juliette?" he questioned, unable to conceal the surprise in his voice and overwhelmed with disappointment that it was not Colette who had come to see him.

"Good afternoon, Lord Waverly."

Her superior smile gave him pause and, as was usually the case whenever Lucien was with Juliette, irritated him. "What are you doing here?"

"Were you expecting Colette, perhaps? I'm terribly sorry to disappoint you."

Her sarcastic yet deadly accurate assessment of the

situation only further irritated his already frayed nerves. *Devil take her!* What did Juliette Hamilton want with him? He advanced farther into the drawing room, stopping near the sofa.

"To what do I owe the pleasure of your visit?" he asked, folding his arms across his chest. She looked directly at him, her blue eyes so similar to Colette's that he almost fell over. Did all those Hamilton sisters have to look so disconcertingly alike?

"I thought we should have a little chat." Her voice was soft.

"Why do you and your sister insist upon going out without a chaperone?" He frowned at her.

Ignoring his question, she inquired instead, "Aren't you the least bit interested in what I have to say?"

"No," he snapped in frustration.

"Please sit down, Lucien, and listen to me."

Struck by the unexpected pleading note in her tone, Lucien felt a sense of unease grow within his chest. Perhaps something happened to Colette. "Is Colette well?"

Juliette flashed a funny little smile. "She's feeling a little under the weather today, but she will no doubt recover soon enough."

Perplexed by Juliette's attitude and at her very presence at his house, Lucien figured he had better find out what she was up to. And with Juliette, it could be anything. Seating himself on the striped damask chair nearest the blue sofa upon which she sat, he commanded, "All right, then. Enlighten me as to the purpose of your visit, Juliette."

She took a deep breath before beginning. "I have something important to share with you, but before I reveal it, I wish to confirm a few points with you first."

Something important? It can only be about Colette. Why else would Juliette be here? Intrigued more than he cared to admit, Lucien wordlessly motioned for her to continue.

"Is it true that you purchased the bookshop from my mother?" she asked.

So Colette had told her. Lucien wondered how the rest of her sisters felt about the news. Hopefully they were happier than Colette was when she found out. "Yes, I did," he stated.

"May I ask why?" She arched a delicate eyebrow in his direction.

"I thought that was obvious. I purchased the shop because I wanted to help your family."

"And Colette?" she asked in a manner meant to prompt more of a response from him.

"Yes, of course, I did it to help Colette as well."

"I know you have feelings for her, Lucien."

"Why are you here, Juliette?" He uttered the words edgily, not wishing to discuss his feelings for her sister when he was not sure of them himself.

Juliette became a little nervous, which was unusual for her. "Well, it seems I find myself in a situation."

"Why does that not surprise me in the slightest?" he asked dryly. Juliette was a master at creating situations.

She ignored his barb and continued. "I know you are in love with Colette, a fact that was made even more obvious to me by the fact that you bought the shop for her. My sister tells me everything, so I know she is in love with you, but you are both too blind to admit it to each other."

Lucien had had just about enough of the Hamilton sisters declaring they knew his feelings better than he did. First Paulette told him he was in love with Colette, and now Juliette had the audacity to come to his own home to tell him how he felt. What was it about that family? They had gotten under his skin somehow and he couldn't shake them. His feelings for Colette alone had him in knots. *Good God, he hoped Colette had not told Juliette everything they had done!* "Are you quite through?"

"No."

Juliette's blatant answer caught him off guard. "No?" he echoed.

"No," she said with determination, her small chin rising up. "I'm not finished yet."

"Well, don't let me keep you," he flung back at her.

"You aren't going to marry Faith Bromleigh after all, are you?"

He could not lie. "No. We agreed we did not suit."

"Thank heaven for small favors!" Juliette exclaimed with a great sigh. "I thought you had taken leave of your senses when I heard you were interested in marrying that one. Really, Lucien, she would have bored you to an early grave—"

"Aside from annoying me, is there a point to your being here, Juliette?" he interrupted with an impatient look, very near the end of his tether with her bold statements and attitude.

"I am only trying to help you."

"If this is your idea of helping me," he said with a grimace, "I shudder to think what you would do if you were trying to do me harm."

Juliette actually laughed, the light sound filling the room. "Well, you do possess a sense of humor after all. I had my doubts that you had one, Lucien. Now would you like me to tell you something that would ease your mind?"

"That would be refreshing."

Again she smiled, tilting her head to the side. "I'm beginning to like you."

"Juliette?" he prompted with impatience. Would the chit never get to the point?

"Very well, then." She swallowed nervously before she spoke. "We are all quite aware of your feelings for Colette and hers for you—"

"Have we not covered this already?"

"If you would you let me finish?" she countered evenly.

"Fine." Jesus, but Juliette Hamilton could drive a man to drink.

"And knowing as we did that you were making a terrible mistake with Faith Bromleigh, Jeffrey and I thought we could do something to help."

His eyes narrowed and he looked at her suspiciously, a gnawing feeling of concern building within him. "To help me?"

"Yes, to help you from making a mistake that would haunt you for the rest of your life," she said simply. "I had this brilliant little plan that if you were led to believe that Colette was going to marry Jeffrey, you would become jealous enough to ask her to marry her yourself, which is what you should have done in the first place."

"You mean to say that you wheedled Jeffrey into lying to me last night about his interest in Colette?" Lucien could barely contain his anger enough to utter the words.

She nodded in admission of her part in the scheme. "But we didn't expect you to flatten him."

"So you and Jeffrey have had quite a good laugh at my expense."

"No! Not at all!" she protested her eyes growing wide. "Honestly, Lucien, Jeffrey and I did this only with the best intentions. We just wanted you and Colette to be happy together."

Lucien's head fell in his hands and he rubbed his eyes with his fingers. He'd made a spectacle of himself last night and punched his best friend, for no apparent reason. No, perhaps there was a good reason. Jeffrey deserved a good wallop for tricking him so cruelly. Wearily he lifted his head and looked at Juliette. "Does Colette know about this?"

Juliette pressed her gloved hands tightly together and leaned forward, her expression quite earnest. "She has no idea, and she had no part in any of this. I swear to you, Lucien. The plan was only between Jeffrey and me. Colette had so much champagne last night, I doubt she is even aware that Jeffrey took us home. She doesn't know anything of what Jeffrey said to you about the two of them, or that you hit him because of it. She would more than likely be angry with us both, if she did know."

"And you think I'm not going to be angry with you?" he snapped.

"I was hoping you would understand that no harm was intended."

"Well, you hoped wrong."

They sat in tense silence for some minutes. Lucien was angry on many levels. At Juliette for meddling. At Jeffrey for conspiring against him. He felt betrayed and manipulated by both of them. But for all that, he could only think of Colette. It seemed he was in love with Colette, and apparently everyone knew it but him.

Finally he looked at Juliette. "So what was your purpose in telling me this now?"

She relaxed somewhat at the softness of his tone. "I wanted to apologize to you. I realize it was a mistake. And I could not bear for you to stay angry with Jeffrey when he was completely innocent in all this."

"I would not say he was *completely* innocent. He did go along with your scatterbrained scheme to dupe me."

"Yes, he did," she agreed, "but only because he knew, just as I did, that it was for the best. He truly has no interest in marrying Colette. He just said that to rile you up."

"And sitting intimately with her on the veranda? I'm sure you had to twist his arm to do that?"

"Well, we had to set it up." She shrugged helplessly. "You had to believe something was happening between them. We didn't expect Colette to drink so much and confide in him."

He had a sickening feeling in the pit of his stomach. "What exactly did Colette confide in Jeffrey?"

Juliette became somewhat flustered, but managed to convey the crux of Jeffrey's conversation with Colette. "Uh . . . that the two of you had been rather . . . intimate of late and—"

"Jesus!" he cried. Did the whole world need to know his private business? Now Jeffrey knew about his relationship with Colette. Now that he thought about it, he was surprised Jeffrey hadn't punched *him* in the face.

"Lucien," she said soothingly. "I realize you don't have any brothers or sisters—"

"For which I am eternally grateful."

Juliette continued as if he had not interrupted her. "My point is that siblings help one another. At least, that is the way it works in my family."

"Yet I assume Colette has no idea you are here with me right now, does she?"

"Of course not."

"So once again, you are taking matters into your own hands and meddling where you don't belong."

She bristled at his criticism. "I wouldn't quite put it that way."

Lucien rose from the chair, looming over her. "Well, I would and I have had quite enough of it. I'll not listen to another word from you. Go home now. And keep your mouth closed and keep yourself out of my business." He turned and pulled the long cloth-covered cord that rang a bell in the servants' quarters.

Unfazed by his ire, Juliette stood and eyed him levelly. "What do you intend to do now?"

"That is none of *your* business. Go home, Juliette." Lucien strode purposefully to the drawing room door and opened it wide, giving her a clear indication that he wished her to walk through it.

"Fine," she muttered in a bit of a huff, stepping toward the door. She turned back to him before making her exit and added, "Just remember that Jeffrey and I were only trying to make sure you and Colette didn't ruin your lives."

"I don't need your help."

"Oh, yes, you most certainly do!" she cried vehemently.

"Good afternoon, Miss Hamilton," he said with finality.

"Good afternoon, Lord Waverly." Her frosty tone left no doubt as to her feelings for him. A footman appeared to escort her to the front door.

With a weary sigh, he shook his head at the strange encounter with Colette's sister. Just as he had guessed, Juliette Hamilton and Jeffrey Eddington together were a dangerous combination. Between them there existed no sense of caution or common sense. What a mess they had created!

Walking toward the window, he pulled back the long silk drapes and peered out at the cobblestone street below. Rain had begun to fall. People with umbrellas hurried by, going about their daily business, living their own lives, trying not to get drenched in the downpour. He pressed his head against the cool pane of glass streaked with raindrops, sorely tempted to put his fist through it in frustration.

Colette. *Colette.*

Lucien did not want to wed Faith Bromleigh and Jeffrey did not want to marry Colette. It should all be so simple. Unfortunately it was not. They said Colette loved him, but Lucien was not quite so sure.

And they all believed that he was in love with her. *Was he?* He had not felt this way when he was wildly in love with Virginia Warren. He felt a thousand times more for Colette than he ever had for Virginia. That should tell him something.

And it did.

His intense feelings for her told him to run as fast as he could from Colette Hamilton.

"Lucien?"

Not turning around at the sound of her now-familiar voice, Lucien stood still and did not immediately answer to the call of his name.

"Lucien, may I come in and speak to you for a moment?"

"Of course, Mother, " he murmured absently, still not facing her, his eyes riveted on the street below and the people walking by, the muffled sound of their footsteps on the wet road.

"I couldn't help but notice Miss Hamilton leaving. She is the sister of your friend Colette, is she not? The one who reads to your father?"

"Yes." He finally turned to look at her. His mother. Lenora stood before him, her eyes full of concern and a yearning that he could not define. Lucien had still not grown accustomed to her constant presence in his home.

"Lucien, I know I have not earned the right to be treated as your mother, but I would desperately like for us to be friends."

"Sit down, Mother. If you wish to have a talk, we might as well be comfortable." With a resigned sigh, he motioned for her to sit. Then he made his way to the sideboard and poured himself a glass of whisky from the crystal decanter. He took a long gulp.

"You're drinking so early?"

He did not even acknowledge her.

Lenora took Juliette's place on the blue sofa and Lucien reluctantly returned to his place on the chair. With his drink still in his hand, he looked at her expectantly.

Lenora wrung her hands in a nervous motion. "You were so young when I left that now I'm not sure how to resume our relationship. You are not a little boy anymore, but you are still my son."

Good Lord, what did she want from him? Hadn't she

hurt him enough over the years? "What is it that you want, Mother?"

"I . . . I'm not sure entirely. I suppose I want us to at least be friendly to each other. Your father has forgiven me, and I have forgiven him, which has eased my heart greatly as well as his." She gazed at him, her fine brows furrowed in sorrow. "But you . . . I don't know how to make it up to you, Lucien. How can I atone for deserting you, my own little son, who was innocent of any wrongdoing?"

Lucien remained quiet for some time, lost in memories of his childhood. There were times he wished his mother had simply died. It would have been easier to bear had that been the case. Easier to explain to his friends. Easier to hold his head up. Then he could have cherished her memory instead of being tormented by her absence. At least he would have understood her death as something beyond his control, whereas he had taken her abandonment personally. He had believed he had been the cause of her flight, for what mother would ever leave a child she loved? "Perhaps you could explain to me why you left? As the innocent party, as you say, I think I have a right to know."

She nodded sadly, her green eyes full of regret and pain. "Yes, I suppose I owe you that much. It's a complicated story, and even when I look back now I don't understand why I did what I did, or why your father did what he did for that matter. We were both foolish and stubborn . . ."

He waited for her to continue, anxious to know what had happened all those years ago to cause her to leave him.

A soft expression came over her face as she spoke. "I fell in love with your father the moment I met him at my coming-out ball when I was eighteen, and I just knew from the first time he held my hand that I wanted him to hold me forever. Simon was charming and handsome and full of life. We married a few months later in a very small, quiet affair. Simon and I were ridiculously happy together and we were over the moon with joy when you were born, Lucien."

Her look of adoration moved him more than he cared to admit. "Go on."

"Oh, how we both doted on you! You were an amazing child, Lucien, truly. So sweet and funny, and so smart. You constantly delighted us. Simon and I wanted to have more children, but I had . . . I could not . . . I lost . . . For years we tried but, for some reason . . . God chose not to bless us with another baby. It was a very stressful and heart-breaking time for me, and your father and I began to have . . . well . . . difficulties, shall we say? Because of that he turned to another woman for comfort. Unfortunately that woman was a dear friend of mine. A very dear friend. When I found out, I became incensed. In an attempt to hurt Simon I became involved with Count Acciani, who was in London visiting his sister. Antonio was young and handsome and madly in love with me, so it was easy enough to make Simon jealous with him. Naturally Simon was furious when he discovered me kissing Antonio one night. We fought bitterly. Terribly. Oh, this is not easy to explain, Lucien."

His mother paused for a moment, unsure if she should continue. With her cheeks flushed pink, her embarrassment was evident.

"Go on, Mother. It's all right," he urged her, fascinated by this glimpse into his parents' past.

"Well . . . Then a small miracle happened, and I discovered I was going to have a baby. I suppose I had made your father a little too jealous, because he refused to believe the child was his, even though it was. I knew without a doubt it was Simon's baby, for Antonio and I had not . . . we had only kissed . . .well . . . you understand how I could know such a thing. Simon, in a rage, did not believe me and had me thrown out of Devon House. He refused to let me see you. Oh, what a terrible scene that was!"

Lucien placed the unfinished glass of whisky on the table and stared speechlessly at his mother. He tried to recall when she left, but could not remember a particular night or event. She was just simply gone one day, like the sun disappearing behind a dark cloud. He felt oddly conflicted at her story. Not knowing what to expect when she began her tale, he was certain he had not expected this.

Her voice grew low. "I had no money and nowhere to go, since my own parents had passed away, and your father had turned all our friends against me, painting me in the worst light. Who else could I turn to but the other man who loved me? Antonio, dear sweet Antonio, took me in when no one else would. I was carrying my husband's child, but no one believed me. Except of course, for Antonio, because he knew the truth. He knew, just as well as I, that it was Simon's child. He even attempted to tell Simon, but Simon would not believe him. So we fled to Italy. I had no other option. It tore my heart out to leave you and your father, but I had no choice. He would not let me back. I wrote you both, letter after letter, for years. But Simon never responded to me, and obviously he did not allow you to see any of my letters to you. I suppose it was easier for him to let you believe your mother was a heartless creature rather than to explain his own jealous rage and stubborn pride. Oh, Lucien, you have no idea how I cried every day, endless tears, over missing you."

Reeling from these revelations, Lucien began to feel tendrils of sympathy grow for his mother for the first time in his life. "And the child?" he asked, his throat dry.

Lenora's eyes became misty. "Oh, I had the child. Simon's child. A beautiful little girl. I named her Katherine, after my mother. Antonio adored her and treated her as his own daughter. We lived in a small villa in Tuscany and everyone just assumed Antonio was my husband. But he knew I was still legally wed to and in love with my husband. He loved me anyway, and he was good to me."

Astounded to learn that he had a sister, a little sister who had to be close to Paulette Hamilton's age, Lucien's head spun. For the last fifteen years he'd had a sister he knew nothing about. "Where is Katherine now?"

"Last year she and Antonio caught a fever . . ." Lenora choked on a sob and fumbled for a handkerchief. "I lost both of them within days of each other."

"I'm so sorry," he murmured, feeling a strange overwhelming sense of loss for the sister he had never known. And somehow, in his mind's eye, he could not help but picture his sister looking like Paulette Hamilton. "I had no idea."

"Of course you didn't," she sniffled, dabbing her eyes with her monogrammed handkerchief. "You were too young to know when I left. And all these years, I stayed foolishly hidden. I should have stood my ground with Simon and let him see Katherine for himself. For all that I named her after my mother, she was the spitting image of Simon's mother. He would not have been able to deny her as his child had he seen her. But I was too afraid he would deny her, too. It was only after I lost Katherine and Antonio that I realized I had nothing to lose by returning to London. And only my son to gain."

He gazed at his mother as if seeing her for the first time. His heart broke for her.

"I returned to London determined to see you and your father, but once I arrived I was overcome with trepidation. I had no idea what Simon had said to you, and I assumed you hated me. When I learned that your father was ill, it only made me more anxious to see him. And you. But it was you I feared the most. I was long accustomed to Simon shutting me out of his life, but if you shut me out too, I didn't think I could bear that hurt. That's why I wrote you first. When you didn't respond I was devastated. And when I finally received your letter, it gave me a glimmer of hope and I could not wait any longer to see you."

That day conjured mixed emotions within him, the joy at seeing his mother again and the anger at her for years of desertion.

She continued to wipe her tears as she spoke. "Seeing your father so changed was quite a shock to me. I still pictured him as I did when I left, young and vital. He is so weakened and frail now."

"He has improved dramatically since you've been here," Lucien stated softly.

"I believe we have come to find a sort of peace between us now. We have been talking about everything that has happened. And I have told him about Katherine, his daughter. Years of pain and regret tend to wear a heart down, making it easier to forgive . . ." Her voice faltered as she looked at Lucien.

Filled with a profound sadness, Lucien moved to sit beside his mother on the sofa and put his arm around her. He held her awkwardly at first. She felt tiny and fragile. Then she kissed his cheek and hugged him to her in a tight embrace.

"I am so sorry, Lucien," she gasped with an agonized sob, finally releasing him. "Your father and I have made a such terrible mess of your life."

"I know now that was never your intention." Feeling the years of heartbreak and the terrible sadness that had affected each of their lives, he was overwhelmed.

"Can you ever forgive me?" she asked, searching his face with her eyes.

He nodded, unable. "I don't know. But I feel better at least knowing the truth."

"Perhaps we can start over? We can at least try to get to know one another again." Her voice was full of hope.

After spending his life wondering what had happened to her and if she had ever really loved him, a small degree of peace settled within Lucien's heart at having her with him once again.

"I know you don't need a mother at your age," she continued, "but I can try to be a mother to you anyway."

"I would like that." He smiled at her, and Lenora began to cry with happiness.

Chapter Twenty-Seven

The Morning After

Colette held her hands to her throbbing temples. Good heavens, but her head ached. She had vague memories of the night before and did not care for any of them. She also had the distinct impression that Jeffrey and Juliette had been secretive about something that had to do with her. Try as she might, she could not recall what it was about.

However, she clearly remembered seeing Lucien with Faith Bromleigh on Lady Hayvenhurst's veranda. Wishing *that* was the image she could not recall, she rubbed her forehead with the pads of her fingertips as she leaned against the counter. She was grateful for the pouring rain outside, if only for the fact that it meant few if any customers would be visiting the shop that day.

"No, Yvette. Don't put that there," she called to her sister.

Yvette spun around, her long blond hair pulled back from her face with a wide cherry-colored ribbon that perfectly matched her dark blue dress with vertical red pin stripes. "Oh. Where does it go, then?" she asked, holding the science textbook in her hand.

"If you can climb the ladder, it belongs on the top shelf. Over there in the science section. Do you see?"

Yvette nodded eagerly. "Oh, I can climb up there."

Her little sister was desperately trying to help her in the shop, something Yvette rarely volunteered to do. Colette had the sinking suspicion that Juliette had put her up to it, for some reason. As Yvette climbed the ladder, Colette folded her arms on the counter and rested her pounding head in them.

She would never drink champagne again for as long as she lived.

Last night had been dreadful.

But not as dreadful as the coming week would be. She did not even know why she bothered having Yvette reshelve the science book, since everything would have to be packed into boxes soon. What difference did it make? They were leaving London and the shop.

She groaned audibly at the thought of the work involved in closing up the bookshop.

"Colette, are you all right?" Yvette yelled from the top of the ladder.

Her sister's shrill voice almost split Colette's skull in two. She mumbled a faint yes, her head still buried in her arms. The light jingling of the bells over the door, which sounded like the clanging of the gates of hell, brought forth another moan from Colette as she slowly raised her head to see who entered the shop.

"Oh, it's you," she whispered and managed to hold up her head with her hands, her elbows resting on the counter. She could not help but notice the ugly bruise under his eye. "What happened to your face?"

"I'll explain that later." Jeffrey shrugged off his wet overcoat and placed it with his hat on the brass hat rack near the door. Turning back to face her, he asked cheerily, "And how are we feeling today?"

His amused smile did not amuse her. "This is all your fault," she muttered.

"I don't recall forcing you to drink that much champagne."

"No, but you started it."

"Now that I will take credit for." He laughed at her then, but added sympathetically, "I know it does not feel that way at the moment, but you will feel better again soon."

"Hello there!"

Jeffrey spun around at the sound of Yvette's voice. She still stood at the top of the ladder, looking down at them both most curiously.

Jeffrey glanced between Colette and Yvette, blinking in surprise. He said to Colette, "I don't believe I have met this one yet."

"This is Yvette. The baby of the family," Colette whispered wearily.

"I don't think I'll ever get over how much the five of you girls look alike," Jeffrey marveled, shaking his head at Colette. "She looks like a miniature version of you with blond hair."

"And I'm not a baby. I just happen to be the youngest," Yvette declared from her perch on the ladder.

Jeffrey made his way over to her. "And I am honored to meet you, Miss Yvette. I am Lord Jeffrey Eddington."

"Oh. So *you're* Jeffrey Eddington. I've heard my sisters talk about you," Yvette murmured, somewhat in awe. If Colette had not felt so terrible, she might have laughed in amusement at the spellbound expression on Yvette's face.

"Good things, I hope?" he asked with a twinkle in his eye.

"I think so," she said hesitantly. "Mostly good things."

Laughing out loud at the implications of her innocently uttered words, Jeffrey gave Yvette the thrill of her life when he gallantly held out his hand to help her from the ladder. With a smile of adoration on her face, she took his hand and gracefully stepped down the wooden rungs.

"Why thank you, Lord Eddington. It's so refreshing to meet a true gentleman," Yvette stated with a touching sincerity that only a thirteen-year-old could show. As if she were the grandest lady in the land, she gave him a proud look.

Jeffrey intuitively sensed how important it was for Yvette to be taken seriously. "I must say it's refreshing to meet a young lady who can recognize a true gentleman when she meets one." Releasing her hand, he bowed elegantly.

Jeffrey certainly had a skill for winning women over with his charm, and Colette knew there would be no living with Yvette after this little interlude. The sophisticated airs she would put on for the next few days would be insufferable.

Yvette asked, "How did you get such a terrible bruise?"

"It seems I accidentally stepped on someone's toes," he explained vaguely.

The door to the shop flew open, bells clanging wildly, and Juliette rushed in, the sound of the rain splashing in the street suddenly louder until she closed the door with a slam. They turned to look at her.

"Oh, it's simply dreadful out there! I'm drenched." And indeed, the hem of her gown was damp past her ankles. Juliette tossed her wet umbrella to the floor with a grimace and glanced up in surprise. "Jeffrey! I didn't know you were here!" she cried.

"I just had the pleasure of meeting Miss Yvette Hamilton," Jeffrey announced to her.

"That's nice," she murmured distractedly. "Yvette, I need to speak to Colette and Lord Eddington privately."

"And you wish for me to go upstairs?" Yvette asked with a gracious tone.

"Would you please?"

"Of course. Again, it was an honor meeting you, Lord Eddington," she said, bowing prettily.

"The honor and the pleasure were all mine. Good afternoon." Jeffrey beamed at her as she turned and left them in the shop. "She's quite a little lady, that one, isn't she?"

"I don't know how you could keep a straight face with the way you spoke to her, Jeffrey," Colette murmured before placing her head back down on her arms.

"Because she is an adorable child," he defended himself. "And your sister."

"Wake up, Colette. I have something to tell you, and it's just as well that Jeffrey is here," Juliette announced as she moved nearer to the counter.

Once again Colette made the tremendous effort to lift her throbbing head. "What?" she asked, noting the guarded glance between Juliette and Jeffrey. "If this is about last night, I don't believe I have the strength to hear it."

Juliette sighed heavily. "It's about more than last night. I think I've made a terrible mess of things."

"What things?" Colette asked in confusion.

Juliette flashed a nervous glance once again at Jeffrey before answering. He shrugged innocently and held up his hands without guilt. Juliette began slowly, "I just came from Devon House."

Colette felt her pulse quicken at the mention of Lucien's home. What had Juliette done? Had she spoken to Lucien? The worried expression on her sister's face caused an uncomfortable unease to spread within her. "What on earth were you doing there?"

"Trying to explain to Lucien that Jeffrey has no intention of marrying you."

Stunned, Colette stared at Juliette blankly, trying to take in what she said, but her aching head seemed to make no sense of the words. "What did you say?"

Jeffrey spoke up. "Last night I gave Lucien the idea that you and I were going to wed. As you can see," he pointed to his face, "the idea did not sit well with him."

"Lucien hit you?" she cried incredulously, her head spinning with their descriptions of the event. She recalled a commotion while on the veranda, and everyone thinking she had fainted. She cringed at the memory. "I don't understand any of this. And I honestly don't think I want to hear any more." With a groan she put her head back down.

"You had better explain it to her from the beginning, Juliette. It's not fair to confuse her when she's in such a bad way." Jeffrey walked toward the counter and began to rub Colette's back. "Poor girl."

Juliette came around and sat on the other stool. She leaned in close to Colette and said, "All right, then. I confess that I should have minded my own business and left things to work out for themselves between you and Lucien."

Colette's head flew up so fast she almost fell off the stool. With her pounding head and pounding heart, she could barely see straight. What had the two of them been up to? And what did anything have to do with her and Lucien? "Between me and Lucien? There is nothing between me and Lucien!"

"There's no need to get so upset," Juliette attempted to soothe her. "We know everything, Colette. We know Lucien bought the bookshop."

The appalled look on her face must have given them both pause, because they looked remorseful. "What have you done?" Colette whispered.

Hesitating and reluctant to reveal the truth, Juliette began slowly. "We knew that Lucien was making a terrible mistake in marrying Faith Bromleigh when he is so obviously in love with you, and we thought we would help the situation along a little, by making Lucien jealous."

Jeffrey continued to rub her back. "So I told Lucien last

night that I had suggested marriage to you and you agreed." He smiled wickedly at her and motioned to the marks on his face. "You see how he reacted to the thought of you with another man?"

Feeling nauseous now, Colette wanted to cry. "Are you sure he didn't simply hit you because you are annoying?"

Jeffrey laughed. "That thought did cross my mind, but as I was lying on Lady Hayvenhurst's veranda, it occurred to me that in all the years I've known Lucien Sinclair, he has never hit me. Not once. Not even when I more than likely deserved to be hit. No, Colette, this reaction could only have been prompted by his feelings for you."

Colette had no response. She did not know what to say. Did Lucien have feelings for her? Had Lucien truly hit Jeffery out of jealousy over her?

Although she knew Juliette and Jeffrey, sweet Jeffrey, were only trying to help her, their meddling in her affairs made her angry.

"After Lucien hit Jeffrey, I realized perhaps that things had gone too far and I went to speak to Lucien this afternoon," Juliette confessed.

"Oh, you didn't!" Colette cried in despair.

Juliette stated tersely, "I did."

"And just how did *that* go?" Jeffrey asked curiously.

"Not well. He was less than thrilled with our little plan," Juliette explained. "But I think he will calm down and come to his senses eventually. The good news is that he is *not* going to marry Faith Bromleigh."

Stunned, Colette stared at them. "He's not?"

"No, he is not," Juliette said. "And he told me so himself."

"There, you see?" Jeffrey added with a grin. "He's in love with you."

Too weak to respond, Colette put her head back in her arms.

Chapter Twenty-Eight

A Change of Heart

"Where have you been?" Lenora asked with a worried expression. "You've been gone for three days."

"I am well aware of how long I've been gone," Lucien responded, continuing up the front staircase of Devon House, carrying a small suitcase.

"But you didn't tell us you were going anywhere." His mother followed close behind him, her anxious words hovering around him.

"I sent word." Unused to having a mother check up on him, he almost wanted to laugh at her anxiety. For over fifteen years she had no idea what he was doing at any given time. Now she was worried.

"Yesterday! Last night we finally received word that you would be home today. Your father and I were worried about you. Where have you been all this time, Lucien?"

He strode into his bedchamber and tossed his bag on a nearby chair. "I just needed to clear my head. I needed to get away. As you can see, I am fine. There is no reason to worry."

Lenora sighed with resignation. "Well, I suppose not, but still . . . We were concerned. Your father said it was not like you to just leave without word. Is everything all right?"

Was everything all right? Lucien was still not even sure. He had left in an attempt to get some clarity, some perspective on things. Time away had only made him more confused. He could not stop thinking of Colette. He had not seen her since the terrible night at Lady Hayvenhurst's when he had punched his best friend. But Jeffrey's words had echoed over and over in his head. As well as Juliette's.

He needed to see Colette. Three days of contemplating his situation with her had left him maddeningly frustrated and still unclear of what to do about any of it. The only blessing was that he had the foresight to end his ridiculous association with the Bromleighs. Nice people though they were, he and Faith would be miserable together.

Colette was something else altogether. He could not stop thinking of her and wanting to be with her. He adored her family, in spite of Juliette's meddling. Colette had completely won over his father. She loved her family, and her loyalty to them was astonishing. He found her intelligent and charming. Lucien respected and even admired her ability to manage the bookshop. She was witty and fun to be with, and of course, there was the sex. He desired her more than any woman he had ever known.

And after his jealous reaction to Jeffrey's plan to marry her, he finally came to the realization that perhaps he was in love with her after all.

He was in love with a woman he was terrified to marry and who, at the moment, wanted nothing to do with him.

"Will you be joining us for dinner?"

Distracted, Lucien glanced at his mother as if just

noticing her presence for the first time. "I'm sorry. No. No, I don't think I'll be able to join you this evening."

"Are you going out again?"

"Yes, I suppose I am," he replied slowly.

"Are you going to see Miss Hamilton?" she asked.

He did not answer.

"She was here yesterday."

He eyed his mother sharply, his heart suddenly racing. *Colette had come to see me?*

She looked at him knowingly and continued talking. "Yes, Miss Hamilton came by to finish the library before she leaves town. In fact, she was here most of the day. She had dozens of books delivered, along with the rest of the furniture. The library looks quite grand now. Wait until you see it. She even read to your father." Lenora paused, thoughtfully tilting her head at him.

Lucien still said nothing, somehow not surprised by Colette's determination to finish the job she agreed to do in spite of their differences. He had grown to admire that quality in her.

"She's a lovely girl. We had a nice little chat, she and I." His mother turned to leave the room. She gave him an enigmatic smile. "Good luck, Lucien."

Looking back at her, Lucien grinned.

The elegant sign on the door of Hamilton's Book Shoppe had been turned to read "Closed," but Lucien ignored it and opened the door anyway. The bells jingled a now-familiar tune as he let himself in the little shop. He should warn Colette to always lock the door when the store was closed. What if a thief wandered into the store with Colette there alone? It was too careless of her not to lock the door.

He stopped short in surprise as he looked around him.

Four pairs of blue eyes stared at him. Juliette, Lisette, Paulette, and Yvette Hamilton stood looking at him curiously. Colette was nowhere in sight. They were in the process of packing books into crates, obviously preparing for their move to Brighton. But what they were planning to do with all the books he had no idea, for certainly they could not fit them all into a little cottage. It pained him to see the shop being packed up.

"Good evening, ladies." He stepped farther into the shop, feeling the chilly reception in their silent and awkward stares.

"In case you couldn't read, Lord Waverly, we are closed," Juliette said in a clipped tone, obviously still angry over their little discussion a few days ago.

"Then you should have locked the door," he rejoined lightly, enjoying the spark that flashed in her eyes when she could not think of a witty response. He looked toward Paulette with a grin and said, "Hello there."

When his faithful ally turned his back on him, Lucien knew he was in trouble with the Hamilton sisters. Then little Yvette, too, turned up her nose and looked away. Something was definitely wrong. To his surprise, the usually reserved and shy Lisette walked forward to greet him with a hesitant smile.

"Good evening, Lord Waverly. Please excuse my sisters. We are a little overwhelmed with packing for our move to Brighton. It is fortunate you are here, since as the new owner, we had no idea what you wanted to do with the bookshop."

He gave her a pointed stare. "I don't wish to do anything with the shop. I want it to remain the way it is. That is why I purchased it, Lisette."

The quizzical look in Lisette's eyes gave him pause. She said nothing and glanced away uncomfortably.

"Ladies, the reason I bought the shop was so that you could remain here," he announced to all of them.

Stony silence filled the room.

Had Colette poisoned all their thoughts against him? He understood, partly, why Colette was angry with him, but he could not fathom why all four sisters looked daggers at him. What had he done that was so terrible?

"You can stop packing the books," he continued. "I wish for them to stay in the shop. Where is Colette?"

Paulette finally spoke to him, her expression searching and apologetic. "Upstairs with Mother."

"May I go up and see her or should I wait?" he asked in a tone that left no doubt in their minds that he would be doing one or the other.

"*Monsieur le Comte,* I believe you may see my daughter now."

Genevieve Hamilton stood tall in the doorway, her hand resting on her ornate, gilt-handled cane. She looked more alive than he had seen her before, more alert. Colette stood beside her.

Lucien could not keep his eyes from Colette. The unreadable expression on her beautiful face made him wonder what she was thinking. Was she glad to see him there? Surprised? Her clear blue eyes stared back at him with a magnetic force, drawing him in. Seeing her chocolate-colored hair pulled up revealing her graceful neck, he was stuck by the overpowering desire to pull her into his arms and hold her to him.

"Good evening, Mrs. Hamilton," he said. "Colette."

"Good evening, Lord Waverly. *Nous voudrions parler en privé. Monte dans ta chambre.* Girls, please leave us. We wish to speak privately. Go upstairs now," Genevieve commanded. Without a word, Colette's four sisters scurried from the room.

Lucien motioned toward a chair for Genevieve to sit.

She shook her head. "*Merci, mais je ne préfère pas.* I shall not stay long. I only wish a moment of your time."

"Of course, Mrs. Hamilton," Lucien agreed. He glanced at Colette, hoping to get an idea of what her mother wished to speak to him about. Wondering what and how much Colette had told Genevieve about their relationship, he asked, "How can I help you?"

"Well, *monsieur*, I have learned that you are the gentleman who has purchased the bookshop from me."

"That is true, yes."

"I see." She gazed at Colette for a moment, then her eyes refocused onto his. "I assume you had good reason for doing so?"

"Yes, Mrs. Hamilton," Lucien said pointedly. "I had excellent reasons. Six of them."

Genevieve smiled faintly. "Yes, that is what I thought, although perhaps one reason motivated you more than the others." She paused in thought, glancing between Lucien and her daughter. "You wish for the bookshop to remain open and for Colette to continue on as she has?"

"That was my intention, yes," Lucien stated.

"We have some arrangements to make, and Colette and I were just discussing them. You have made it possible for my daughter to keep this shop, which she loves so much, while setting me free. And for that I thank you from the bottom of my heart."

"You are very welcome."

"I believe you two have some important matters to discuss, so I shall leave you now. *Bonsoir, Monsieur le Comte. Je vous remercie du fond du coeur.* Good evening." With that Genevieve Hamilton turned and walked from the room, leaving him alone with Colette.

They stood awkwardly with each other, before Lucien reached into his jacket pocket and pulled out a sheaf of papers tied with a ribbon. "I have something for you, Colette."

"I don't want anything from you." Her words were terribly cold and nothing less than he expected from her.

"I realize that, but please take this anyway."

Hesitantly, her hand reached out to take the papers. Before she had them in her grasp, he pulled them back and grabbed her hand in his. Slowly he dragged her toward him. Her feet reluctantly stepped forward across the wooden plank floor. When she was close enough, he cupped her face in his hands. "I know you are angry with me, and you have every right to be, because I have behaved like a fool. But I want you to know something first."

Colette glanced up at him, eyeing him suspiciously, but he noted that she also seemed nervous.

"I love you, Colette Elizabeth Hamilton. I love everything about you, from your pretty blue eyes to your sexy mouth to your adorable, meddling sisters to your working in the bookshop to the way your kisses drive me wild. I love the color of your hair and the shape of your nose. I've made myself crazy thinking it would never work between us. I have tried for weeks to deny my feelings for you, and I simply cannot do it any longer."

Colette couldn't breathe. A million thoughts raced through her head, not one of them coherent. Had Lucien just said the words she had longed to hear? "Lucien, I . . . I think . . ."

"Don't speak yet." He pressed the papers into her hand. "Look at this before you say anything."

With her heart thumping wildly in her chest, her fingers trembled as she untied the ribbon and unfolded the pages he had given her. At first she could not believe what she was seeing. She glanced up at him in uncertainty. His gorgeous green eyes twinkled in response. She returned her gaze to the sheet of paper in front of her on which Lucien had written her favorite poem, *Who Ever Loved That Loved Not at First Sight?* by Christopher Marlowe. The first line, "It lies not in our power to love or hate . . ." swam before her eyes.

"I think I fell in love with you the moment I met you, Colette, but I was too blind to recognize the truth."

"Lucien," she began, but he interrupted her again.

"And just so you are aware, I did not buy that poetry book for a 'lady friend,' as I led you to believe. I kept it for myself and read page seventy-four thinking of you. I could not get you out of my mind from the day I saw you here in the disordered shop with dust in your hair and dirt on your face. You were still the most beautiful creature I had ever laid eyes on."

Speechless, Colette stared at him. *Lucien Sinclair loves me?* And had loved her from that first day? She could not take in such momentous news.

"Look at the next page," he coaxed her with a warm smile that caused her heart to flutter wildly.

She shifted the papers and read the next page, recognizing it immediately as the deed of ownership to the bookshop. However, what caused her to catch her breath and almost sink to her knees was her name. There in black ink on a white page was printed the name of the new legal owner of Hamilton's Book Shoppe. It was her name, Colette Elizabeth Hamilton. Lucien had put the shop in her name when he bought it. It now belonged to her.

"Lucien?" She could barely speak, for her throat had gone as dry as a desert.

"Yes, it is yours." He placed a sweet kiss on her lips. "I realize that you are under the mistaken impression that I bought the shop as a way to compensate for not marrying you after that night we were together. But, Colette, I bought the shop before anything happened between us. Weeks before we became intimate, if the truth were told.

I never thought you would end up in my bed, and I never would have purchased the bookshop as a way to 'buy you off,' as you so eloquently phrased it one time."

Colette actually blushed at his words. "Why did you buy it, then?" she managed to ask when she was able to breathe again.

He looked flustered and then admitted, "At first I told myself I bought it to help your family. Which is true to an extent. I care for your sisters very much, and I thought it would make things easier for all of you if I were to help. When I learned that your mother was selling the place, I knew immediately how devastated you would be. I wanted you to keep the shop and make it the huge success I knew only you could make it. I didn't want any of you to feel indebted to me in any way, so I kept it anonymous."

Pausing, Lucien took a deep breath and gazed at her with longing that she felt to the tips of her toes.

Overcome with emotions, Colette noted the date at the bottom of the page. He *had* purchased the shop before they had made love together that night at Devon House. He bought the shop for her, knowing just how much it meant to her.

"That is the sweetest and the most thoughtful thing anyone has ever done for me," she whispered breathlessly, afraid she might burst into tears. "I don't even know what to say to you."

"Say that you will marry me." With his green eyes pinned on her, she could not move, could not think of anything but him.

"You want to marry me?" Her voice quaked and her heart flipped over.

"Yes."

It suddenly seemed as if the world as she knew it had simply turned upside down and nothing made sense anymore. She began to babble, "But the bookshop is . . . I thought . . . I want to work . . . You want—"

"I want you, Colette." He placed his hands on her shoulders and she shivered from the contact. "I've come to realize that I am proud of you and the work you have accomplished here. I want you to continue making the bookshop a success." His tone was filled with determination.

"But a countess . . . a marchioness . . . Your wife cannot work in a shop."

"*My* wife certainly can if she wants to. If *you* want to, Colette. I have no doubt that you can do anything you put your mind to doing."

Colette opened her mouth to speak. She closed her mouth. She opened it once again and then closed it, unable to utter a single word. She was stunned. Lucien loved her and wanted to marry her, and it did not matter to him if she still worked in the bookshop. *My bookshop.* He had given it to her. He made it possible for her to keep the shop forever. Her heart flipped over in her chest.

"Oh, Lucien, do you mean that?" she finally gasped, her voice surprising her by sounding higher than usual.

He pulled her into his arms, the papers spilling unheeded to her slippered feet on the floor. He leaned in close to her, slanting his mouth over hers, and crushed a kiss to her lips. "Yes, I mean that."

With her mouth close to his, inhaling the scent of him, she whispered on a shaky breath, "Thank you."

"What about 'yes'?"

"Yes?" she asked, confused by his question.

His emerald green gaze penetrated her entire body. "Will you marry me?"

Recognition dawned. "Oh, yes!" She pulled his head to hers, spreading her fingers into his thick, dark hair, and kissed his lips. This was what she wanted more than anything in the world. "Yes, I will marry you."

"I love you, Colette."

"And I love you, Lucien, with all my heart."

And that heart of Colette's pounded with anticipation as Lucien's mouth covered hers with a kiss. Slowly he began to walk her backward in the direction of a certain bookshelf in the history section.

Chapter Twenty-Nine

The Family That
Plays Together...

Colette grinned while her husband laughed with her sisters as they all gathered around him for a photograph. After their wedding ceremony earlier that morning, Lucien had specially arranged for one of the city's best photographers to come to Devon House to take a family portrait. The new art of photography was all the rage in London, and Lucien wanted a photograph of the entire family to commemorate the occasion. With Genevieve, Juliette, Lisette, Paulette, Yvette, Simon, and Lenora standing beside them, she and Lucien posed in front of one wall of fully stocked bookshelves in the newly renovated Devon House library.

The rather short and anxious photographer instructed them to hold very still while he arranged the camera. The large wooden camera rested on a tripod, and he fiddled with brass knobs before he lifted a dark cloth and huddled beneath it.

Before he could take their picture, however, Juliette called out, "Wait! Where is Jeffrey? He needs to be in this picture, too."

"Yes, he should be with us," Colette agreed, moving from her carefully posed position beside Lucien. After all they had been through together, Colette now considered Jeffrey as not just a friend but as a part of her family. She also sensed how much it would mean to him to be in this family portrait with them. And he had just returned from Paris to attend their wedding and serve as Lucien's best man.

"You cannot move!" the photographer wailed.

"I'll go and get him," Lucien volunteered, lifting his hand from where it had been strategically placed on Colette's shoulder, but not before caressing her lightly. "I shall only be a moment," he explained to the photographer.

He left the library to retrieve Jeffrey, who was more than likely still mingling with the other wedding guests in the grand salon. After Juliette's little scheme to make Lucien jealous, which actually had some merit to it after all, Lucien and Jeffrey had enjoyed a good laugh over Jeffrey's part in it.

"Don't anyone else move!" the frustrated photographer pleaded with them, throwing his hands up in the air at the groom's departure.

Of course no one listened to him. Juliette immediately began telling Lisette that she was blocking her, while Paulette and Yvette giggled. Lenora, Simon, and Genevieve chatted amiably together.

Lucien returned momentarily with his friend following behind him. Jeffrey looked slightly befuddled and somewhat embarrassed. "I thought this was a Sinclair-Hamilton family portrait. Are you sure you wish for me to join you?"

A resounding chorus of "Yes!" answered his question. He smiled and thanked them, following the photographer's anxious instructions for him to stand behind Yvette.

"Now, you must not move again. Remain very, very still," the photographer murmured before diving beneath the camera cloth again.

Adjusting the long train on her sumptuous bridal gown of embroidered white silk and satin, Colette smiled as Lucien once again placed his hand upon her shoulder. This photograph, the first Colette had ever had taken in her life, marked a special day. It was not just her wedding day, but the beginning of her new life. With Lucien's encouragement and support she could now make Hamilton's Book Shoppe the premier book store in the city. There was nothing she could not do.

She stood perfectly still waiting for the photograph to be taken.

Everything had turned out so well. Her sisters would now be living with her and Lucien at Devon House. Simon, her new father-in-law, had been thrilled at not only gaining Colette as a daughter-in-law, but in also gaining her four sisters. Lenora had been warm in her welcome of Colette into the family, and Colette knew instinctively that they would become good friends. And even Genevieve was happy with the union. She had agreed to spend part of the year in Brighton and part of the year in London with them. Uncle Randall and Aunt Cecilia, who had attended the wedding, were more than pleased with Colette's marriage to Lucien. Aunt Cecilia had actually kissed her on the cheek with glee!

But the best part of all was Lucien.

She glanced up at him just as the photograph was finally taken.

"And that is it!" the photographer shouted gleefully.

Lucien kissed her, whispering, "I love you."

Happy beyond words to be married to the man she loved, she kissed him back, not caring that their parents and her sisters were all watching them. As everyone began to move from his or her positions an overwhelming sense of love flooded Colette.

Lucien took her hand in his, pulling her to his side. She moved toward him eagerly. "Doesn't the Countess of Waverly look beautiful today?"

"Oh my, that's me, isn't it?" she murmured, still not used to the idea of being a countess. But it was exciting to be a countess in charge of a bookshop!

"Yes, that's you," he whispered in her ear.

A little thrill went through her. She had fallen in love with Lucien Sinclair that first day he entered her bookshop, and now he was her husband. Nothing could make her happier.

She tilted her head up to his, ready for another kiss.

And he kissed her.

Dear Readers,

Thank you for reading *When His Kiss Is Wicked*. I hope you enjoyed meeting the five Hamilton sisters and reading about Colette Hamilton and the Earl of Waverly as much as I enjoyed writing about them.

But what about the other four sisters, you ask? Do Juliette and Lord Eddington ever get together? Does Hamilton's Book Shoppe become a success? Here's a sneak peek at the first chapter of my next, as yet untitled, book. As you recall, Juliette Hamilton is as passionate as she is rebellious. She is determined to live her life her way, without anyone telling her what to do—which will bring her a great deal of excitement and romance, not to mention a few harrowing misadventures. Of course, the irrepressible Lord Jeffrey Eddington plays a special role, as well as a few unforgettable new characters, including a very handsome, very sexy sea captain with a secret of his own.

So read on to get a little preview of the next story in the Hamilton series . . .

Thanks for reading!
Kaitlin O'Riley
www.KaitlinORiley.com

London, England
Summer 1871

The evening Captain Harrison Fleming came to supper at Devon House was the night Juliette Hamilton finally made up her mind to run away.

That had been three weeks ago.

Now Juliette held her breath, her heart pounding an erratic rhythm against her chest, waiting silently in the shadows as the small group of sailors, laughing and talking in boisterous tones, walked by oblivious to her presence. *Oh, God, she was really doing this.* She was actually leaving. Leaving her sisters. Her family. Her home. A strange thrill coursed through her veins and she took a deep breath of the briny night air to fortify her shaking legs. She peered cautiously from her hiding space on the dock behind a stack of large oak barrels filled with she knew not what.

The moonlit water glistened as still as glass beside the now empty dock.

All her planning had come to this moment.

There was the *Sea Minx*, docked just where Captain Fleming had said it would be.

When the last sailor had disappeared up the gangway of the ship, Juliette pulled the black cap down over her head to heighten her boyish disguise and took another deep breath, before scurrying on silent feet after them, up the ramp onto the deck of the *Sea Minx*.

Juliette had somehow managed a minor miracle by reaching the dock and boarding the ship without being detected. Now began the more challenging aspect of her plan. She needed to remain hidden until they were well out to sea, when it would be too late for Captain Fleming to turn back and bring her home. Unsure where to go next, she hesitated for an instant before she ducked through a low doorway into a narrow, dimly lit passageway. Hearing male voices and heavy footsteps approaching she opened the nearest door in a blind panic and quickly found herself inside what appeared to be some sort of small storage room.

Unpleasant smells accosted her immediately, and once again she held her breath, not daring to move until the voices passed by, as her eyes slowly adjusted to the dimness. When the passageway quieted and she no longer heard voices, Juliette softly exhaled before daring to draw another breath. *Now what?* Her plan had not been so detailed as to exactly what she would do once she finally boarded the ship, aside from keeping out of sight until they had already set sail. Now she fumbled about in the cramped, dark space awash in sour smells until she found a small wooden crate upon which to sit. Thrilled with this bit of good fortune, she sat and nervously patted the little satchel she had brought with her.

She had brought enough food to last her a few days if she ate sparingly, a photographic card of her family which was taken at her sister Colette's wedding last fall, letters with her friend Christine Dunbar's address, some clothes, and her savings. Once she reached New York she would seek out her friend.

Then her adventure would really begin.

She had finally done it! She had successfully boarded Captain Fleming's ship! She hugged herself in disbelief, a little stunned that she had actually accomplished her goal.

A rather strong pang of regret filled her at the thought of her four sisters when they discovered her note of explanation she had left in her bedroom. By morning her sisters would undoubtedly be overcome with worry and panic at her unexpected departure, but there was no help for it. It was time. Juliette had had to seize this opportunity to leave. She simply had to. She wanted to be free and independent and this was the only way.

As she sat in the dank and malodorous gloom, she felt the ship suddenly begin to rock beneath her and pitch forward. Loud shouts and excited cries could be heard above deck. Her heart lurched. *This was it!* There was no turning back now. The *Sea Minx* was sailing out across the Atlantic Ocean to America. Her fate was sealed, for better or for worse. For a fraction of a second she regretted her crazy desire to venture out and see the world, but then she held up her chin and grinned to herself in the dark.

She had always longed for an exciting adventure, a chance to visit exotic locales, to meet new people. However, she had not envisioned doing so in such furtive secrecy.

But that night at Devon House three weeks earlier she knew within an instant that Captain Harrison Fleming had unwittingly presented her with an advantageous opportunity to escape her regimented existence.

Perhaps it was when Captain Fleming described his

beautiful clipper ship, the *Sea Minx*. The color of his eyes seemed the exact shade of the ocean on a stormy gray afternoon. Or maybe it was when he regaled them all with tales of his life at sea and his adventures in ports around the globe. He had actually *been* to exotic and foreign lands. India. China. Africa. America. The Caribbean. Captain Fleming was living the life she had only dared to dream of and it fascinated her to hear him speak.

Juliette's brilliant scheme came to her in bits and pieces throughout the lengthy eight-course meal. She could not quite pinpoint the exact moment that the idea to stow away on his ship popped into her head, but by the end of that intimate supper party at Devon House, the beginnings of her plan had everything to do with the charismatic Captain Fleming. As soon as she learned that the adventurous sea captain planned to return to New York shortly, Juliette knew just what she had to do. She might never have this chance again.

He was her only means of getting to New York. She had to sail with him.

She had barely been able to finish her dessert for containing her wild excitement at this revolutionary idea.

"Look at Juliette, would you? She looks like the cat that ate the canary," Lord Jeffrey Eddington had remarked to everyone gathered around the dinner table, an amused smile lurking on his boyishly handsome face, his merry eyes dancing. "Tell us now what is going on in that pretty head of yours, Juliette. Whatever are you scheming about now?"

Juliette had flashed him an irritated glance while trying to maintain an innocent expression. Leave it to Jeffrey to notice the slightest bit of change in her. In spite of being her dearest friend, he could be quite exasperating at times. If Jeffrey even suspected what she was plotting to do he would see to it that Juliette was locked in her bedchamber and under twenty-four-hour guard for the rest of her life.

She had to be very careful with him. He could spoil everything.

"I simply enjoy listening to Captain Fleming's adventures of life at sea," Juliette had answered Jeffrey cooly, glancing toward the tall and rugged looking man who sat to the right of her sister, Colette. They had all just been introduced to Captain Fleming that evening, because her brother-in-law, Lucien Sinclair, the Earl of Waverly, had invited him to stay at Devon House while he was conducting business in London. Apparently the two men were good friends, although Juliette had a difficult time imagining her staid and very proper brother-in-law being friends with the rather daring captain.

At her remark to Jeffrey, Captain Fleming questioned her across the long, elaborately set table. "Is that so, Miss Hamilton? And just what part of my story did you find so interesting?"

His exotic accent added to his charm, Juliette acknowledged. He sounded very American, which, of course, was only natural considering he was born in New York, but she found it intriguing nonetheless. He was vastly different from any man she had ever met in London. Juliette stared boldly into his stormy gray eyes. "I believe it was the part where you described your journey from New York to San Francisco. I felt as if I were on your ship."

He smiled at her, and Juliette felt her heart flutter erratically. How peculiar! She had never met a man who made her heart race before. Nor had she ever expected to. At least not here at Devon House.

But she had always held out a vain hope. All through the Season last year, when her Uncle Randall had forced her and Colette to find husbands, every man she had met had bored her to tears. While Colette had been fortunate enough to fall in love with the wealthy Lucien Sinclair, the Earl of Waverly, and rescue the family from financial ruin and save the family bookshop, Juliette had had a more difficult time. Aside from becoming fast friends with Jeffrey Eddington, she had not met a single gentleman who held her interest for more than a minute. To be completely honest with herself, she knew she scared the trousers off most of the men and she took a perverse delight in doing just that. All she had to do was say something even remotely opinionated and they did not k now what to do with her. Despite her behavior, most of them became besotted with her anyway, declaring their love in the most embarrassing manner. The rest saw her as a challenge, something that they could tame or subdue. Juliette despaired of ever meeting a man who lived up to her expectations. Not even her darling Jeffrey.

No. She needed to leave London.

Not that her life in London was at all terrible. Leaving was something she simply had to do. She had harbored this unappeased restlessness inside of her for as long as she could remember and she felt smothered. If she didn't get away from London, away from the tightly bound rules of society, even away from her family as much as she loved them, she knew she would go mad. Stark, raving mad.

Now she found herself on a ship captained by a man she barely knew. What would Harrison Fleming do when he discovered her? Would he be angry with her? Most likely. Would he punish her somehow? Perhaps, but she doubted it. Most men were full of bluster but would never lay a finger on her. Would he immediately turn the ship around and drag her back in humiliation to face Colette and Lucien? She could bear almost anything rather than that. She had come so far. She could not return now. All she had to do was remain undetected for a day or two. Aware that Captain Fleming had a schedule to keep and needed to arrive in New York before the end of the month, she doubted he would lose valuable time by sailing back to London simply to return her.

At least Juliette fervently hoped he would not.

She presumed he would be forced to keep her until they arrived in America with a plan to send her back on another ship, but by then she would have arranged to stay with her friend Christina. It was a good plan. In fact, it was the most daring she had ever come up with.

She sighed heavily, wondering how long she would have to remain in this squalid hole, but she would stay there a month if she had to. If that was what it took to get her to New York, she would gladly do it. Her legs were slowly falling asleep and her lower back was beginning to ache. She managed to lean the satchel behind her as a sort of makeshift cushion for her back. That helped a bit. There being nothing else to do, sitting there in the dark, she closed her eyes. Allowing the gentle sway of the ship to lull her, she drifted asleep.

Suddenly the door flung open with a clatter. Surprised by the unexpected intrusion, Juliette screamed shrilly, covering her mouth with her hand in a belated attempt to silence herself. She could not be found yet. *It was too soon!* Filled with bitter disappointment, and admittedly fear, she glanced up at the person responsible for ruining her hiding place.

A young man, his face awash with disbelief, stood in the dim lantern light of the passageway, startled speechless by her presence in the storage room. They stared mutely at each other for a moment before he recovered his senses. With a disapproving frown, he cried, "Hey now there, lad! We don't allow stow-aways on board the *Sea Minx*."

He obviously referred to Juliette's disguise. Having sweet-talked one of the storter stable boys from Devon House into giving her his old clothes, she had donned trousers, a shirt, and a tweed cap. She thought she looked quite passable. And wearing trousers was most freeing, making her feel even more reckless and independent. No wonder men wore them! This sailor naturally assumed she was a boy. Juliette did not dare to move.

"You'll have to come with me to see the captain." The young man grabbed Juliette's arm and yanked her roughly to her feet. As she stumbled into the passageway and the light fell across her face, he shouted, "Bloody hell!" He snatched the cap off her head, and her long dark hair fell in soft waves to her waist. "You're a girl!" He stepped back from her in astonishment, his eyes round.

"Of course, I'm a girl, you simpleton," she snapped at him, irritated that she should be found out so soon by this mere slip of a boy. Her entire plan was ruined. All her dreams now destroyed. She would never get to New York. Harrison Fleming would surely to take her back to Devon House this very night for they couldn't be more than an hour or two out to sea by now.

"Wait until the captain sees you," he whispered, shaking his head.

Reaching down to grab her tapestry-embroidered satchel, she thought to herself, *"Yes, just wait until the captain sees me."* Juliette cringed inwardly at the thought of facing him. There was no help for it. Besides, he was merely a man. Like all the other men she had ever known. She could handle him easily enough. There wasn't a man yet that she hadn't. She squared her shoulders and followed the young sailor down the narrow passageway toward the captain's cabin.

The door opened into a gorgeous anteroom with wood-paneled walls and gilt-framed maps. A round table with six leather-backed chairs dominated the room. Another door opened partially to reveal the captain's private quarters. She could see a large bed within. Her eyes flashed back quickly to the oak desk, behind which stood Captain Harrison Fleming.

"I found a stow away aboard, Captain. *A girl.* She was hiding in the storage room," the sailor explained.

Ignoring her rapidly beating heart, she stared up at the imposing figure who was in charge of the *Sea Minx* and, unintentionally, Juliette's fate.

"Thank you for bringing our unexpected visitor to my attention," Captain Fleming said with an even-toned voice, although his intent sea colored eyes never left Juliette's face. "You may leave us now."

As the young boy respectfully nodded his head and quit the room, Juliette was left alone with Captain Fleming for the first time. She had been in his company on many occasions during the past few weeks while he visited London, but never alone. Each time she had thought him quiet and somewhat disinterested in her, which had been surprising. Every man she had ever met could not seem to help but lavish her with attention, even the painfully shy ones. Now it seemed that the aloof Captain Fleming was finally giving her his undivided attention. And that made her uncharacteristically nervous.

He continued to stare at her. His stormy gray eyes, with startlingly long lashes, bored into her. She waited in silence, a strange tingling sensation building within her.

Juliette suddenly came to the realization that he was made of sterner stuff than she was accustomed to seeing in most men. He had the bearing of a pirate and beneath his cool surface he seemed to possess a sense of tightly leashed desire as if he kept this emotions on a close rein. With a high forehead, aquiline nose and rakish mouth, he exuded a rugged, very masculine handsomeness. He was quite taller than average, with broad shoulders, sun-streaked hair and gray eyes. His bronzed skin declared boldly that he spent much of his days out of doors. Yet for all his commanding presence, there was nothing aristocratic about him.

"Well, Juliette, it seems you have created quite the situation on my ship."

She raised one eyebrow at him for stating the obvious while noting he had dispensed with any formality by not addressing her as Miss Hamilton. Being that she had brazenly stowed away, she supposed the need for propriety had passed.

"I merely wish to go to New York to visit a friend."

"Why didn't you simply ask me to take you?"

Most men she knew would be beside themselves by now, yet Captain Fleming seemed remarkably calm at her presence. That impressed her. "My family would never allow me to go. In fact, my mother expressly forbade my going to New York."

"Ahh, I see." He nodded his head, crossing his arms across his broad chest.

His white shirt was partially unbuttoned and Juliette could not help but notice the bare expanse of tanned skin. She swallowed and forced herself to focus on his face. But that also was dangerous. He was a very handsome man. Yes, he was. Definitely.

"I should take you home directly."

"I wish you wouldn't," she managed to respond. If he took her back now, she would die of disappointment.

"Your family must be sick with worry by now."

Once again guilt surged within her at the thought of leaving her sisters in such a manner. But truly, she had no other recourse. "I wrote them a letter, explaining what I was doing and asking them not to worry about me. They won't find it until the morning when I don't appear at breakfast."

"Well, you have thought of almost everything."

She challenged him. "Almost?"

"Everything except one."

They stood in tense silence, regarding each other with undisguised wariness. Her heart hammered erratically in her chest. Oh, she *had* definitely underestimated Captain Fleming. Of course he would never harm her. He was a friend of her brother-in-law and had been a guest in their house. Still, a strange sense of nervousness engulfed her at his masculine presence and she trembled. Odd, she had never felt nervous with a man before.

Stepping from behind the desk, Captain Fleming moved closer to her and she sucked in her breath at his nearness. He loomed over her and the mysterious scent of him made her weak-kneed.

"It seems you did not consider me in your little plan to flee to New York," he breathed. He leaned in closer to her face.

Unconsciously she inched away from him. He pressed closer, his intense gray eyes on her, his lips hovering near her cheek. The heat of his breath made her shiver and his whispered words left her speechless. She had backed up against the table and could retreat no farther. She had no choice but to face him.

"You did not factor me into your plan, Juliette."

She stared helplessly at him. This handsome sea captain who held her fate in his hands. This man who embodied all the adventurousness she harbored in her soul. He was close enough to kiss her and for a wild, panicked moment Juliette hoped he would.

His whispered words brushed her lips, causing her to stop breathing altogether.

"Or what I plan to do with you."

About the Author

Kaitlin O'Riley fell in love with historical romance novels when she was just fourteen years old, and shortly thereafter she began writing her own stories in spiral notebooks. Fortunately for her, none of those early efforts survive today. She is still an avid reader and can often be found curled up on a sofa with a book in her hands. Kaitlin grew up in New Jersey, but now she lives in sunny Southern California, where she is busy writing her next book. Please visit her on the web at *www.KaitlinORiley.com*.

More by Bestselling Author
Hannah Howell